THE SAVAGE DAWN

The SAVAGE DAWN

MELISSA GREY

✳

DELACORTE PRESS

All rights reserved. Published in the United States by Delacorte
Press, an imprint of Random House Children's Books, a division of
Penguin Random House LLC, New York.

Delacorte Press is a registered trademark and the colophon is a
trademark of Penguin Random House LLC.

Visit us on the Web! randomhouseteens.com

Educators and librarians, for a variety of teaching tools, visit us at
RHTeachersLibrarians.com

Library of Congress Cataloging-in-Publication Data is available
upon request.

ISBN 978-0-385-74469-0 (hc) —
ISBN 978-0-375-99181-3 (lib. bdg.) —
ISBN 978-0-385-39101-6 (ebook)

The text of this book is set in 12-point Fairfield.

Printed in the United States of America
10 9 8 7 6 5 4 3 2 1
First Edition

TO YOU, THE READER,
FOR STICKING WITH ECHO UNTIL THE END

PROLOGUE

It had been so hungry for so long.

Hungry and cold, wandering the abyss, alone and unmoored. A solitary shadow lost in a dark sea.

No, It had not been hungry. Hungry was too gentle a word for what It had felt. It had been ravenous. There was a great, yawning chasm inside It that ached to be filled.

But there was nothing with which It could soothe Its hunger, slake Its thirst. There was just the nothing in which It was suspended. Trapped. Caged. It was the only thing that existed, adrift in all that nothing. It, and the bright shining Light of Its seal. The bars of Its cage glowed with a warmth upon which It wanted to burn Itself. But try as It might, It could not reach the light. The light remained, like an end to Its long torment, out of Its grasp.

Until one day, the Light went out.

It did not understand where the Light had gone, but It felt a release the moment the Light disappeared. Like air rushing into a vacuum. The Light had departed and the Darkness inched forward, through the void, waiting to be burned. Waiting for the Light to reappear, casting It back into the solace of the shadows, but there was nothing.

Nothing. Except a door, left ajar in the Light's wake.

It rushed through the opening left in the absence of the Light and broke free of the cage It had known for so long that It had forgotten there was anything else in the world.

And, oh, what a world it was.

It had forgotten what it felt like to be free, to be able to soar across the skies, as unstoppable as a storm. Like a wild beast It fed on the first thing It found, a village filled with life and love. It devoured that place, shrouding it in darkness, but the meal was a small one, which only served to whet Its appetite for more.

There were lights and sounds and people. The people It favored so. Their screams were delicious, coating the insides of Its empty belly, easing the growling ache that had taken up permanent residence there. It had been so empty, but now . . . now, It could feast. It gorged Itself on the things It found, yet still, It felt a tug.

The Light was not gone. Not truly. Not completely. The Light was there, somewhere, in the world—the great, wide world, with its sumptuous offerings and delectable woes— and It realized now what the Light had been. Not solely a cage—though it had been that—but a complement. A companion. They needed one another to exist. It had despised the Light. Hated it with every particle of Its being, and that hate had sustained It, but without the Light, there was no counterpoint to Its existence. No balance.

And so It sought out the Light. Sniffed out where its

presence was strongest. Through this world It floated, drawn to places where that other thing burned brightest. There, It planted Its seeds of sorrow, drank Its fill from the dead and dying. Another feast It had found, this one a familiar taste, so like the little beasts that had locked It away, all those eons ago. It took particular delight in the flavor of the suffering. The pain almost sated the hunger. Almost, but not quite. There was still something missing. Something vital.

But try as It might, It could not tether Itself to the world. It did not belong. It was other, like the Light. But the Light had found a place to call home. A port at which to anchor. It had nothing. Nothing but a vague sense of self-awareness. Of the things that were It and not It. It wandered the world, as lost as a frightened child, until It heard her calling Its name.

It had forgotten that It even had a name.

Her shout was the roar of a dragon, all fire and smoke and ash. It could smell the blood in which she bathed, and It shivered with anticipation. It fed on death and woe, and that was what she brought with her. Across the unfathomable distance of the void, It felt her cry, her longing, and It strained to find her, to reach for the feast she had prepared for It.

It answered her call with one of Its own: *Who are you?*

It sensed the moment she heard Its voice, cutting through the sound of the screams of those she betrayed. She paused, her sword dripping with the blood of sacrifice.

I am Tanith, she said. *I am the Dragon Prince.*

That was not the answer It craved. Names were meaningless in the abyss, and titles even more so. Darkness desired no label. It repeated Its query, delivering it with enough force to make her stumble, despite the distance that divided them.

Who are you?

It needed to know. It needed to be sure.

She seemed to understand then. *I am death,* she said, her voice echoing across the distance. *I am destruction. I am yours and you are mine. Come to me, kuçedra. Come to me and give me your strength.*

Her want was so fierce. It knew, with stunning clarity, what she yearned for: power for herself, for her people, enough to remake the world in her image, to destroy everything that wasn't what she wanted. The magnitude of her hunger matched Its own. Her desire was a beacon, and It followed that beacon to shore.

Kuçedra. That was Its name. It was a fine name, a name to be feared. It was this name she called out, allowing herself to find It, for It to find her. Perhaps there was power in names after all.

CHAPTER ONE

The Agora had, in Echo's modest lifetime, never been this empty. On an average day, it was packed to the rafters with a wild assortment of characters selling everything from mismatched tea sets to magic potions of varying efficacy. The majority of the shops were owned and operated by Avicen, most of whom had evacuated when their safe haven—the Nest—proved to be less safe than they'd thought.

Echo walked past shuttered storefronts, gravel crunching beneath her boots. Beside her, Rowan kept a watchful eye on the stragglers who had refused to abandon the once-bustling market in the wake of the Nest's fall. His hands were thrust into his pockets; he would have looked like he was out for a casual stroll if not for the tension threaded through his back and the tightness of his jaw. The Agora was not the same as it had once been, but then, Echo thought, none of them were.

The gaslights that illuminated the Agora's cavernous

interior cast a greasy yellow glow over the bare tabletops and darkened windows. Gone was the plum-feathered Avicen woman named Crystal who had peddled a bizarre collection of knickknacks culled from all over the globe. If you were looking for buttons to adorn a Victorian-era waistcoat, she was your girl. If you were in the market for a shrunken head—cursed, naturally—pilfered from an obscure cultist tribe in the depths of the Amazon rain forest, she was also your girl. But now her little kiosk stood empty, bare of its eccentricities and strangely morose in the Agora's gloom. Also gone were the blacksmith—an Avicen by the name of Othello who had a deep and abiding obsession with speaking in iambic pentameter—and the cobbler and the baker. The cobbler had repaired more than one pair of Echo's boots over the years, and the baker would sneak her treats when his wife wasn't looking in exchange for the latest issue of *Spider-Man*. She'd spotted the cobbler in one of the overcrowded rooms in Avalon Castle, where those who'd survived the attack on the Nest had sought refuge, but the baker was listed among the missing. A wall in the castle's foyer had been requisitioned as a board for people to post notices of loved ones unaccounted for, though Echo had let her gaze wander to it only once, and only for a few seconds. It made her feel as though icicles were sprouting inside her stomach, spearing her tender organs with their sharp chill. There were too many names on that board she recognized, too many faces she knew. There was nothing she could do for the lost and the dead. At least, that was what she told herself.

She wondered if Crystal had survived the attack on the Nest. Echo hadn't seen her photo on the board, but she hadn't pored over every single one. She'd spent a few days raking her eyes over the haunted faces of the refugees at Avalon, but doing so had threatened to drive her mad. It was easier, Echo found, to wonder about the people whose faces she didn't see. She couldn't bear to think of them as dead, and if by some miracle they weren't, she couldn't bear to see the accusation she feared would be in their eyes. Not all of the Avicen blamed Echo for the tragedy that had befallen them, but enough of them did to stoke the embers of guilt in Echo's heart to a roaring fire.

Echo and Rowan stuck to the edges of the Agora to avoid the few vendors who had bothered to stay—warlocks, every last one of them, probably selling mummified kittens in jars or something equally horrific. Their pale gazes burned holes in her back. They watched, but they didn't approach. A small part of Echo hoped they were afraid of her. Warlocks were bad—the kind of bad that should exist only in fairy tales where tricksters spirited away firstborns or made princesses spin gold until their fingers fell off. They were as monstrous as humans could make themselves, and if monsters were afraid of Echo, then maybe she stood a chance in the messed-up fairy tale her own life had become.

Her footsteps slowed as she approached her destination: Perrin's Enchanting Essentials.

"Wait outside?" she asked Rowan. She didn't like the look of those warlocks, even if she was newly fearsome. Judging by his terse nod, Rowan didn't like the look of them either.

"Hurry back." He took up a position by the door, looking every inch the strapping Warhawk recruit, despite his civilian clothes. He had changed too, just as much as Echo had. With a small huff, Echo steeled herself to enter the shop.

The door swung open with a weak squeal. The hinges

were rusty, something that happened to metal with ease down in the Agora, yet Perrin had been fastidious about maintaining his shop; he'd taken such pride in it. But he wasn't here anymore, not to oil the hinges, nor to wipe down the glass countertops, nor to refill the small bowls of fragrant flowers placed strategically around the room. The flower petals had long since wilted, and the display cases had collected a heavy layer of dust. Handprints cut through the grime in spots, evidence that someone had tampered with the protective charms Perrin had placed on the cases to guard their contents. Those cases stood mostly empty now, ransacked of anything of even moderate value. Shame flooded Echo at the sight. It hadn't occurred to her that no one would be around to tend Perrin's shop after . . . well, after.

If she was completely honest with herself—and she avoided that more often than she cared to admit—she had deliberately skirted memories of Perrin. She hadn't wanted to remember him. Not his life. Not his death. Memory was a burden borne by the survivors. Dying, Echo knew now, was easy. It could be painful or frightening or any number of things, but when it was done, it was done. She had died once before. She knew, better than most. It was living that was hard. Moving forward when memory wanted nothing more than to pull you back . . . that was the real challenge. Like Sisyphus pushing his boulder uphill for all eternity, it was a battle that could not be won. But the living kept trying because that was what it meant to be alive. To keep going lest the boulder crush you under its weight. That would be giving up, and giving up was not an option. It hadn't ever been, not for Echo, not since stabbing herself in the heart and tying her life inextricably to the fates of thousands.

Echo walked toward the back room of Perrin's shop, where she knew he kept the stuff too expensive or rare or downright dangerous to display. The skin between her shoulder blades prickled as if she weren't alone. A glance around showed that she was, but the feeling lingered. Ghosts, then. Or guilt. Sometimes it was hard to tell the difference. Even if she didn't want to remember Perrin, it was only a matter of time before memory—fickle, cruel thing it was—caught up with her. She didn't want to remember the first time she'd entered this very shop, hand clutching the Ala's, eyes as wide as saucers, as she took in the utterly disorganized assortment of glittering wares. Didn't want to remember the cookie he'd given her when he caught her eyeing the open box of macarons on the countertop—it had been raspberry-flavored, and the cloyingly sweet filling had stuck to the roof of her mouth. She didn't want to remember the first time she'd accepted a job from him; for some reason, he'd wanted a 1961 Mickey Mantle baseball card—"Mint condition or don't bother darkening my doorstep, please"—and so Echo had tracked down a collector, slunk into his office, and swiped the card from his album when he was out to lunch. Perrin had given Echo a six-month supply of shadow dust in exchange, teaching her the ways of the Avicen's barter economy.

And that was how she'd decided she ought to be a thief instead of a mere pickpocket. She'd discovered something about herself: she was good at stealing other people's things, really good. The knowledge that she'd developed such a talent filled her with a confidence she'd never had before. She didn't want to remember how much the person she was now had been shaped by Perrin's request for a baseball card. And she did not want to remember the last time she had seen him, eerily motionless, either dead or dying, reduced to nothing more than a pile of rags huddled in the corner of a damp dungeon in the belly of Wyvern's Keep. She hadn't said goodbye; she'd been angry at him. He'd told the Drakharin about her—what she did, where to find her—and it hadn't mattered to her then that the information had been tortured out of him or that he'd died scared and alone and in pain.

Regret clawed at Echo's insides like a beast fighting to break free. Her vision blurred as she rifled through the back room, messier than it had been even when Perrin was alive. His records were less of a system and more of a loose constellation of papers strewn about his desk, crammed into drawers, and spilling over densely packed bookshelves. What she was searching for would be hidden, most likely. Perrin had managed to track her for the Drakharin using a bracelet he'd fashioned from braided leather, shiny beads, and his own feathers. Echo had left the bracelet in her cell in Wyvern's Keep, but she knew a tracker was no good without a way to track it. He'd probably used a scrying bowl or a mirror or something like that to locate the bracelet, which he knew had been attached to Echo. The same bracelet Caius and his Drakharin agents had used to find her when she'd been hunting down the objects Rose had scattered around the globe, a scavenger hunt that led straight to the firebird. The feathers were what made locating it possible. A little biological material, a clever enchantment, and a reflective surface to tie a charm to, *et voilà*: a tracking spell so easy even a modest shopkeeper could use it. If Perrin had been around for Echo to ask why he'd done it, he probably would have said it was to keep an eye on her. But he wasn't around, so she couldn't ask. She shoved a pile of books off a box, flinching when the noise reverberated through the abandoned shop. The counterpart to the bracelet had to be here somewhere. If it wasn't, then their only lead to find Caius was dead. Dead, dead, dead.

She should have said "Goodbye."

She should have said "I'm sorry you got dragged into this mess."

She should have said "Thank you for the macaron. It was lovely and I was so hungry and you were kind when I had known so little kindness."

But she hadn't said any of those things. She had left his broken body to rot in that dungeon, and now there was no one left to say anything to at all.

Echo stepped over broken glass and collapsed tables, making her way to the office where Perrin kept his account books.

The room itself was modest. Large, heavy tomes bound in unassuming brown leather lined the shelves, their spines embossed with golden dates spanning back to the late nineteenth century. The Agora had been around for a long time. When it was established, the island had been a Dutch colony by the name of New Amsterdam, and the market had weathered the years since. Perrin's records were meticulously arranged in chronological order on shelves that covered every inch of wall space. The books' bindings had been worn smooth by age and handling. The business had operated, like most Avicen enterprises, on a complicated bartering system. Echo's involvement with Perrin had been relatively simple. He had requests. She fulfilled them, acquiring goods out in the human world that were difficult for an Avicen to come by, and in return, he kept her in a steady supply of shadow dust.

But she knew from watching him work in the shop that his other arrangements had not always been as simple. The shopkeeper had woven a complex web of favors and debts, and each of these books was a record of every transaction he had performed in the year stamped on its spine. The books had obviously been pulled off the shelves with frequency. There was a scant bit of dust on them from the months of neglect, but they still showed signs of once-regular usage. Echo had no doubt that Perrin remembered, with the aid of his detailed record keeping, every favor owed him by the Avicen—and occasional warlock—who passed through his shop. A less discerning eye might not have caught the slight aberration among the books, but Echo, who spent the vast majority of her life surrounded by books in various states of disrepair, noticed it.

A single ledger, almost identical to its neighbors. The year, written in faded golden lettering on its spine: 1961. Echo snatched at a fragment of memory: Perrin, listing the greatest baseball teams in the history of the sport during one of the slow days at his shop, when Echo had come around looking to stock up on shadow dust only to find herself roped into one of his diatribes on sports. She couldn't remember most of what he had said, but she remembered the enthusiasm in his voice as he'd described the virtues of the 1961 Yankees: victors of that year's World Series after defeating the Cincinnati Reds in five games; home to both Mickey

Mantle and Roger Maris, who were famous for racing to beat Babe Ruth's home run record. The memory would probably have remained buried deep in Echo's subconscious if not for the condition of the ledger.

The spine was not cracked.

The leather showed signs of handling, particularly near the top where someone would have pressed their fingers to the book to pull it off the shelf. But unlike every other ledger in the office, it showed no sign of having been opened repeatedly. This book was not for reading. She rested her hand atop it and pulled.

The ledger did not slide off the shelf as it should have. Instead it angled forward like a lever. Echo continued applying gentle pressure to the book until she felt a click. The shelf swung toward her, revealing a shallow alcove set into the wall.

"Jackpot," Echo whispered.

Inside the alcove were the treasures Perrin didn't want found, some more obviously valuable than others. A triptych frame housed three tintypes of Avicen whom Echo had never seen before; the Avicen in the pictures were all short, like Perrin, and one of the younger ones had his deep-set eyes. Family, most likely. If the photos had been tucked away in this secret alcove, they had probably meant a great deal to Perrin. He would never be coming back for them, and it seemed wrong, somehow, to leave them there, forgotten. Echo slung her backpack off her shoulders and unzipped it. She carefully folded up the triptych and wrapped it in a scarf she found wadded up at the bottom of her backpack. Perhaps the Ala would know if Perrin had any surviving relatives who would appreciate the pictures. If not, then Echo would keep them, and even if she did not know the names of the Avicen in them, she would remember their faces. For Perrin.

On the alcove's uppermost shelf, she found what she was looking for: a silver bowl, decorated with ornate etchings scrolling around its exterior. It was a scrying bowl. The same one Perrin must have used to track the bracelet he had given her. Inside the bowl's basin was a ball made up of multicolored rubber bands. Echo put it aside, extremely doubtful that it was related to the bowl and its use. Perrin's hoarding habits had always skirted toward the peculiar.

The bowl was heavy in her hands, far heavier than it looked. It must have been made out of solid silver, and not merely plated in it. The designs carved into the sides depicted roses tangled up with vines, and long, willowy branches of blossoming mugwort, with its distinctive thin, sharp leaves. Both flowers were common in divination rituals, and Echo suspected that carving them into the silver had amplified the magic of the bowl. She held it in both hands and breathed deeply. The Ala had been trying to teach her meditation techniques, but so far, Echo had proven to be an atrocious pupil. It was so rare for the wheels in her mind to stop spinning long enough for her to find that calm place the Ala insisted was there. Echo tried it now, pulling in slow, languid breaths, focusing on nothing but the silver bowl. The weight of it. How it felt in her hands.

Her eyes closed. In the silence, she listened for the sound of the blood rushing through her veins, the beating of her heart, the flow of air in her lungs. And then she found it. That calm place. Once she was there, she knew exactly what the Ala had meant during those interminable lectures.

She was hyperaware of the nerve endings in her skin. All her senses were heightened. She heard a mouse scuttle across the floor in the main room of the shop, the faint murmur of voices out in the Agora as the warlocks went about their business. The silver bowl was cool against her palms, and the more Echo focused her attention on it, the more she noticed about it. There was magic in it, worked into the metal itself, perhaps by whoever had done the carvings.

No ordinary bowl would hum with that kind of energy.

Echo opened her eyes. The sensation of magic left her in a dizzying wave, like air rushing from her lungs after a punch to the gut. The Ala had mentioned something about disengaging from a meditative state, but Echo hadn't really been listening. Now she wished she had. She took a moment to steady herself. Her skin felt like it was stretched a little too tight over her skeleton, and the sounds that she had noticed had retreated back into silence, too slight or far away for her to hear them. She made a vow to herself to actually listen when the Ala was imparting wisdom the next time they sat down for a chat. There was so much for Echo to learn, so much that she did not understand. Arming herself with knowledge had always been her way of making herself not feel quite so helpless. Even when she had been a tiny runaway, living off stolen scraps, she'd had the books in her library to ground her. Listening wasn't as easy as reading, at least not for Echo, but she made a silent promise to do better in the future. The Ala needed Echo at her best. All of her friends—her family—did.

Caius did.

And that was what she would give them.

Echo put the bowl in her backpack and zipped it up. She

gave the room a final, cursory glance. Maybe the Ala could send someone down here—if there was anyone to spare—to gather Perrin's things. Or maybe even take over the shop. The world would return to normal. Echo would make sure of that. Or die trying. Either way.

She slung her bag over her shoulder and exited Perrin's Enchanting Essentials, possibly for the last time.

Rowan quirked a questioning eyebrow at her as she joined him. "Did you find it?"

She nodded. "Right where I thought it would be."

"Good," said Rowan. "Let's get out of here before those warlocks find the courage to try to catch themselves a firebird."

"You know, I think I liked it better when no one paid me the slightest bit of attention." But those days, Echo mused, were long gone. She was someone now, whether she liked it or not.

Armed with the newfound scrying bowl, Echo made her way out of the Agora, ignoring the curious stares of the warlocks and Rowan's answering glares. She felt lighter as she left, soothed by the fact that she was being productive, that she had purpose. With a skip in her step, she exited the market's secret entrance, in the hot dog restaurant on St. Marks Place, and breathed in some not-so-fresh city air.

Onward and upward, Echo thought. There was work to be done. She had a locator spell to learn and a lost prince to find.

CHAPTER TWO

"**W**e need more power."

Disembodied voices broke through Caius's half-conscious haze. For hours, he had drifted in and out of wakefulness, only vaguely aware of the hands that propped him up and moved him from place to place as if he were nothing more than an inconvenient sack of potatoes. He was not blindfolded, but he might as well have been. His eyes stubbornly refused to open to let him survey his surroundings; they were still bruised and swollen from the two punches that had knocked him out. The force of a gauntleted fist crashing into his head had been more than enough to put him to sleep for an indeterminate amount of time. Hours, maybe. Gods, perhaps even days.

A different voice responded to the first. This one he recognized, and the familiarity of it made Caius's stomach turn.

"Bring him to me."

Hands seized him once more and hefted him upright so

that he was almost standing, even though his legs did not seem inclined to support him. He sagged between his captors, and a small part of him wished that they would let him fall, that they would allow him to slip into the sweet oblivion of unconsciousness. An armored fist to the face seemed preferable to facing the person who had just spoken.

He did not want to look upon his sister and see what she had become. Tanith, it would seem, had other plans.

Although he could not see his surroundings, Caius could tell the space was damp—there was a faint scent of decay permeating the air, reminding him of long-dead plants and the whiff of rot he associated with the catacombs deep beneath Wyvern's Keep. They were underground. Probably very far underground.

He tried to take stock of what his other senses told him about the space in which he was being held and the number of people holding him. His sister was one. The soldiers on either side of him were two more. Firedrakes, he assumed. There was a faint scuffle of boots about two or three yards to his left, if he correctly judged the distance the sound traveled. Armor creaking off to his right. Pages of a book flipped behind him accompanied by the tinkling chime of glass settling against glass. Too small and delicate to belong to something large, Caius noted. Perhaps the small vials carried by healers or mages.

Seven people, then. Maybe eight. Healers often performed their duties solo, but Drakharin mages operated in pairs. In front of him, where Caius assumed his sister was, another voice whispered something in unintelligible Drakhar. Eight people, then. A paltry number to hold a Dragon Prince captive, even a dethroned one. If he was in fighting form, eight opponents would not present much of a challenge, even if he were unarmed. The body was a weapon; Caius's trainers had drilled that into him from an early age. He had molded his to be as strong and as deadly as steel. Few could meet him in combat and live to tell the tale. His sister would have tried, but he had bested her in the sparring ring more times than he could count. On a good day, they were very nearly evenly matched, though Caius's height and reach gave him a marginal advantage.

But today was not a good day.

The two soldiers holding him up dragged him forward a few feet, only to dump him unceremoniously on the ground. Caius was so exhausted, so thoroughly drained from his ordeal thus far, that he barely registered the pain of his knees smacking into hard stone.

Fingers brushed against the bruising on his face and he fought not to flinch. It was an instinctive response. A Dragon Prince does not cower. A Dragon Prince does not show fear. But then, he was no longer a Dragon Prince.

"Always so brave," said his sister. She pressed at the center of the worst bruising on his cheekbone, and the pain was so severe, he thought he might vomit. Maybe that would serve her right, to have the brother she tormented spew his sick all over her shiny golden boots.

Her hand retreated, and it was only then that Caius realized what had felt so wrong about it. Aside from the obvious.

Her skin was cold.

Drakharin tended to run hot; their core temperature exceeded that of both humans and Avicen. But Tanith possessed a unique ability, once common among their kind, now extremely rare. Fire danced in her veins, the same way the power of the in-between lived in Caius's. Fire was her element to call, and it had always felt as though it were simmering below the surface of her skin, as if her skeleton were made not of bone, but of blazing embers.

But now her skin was cold. Unnaturally so.

"You know I take no pleasure in this," said Tanith.

Caius could not resist the urge to spit at her feet. Without sight, he couldn't aim, and wasn't sure if he'd hit her, but the disgusted noise she made at the display proved that he had made his point. He decided to drive it home with a single word: "Liar."

A fist seized his hair, yanking his head upward. When Tanith spoke next, it was not to him, but to one of the healers or mages who'd been fiddling with the books and glass vials behind him.

"Heal him." The words did not match his sister's tone. This would be no benevolent act of healing. An undercurrent of violence lived in that command, promising more pain to follow. Caius gritted his teeth. He would not cower. Not now. Not ever. Tanith continued speaking, each word more poisonous than the last. "I want him to see me when I reduce him to nothing. I want to watch the light go out of his eyes."

The warm glow of healing magic washed over Caius as the healer obeyed Tanith's order. It wasn't a complete healing; the throbbing of the bruises on his face eased and the headache that had lingered since he regained consciousness faded, but the limited relief only made him more aware of the cuts and bruises on the rest of his body.

"Open your eyes, Brother." Tanith relinquished her grip on his hair. "Look. See what I have wrought."

Caius did as she commanded, quelling the urge to rebel out of spite. Light seared his vision as his eyes adjusted to being used for the first time in days. Even as the initial burn faded, he couldn't quite make sense of what he was seeing.

They were not in the catacombs beneath the keep; they were in a tomb. Alcoves set deep into the walls housed skeletons gone yellow with age. Caius caught sight of random weapons and pieces of armor: the broken blade of a bronze sword here, the pale green of a rusted helm there. The walls themselves were made of bones packed so tightly together that they appeared at first glance to be stone. Every few inches a row of teeth or an empty eye socket protruded from the wall, a grotesque reminder of the materials that comprised it. By the time Wyvern's Keep had been built, the fashion of burying the honored dead in palaces of bone had long since passed, but Caius recognized the style of architecture. This was a warriors' tomb, where victors were laid to rest among the remains of the vanquished.

The walls, however, were not the room's most arresting sight. Set into the middle of the floor was what appeared to be a large, round metal seal. A crest had been etched into its surface; Caius did not immediately recognize the language of the text encircling it, but the symbols were familiar. He had come across similar pictographs in his research when he was hunting for the firebird. It was an ancient writing system, the secrets of which he had assumed were long lost.

A crack ran through the center of the seal, and from it arose the telltale black tendrils of the in-between. Caius could feel the magic pulsing through the rift. It was like the song of a siren beckoning sailors closer, aching for the satisfying destruction of ships crashing against rocks. It called to him, stronger than any normal gateway. There was something distressingly not right about the scene.

As he watched, the crack grew wider, and the power emanating from it became suffocating.

"You heard what the mage said," came Tanith's voice. Caius tore his eyes from the seal to look at her and immediately wished he hadn't.

The crimson had bled out of her eyes and been replaced by an inky black, which made it seem as if another mind was looking out from behind his sister's eyes. Dark veins ran up her bare arms, twisting and twining like the branches of a tree in winter. The color had been drained from her lips, giving her the sickly, pale appearance of a corpse dredged up from a river. Caius wanted to close his eyes again. The thing standing in front of him was not his sister. He could not think of her as such. His sister had been a being of fire and gold, blood and steel. This . . . this was something else entirely.

Cold fingers clamped around his chin. The second Tanith's skin touched his, he felt the energy seep out of him. He had so little left to give that it reduced him to a slow trickle, a painful sludge. Tanith pulled his power from him as if she were gutting a beast she had felled in a hunt.

"I need more power," said Tanith. "And you, Caius, are the perfect conduit. You are my blood, my flesh. We once shared a womb, and now we share magic." Caius's vision blurred at the edges as his sister continued to talk. "Isn't it wonderful?"

It was not.

Finally, his well of power ran dry and she released him.

It took everything he had not to slump to the floor, half dead. He felt as bad as Tanith looked.

As he watched through slitted eyes, Tanith turned to the seal and projected her stolen power toward it. With the screech of metal snapping, another crack split the surface. Then another. And another. Magic churned the air, wild and uncontrolled, threatening to devour them all. The mages Caius had heard before threw up a barrier around the seal, a flimsy circle of magic that wouldn't hold all that erratic power for long. The wrongness of it all compounded. He didn't understand what he was seeing, but he knew it wasn't right.

"What are you doing?" Caius asked, looking at the broken seal. His voice echoed inside his head, rattling around his skull painfully. The minor healing had already been undone by Tanith's leaching of his power. "What is this?"

The thing that was not his sister turned from the seal and fixed its unsettling black gaze on him.

"For a new world to be born, the old one must first make way." Tanith's lips split into a ghastly smile as she gazed at the cracked seal. "This, my dearest brother, is the end. And the beginning."

CHAPTER THREE

"You know, I've never actually eaten a hot dog from here before," Rowan said. He zipped his track jacket all the way up to his chin and thrust his hands into his pockets.

Echo looked up at the board behind the counter at Crif Dogs. They had just emerged from the phone booth at the back of the restaurant after exiting the Agora. No one had looked askance at two people making their way out of the very small booth. The hidden market might have been practically abandoned, but the entrance enchantment that encouraged potentially curious onlookers to avert their gazes held firm. Echo wondered if the magic would need topping up soon. She wondered who would do it.

"Do you want one?" Echo asked, hefting her backpack higher on her shoulder. The bowl was heavy, but also comforting in its heft. "I think I have enough cash on me."

At the prospect of a potential sale, the blue-haired girl

behind the counter lowered her magazine to peer at them over its pages.

Rowan shook his head. "Nah," he said. "Wouldn't want you to stoop so low as to exchange actual money for food."

The blue-haired girl rolled her eyes and went back to reading her magazine.

"Yeah, I'd hate to make a habit of that," Echo said, trying to keep her tone light, but unable to fight the note of impatience that seeped into it. "Besides, I kind of just want to get back to Avalon and the Ala."

"Right," Rowan said as he reached for the door. The little bell on top of it jingled as they left the shop. "Princes to save."

"Just another Tuesday," Echo said.

Rowan's words were flippant, but they made something tighten in Echo's chest. She hoped there was a prince left to save after Tanith was done with him. A brisk wind bit into their cheeks as they made their way westward on St. Marks Place toward the Astor Place subway station. Summer had fled and autumn had snuck up on Echo without her noticing the change of seasons. One day it had been muggy and hot; the next, falling leaves and pumpkin-flavored everything. Time was marching on faster than she liked, and every day that went by without Caius felt longer than the last. Echo trudged ahead, hands burrowed in the pockets of her leather jacket, head down against the wind.

An elbow jostled her in the side when she went three blocks without uttering a single word. Echo shot Rowan a look. It was still hard to be near him, but it was getting easier. Slowly. There was too much baggage between them for reconciliation to be swift and painless.

"You all right?" Rowan asked, even though Echo was pretty sure he knew that she wasn't.

She nodded, and he let her have the lie. "Yeah, I'm just . . ."

"Worried about him," Rowan supplied when her sentence failed to find its ending.

"I know you don't like talking about Caius," Echo said.

They drew to a stop across the street from the subway station and waited for the light to change. A bus rolled past, spewing acrid fumes.

"Caius is okay," Rowan said, tapping one foot as the light switched from green to red and yellow cabs, undeterred by traffic laws, blasted through the intersection. "I've decided that if you like him, he can't be that bad."

Echo's eyebrows crept up. "Never imagined I'd hear you say that."

Rowan ducked his chin into the high collar of his jacket, long legs gobbling up the crosswalk as Echo broke into a half jog to keep up with him. "I don't like seeing you sad. And him being gone is making you sad, so I'm gonna help you get him back."

Echo let his words marinate as they clambered down the steps into the train station. It was late morning on a weekday. The platform wouldn't be too crowded, and the utility closet on the far end of the northbound track was usually secure as a gateway to the in-between.

There was no attendant in the station booth, so Echo hopped the turnstile. Rowan swiped his MetroCard behind her. He'd always been more lawful than she was.

They were halfway down the platform when Echo spoke again. "Thank you," she said.

"What for?" Rowan asked. He already had the pouch of

shadow dust in his hand, ready to smear some on the door-jamb.

Echo shrugged. Things felt complicated, and if there was one thing she hated having to articulate it was complicated feelings. "For being my friend," she said succinctly.

Rowan paused in front of the utility closet. The train must have just left the station because the platform was empty save for a woman surrounded by bags and a shopping cart who was napping on a bench about twenty feet away. After the attack on Grand Central, the 6 train didn't go north of the next stop, Union Square anyway.

"I'm your friend no matter what," Rowan said. "I know things have been rocky between us and we can't go back to the way things were, but I've always got your back." He chucked her under the chin. "Even when you're being a butt-head."

The tightness in Echo's chest eased a fraction of a milli-meter. "Butthead is my middle name."

Rowan laughed as he dipped his fingers into the pouch. They came away stained with the rich blackness of shadow dust. "That's unfortunate."

He smeared the dust on the frame of the door before cracking it open. The hinges squealed. "M'lady," he said as he offered Echo his hand.

They had traveled through the in-between like this countless times since childhood. She knew the feel of his hands as well as she knew her own. Every knuckle, every muscle. Echo slipped her palm into his, lacing their fingers together. "After you," she said.

They stepped over the threshold and everything went black. Echo pictured their destination: the Hudson River shoreline, where they would find the small boat, cloaked with the same enchantment that made the phone booth at Crif Dogs so inconspicuous, that would take them back to Avalon Castle. No one would bother it until they got there. In a few minutes, they would be home and one step closer to finding their lost prince.

Echo had a moment to orient herself in the impenetrably dark void that was the in-between before she noticed that her hand was holding on to nothing.

Rowan was gone.

Echo fell to her knees when she emerged from the darkness, her hands clutching at the dirt as if she could summon Rowan through sheer force of will.

He was gone. His hand had slipped from hers and he was gone.

Echo looked around wildly, hoping against hope that her mind was simply playing tricks on her, that she would find him standing somewhere nearby, as nonchalant as ever and wondering why she was acting like a crazy person.

All she saw was long yellow grass swaying in the wind and errant scraps of garbage that had floated down from the highway. An empty Cheetos bag fluttered in the breeze beside a crushed Budweiser can. The boat bobbed in the water about a hundred feet down shore from where she stood.

She was alone.

No. No, no, no, no.

To be lost in the in-between was to be lost forever. There had been recent reports of it acting strangely, but Echo hadn't given them much thought. She had been too focused on searching for Caius, on cobbling together a plan to find him. Nothing else had mattered. Until now.

Rowan was *gone.*

Echo slid her backpack off her shoulders, unceremoniously dumping its contents onto the pebbly shore as she rummaged for the pouch of shadow dust. Maybe he hadn't left the station. Maybe she could find him if she went back. Maybe—

Her phone rang.

Echo ignored it, cursing the mess her backpack had vomited up. Crumpled candy wrappers and empty water bottles and a gleaming silver bowl and an army of highlighters. A scented candle. Two issues of *Wonder Woman,* for some reason. The pouch was small, and easy to miss. Echo unzipped the exterior pockets of her bag and searched each one. It was in there somewhere. It had to be. She never left home without it.

The phone rang again and again as tears clouded Echo's vision.

The ringing stopped, then started again before the particulars of the sound registered in her addled mind.

The *Star Wars* theme song.

Rowan's ringtone. The one he'd programmed into her phone one afternoon.

So you'll always know it's me, he'd said.

Echo picked up the phone, nearly dropping it in her haste to swipe the screen to answer the call.

"Hello," she said, voice thick with fear and hope and a jumble of a thousand emotions she couldn't name.

"Echo."

Rowan's voice sent a wave of dizzying relief through her,

one so powerful she had to sit down, heedless of the sharp pebbles digging into the seat of her jeans.

"Rowan? Are you okay? What happened? Where are you—"

"Lincoln Center," he interrupted. His voice was nearly drowned out by an announcement over the subway station's public address system. "Somehow. I'm fine," he said, even though he sounded as frazzled as Echo felt.

She squeezed her eyes shut and thanked the gods for their mercy.

"Where are you?" Rowan prompted when the only sound Echo felt capable of emitting was a reedy sigh.

"Near the boat." She could feel tears cooling on her cheeks. She hadn't even realized they'd fallen, so great was her relief.

"Go on ahead," Rowan said, sounding out of breath as he navigated the station platform. From what Echo could make out over the connection, it was crowded with commuters. "I'll meet you there. I'm gonna take the long way home." He let out a shaky laugh that didn't fool Echo in the slightest. He was scared. "I don't know what the hell happened back there, but I'm not really feeling in-between travel right now."

"Okay," Echo said, voice barely above a whisper. The ordeal hadn't lasted more than two minutes, but she felt wrung out. Emotionally. Physically. Spiritually. "Be safe."

"I will," Rowan replied. "Go home. I'll meet you there."

He hung up and the line went dead. The phone slipped through Echo's limp fingers. A full-body tremble seized her. That had been too close. She had already lost one person she loved. The thought of losing another was almost too terrible a weight to bear.

With unsteady hands, Echo gathered up her belongings and shoved them into her backpack. Equally unsteady legs carried her toward the boat. She clung to the knowledge that Rowan was safe, that she hadn't lost another person. This was her life now. An endless parade of fear and uncertainty, marked by moments of blinding terror.

A manic laugh erupted from her throat as she clambered into the boat.

"Just another Tuesday," she said. Unable to stave off another peal of unhinged giggling, she was glad that the river was the only witness to her unraveling.

CHAPTER FOUR

The sun beat down on the back of Dorian's neck, and though his palms were slick with sweat, his grip on his sword remained steady. Even with only one functioning eye, he could see the crowd forming along the edges of the courtyard. He hadn't been alone at the start of his training session—he was never alone in Avalon, not truly, as there was always at least one Avicen watching his every move— but the small cluster of Warhawks had grown over the course of the past hour. Their rapt attention was focused on him as he sliced open yet another training dummy, its burlap stomach spilling hay like intestines from a gutted corpse. At its wooden feet lay the remains of two other dummies, both in equal states of disrepair. Someone had attached a soccer ball to the neck of one and drawn a crude smiley face on it; a swing of Dorian's sword had decapitated the dummy, and its dead eyes seemed to stare at him in judgment.

Rending the dummies limb by limb had done little to

quell the storm in Dorian's heart, but it made him feel marginally less awful. His default state of being since Caius's abduction vacillated between abject agony and bone-crushing guilt. Right now, with his muscles aching after the first good workout he'd had in weeks, his mood hovered near simmering despair. An improvement, however slight.

He lowered his sword as he gazed upon the destruction his frustration had wrought. Sweat glued his shirt to his back, and he was thankful that the afternoon had brought with it a brisk wind, even if there was no reprieve from the heat of the sun.

Behind him, a familiar voice tutted in disapproval.

"What on earth did that poor, defenseless dummy do to you?"

The sound of Jasper's voice teased an involuntary smile from Dorian's lips as he turned. It vanished almost as quickly as it had appeared, though Dorian had no doubt the change in his expression had not gone unnoticed. Jasper was far too perceptive for his own good, and most certainly too perceptive for Dorian's good.

Dorian wiped the sweat from his brow with his free hand as he sheathed his sword. It felt good to have the sword back. It would be folly to say that the Avicen of Avalon trusted him—centuries of war and hate would take longer than a few weeks to unravel—but he had worked tirelessly beside them in the wake of Tanith's attack on the island, bloodying his hands as he dug through the rubble to reach survivors. Although they would never forget years of Drakharin savagery, they remembered that Dorian had helped them in their darkest moment.

Dorian was an oddity to them, and they watched him

with a mixture of fascination and fear. Few of the Avicen at Avalon had ever seen a Drakharin fight, and the ones who still held him in contempt for being who and what he was could not resist the opportunity to watch one train. The Warhawks had been devastated by the disasters that had befallen them—the kuçedra had attacked their home in the heart of New York City, then Tanith had wreaked havoc on their refuge at Avalon—and the ones who remained standing took a perverse amount of pleasure in critiquing Dorian's form. He didn't mind. So long as he had a sword in his hand, they could disparage him all they wanted. He was confident in his skills, and nothing anyone said would convince him that his swordsmanship was anything less than impeccable. And while it felt strange to have an audience as he violently worked out his frustrations, there was the possibility they might learn something by watching him. He had noticed more than a little sloppy sparring when he observed the surviving Warhawks in the training yard.

One of those Warhawks—Sage, an incongruous name for one so perpetually surly—had pushed the sword into Dorian's hand a few days after the attack. "You're no good to us defenseless," she had said, "and I cannot be bothered to defend you."

Not that Dorian needed defending, especially from a soldier less than half his age, but it was the closest to approval he was likely to get from one of the few Avicen of rank left standing.

As he faced Jasper, he schooled his expression into something he hoped was neutral.

"I didn't like the way it was looking at me," Dorian said.

"I can see that." Jasper laughed, and though the mirth

didn't quite reach his eyes, the sound made something deep in Dorian's chest twinge with longing. Jasper hopped down from the crumbled wall upon which he had been sitting as he watched Dorian hack away at wooden foes, and made his way to the pile of debris Dorian had spent an hour creating. Jasper kicked the soccer ball head to a cluster of Avicelings who had been watching Dorian practice. They scampered over to the ball, reclaiming it. With a tight smile, Jasper made his way back to his perch and sat down, his sharp amber eyes lingering on Dorian.

It still startled Dorian, even now, how he found himself reacting to Jasper's presence. It wasn't simply that Jasper was distractingly beautiful—and knew it. Dorian liked to think he was strong enough to resist a pretty face. Gods knew he had long experience doing just that; his position as captain of the royal guard had made him one of the most sought-after companions among the Drakharin, yet he had welcomed none of the nobility's perfume-soaked advances. For so long, Dorian had held only one person in his heart, but Jasper had somehow, against all odds, made room for himself there. It had taken Dorian months to welcome the intrusion, and only minutes for the fragile thing growing between them to collapse. For how could he allow himself to find happiness with Jasper when he had so thoroughly and shamefully failed the person to whom he had pledged his love and loyalty?

You are my prince and I will follow you anywhere.

Dorian had spoken those words a thousand times. It was the truth he'd held most dear for more than a century. He had meant the words each and every time he'd uttered them, and there hadn't been a single doubt in his mind that he would be there, by Caius's side, to follow through on them when the time came. But when his prince had needed him the most, Dorian had been miles away, ignorant of the danger Caius was in. It was the most solemn oath Dorian had ever taken, and he had failed to live up to it. He had failed Caius. And for that, he would never forgive himself. Not until Caius was found. Not until Dorian knew Caius was safe. And probably not even then.

There was no time for a dalliance in his life. Not even with someone who insisted, rather impudently, on looking like *that*.

Sunlight danced along Jasper's hair-feathers, breaking into beautiful, prismatic light. The purple feathers weren't merely purple, they were indigo and fuchsia and the deepest violet. The blues shimmered like ocean waves, and the shades of green fluctuated like the rustling leaves of a tree canopy in a soft breeze. Jasper's bronze skin shone in the light. He was silent, as if allowing Dorian a moment to revel in his magnificence.

Dorian let himself revel, just for a little while. Self-flagellation might have been the order of the day, but he had never claimed to be a saint.

The corners of Jasper's lips ticked upward, as if he were reading Dorian's thoughts and found them most satisfactory. "Enjoying the view?"

Heat flooded Dorian's cheeks and he turned around quickly, on the pretense of tidying up the savaged training dummies, but the widening smirk he caught on Jasper's face before it was lost to view told him that he had hidden nothing. To gawk was one thing. To be caught gawking was something else entirely. His embarrassment scrolled in patchwork red across the back of his neck. He rubbed at the skin there, hoping—in vain—to mask it.

The sound of shoes crunching over gravel heralded Jasper's approach. It was never wise to sneak up on a person wielding a wickedly sharp blade, and Dorian was strung as tightly as a bowstring. He was sure the tension in his shoulders and down his spine was painfully obvious to Jasper's keen eyes.

"You know," Jasper said, without waiting for Dorian to gather the courage to meet his gaze, "I've watched you come out here every day since Caius was taken and run yourself completely ragged." The air by Dorian's shoulder felt disturbed, as if a hand had reached for his arm only to pull back at the last minute. "I know this is hard for you. Hell, it's hard for me to watch you punishing yourself like this. And I know I'm not always great when it comes to dealing with feelings and all that messy emotional nonsense, but I'd make an exception for you." A soft sigh. "You can talk to me. I hope you know that."

"There isn't much to say." Dorian went to retrieve the supplies—a rag, some oil, a whetstone to keep his blade sharp—he'd tucked away in a corner of the courtyard. "I was his guard, and I failed to guard him."

Jasper wormed his way between Dorian and the wall he was stubbornly facing. Dorian took half a step back before he realized how cowardly that made him look. He held his ground, which put Jasper less than a foot from him. It was the closest they had been, physically, in weeks. Dorian had pulled away from the comfort he knew he would find with

Jasper. Strange, to know that he would find such comfort in someone belonging to a race he had thought he'd hated. But he didn't deserve it. Not until he'd made things right.

Their proximity was not lost on Jasper, who looked at him through half-lidded eyes. "Dorian."

"Jasper."

"Talk to me. You need to talk to someone."

Dorian tossed the rag to the ground with a frustrated growl. "There's nothing to say."

With that, Dorian turned on his heel and made his way toward the castle. He didn't know where he was going; he didn't much care. He just needed to get away from Jasper. Away from the hurt in those golden eyes, from the powerful punch of longing that punctuated each beat of Dorian's heart.

Rapid footsteps echoed behind him. "Dorian!" Jasper called out. "Wait."

Dorian paused, squeezing his eyes shut. He had evaded Jasper's direct attentions for weeks, but he knew it was only a matter of time before Jasper made their confrontation inescapable. Dorian was surprised it had taken him this long. Perhaps the delay had been Jasper's attempt to respect Dorian's obvious despair.

"You can't run from me forever, you know." Jasper stopped right in front of Dorian. Another evasion would require Dorian to step around him. He didn't want to. Not really. Not even if the thought of enjoying the slightest warmth of Jasper's nearness made the clawed monster inside him roll around in his guilt like a pig in slop.

Dorian raised his eye to meet Jasper's. "I'm surprised you let me run this long."

"You should be," Jasper said. "I'm not known for my patience."

"I don't know what you want me to say," Dorian admitted, even though it was a lie. *You rotten coward.* He knew exactly what Jasper wanted him to say. He just wasn't strong or good enough to say it.

"There's plenty I'd like to hear you say," Jasper said. "Sweet nothings, dirty limericks, raunchy confessions. The list goes on."

"Jasper—"

"But the thing I most want is an explanation." Jasper held up a hand before Dorian could argue. "I know things have been hard for you. Losing Caius was . . . rough."

"Rough," Dorian repeated, with a huff of humorless laughter. "That is a gross underestimation."

Jasper plowed on as if Dorian hadn't spoken. "But something happened between us, and even if it was just that one night and it'll never be anything more"—his expression flickered as if he was fighting not to betray the intensity of his emotion—"I want to hear you say it. You can't just ignore it. Please don't ignore it."

Please don't ignore me was what Dorian heard. Something had happened between them. And no matter how desperately he tried, Dorian couldn't ignore it. He replayed those stolen moments in his head every time he closed his eye. The feel of Jasper's lips against his, moving with a tentativeness that had surprised Dorian. The softness of the feathers he'd run his fingers through as his hand cradled the back of Jasper's neck. The tingle of Jasper's breath against Dorian's neck. Each and every moment, preserved with stunning clarity, as if not a single second had passed.

Dorian's heart twisted in new and interesting and torturous ways.

"The last thing I want to do is hurt you," Dorian said, and he meant it. He meant those words just as he'd meant the words he'd said to Caius so many times.

"Then talk to me."

"And say what?" Dorian snapped. Jasper took a step back, and Dorian's regret was instant. He was angry, but Jasper had done nothing to deserve being the target of that anger. Other than exist. Dorian sucked in a fortifying breath. "I'm sorry. I just—"

"I can't understand if you don't tell me what's going on in that head of yours," Jasper said, reclaiming his place in front of Dorian.

Dorian let a full minute tick by while he measured his words. "When I was with you, I didn't think about anything else. I didn't want to."

"And that's a bad thing?" Jasper asked.

Dorian shook his head. "No. Yes. I don't know. All I know is that I was enjoying myself and Caius was suffering and I wasn't there for him. I should have been. But I didn't want to; I wanted to be with you."

Jasper pulled his lower lip between his teeth. Dorian resisted the urge to close the space between them and pull that lip into his own mouth.

"And now you're punishing yourself for that," Jasper said.

Dorian sighed. "I suppose I am." He didn't like the way it sounded when phrased like that, but the truth of it was impossible to deny. "It's just . . . I feel so powerless. I swore an oath to protect Caius, and now I don't know where he is or how to get him back or if he's even still alive. Every waking moment I think about him being held captive by a sadistic monster, and it's killing me."

"Did it make you feel better to say that?" Jasper asked.

"No."

This time, Jasper didn't stop himself from laying a hand on Dorian's arm. His touch was electric. Dorian's bicep twitched under the gentle pressure. But he didn't move back. He didn't push Jasper away. He didn't want to. Gods, he was weak.

"You'll find him," Jasper said. "Echo told me she was working on a way to track him down, and that girl is as stubborn as an ox."

"It isn't Echo's responsibility," Dorian said. "It's mine."

Jasper pinched the bridge of his nose. "You aren't a one-man army, Dorian. You don't have to bear this alone. That's all I'm trying to say. Look, you said your contacts inside Wyvern's Keep had spotted Caius, right?"

"Two weeks ago. Then Tanith left with him and there's been no sign of him since."

"Okay, well, say we get confirmation that he's there," Jasper said. "What are you going to do? Storm the keep? All by yourself?"

"If I have to."

"Dorian—"

"You wouldn't understand."

Jasper narrowed his eyes, and a faint twinge of something like guilt prodded at Dorian's conscience. "You think I don't understand loyalty? I know I don't have the most sterling reputation, but I thought we were past that."

"No," Dorian said. "I didn't mean that. It's . . . different. It's more. I don't know how to explain it."

I was in love with him for a hundred years went unsaid.

Jasper was never one to give up without a fight. "Try."

Dorian snorted. To explain his and Caius's connection was far easier said than done. Caius had saved Dorian's life and given him a purpose. He had given Dorian friendship, loyalty, unwavering faith. Each morning, Dorian had risen with a light heart, knowing that the path before him was clear: to be beside Caius, to protect him, to be his second. Love was the least of what Dorian had felt for Caius. There was no Dorian without Caius. Without Caius, Dorian would have bled out on that beach, another nameless casualty in a war that had already claimed so many before him, so many after. But he didn't have the words to say that aloud. Verbalizing it made it seem paltry. Words would never be enough. So he told Jasper the only thing that made sense to him: "I owe him everything."

Jasper held Dorian's gaze for a long moment. The sun was setting behind him, its dying rays skittering over the gleaming ridges of his feathers. Jasper blinked his long-lashed yellow eyes slowly as he breathed in deeply, as if a great decision had just been made. "Fine."

What? "Fine?"

Jasper heaved a dramatic sigh as though Dorian were being unbearably stupid on purpose. "I mean, fine. I will help you find Caius. We'll save him and he'll be fine and you can move past this unseemly self-flagellation phase and I can get back to living my life and not feeling guilty about every double entendre I throw your way."

"Jasper, I'm not asking you to—"

"I don't care," Jasper said. "He matters to you, so no

matter how much his smug, handsome face grates on my nerves, and *it does*"—he said this with a knowing look, as if the entire history of Dorian's painful, one-sided love were written across his forehead—"then he matters to me. So I'll help you however I can. We'll find him and then we'll bring his smug, handsome face back in one piece."

Dorian didn't know what to say to that other than "Thank you." Two little words, but they contained multitudes. *Wait.* "You think Caius is handsome?"

"Of course I do," Jasper said. "You have impeccable taste in men. I'd be insulted if he weren't."

Dorian couldn't help but smile at that, at least a little. "You're ridiculous. I hope you know that."

Jasper's shoulders rose in a nonchalant shrug. "Some may find me so. Besides, I owe him, too."

"For what?"

The question was greeted with an enigmatic grin. "You."

"Me?"

"No, the other Dorian. Yes, you."

The Avicen at the other end of the courtyard had drifted off, but Dorian was keenly aware of the few who remained within earshot. He knew that every word, every gesture was being reported to Sage and the Ala and whoever else was in charge of ensuring the safety of the Avicen's refuge. He wasn't sure he wanted this conversation to go any further, but curiosity was a bright, burning thing. "What does that mean? A straight answer, please."

"The day we first met, when you were bleeding all over my white carpet and Egyptian cotton sheets—"

"Yes, yes, I've heard this complaint a thousand times."

Dorian rolled his eye skyward. "My apologies for the inconvenience."

"Well, you and Caius and Echo were in a tough spot and you needed my help. Caius and I made a deal."

Dorian did not like the sound of that. Not one bit. "What kind of deal?"

For what was likely the first time in his life, Jasper had the grace to look marginally abashed. "Long story short, he agreed to stay out of my way while I courted you."

The manner in which Jasper hedged his words made Dorian think that the deal, whatever it was, hadn't been framed as innocently as that, but to complain about it now would have been the height of hypocrisy. He wasn't distraught over how it had worked out. Not entirely. Not when Jasper had so deftly worked his way past Dorian's defenses and made him feel things he'd long since given up hope of ever feeling.

"Is that what you call this?" Dorian said. "Courting?"

"Oh, I'm sorry. Did you want flowers? I'm sure I could scrounge up a nice bouquet."

Jasper eyed a clump of stubborn weeds sprouting through the cracks in the flagstones. "Those would look lovely on your windowsill."

They were the saddest little weeds Dorian had ever seen. "You wouldn't."

Jasper came even closer to Dorian, daring him to step back. He didn't. A tentative hand reached up to touch the edge of Dorian's jaw. There was a scar there, barely visible. It had the same white tint as the other scars on his face. There were so many. He didn't even remember how he had acquired that one. A cool fingertip traced the line of the scar.

Dorian flushed. It was the most he had allowed himself to be touched in weeks.

"Don't shut me out," Jasper said, his voice a hairsbreadth above a whisper.

Dorian swallowed thickly. He was both intensely aware of the Avicen still watching them and wholly unconcerned by their presence. Let them run to Sage and tell her all they saw. Let her know that he was wrapped around the finger of one of her people.

Weak, weak, weak.

It would be so easy to lean in, to slide his cheek against Jasper's open palm, to let himself rest his burdens at Jasper's feet just so he wouldn't have to carry them for a short while. But he had sworn an oath, and he would let nothing get in the way of that. Not even the face of temptation itself.

Dorian stepped away. Hurt flashed in Jasper's eyes. It was gone as quickly as it had appeared as he schooled his achingly perfect features into something almost nonchalant. *Almost.*

"I'm sorry," Dorian said.

Jasper turned away. "Don't be."

His steps were light as he made his way out of the courtyard. Anyone who didn't know him would have mistaken his posture for one of ease. But Dorian knew. Disappointment was written in the way Jasper moved, the set of his shoulders, the tightness in his hands. The refusal to look back, to see the regret written just as clearly on Dorian's face.

Weak, he told himself. *Weak, weak, weak.*

CHAPTER FIVE

The boat ride had not been long enough for Echo to pull herself together. Rowan had called again to let her know he was okay, and the sound of his voice had been a balm to her nerves. She'd sat in the little boathouse on the eastern side of the island, soothed by the sound of birds chirping and water sloshing against the wooden beams of the dock, for what felt like an hour before she'd calmed down enough to make her way upstairs. The second she opened the door, the sweet aroma that greeted her made her feel almost normal again.

Scent, it is said, is the sense tied most closely to memory. Echo couldn't remember where or when she had read that, but it rang true. The candles distributed throughout her bedroom, crowded on every level surface, were testament to that. Each one had a unique scent that reminded her of someone she had lost. She wasn't much for funerals, but she had found a way to remember the dead in her own fashion.

There was a balsam fir candle for Holly, the Avicen woman who had sold Christmas ornaments in the Agora year-round. Christmas was a Christian holiday, and the Avicen did not celebrate it, but Holly loved bright, shiny things, and the decorations most associated with Christmas—poinsettias, icicles, pinecones, and, most important, glitter—were not out of place during the winter solstice festivals the Avicen celebrated. She had even taken to stocking candy canes once she learned how much Echo loved them. Holly had been at the Nest when it was attacked, and she had not made it out alive.

She had not been the only one. Far from it. Over the past few weeks, Echo had collected a modest trove of treasures, one for each person she held dear. Most were candles, but when she couldn't find a suitable candle, she substituted another item.

There was a vanilla-scented candle for Ainslie, the apothecary. A cinnamon one for Hazel, the baker who'd always slipped Echo a few truffles whenever she stopped by.

A small eagle, carved out of wood, for Altair, a man Echo had only begun to know, a man she'd thought she despised and who she'd thought despised her in turn. But he had been, like most people, far more substantial than she'd realized. Echo mourned that she had only begun to see how much love he'd had in his heart before Tanith had torn it out of his chest. He'd loved his people. He'd wanted them safe, protected. He'd died for that love, and Echo would carry that memory with her until she met her own end.

A fat yellow, citrusy candle for Garland, the young Avicen who'd joined the ranks of apprentice healers the same week Ivy had. Echo hadn't procured that candle—she had come back to her room one day to find that Ivy had added it to the collection without a word. Echo hadn't told anyone what she was doing with the candles or why; it was no one else's business how she mourned. But Ivy knew. They'd been sharing a room since the Ala had ordered everyone to double up to make space for more refugees. Tales of Echo's defeat of Tanith—however temporary—and her subsequent warding of the island had spread far and wide, and each day brought with it a new face, desperate for the safety Avalon provided.

Ivy had watched silently as Echo amassed her collection of candles and trinkets. She hadn't pushed for an explanation or begrudged Echo the space. After a time, Ivy also started adding to the collection. The candle for Garland had been the first, but her contributions had not ended there. She had acquired a small bowl of colorful beads, their vibrant hues the same shades as the feathers of some of the Avicen who had not escaped the Nest; a porcelain unicorn; a sprig of dried lavender; a painted wooden knight from a chess set; and a *maneki-neko,* a little white cat with an upraised paw said to bring luck to shop owners. Echo knew who some of the items were meant to commemorate, but not all, and she didn't prod Ivy for explanations. If Ivy wanted to share, she would do it in her own time.

Their little collection grew and grew, taking over the surfaces of the room. It reminded Echo of a German word she'd come across in a book: *Habseligkeiten.* A meager collection of treasures that might appear to possess little value but that held great meaning for their owner. It fit their memorial, as strange and varied and cobbled together as it was.

Before meeting up with Rowan to go to the Agora, Echo had made an unplanned stop. She had struggled with finding the right object for weeks, but she had finally spotted it in the window of a gift shop on St. Marks Place. The contents of her backpack clanked together, glass bumping against silver through the newspaper she had stuffed between items. Her boots dragged along the worn stones of Avalon's courtyard. Stares followed her, as they always did, as she made her way through the foyer, up the grand staircase, and down the labyrinthine corridors that led to the room she shared with Ivy. It was situated as far from the rest of the castle's inhabitants as possible—knowing that Echo needed her space, the Ala had quietly reassigned her to a more secluded room.

One last flight of winding stairs left her by the uppermost room in the castle's highest tower. She could feel the draft that perpetually wafted through the room despite its thick wooden door. For the sake of privacy, she and Ivy had sacrificed the possibility of ever being warm. They could not have their cake and eat it too.

Echo pushed open the door slowly. The room was so small that on more than one occasion, she or Ivy had slammed the door into the other when they opened it too quickly.

"You're good," came Ivy's soft assurance from the other side of the room. She sat on the window seat Echo had fashioned from a wooden crate and a few scraps of fabric too small to be good for much else. Her nose was buried in a book, and the late-afternoon sun provided enough light for Echo to read the title: *Herbalism and the Healing Arts.* A stack of similarly themed books sat on the floor at Ivy's feet. The Avicen's central leadership and fighting arm weren't the only groups devastated by the attacks. The healers had also seen their numbers diminished. They were often the first to rush toward disaster, but unlike the Warhawks, they had no armor to protect them. Ivy had lost time in her training while they'd been on the run in London and she was determined to get back on track. That Ivy would resume her studies wasn't even a question; the Avicen needed her and she would be there for them.

Echo kicked the door shut behind her and unslung her pack from her sore shoulders. The bowl and the addition to their memorial weren't the only items with which she had returned. She unzipped her bag and dumped its contents onto the bed. Curiosity drove Ivy from her perch to inspect the spoils of Echo's trip into the city.

"Where's Rowan?" Ivy asked.

"He got lost on the way back," Echo said.

Ivy froze. "What?"

"He's okay. It was the in-between. It spit him out on the Upper West Side, but he's on his way. He's okay. Everyone's okay."

A frown creased Ivy's brow. "That's not good."

"No, ma'am, it is not," Echo agreed, injecting bravado she didn't quite feel into her voice. "But everyone's alive and accounted for, so I'm counting it as a victory."

She set aside the silver bowl, ignoring the drumbeat of urgency she felt when she touched it. As much as she wanted to use it right away, she still lacked several key ingredients required for the locator spell. Until each item was found, the bowl—despite the enchantments laced through its metal— was about as useful as a candy dish.

Ivy reached for the heavy textbooks Echo had plucked off a shelf at Enchanting Essentials. One was an anatomical text—similar to *Gray's Anatomy* but with chapters devoted to

Avicen and Drakharin anatomy—and the other was a compendium of spells, potions, salves, and poultices for treating wounds of the magical variety. Both had been among the Ala's extensive library, and like everything else the Avicen had left behind, they had been lost to the mage fires that had cleansed any trace of the Avicen's existence. The fires were a contingency plan they had hoped never to use.

"You found them," Ivy said, her tone reverent. She traced a finger down the gilded spine of one book as if it were actually gold. "Echo . . . thank you."

Echo shrugged off Ivy's gratitude. Her heart was still too heavy to allow for any amount of graciousness. She felt Ivy's gaze on her as she sorted the rest of the items: a few more books for the Ala, some glass vials for the bloodweed elixir, a half-crushed box of granola bars. Ivy remained silent until Echo picked up the last object: a candle in a heavy glass jar, its label sporting a cheery illustration to accompany the name of the scent.

"'Cookies and Cream,'" Ivy read. She met Echo's gaze with a knowing smile, her eyes a touch watery.

Echo nodded. She rearranged the items on the windowsill to make room for the candle. They were running out of space, but this one required a decent spot. "For Perrin."

"I think he would've liked that," Ivy said. She fished a box of matches out of the milk crate that functioned as an end table and lit the candle. Its scent was sugary and artificial, but it was enough to make a lump form in Echo's throat.

She and Ivy stood in silence for a while, watching the candle's meager flame flutter to and fro. The room's perpetual draft refused to let it burn calmly. It was a peculiar vigil, and not one likely to be understood by anyone outside of that room, but that was what made it fitting.

Echo knocked her shoulder into Ivy's. The harsh reminder of the fragility of life and the inevitability of mortality was making her maudlin. "I'm glad you're here," she told Ivy. She didn't say that enough, especially considering their lives could be snuffed out any day, as easily as Perrin's or Altair's or those of any of the dozens of people they'd lost in the past few months.

"Are you getting sappy on me?" Ivy asked, rubbing her eyes in a valiant attempt to conceal their wateriness.

"Maybe." Echo thrust her hands into her pockets. "I just wanted to say thank you. Thank you for being the Ron to my Harry. The Samwise to my Frodo. The Tom to my Huck."

Ivy let out a sniffling laugh. "I get it. I love you, too."

"The Watson to my Holmes—"

"Please stop."

"The Horatio to my Hamlet—"

"Echo, everybody died in that play."

"—except for Horatio. The Sancho Panza to my Don Quixote."

"The Sancho who?"

"The Piglet to my Pooh."

"Okay, now you're just insulting me."

A knock on the door interrupted them.

"Come in," Echo called, hastily wiping moisture from her eyes. The tears hadn't quite fallen, but they'd been close. The banter had helped. Ivy gave Echo's shoulder a quick squeeze, her eyes similarly red-rimmed.

The door was pushed open slowly, and a head covered

in tawny golden feathers appeared. Rowan peered into the room. His sweaty hair-feathers stuck up at odd angles and his cheeks were flushed. He must have run all the way up the stairs.

Ivy broke the silence first. "Hey, Rowan. Heard you took the scenic route home."

Echo hadn't even realized she and Rowan had been staring at each other like slack-jawed idiots. She shook herself internally and launched herself at him.

"Hey," Rowan said, sliding through the door that never quite fully opened. The second he was inside, he had an armful of Echo.

"I'm glad you're safe," Echo said into his neck.

"Yeah," he said, squeezing her back. "Me too." The hug went on for what felt like an eternity, but Echo was reluctant to let him go. He was so solid in her arms, so real and alive and *safe*. Only when Ivy cleared her throat did Echo step away.

Rowan took a moment to rake his gaze over the odd array of trinkets and candles and mementos placed around the room. His eyes landed on the still-burning cookies-and-cream candle. He looked at Echo, and there was no hesitation in his expression. Just empathy, raw and open. "For Perrin?"

Sometimes she forgot how well he knew her. Almost as well as Ivy did. In some ways, even better. Echo held nothing back from Ivy, but Rowan had awakened parts of her she hadn't known existed. She answered him with a nod, not quite trusting the steadiness of her voice.

Ivy climbed over the stack of books she'd been reading

and settled on the bed. With three people in the room, there was no place else to comfortably sit. Or stand. Or exist, really.

"You sure you're okay, Rowan?" Ivy asked. "Echo said the in-between was acting wonky." Ivy might have been Echo's best friend, but she was Rowan's, too. They had begun to grow apart once adolescence had dug its claws into them—Rowan and Echo's relationship playing no small part in that—but the events of the past several months had erased the petty differences that divided them. They were family, all of them, for better or worse.

Rowan pushed aside a pile of clothes Echo hadn't bothered to fold. Why fold clothing if you were just going to wrinkle it with wear? He perched on the bed next to Ivy and wiped at the sweat on his brow with a towel he'd draped across his shoulders.

"I'm fine," he said, even though Echo could see he was still a bit shaken and trying to hide it. "I ran into the Ala on my way up here. There's a meeting in the library in five."

Ivy reached across him to pluck a bottle of water from their stash in the crate beside the bed and offered it to him. He accepted it with thanks and then downed half of it in a single gulp.

"You smell," Ivy said helpfully.

"Like a bouquet of beautiful roses," said Rowan.

"And sweat," Echo added. "With a hint of old cheese."

It was comfortable, the three of them insulting each other. It almost felt like old times.

Rowan sniffed his armpit. "I do not smell of old cheese."

"Anyway," Ivy said, drawing out the last syllable to signify how done she was with the topic of Rowan's body odor. As if she hadn't started it. "Who's going to be at this meeting? What's it about?"

Rowan eyed the silver bowl. "That, I'm guessing. And my jolly jaunt to the Upper West Side."

"Okay," Ivy said, clapping her hands once and pushing herself off the bed. "I don't know about you two, but I don't want to keep the Ala waiting."

Rowan finished off the water and left the bottle on the box serving as Echo's nightstand. "Me neither."

"Great," Ivy said. She looked from Rowan to Echo before coming to a decision. "I'm gonna go." She smiled at them both. "It's nice to see the two of you getting along. Your angst was getting tiresome." With that, she left.

Echo snorted, then grabbed her bag. She could feel Rowan's eyes on her as she put aside the things she didn't need and replaced the things she did.

A heavy sigh sounded as he stood. "Ivy's right."

"She usually is," said Echo. She risked a glance at Rowan. "I really hate that about her."

The smile that graced his lips was reluctant but sincere. "Me too." He wrung his hands, looking older than his eighteen years. "Look . . . I just had a brush with death, and it got me thinking, because mortality is terrifying and you deserve more than what little I said at the train station. Things between us have changed since . . . since Ruby"—he stumbled over the words as if tripping over the memory itself—"and I just want us to be okay. I want us to start over. As friends, if nothing else. I don't want all the terrible things that have been thrust upon us to ruin that. You may not be my girlfriend anymore—and I'm fine with that, I am, I've changed, too—but you're still my best friend. I don't want to let you go."

"Maybe you should," Echo said. "Everyone who gets close to me gets hurt, kidnapped, or killed."

Rowan stepped over the mess on the floor and went to Echo. His hands came to rest on her shoulders, a comforting weight. "And none of that is your fault." He gave her a playful shake. "You hear me?"

Echo couldn't help the upward tic of her lips. "I hear you," she said. Her small smile faded. "But I'm not sure I believe you."

"Well, tough cookies. Because I'm right," said Rowan. He tapped one knuckle against the underside of her chin. "You aren't the reason any of this has happened. This is a lot bigger than you or me or Caius or even Tanith. You're not to blame for anyone getting hurt, but if I know you, you'll figure out a way to help them. You always do."

Echo laid her hand atop the one that still rested on her shoulder. His skin was warm. "Thanks," she said. "I needed to hear that."

Rowan looked as if there was something more he wanted to say but, for whatever reason, wouldn't. He slid his hand out from under hers and stepped away. "Anytime," he said, with an air of finality. Echo could practically see the walls he was erecting between them. "But Ivy's right. We shouldn't dally. The Ala gets cranky when she has to wait."

CHAPTER SIX

The library of Avalon Castle had once been beautiful.

When the Avicen first sought refuge on the island, the shelves of the library had been bare. In place of books, cobwebs had taken root, crowding into the empty spaces. Loose pages of tomes long disappeared littered the floor like carpeting, waterlogged from the rain let in through the holes in the ceiling. The chandelier that had once hung proudly above the room's center had fallen, its chains rusted from decades of neglect. Echo had commandeered the aid of Rowan and a few of his Warhawk friends to move it—the half-destroyed brass monstrosity was heavier than it looked—and it still sat, neglected, in a corner of the library, a mournful reminder of the glory days of Avalon. The Ala had taken to using it as a place to dry her laundry. An ignominious end for such a grand furnishing.

The paper mulch had been swept away, revealing hardwood floors that had seen better days. Beneath the rotting floorboards was solid stone, impervious to decay. Each day, the shelves rediscovered their purpose as the Ala filled them with books salvaged from her chamber at the Nest by the mages who had gone to clear it out before human authorities could discover signs of the Avicen's habitation beneath Grand Central. Echo had added to the collection with books found in her travels. She wanted to help the Avicen rebuild—she was not Avicen by blood, but they were the family who had taken her in when her own had proven too hostile to ever be a home. Echo carried one of the volumes of what she assumed to be Avicen mythology she'd found in Perrin's shop, along with the triptych she'd taken from the hidden alcove in his office. The book she would contribute to the Avicen's modest but evolving library—it wasn't right for so much of their written history to be lost. Echo knew what it was to be untethered. She'd felt that way when she'd first run away from home, before she'd settled into the library on Fifth Avenue. Nothing anchored the soul like a story, and the Avicen had left behind so much at the Nest.

In its current state, the library was less than halfway to what could be labeled good repair, but it was comfortable enough. Echo sat down on one of the wooden benches that the Ala had unabashedly relocated from the castle's garden to what was now, inarguably, *her* library. She used the room to meet with the remaining Warhawks, to convene informal councils on how food and necessary supplies would be distributed to the refugees housed within the castle, to plan their steps into an uncertain future. It wasn't as homey as her chamber at the Nest had been. Echo let herself indulge in a moment of longing for the place that had been her second home; she missed the soft couches and the mountains of pillows and the welcoming glow of candlelight. It had been a place of solace and safety for her. After a turbulent childhood, it had been one of the first places where Echo had found peace. And now it was gone, like so much else.

Dorian and Jasper had claimed the only other viable seating in the library—a cozy nook in front of a picturesque bay window—while Helios, the Drakharin Ivy had brought home, sat on the floor nearby. They were a motley crew, but they were her motley crew. Their presence soothed the parts of Echo that ached when she let herself dwell too long on the sadness nibbling at the edges of her heart.

Echo reached for the box of Gushers she'd swiped from a grocery store on her way home. At least there were still snacks. There would always be snacks, so long as she was alive and able to steal them. She offered one of the pouches to Ivy, who politely declined, and another to Rowan, who took not only the proffered one but also the one Echo had claimed for herself. *Greedy bastard.* Echo replaced her stolen Gushers and tried to open the foil package as quietly as she could while the Ala spoke. Jasper chomped unabashedly on a handful of sugary cereal, also stolen, straight out of the box.

"Thank you for coming," the Ala said, as if any of them would decline an invitation from her. As the only surviving member of the Council of Elders, she was the de facto leader of the Avicen.

"Thank you for having us," Jasper said. He shook the box of cereal in his hands, peering into it dolefully. "Though I must say the refreshments leave something to be desired."

"Then steal your own food, Jasper," Echo said around a mouthful of Gushers. *Ingrate.*

Before Jasper could fire off a retort, the Ala cleared her throat. "We have much to discuss, and little time to waste on the merits of junk food." She picked up a notebook from the writing desk that had been one of the few bits of furniture in the library worth salvaging. For as long as Echo had known the Ala, her mind had appeared to be fathomless, full of a seemingly infinite store of knowledge gleaned from a millennium of existence. But now Echo noticed moments when the Ala would trail off mid-sentence. Her onyx eyes would glaze over and, for a few seconds, it would be as if she weren't there. She always shook it off and claimed it was nothing, but Echo had seen the same lapse in the other Avicen who had fallen under the kuçedra's enchanted slumber and been awakened by the elixir Ivy concocted. They had returned, but it was as though parts of them were still missing, still trapped in the darkness in which the beast had shrouded them. They were back, but they weren't quite whole. The Ala had never needed to write things down to remember them before; now she used notes like a crutch, lest she forget during those awful, lost moments.

The Ala ticked off items on the list she'd written, mumbling to herself before looking back up. "Rowan," she said, "you've had quite the journey today."

Rowan nodded. "That's one way of putting it," he replied. "The reports of instability in the in-between we've received—people exiting from gateways they never intended to travel to and others getting lost—weren't just rumors like we'd hoped. I found that out firsthand, and really wish I hadn't."

The Ala rubbed the bridge of her nose. "This is the last thing we need right now."

"But that happens, doesn't it?" asked Helios, the newest

Drakharin stray. "People don't focus strongly enough on their destination, or they get distracted and get lost."

Rowan frowned as his gaze moved from the Ala to the Drakharin seated on the ground. He'd grown used to Dorian, to a degree, but Helios seemed to be having little luck thawing Rowan's icy demeanor. Echo was willing to bet it had to do with Ivy. Although Rowan would never admit it aloud, she knew he felt protective of Ivy, and she had no doubt that the amount of time their white-feathered friend had been spending with a new Drakharin was failing to sit well with Rowan. Nevertheless, Rowan answered Helios's query. "Rarely. Not as frequently as it's happening now, and almost never with people experienced with traveling through the in-between, especially if they're going from one familiar place to another using gateways they know well. And I didn't mess up."

A deeply unsettling thought occurred to Echo. "Do you think the in-between acting all wonky is my fault?"

"How in the world could that possibly be your fault?" Rowan asked. "I know you're the firebird and all"—he said it so casually, as if it were a perfectly normal thing for a human girl to be—"but don't you think that's giving yourself a little too much credit?" He said the last bit with a small grin to soften it.

"Echo might be right," said the Ala.

Echo grimaced. Usually she adored being right. Now was not one of those times. "I was sort of hoping you'd tell me I was insane to even consider it."

"Everything in this world requires balance," said the Ala in her most professorial tone. "You disrupted it when you welcomed the firebird into the world. Into yourself."

"Yeah, but the kuçedra was supposed to be the counter-balance," Echo said. "I mean, that was the whole point of it, right? The light and the dark, the action and the reaction. It's physics. Fancy physics. With magic."

The Ala huffed a soft, joyless laugh. "You and the new Dragon Prince tore holes in the world—"

"Sorry about that."

"—and it would stand to reason that there would be consequences," the Ala finished, ignoring Echo's interruption. "But it's all theoretical at this point until we've had our mages study the phenomena further. I'll look into it myself when I have a chance." An unlikely scenario, considering the Ala was the only one holding the huddled masses of Avicen together. Her attention wandered briefly, but she snapped out of it before anyone besides Echo noticed. The Ala glanced down at her notebook and then redirected her gaze to Dorian. "Any word from your contacts within Wyvern's Keep about the Dragon Prince's whereabouts?"

"Which one?" Jasper muttered, earning a glare from Dorian.

"Either will do," the Ala said, as if it had been a serious question. Jasper had the grace to look properly chastened. "Find one, you find the other."

Wherever Tanith was, Caius was likely to be. Echo leaned forward in her seat, hoping that Dorian had gotten further in his search than the last time he had checked in. Her heart sank when he shook his head. "No. Tanith hasn't been to the keep in at least a fortnight. She's sent messengers there, but so far I haven't been able to track them and learn where she is or what she's up to."

"And Caius?" Echo asked. A presence at the back of her

mind pressed against her thoughts, like a ghost leaning in to better hear the answer. *Not now, Rose.*

Dorian clenched his jaw so tightly, Echo could see the tendons working beneath his skin. "No sign of him either."

"I would not give up hope just yet," said the Ala. "I find it highly unlikely that Tanith would go through the trouble of kidnapping her brother just to kill him once she had him alone."

"You're assuming she's being governed by reason," said Dorian. "The Tanith I knew would never stage an assault on an island in the middle of the Hudson River. She isn't herself. Not anymore. Not with that . . . *thing* inside her."

"Be that as it may," the Ala said, "finding the Dragon Prince—both of them," she added in a mollifying tone when Dorian bristled, "is our first priority."

"I may have something to help with that," Echo said. She was hoping they wouldn't need it, but if there had been no sign of Caius, then it was their best—and only—plan.

She retrieved the silver bowl from her backpack and held it on her lap. "It's Perrin's scrying bowl. He used to it to track the bracelet he gave me. He'd woven one of his own feathers into the braided strap. The tracking spell he worked into it must require something to latch onto, like a feather or hair or a personal belonging. I don't really know the details, but I was hoping you might."

She handed the bowl to the Ala, who gave the intricate carvings on the side only a cursory glance. Her eyes drooped closed and she went very still. Everyone waited, silent. After a few moments, the Ala opened her eyes and smiled. There was sadness in that smile.

"It's a clever bit of spell work," said the Ala. "Your instincts were right, Echo. This bowl can be used to track down certain items, but it needs to be linked to some physical part of the person you seek. As you said, a feather or a lock of hair would suffice. However, unless Caius had the forethought to gift you with a few strands of his hair, then I do not think—"

"What about blood?" Dorian asked, none too politely.

The Ala blinked at him, no doubt silently delivering the litany Echo had heard a thousand times before about the impudence of younger generations, which, considering the Ala's advanced age—she was a thousand years old, give or take a few decades—consisted of pretty much everyone. Aloud, she said, "Blood would do. It would be even better than hair or feathers, as it is commonly more potent when deployed in magic such as this. Even a few drops would be inordinately useful, but unless you're carrying a bottle of it around—"

"Which would be intensely weird," Echo said.

"—then I'm afraid we're back at—what's that saying?— square one."

"Rest assured, I do not make it a habit of carting blood around with me, but I do know where we can acquire a sample of Caius's," said Dorian.

"Where?" asked the Ala.

"Wyvern's Keep."

"Oh, hell no," Ivy said.

Echo patted Ivy's knee. Of everyone in the room who wasn't Drakharin, Ivy had accumulated the most visits— two—to the keep. Neither one had been overly pleasant. "We're not sending you back there. No matter what."

Not to mention the fact that a ruse similar to the one

that had tricked Tanith the first time wouldn't work a second time.

"We don't need to send anyone in," Dorian said. "Helios passed along the pendant Ivy smuggled into the fortress. It's connected to the blade of my sword. We can use them to communicate with my agents inside the keep. There are some still loyal to Caius, and they've been laying the groundwork for an uprising from within. They can acquire the blood, and if the gods smile upon us—"

"When do they ever?" Jasper muttered.

"—they will be able to smuggle the blood out of the keep and into my waiting hands."

"Question," Echo said. "Why is Caius's blood lying around the keep? That seems unsanitary."

Dorian rolled his eye. "It's not 'lying around the keep.' It's in a vault, along with the blood of every other Dragon Prince elected since the title came into being. Part of the coronation rituals requires a ceremonial bloodletting. It's meant to symbolize that the elected prince will willingly shed his or her blood for the good of the Drakharin people. The office of Dragon Prince is about more than just having power over our people. The prince belongs to them, body and soul. The blood is collected in a vial and stored in a secure location for posterity. And to remind both prince and pauper of the nature of the Dragon Prince's sacrifice."

"How difficult will it be for your agents to access the vault?" the Ala asked.

Dorian shrugged. "It's hard to say. At least one guard is stationed at the vault at all times, but it's more of a formality than anything else. If Tanith suspects we might attempt to steal the blood, for whatever reason, then she may have assigned more guards to it. As far as I know, there have not been any changes in the guard rotations for that section of the fortress. According to the last report my agents sent me, only the exits and entrances have had additional forces assigned to them. Tanith has also doubled up the scouting parties in the surrounding area. Getting the blood out of the keep might be harder than getting into the vault itself."

The Ala nodded. "See what you can do. As challenging as it seems, it might be our only way to find Caius and, through him, Tanith. Our scouts have spotted her or her operatives all over the globe, but there doesn't appear to be a pattern to her travels. There must be one, but we have not yet seen it."

Echo fidgeted in her seat. She knew she should be more concerned with whatever plan Tanith was concocting, but all she could think of was that they were closer to figuring out where Caius was—and whether he was even still alive—than they had been in weeks. Ivy bumped her shoulder against Echo, as if sensing her agitation. The Ala began to hammer out details for how to proceed, with Dorian and Helios chipping in with knowledge of the Drakharin when needed, but Echo was only half listening. She said a silent prayer to the gods she wasn't sure she believed in, that Caius would hang on just a little bit longer.

We're coming for you, Echo thought. *All you have to do is stay alive.*

CHAPTER SEVEN

Caius didn't know where he was.

The uncertainty assaulted him on two fronts: geographically and existentially. He had no idea where in the world his body was. Not that it particularly mattered, he had to admit. Each and every day was the same: an endless parade of misery through the hellish landscape he now called home. He had thought that time would help him grow accustomed to the pain of having his life force, his vitality, the very thing that made him more than simply a sack of bones and meat, drained to top up his deranged sister's power stores, but the days turned into weeks, and his naive notion was proven indubitably wrong.

Yet more than the question of his location—he was vaguely aware of having left Scotland, but beyond that, the specifics remained a mystery—the certainty of his being was fuzzier than he preferred. It was hard to tell sometimes whether he was even in his own body. He felt, on occasion, like he was floating through the void of the in-between, lost to the darkness that lived between all the heres and theres of the world, stuck in a limbo that defied the senses. The pain followed him into that void even when he wasn't aware of his own body; it had invaded his consciousness, depriving him of a single moment's rest, refusing him the sweet embrace of oblivion.

Death would have been a kindness.

"Wake up, Brother."

A damp cloth was pressed to his chapped lips, and the sensation dragged him out of the void. His throat was parched. He would have killed for a drink of water, but he wasn't sure he had the control of his muscles to swallow anything successfully. He wasn't sure any Dragon Princes had ever met their end by drowning in bed, and he wasn't keen to be the first, even if he was currently dethroned.

The cloth was removed. With his eyes still closed, Caius worked his jaw, testing its range of motion. He hadn't eaten anything for days, he'd been so ill, and even the small motion was enough to send bolts of pain shooting through his skull. The dehydration certainly wasn't helping. Whatever Tanith was doing to him was killing him, slowly but ever so surely.

A gentle hand traced the planes of his face as his sister's voice murmured soothing nonsense in Drakhar. When Caius failed to open his eyes, the touch went from soft to sharp. Fingers clutched his jaw as Tanith jerked his head to one side.

"I said, 'Wake up, Brother.'" Tanith's voice was unrecognizable. She'd never spoken in the high-pitched lilt favored by some of the ladies at court, but then, she'd never been much of a lady either. Tanith's speech had always been sharp and deadly; now Caius could hear something insidious laced through it that wasn't *Tanith*. The kuçedra—housed in Tanith's body after she'd bound herself to it—had poisoned her so thoroughly that its stain could be heard in her clipped vowels and her harsh, grating consonants.

Caius's eyes blinked open. The room was illuminated by a single candle on the small table beside his bed, but even that meager light sliced through his head with the ferocity of a blow from an ax.

"Go away," he mumbled, his voice as rough as gravel.

"Now, now. No need to be impolite." Tanith dabbed at his face with the cool washcloth.

He hated how soothing it felt. He wanted to smack the cloth from her hand, but his arm managed only to twitch about on the sheets. Rebellion of the physical sort was beyond him. He would have to make do with words. "Leave me to my nightmares. They're far better company."

The washcloth retreated. Tanith peered at him with her horrible, blackened eyes. There was hardly any red left to the irises. The kuçedra was colonizing her body, inch by condemned inch. "Must you be so disagreeable?"

"You kidnapped me. You stole my magic. You had me beaten."

"Yes, but the pain was only to make you more pliant. You fought me when I tried to borrow your power. It would have been much easier for you to bear if you had not resisted."

This was not his sister. Caius pushed himself to sitting, despite the intense wave of nausea that passed through him with every pained movement. His body was a litany of complaints.

"And why did you need my magic?" Caius had little hope of receiving an honest answer from the thing that was not his sister, but he had to ask. "What was that seal? And why did you break it?"

Tanith tsked and dabbed at the fresh beads of sweat on his forehead with a tenderness at odds with her steely gaze. "One would think that with as many books as that ostentatious library of yours has, you would hardly need me to explain such things to you."

"Indulge me."

"It is as I said," Tanith began. "In order for a new world to begin, the old must first make way."

"What new world?" Caius pressed.

"Ours." There was a gleam in Tanith's eyes that spoke of chaos. "Do you wish to live in a world where we are beholden to the whims of an inferior species? Where humanity dictates the terms and conditions of our existence? Where we live in fear of discovery, of extermination?"

There was logic in her words, and that was precisely what made them so insidious. "No," Caius said, "but I have a sneaking suspicion your noble intentions will come to a bitter, bloody end."

"Nothing worth doing is ever easy." His sister placed the washcloth on the bedside table and plucked at a loose thread on the sleeve of her gown. The old Tanith—the real Tanith— would never have tolerated such slovenliness. But this new being, this entity wearing her skin, appeared to have greater and more terrible concerns. "The seals are a stopgap. A dam. They are the lock that holds back that which lies beyond."

"The in-between," Caius said. The sickly feeling that had washed over him when the seal had ruptured returned, with friends in tow: Fear. The first inkling of panic.

Tanith nodded. "Yes, the in-between. For so long, we've viewed it as a passive force, a river to be crossed. But it can be so much more than that. It *is* so much more than that."

Caius shook his head, alight with the bright and vicious spark of disbelief. "You intend to weaponize the in-between?" To attempt that was insanity. It was insanity to even *consider* such an attempt, as breaking the barrier between worlds would result in nothing but destruction. "Do you hear yourself when you talk? Or does that beast you bound yourself to control your mouth with a hand up your ass like a puppet?"

A fist cracked across Caius's face. He fell back against the headboard. The pain was nothing compared to how satisfying it had felt saying that. He smiled, wincing at the pull on the fresh cut on his lip. "Touched a nerve, did I?"

Flames crackled around Tanith's fist. Something dark slid behind her eyes, blotting out the remaining sliver of crimson. The fire in her hand turned black, and then it was gone.

"You provoke me. Why?"

He shrugged one shoulder. Shrugging both would have been too painful. "Boredom."

A blond eyebrow arched. For a moment, his sister looked like herself again. "Would you be better behaved if I sent up a book?"

"Do you think my compliance is that easy to buy?" Caius asked.

"Every soul has its price," Tanith said. She looked at the hand that she had used to strike him. It was still curled in a fist. Her fingers unfurled slowly, as if she had to fight to make them do so. "I know that better than most."

Her moment of self-awareness was far too little, far too late. But her suggestion had merit, even if she didn't know it. Yet. She had been the only person to darken Caius's door since she had deposited him back in his bed at Wyvern's Keep. If only he had an opportunity to see someone else, to talk to them . . . perhaps hope was not entirely lost.

"Fine," Caius said. All he needed was a sympathetic ear, and there was no shortage of those in the fortress, even if Tanith was too blind to see them. Her cruelty had started to fray her already fragile support. All his people needed was a push in the right direction. He might not be in a fight at this particular moment, but even from the confines of his sickbed, he could still help the people to whom he'd sworn himself prince.

"I'll be a good boy." He hoped Tanith didn't hear the lie in his voice. "But it had better be a good book."

CHAPTER EIGHT

The dream was never the same, not exactly, but it was similar, and it happened every night. It seemed to be the only dream Echo could remember. If her subconscious entertained other flights of fancy during her sleeping hours, her mind didn't see fit to retain the details. She knew just what her dreams would serve her the moment she laid her head down on the pillow. Though she'd fought off sleep as long as possible, burying her growing exhaustion in the stack of books beside her bed, slumber won, as it always did, and pulled her into its wicked embrace.

Echo stood in a hall of mirrors. Not just any hall of mirrors. No, this was *the* Hall of Mirrors. The one that visitors to the Palace of Versailles had marveled at since Louis XIV, the Sun King, had commissioned its building during his reign.

Echo had been to Versailles once, on an ill-advised and illicit journey with Ivy when they'd both been far too young to navigate the in-between alone. But the Ala had forgotten all about Echo's sticky fingers and left a pouch of shadow dust sitting on her desk, and, well . . . Echo had never been one to ignore an opportunity when it was so clearly (and carelessly) presented to her. And so she had absconded with the shadow dust—she never stole, she *absconded*—and she and Ivy had run away, entertaining the grand notion that they would be able to live in Versailles like Claudia and Jamie Kincaid had lived in the Metropolitan Museum of Art in Echo's favorite childhood novel, *From the Mixed-Up Files of Mrs. Basil E. Frankweiler.* They'd barely set foot through the sloppily opened gateway in an abandoned subway tunnel when the Ala's hands had clamped down on their shoulders like steel grips. But the Ala, though stern in her reprimands, had indulged their whimsy and escorted them to Versailles anyway. After hours, of course.

Now there was no comforting warmth of Ivy's hand in Echo's own, no steady swish of the Ala's skirts over polished marble. There was only the velvet cloak of night, the silver spill of moonlight, and the whispers of the dead.

One side of the corridor—impossibly long, far longer than it was in reality—was dominated by a series of floor-to-ceiling arches, each inlaid with a mirror designed to reflect the windows on the wall opposite.

Echo ignored the mirrors for now. The mirrors were her least favorite part of the dream. Instead, she let her feet carry her to the bank of tall windows to gaze outside, hoping that for once, her mind would supply her with something beautiful to look at. She should have known better.

She knew from experience that the windows in the real

palace looked out on the sea of manicured gardens of which Marie Antoinette had been so proud.

But there were no gloriously sculpted hedges or cheery, babbling fountains or verdant lime avenues. There was only darkness, a great and endless abyss. Echo pressed a palm to the glass and felt the darkness pulse, as if it could feel her heat through the window and it wanted—no, *needed*—to reach out for her, to claim her warmth and life for itself.

Echo snatched her hand away from the glass and clutched it against her chest. Her palm tingled with the memory of sensation.

Maybe the mirrors weren't the worst part. Maybe looking within oneself wasn't nearly half as bad as whatever lurked outside.

Her steps were unsteady as she stumbled back, away from the windows and the darkness begging to be let in.

It's only a dream, she reminded herself. That was cold comfort. A dream was as good as a prison while one was trapped inside it, and Echo knew that the cage would open only when she faced her current self and all the selves that had come before.

She turned toward the bank of mirrors and gazed upon her reflection.

Brown eyes stared back at her. Smudges marred the skin beneath her eyes, evidence of the exhaustion built up by nights of restless sleep. Her complexion, once a healthy tan, almost the color of sand, was sallow and pale. The girl in the mirror wore what Echo had come to think of as her battle armor: Dark jeans. Sturdy boots. A leather jacket. A T-shirt bearing an image of Alice sitting down to tea with the Mad

Hatter. After seeing the shirt at the Strand, Echo had actually paid for it, albeit with money pickpocketed from an investment banker she'd stood beside on a crowded subway platform. But she had *paid*. Echo didn't steal books, and she didn't steal from bookstores. Even a thief needed a code of honor.

The image of herself was not a surprise. The first thing Echo saw in the mirrors was always Echo.

A persistent itch tingled beneath her shirt, right over her heart. Echo's hands curled into fists at her sides, but no matter how much she tried to resist, this part of the dream would not be denied. The itch evolved into a steady burn, as if her skin were peeling away to expose the rot beneath. Biting back a curse, Echo raised her hands to the collar of her shirt and pulled it down, exposing her collarbone and, directly beneath it, the black mark staining her skin. Darkened veins, more charcoal than black, branched from the center of the scar, reaching for the hollow of her neck, the ridges of her rib cage, any untainted skin it could get to.

As Echo watched, the scar grew, consuming the tan flesh around it, propelled by the beating of her heart. She placed her free hand over the mark to hide it from sight, but to no avail. The infection spread from her chest to her fingers, clinging to her skin as if she'd dipped her hand in oil.

She stopped fighting it and simply watched in morbid fascination as the darkened veins slithered up her wrist, along her arm, around the curve of her elbow.

If she didn't fight it, it didn't hurt.

It had taken Echo several sweat-soaked and sleepless nights to figure that out.

She walked down the hallway, the expanse stretching

out before her as far as the eye could see and then, no doubt, farther.

Daylight spilled from the second mirror, as brightly as if it were a window. It was, in a way. To another world, another life.

Echo met the eyes in the mirror. Brown, but not the same brown as her own. Darker. Harder. Striated black-and-white feathers instead of chocolate-brown hair. Skin the color of pale sand, a shade lighter than Echo's.

It was strange to see Rose so directly even now, after nights of the same dream, twisted and mutated, but always the same. Always herself. Before, Rose had appeared to Echo as fragments, the way people did when they existed only in memory.

Rose stared out at Echo, her gaze expectant. Echo raised her right hand and Rose mirrored the action, her own fingers approaching the glass at the same speed as Echo's, as if she truly were a reflection.

"Echo," said Rose, her hand inches from Echo's. Her eyes narrowed. "Run."

The mirror shattered the moment Echo's fingertips touched its surface, fracturing Rose into a thousand scattered shards. The darkness beat against the windows, clamoring to be let in. A crash sounded from the hallway behind her. Echo glanced back. One of the windows had been smashed from the outside, and shadows were writhing through the jagged opening, spilling across the marble floor.

Echo ran.

Mirrors streamed past as she sailed by. In each, a vessel of the firebird, forgotten by time, but not by the firebird itself, called out to Echo. Some she remembered from dreams past; some were new. She recognized a Drakharin woman with white-blond hair in warrior braids who shouted, "*Cha'laen*"—the Drakhar word for *sister*—but Echo's passage was too swift to make note of anything other than the woman's distinctive scales and the bow and quiver full of arrows slung over her shoulders.

The vessels called to her in a hundred languages, half of them dead, but they all said the same thing.

Run.

And she did. But no matter how fast she ran or how far, she could never escape the darkness.

CHAPTER NINE

The garden had quickly become Ivy's favorite place in Avalon Castle. It wasn't quiet, not with its proximity to the rubble-strewn area of the courtyard that the surviving Warhawks used as a sparring ground, nor was it particularly beautiful, considering that two of the four walls surrounding it had crumbled during Tanith's attack. In spite of all that, Ivy found a sort of peace when she was working there, snipping leaves to muddle for tea or pulling up roots to create poultices for minor wounds and burns. There was something about the feeling of dirt underneath her fingernails that made her feel accomplished. It sounded trite, even in her own head, but there was an honesty to working with her hands that Ivy found reassuring in a world filled with uncertainty and brutality. And it helped that the view was spectacular.

The object of her gaze turned, as if feeling her eyes grazing the side of his face. In the late-morning sun, Helios's black hair shimmered in shades of midnight blue. The iridescent dusting of scales at his temples reminded Ivy of the clear glitter nail polish Echo had shoplifted from Sephora as a Christmas gift for her last year. The Avicen didn't celebrate that particular holiday, but Ivy would never turn her nose up at presents. Thinking of Helios and glitter brought a small smile to Ivy's lips, a rarity these days. Helios mirrored it with one of his own.

"Something funny?" His English was flawless, though his accent was slightly thicker than Dorian's or Caius's. Ivy assumed he had spent most of his time speaking in his native tongue with his fellow Firedrakes before he turned his back on them to help Ivy escape Wyvern's Keep. The memory of her time there made her smile falter. She mentally batted the recollection away as if it were an annoyingly persistent mosquito.

Helios noticed the change in her demeanor. He leaned back on his heels, brushing the dirt from his hands onto his already stained jeans. "Are you all right?"

Ivy took a deep breath, inhaling the scent of the herbs around her, finding solace even in the bitter aroma of the bloodweed roots she was planting. She pulled off her heavy gloves—a necessity when dealing with bloodweed, as its leaves had the tendency to sting—and sank her fingers into a patch of moist dirt. It had rained during the night, and the soil was ripe for gardening. She could feel the magic buried in the earth like a subtle vibration. The spell that Echo had worked in the heat of battle had seeped into the very foundations of the island, working its way through every inch of soil and stone, creating a protective barrier between the island and the rest of the world. The magic even felt like Echo, though if Ivy tried to verbalize *how* it felt like Echo, she would have found words to be too reductive, too simplistic to describe the magic's familiarity. Every living thing had an aura about it. Not the kind that human new age books liked to talk about, not exactly. It was as if every person, every animal had a unique flavor—or perhaps a unique perfume—that was theirs and theirs alone, one that was created through an accumulation of all of life's experiences, of all the people they had ever met, of all the places they had ever been. Part of Ivy's training as a healer was learning to read auras, to understand them. One of the truths about medicine—human or Avicen—was that patients were unreliable narrators of their own condition. Some people would downplay their pain, either because they wanted to act tough or because they had grown so accustomed to its presence that it simply didn't seem as big a deal as it was, while others oversold their symptoms. But auras were honest. Auras did not lie or exaggerate or understate. A person's aura told the truth of their distress. Ivy could always tell when Echo was feeling unwell or frightened or elated, without needing Echo's words to confirm the diagnosis. Ivy spent more time with Echo than she did with anyone else, and therefore she knew the feeling of Echo's aura better than anyone else's. She felt it now, coursing through the soil of Avalon island. It comforted her, as it did when Echo was present. Her friend was elsewhere, but a part of her remained.

"Ivy?" Helios prompted. "Are you all right?"

"Yeah," Ivy replied, pulling her fingers from the dirt. "I'm okay."

She looked back at Helios to find him quirking a disbelieving eyebrow at her. "Is that an 'I'm okay' as in 'I am actually okay,' or is that an 'I'm okay' as in 'I am not at all okay but I do not wish to discuss it at this time'?"

"I'm okay, truly," Ivy insisted. "I was just . . . thinking."

"Ah, yes," Helios said, rubbing his chin as if deep in thought himself, and unintentionally smearing dirt on his face. "Thinking. A dangerous activity. I try to avoid it whenever possible."

Ivy chucked one of her gardening gloves at him. He caught it with a smile. Instead of returning it to her, he plopped the glove down on top of his own, which he only wore when handling bloodweed. He reached into the basket of herbs Ivy had instructed him to pick and retrieved a small purple blossom that was often used to treat ailments of the head and stomach. He held the flower out to her and said, "Peony for your thoughts?"

Ivy groaned, but she accepted the flower, hoping the blush she felt rising in her cheeks wasn't too violent a shade of red. "Two things," she said. "One: that's rosemary, not a peony. And two: that was a terrible pun and you should be ashamed of yourself."

"Be that as it may," said Helios, "my question still stands."

Ivy wanted to insist that she wasn't avoiding his question, but since she was, she grasped for a diversion. The clouds above shifted, strengthening the sunlight falling on the garden, and Ivy's eyes alighted on a glint at Helios's throat. A thin gold chain disappeared into the collar of his shirt, but the subtle form of what looked like a pendant showed beneath the fabric. "What's with the necklace?" she asked. She'd noticed it weeks ago, and as far as she could tell, Helios hadn't taken it off once.

Helios's hand rose to lightly touch the pendant. "This?

It's just a locket. I've had it for so long, I don't even feel its weight anymore."

Something too close to jealousy for Ivy's liking fluttered in her chest. "Did you leave a special someone back at the keep?"

Helios cut her a sideways glance, informing her without words that she was hiding nothing. "Yes," he replied, "but not the way you're imagining."

Warmth suffused Ivy's cheeks. "Oh?"

By way of explanation, Helios pulled the chain from beneath his shirt and placed the locket in his palm. It was a humble piece, its square, golden surface burnished to a reflective shine. He popped open the clasp to reveal two portraits, one of an older woman and the other of a young man who bore a striking resemblance to Helios. "My mother and my younger brother," he said. "She passed away some years ago, but Hermes is still alive. As far as I know, anyway." His fist closed around the locket, blocking the portraits from Ivy's view.

"Where is he now?" Ivy asked.

"He works in the kitchens at Wyvern's Keep," Helios replied, snapping the locket shut and tucking it back into his shirt. "He was never much of a fighter, so he didn't follow me into the Firedrakes, but he's a genius in the kitchen. He made the almond cakes I brought you." He sighed. "I hope Hermes is unimportant enough to escape Tanith's notice. My leaving put him in danger, but he was always telling me I ought to do what's right, no matter the cost."

"I'm sure he's fine," Ivy said, even though she was sure of no such thing. She wasn't cruel enough to say anything else.

Helios scoffed softly. "I hope you're right." He blinked up

at the sky, squinting against the light. "I want to make him proud. And I want to keep him safe. I'm not sure I can do both." He looked back at her, his expression rearranging itself into one of curiosity rather than concern. "And don't think I didn't notice the redirect. You're avoiding my question." For good measure, he repeated it: "What's on your mind?"

"I'm not avoiding the question," Ivy said. "I honestly don't know where to begin."

Helios sat on the ground, legs crossed in front of him, supporting his weight on his elbows. He turned his face toward the sun, soaking up the rays like a contented cat. He rarely went outside. The Avicen distrusted him, and while the Ala had made it clear Helios was a defector and therefore on their side, he kept to his room, unhappy that he made them so uncomfortable. In the herb garden, with Ivy, he was safe, mostly because only the healers and kitchen staff were allowed there, and they were far too busy fixing and feeding a castle's worth of refugees to grumble about one lone Drakharin. Ivy had overheard one of the senior healers say she didn't care if Helios had scales so long as he made himself useful, which he was very good at doing.

"You might feel better if you talk about whatever it is," Helios said, cracking open a single lemon-yellow eye to squint at Ivy. "Feelings are like wine: they need time to breathe."

"That was unusually poetic," Ivy said. She abandoned the bloodweed. They were running dangerously low on bloodweed, and so far, she and Helios had managed to cultivate only a tiny bit more. It was an astonishingly difficult herb to grow, as Ivy had discovered, which was not the least of her grievances.

She moved to sit next to Helios, close enough to touch

him, even though she didn't. "Where do I start? There's the issue of the bloodweed. If that monster attacks again, we don't have nearly enough to treat any victims. We barely had enough to help the people here. Not to mention the fact that there is a hospital full of people in Manhattan—human people—who are suffering from the same ailment, and I don't know how or even if we can help them. Just because the bloodweed works on us doesn't mean it's compatible with human biology."

Now that Ivy had started, she wasn't sure she'd be able to stop.

"And then there's the issue of my best friend running off on another dangerous and deadly mission to save a guy being held captive by one of the vilest individuals I've ever had the misfortune to meet. And that's the best-case scenario. Caius could be dead for all we know, and Echo could be putting herself right into the trap that vicious bitch has left for her."

"Such language," Helios said without a hint of judgment. "Go on."

Oh, would she ever go on. Gladly. The words bubbled up as if they'd been boiling inside her.

"Echo is out there risking her life and I'm sitting here planting godsdamn weeds that insist on dying if the wind doesn't blow right. I've lost my home, I've lost people I've known since I was a child, and I don't want to lose her, too. I can't. I wouldn't survive that. But I'm here, and she's . . . I don't know where she is, but it's not here, and there's nothing I can do to help her." The words came out in a messy tumble, backed by such force that it felt as though they stole all the air from Ivy's lungs.

"And that's where you're wrong," said Helios. "You might

not be fighting by her side, but you are helping her. Right here, right now." He motioned toward the fragile crimson stems that had reluctantly taken root in the soil under Ivy's care. The bloodweed was in a shady corner of the garden; Echo had found it in an underground cave, but the plant seemed to require at least a small amount of light to flourish. The mountain in which the cave had been located, Echo had told Ivy, had bled magic from its very stones, and she was willing to bet that, in the absence of sunlight, magic had helped the weed grow. Short a magic mountain, a shady patch of soil was the best Ivy could do.

"This bloodweed didn't grow itself," Helios said. "And there are a lot of people inside the castle right now who are alive because of you."

Ivy blushed under his praise. "All I did was follow instructions on how to make the elixir. That text we stole from the keep contained everything we needed to figure it out."

Helios laughed then, a bright, cheerful sound. "You say that as if it were easily laid out for us, not wrapped up in cryptic language and ancient nonsense. Creating that elixir was nothing short of genius, and you shouldn't sell yourself short." He reached out to touch the herbs in the basket beside him, sliding a gentle finger along the delicate petals, tracing the veins of the leaves. To both Helios's and Ivy's surprise, they had discovered he had a natural gift for cultivating plants. The herbs Ivy used required a delicate touch, and she had not expected to find that in the hands of a Firedrake.

"If there's anything I've learned from spending time with you," he continued, "it's that fighting on the front lines isn't the only way to make a difference." He closed the distance between them, laying a gentle touch on the back of her hand. He moved slowly enough that Ivy had time to pull away if she wanted to. She didn't. "I know you want to be out there with Echo. From what I've seen, she is more than just a friend, she's your sister. And I know that telling you not to worry about her would be a waste of breath, but she isn't alone and neither are you. For what it's worth—which probably isn't much—you have my help, whenever and however you may need it."

Ivy was hyperaware of the points of contact between them, of the fact that they were not quite alone, of the castle tower windows that overlooked the herb garden. Anyone who peered out one of those windows would be able to see Ivy sitting beside someone she once would have considered her enemy, his hand on hers, her eyes on him. Being around Dorian and Caius had changed Ivy. She found that she could hate individuals just fine—Tanith was proof of that—but hating entire groups of people took entirely too much effort.

Helios was looking at her as if he expected her to say something, but the words that had come so freely before now seemed to escape her. "I . . . Thank you." It felt inadequate, but it was all she had. Helios barely knew her, and yet he placed enough faith in her to say something like that.

"Your people need you now more than ever," Helios insisted. "As you said, so much has been lost, and that includes the people they relied on to take care of them. But you can do that for them now. I am confident you can."

"How?" Ivy asked. "How can you possibly know that?"

"I know that you put yourself in harm's way to do the right thing, that you walked into the lion's den, head held high, even though you had to be terrified that you might not walk out. What you did at the keep required an extraordinary amount of bravery, and not once did you falter. I know everything I need to know."

Helios stood, brushing the dirt off his knees and retrieving their gloves. The power of speech had entirely failed Ivy. She watched, silently, as he picked up his basket of herbs with one hand and held out the other to her. She accepted it, allowing him to pull her to her feet. His hand was so warm in hers, warmer than an Avicen's, warmer than a human's. The people of the Dragon seemed to run hotter than everyone else. His grip lingered for a few moments longer than necessary. His back was to the tower, but Helios knew as well as Ivy did that they were probably being watched. She fought the overwhelming urge to hug him.

"Thank you," she said quietly so not even the keenest ears could overhear. "I needed to hear that."

Helios grinned, and something fluttered in Ivy's chest. "Like I said, I've got your back." He bent down to pick up Ivy's basket as well. He seemed to enjoy doing things like that, although such gestures seemed slightly old-fashioned to Ivy. She was perfectly capable of carrying her own baskets and boxes and bags, but it was nice to have someone who wanted to help her. She felt lighter now that she had shared her burdens, that she had let Helios carry some of the weight.

"What's next on the agenda?" Helios asked. He looked unbearably charming with his arms full of flowers.

They'd distill elixir from the bloodweed they'd just gathered. Then they'd go to the hospital, where the human victims of the kuçedra were being kept, and administer the elixir. Ivy hoped it worked as well on the humans as it had on the Avicen. Their biology was similar, though not identical. But then, magical healing wasn't as exact as modern medicine. It was always a bit of a guessing game.

Ivy drew a steadying breath, inhaling the powerful scent of herbs. Helios was right. People needed her, and she knew what she could do to help them. "First we brew some magic potion. Then we save some lives."

CHAPTER TEN

There was nothing to do but wait.

The log cabin to which the Ala had given them directions stood alone in the forest, its walls half devoured by crawling ivy. On the roof sat a squat chimney, which, during daylight hours, would look perfectly charming belching up woodsmoke. The cabin was modestly appointed: two bedrooms, a small sitting room with a fireplace, and a kitchen that was empty save for a few pots and pans and a lonely box of baking soda in one of the cabinets. The Ala had possessed the foresight to send them with food, all of it healthy. The cabin provided a most picturesque place to wait.

Echo hated waiting. She hated it more than most things she hated: spiders, the texture of oatmeal, people who dog-eared pages in library books. Waiting rankled her in a way few things did. Especially when she had no option but to do it.

The wards that kept Avalon safe prevented the type of

magic they were about to attempt. Locator spells didn't work on the island for the same reason the in-between was inaccessible. The wards jammed the magical frequencies, and the new cloaking spells the mages had erected under the Ala's supervision added an even stronger layer of protection. It was like painting a window black. No one could peek in, but you couldn't look out, either.

"Don't worry. They'll be back soon enough," Rowan said. With a wooden spoon, he pushed around the chopped vegetables frying in the pan he'd scoured for ten minutes before deciding it was fit for use. Rowan knew how to cook precisely one thing—stir-fry—and only because it required little more than throwing a medley of edible items into a pan and applying heat. He took an inordinate amount of pride in this feat.

Echo watched him cook. There was an ease to his posture she hadn't expected, not after everything he'd been through. Not after being displaced by the in-between like that. Before they'd stepped through the gateway that led them to the cabin, he'd hesitated, but he hadn't said anything. He'd simply gritted his teeth and plunged into the void, his hand clammy in Echo's. Now he hummed a jaunty tune, one that Echo only vaguely recognized as a pop song popular last summer, as if nothing had happened.

"Are you sure you're okay?" Echo asked.

"I'm fine," he said, words clipped. But his shoulders crept slightly upward. He kept his back to her, but she saw the relaxation drain from him, replaced by taut strings of tension. Rowan had been fine, and Echo had gone and ruined it.

Shit.

"I'm sorry," she said, "I just—"

"It's fine," Rowan interrupted. "I just don't want to talk about it." With a sigh, he glanced at her over his shoulder. "It was scary, and I don't like being scared."

"Okay," Echo said, nodding.

Rowan turned back to the pan, wooden spoon pushing the diced vegetables around. Echo wished he'd start humming again. He didn't. Seconds ticked by in silence. Then minutes.

"I have a new word for you," said Rowan. The statement had the air of a peace offering.

Echo accepted it. "Hit me."

"Shash biza'azis hólóní." Rowan enunciated each syllable with the careful precision that came only from practice.

"That's a mouthful. What does it mean?"

"It's the Navajo word for *koala*. It literally means 'bear with a pocket.'"

Echo's fingers ceased their restless drumming on the kitchen table. "I love it."

And she did. But it was only a temporary balm. The restlessness returned. She got up. Paced. Sat back down. Chewed on a half-broken nail. Got up again.

She really did hate waiting.

"Will you stop pacing like a caged tiger?" Rowan glanced up from the sizzling pan. "You're driving me nuts."

"I'm not pacing," Echo said as she paced. "I'm wallowing in the winter of my discontent."

Rowan rolled his eyes and went back to the stir-fry.

Dorian and Jasper were off awaiting the arrival of one of Dorian's contacts within Wyvern's Keep. Thanks to the mirrored pendant Ivy had delivered to Caius's network of loyalists inside the keep's virtually impregnable walls,

Dorian and those still loyal to Caius were able to communicate. The mirror was magically tethered to Dorian's sword. If he wrote something in blood on the steel blade, it would appear on the mirrored side of the pendant within the keep. As far as Echo knew, Dorian and his allies were communicating via a kind of symbolic Morse code or Drakhar runes or something. She hadn't paid much attention to the details.

"What if Dorian's contact doesn't show?" Echo asked. It wasn't the first hypothetical she had posed in the hour since Jasper and Dorian had departed the cabin, and Rowan answered it with a magnanimity born of patient repetition.

"They'll show."

"Yeah, but what if they don't?"

Rowan's shoulders rose and fell with an inaudible sigh. He was probably counting to ten. "If they don't show, then we try again." Echo opened her mouth to pose another pessimistic question. She was full of them. But Rowan continued. "And if that doesn't work, then we'll find another way."

There was no other way. They had spent weeks racking their brains trying to think of another way, but this was all they had come up with. Echo swallowed her objections and accepted Rowan's determined optimism.

"You're being awfully nice about all this," Echo said.

Rowan placed the wooden spoon on the countertop and wiped his hands on a towel he'd thrown over his shoulder. He looked awfully domestic.

"You're my friend," Rowan said.

That was a gross simplification of the mess of their entwined lives, but Echo allowed it.

"And no matter what, I don't like to see you suffer. I know

you feel responsible for what's happening to Caius, which I think is absurd, but I also know there's no talking you out of something once you've decided to shoulder the blame."

It wasn't the first time they'd had this conversation. They both let a long moment pass in silence, an acknowledgment of the back-and-forth they now knew by heart. There was no need to repeat it all out loud.

"And," Rowan said, turning back to his stir-fry, which was sizzling quite happily, "even if I don't like him, I can admit that Caius is maybe not a completely terrible person and he probably doesn't deserve whatever his batshit insane sister is doing to him."

That was the nicest thing Rowan had ever said about Caius.

"Color me shocked," Echo said.

"I know," Rowan said. "I'm really growing as a person."

Before Echo could hit him with a witty retort, the phone in her pocket rang. She dug it out as Rowan stirred the vegetables with a studied fastidiousness. The Ala's number flashed across the screen. Echo answered with a swipe of her thumb.

"Miss me already?" Echo said.

"I have a task for you." The Ala's clipped tones were all business. So not a social call, then.

"Well, hello to you, too," Echo said. She thumped the heel of her boot on the floor to get Rowan's attention. He turned the burner down and joined her at the table. Echo put the phone on speaker. "What's going on?"

"Our scouts have come back to Avalon with some interesting reports. While you wait for your friends to return, I would like you to follow up on the reports. I do know how much you loathe waiting."

Echo suppressed a sardonic grin. "Define 'interesting.'"

"Drakharin," the Ala said. "In Avicen territory."

Rowan leaned closer to the phone. "What makes this incursion special? We have spies in their territory. That's always been the case."

"According to my scouts, these individuals don't look like spies. Or warriors," said the Ala. "They appear to be civilians. And aside from avoiding human settlements, they don't seem to be hiding. It's almost as though they want to be found."

Echo frowned. "That's unusual."

"Most unusual, yes." The Ala's voice went distant and muffled as she spoke to someone nearby. When she returned, her voice sounded harried. "As we are short on numbers, I was hoping you would be able to track these Drakharin down and assess the situation. They might react better to you than to Avicen scouts."

Echo wiggled her fingers. "Because I'm feather-free?"

"Indeed." Another short, muffled conversation followed. The Ala sounded impatient, a trait she seldom displayed. "I'll send you the location. I take it this won't be a problem."

The scent of smoke drifted through the kitchen. Rowan jumped up with a bitten-off curse. His vegetables were burning.

"Nope," Echo said. Rowan was frantically waving the towel in the air to clear the smoke. The stir-fry was a lost cause. Maybe they'd be able to pick something up on the way. "Not a problem at all."

* * *

Echo blinked against the beaming Cairo sun as she peeled off her leather jacket. Normally, she didn't balk at wearing layers, no matter how inappropriate the climate—the leather jacket suited her aesthetic—but the heat was oppressive. When she said as much to Rowan, he merely shrugged and said, "Could be worse. At least it's a dry heat."

At least. Echo still wanted to crawl out of her skin and die.

The Ala had sent Echo a set of coordinates via text message. She had also appended a series of incomprehensibly selected emojis to the end of the text, as was her fashion. Echo didn't know what an alien head, smiling poop, and a wineglass meant, but ever since she had shown the Ala how to send them, every text from her was punctuated with an increasingly incongruous and baffling array.

Echo had replied with a simple "Thanks. On it," followed by her own emojis: baby chick hatching from a shell, fire, stars. She thought it made a good enough signature for the firebird.

The Ala's instructions had led them to a bustling Cairo side street in a neighborhood teeming with tourists and locals alike. Sidewalk stands were packed from top to bottom with vibrant fabrics and hanging lamps in all colors of the rainbow. Echo wondered if they were authentic, or the schlock put out to tempt tourists' wallets. Probably the latter.

"It's weird that Drakharin would come this far into a city as populated as Cairo," Echo said. "They're usually a lot warier of humans than the Avicen. Centuries of isolation doesn't exactly enamor them of being in close quarters with a race they don't like."

Rowan squinted at the map they'd picked up from one of the vendors. The compass on his phone had stopped working once they'd exited the in-between in Egypt, so they'd had to resort to analog means to track down the Drakharin the Avicen scouts had spotted.

"Maybe they were being followed," Rowan said. "This is pretty much the last place their own people would think to look for them. Too many humans. That's why the Avicen stayed in New York even after the population boomed way back in the day. We're pretty much hiding in a crowd. Maybe they took a page out of the Avicen playbook." He glanced up from the map to read the street signs. "We should be close."

They ventured down a series of twisting side streets that led them farther from the tourist area. Stray cats darted between their legs, absolutely fearless in their hunt for their next meal. The windows in this part of town were either dark or boarded up. Graffiti in at least three different languages was splashed along the walls.

"Hey," Echo said quietly, her voice hardly above a whisper. She came to a stop in front of a freshly painted section of graffiti, written in a language she doubted few in Cairo understood. "This is Drakhar. A protection rune, I think."

She had seen Caius paint such runes on the interior walls of their warehouse hideout in London. Every few days, he or Dorian would refresh them with a new coat of paint. They'd used white paint, the same color as the wall, so the runes would be less noticeable, but this one stood out. It was in bright green paint, which had dried in rivulets as it dripped down the wall. The angular shape had been drawn in a shaky hand, so unlike the careful, clean lines of Caius's runes. Whoever had drawn this one had been scared, in a hurry, or both.

A heavy metal door, plastered with peeling signs for

events long since past, stood not too far from the rune. Droplets of the same green paint had splashed on the ground, and the doorknob was streaked with faint green smears, as if someone had hastily wiped their hands before using it.

Rowan headed toward the door, but Echo pulled him aside and shook her head. Better for her to go first. Rowan could pass as human to an unsuspecting eye, but Echo *was* human. For the most part. If there were Drakharin hiding in the building, they might be spooked by the sight of an Avicen barging into their safe house. The scouts had said they didn't appear to be skilled at combat, but it wouldn't take more than one frightened lookout with a sharp weapon to start a fight that could potentially end in tragedy.

The door was locked, but Echo made quick work of it with the small lock-picking set she kept tucked in the interior pocket of her leather jacket. She never left home without it. She was just glad the lock wasn't a dead bolt or something else that would require more advanced tools. The door was ancient, but its hinges had been recently oiled, and it opened without a sound.

Echo entered the building, Rowan close behind her. A naked lightbulb hung from a chain in the middle of the room, casting a weak, flickering glow that didn't quite reach the shadowy corners. There was nothing in the room save for a rickety table with a broken leg shoved into one corner and a pile of broken wood slats. Near the door was a can of paint. Green, like the rune outside. It was the only thing in the room not covered with a liberal coating of dust.

There was a door in the far wall that led to a staircase. Echo stopped on the landing, straining to hear even the slightest sound. There was none. It was quiet, but not a casual quiet. It was a deliberate quiet. There was a quality to the silence that made her think of mice holding their breath, waiting for the falcon overhead to fly away. The only way to go was down, so that was where Echo and Rowan went.

Their footfalls were loud as they descended, even though Echo tried to keep her tread as light as possible. Whoever was down there would hear them coming. She could only hope that they were the "ask questions first, shoot later" type. She had survived a great many things in the past several months, but she wasn't sure she would walk away from a slug to the chest. The Drakharin shared the Avicen's distaste for modern human weaponry, but there was a first time for everything.

At the foot of the stairs was a wooden door emblazoned with the same protective rune as the wall outside. Echo pressed a finger to her lips, gesturing for Rowan to stay silent. He mimed locking his lips closed and then throwing away a key. *Nerd.*

Echo took up position on one side of the door while Rowan mirrored her on the other side. She crouched low and slowly turned the knob. A shuffling sound came from behind the door, like people scurrying out of the way. Echo pushed the door open and waited for an attack that did not come.

She met Rowan's eyes. He shrugged. Echo peered around the doorframe. The room was dark, but the smoky scent of candles recently snuffed out wafted through the air. A faint whimper broke the silence.

"Hello?" Echo called out, keeping her voice quiet. "We come in peace."

Rowan arched a bronze eyebrow at her. She mouthed,

What? It seemed as good a thing to say as any. And it was true.

When no reply came, Echo stood. With her hands held up to show that she wasn't carrying a weapon—a *visible* weapon, unlike the dagger tucked into her boot or the fire that tingled beneath her skin at the prospect of being used—Echo entered the room. The dim light from the stairwell penetrated only so far, but she could discern a few figures in the darkness.

More scuffling. An intrepid soul broke away from the group to come to the forefront. A female voice said something in Drakhar that lilted upward at the end. The intonation made Echo think it was a question, but she had no idea what the woman had said.

"I'm going to turn on the lights," Echo said, hoping they could understand her.

The fire inside Echo wanted out. It was easy to call a tiny bit of it forth. Less easy was stopping the flow once it started. Echo snapped her fingers and the candles she had smelled upon entering sprang to life, unnaturally white flames shooting from their wicks before settling into a more conventional tongue of fire.

Startled gasps shivered through the group. There were about a dozen of them, not counting the ones hiding in the back who Echo couldn't see. Men, women, and children in tattered garb who looked like something out of the eighteenth century. All Drakharin. None of them armed. The one who had come forward was staring at Echo in open mistrust. When Rowan followed Echo into the room, the woman swore and grabbed for an iron poker resting against the wall beside her. A frightened child broke from the group to run toward the woman, throwing her little arms around the woman's waist.

"Oops," Rowan said. Echo shot a quick glance behind her. He'd taken off his hat, and in the candlelight his feathers gleamed in all their tawny brilliance. The Drakharin responded to the sight of an Avicen as Echo had thought they might.

"It's okay," Echo said softly. "He won't hurt you. We heard you were here and we thought you might need help."

It wasn't entirely the truth—they could have been hostile, for all Echo had known—but their current state made it painfully obvious that they *did* need help. Desperately. Their clothes were dusty from travel, worn through in places and held together by careful mending. The adults looked gaunt, their cheeks hollowed in a way that spoke of long periods without adequate sustenance. The children didn't appear to be as malnourished. The elder Drakharin had probably rationed their supplies among themselves, giving the children the lion's share of food. They went hungry so the little ones could eat. Echo was no stranger to hunger. She knew the feeling of an empty stomach cramping around nothing, and she wouldn't wish it on her worst enemy.

One of the Drakharin stepped forward, a woman of apparent middle age, though her kind matured like the Avicen. When they reached physical maturity, the aging process slowed considerably, depending on how powerful their personal magic was. At nearly a thousand years old, the Ala didn't look a day over thirty, but she was easily one of the most powerful beings Echo had ever met. This woman could have been in her midforties, maybe fifties. For all Echo knew, she had seen five centuries in her life, not five decades. A little girl clung to her legs, and though one of the Drakharin men tried to pull her away, she refused to budge, burrowing deeper into the woman's leg. She peered around the woman's knee, her eyes as round as saucers. She couldn't seem to decide whom she found more fascinating: Echo or Rowan. Her gaze bounced between them frantically. A smattering of barely visible scales peppered the bridge of her nose.

"The prince told us to find you," the woman said. The child huddled even closer to her, hiding her face in the woman's skirts.

"The prince?" Echo said. Pricks of unease marched down her spine. This was a trap. They'd walked right into a freaking trap. "Tanith?"

The woman shook her head rapidly, her eyes wide and pleading. "No. The true prince," she said in a rush, tripping over her words. "He said that you would help us." She eyed Rowan with a wary look. "He said the Avicen were not our true enemy. Not many believed, but we had no choice. The prince"—she shook her head as if dislodging something stuck—"the false prince, his sister . . . she has gone mad with power. It is not safe for us there. There is nowhere safe for us now." She lowered her gaze to the floor, then dropped to her knees in a gesture of supplication. Her companions followed suit. "We are at your mercy, Firebird."

Echo stepped toward her, but stopped when the woman cowered and pushed her child behind her. "Echo. My name is Echo. You don't have to call me Firebird. And you really don't have to grovel." The woman didn't budge. "Please stand up." She didn't. "Pretty please? With a cherry on top?"

The ragged group of Drakharin rose, uneasy, as if they didn't trust her not to punish them for not showing the appropriate respect. It made Echo wonder just how badly Tanith had been mistreating her own people, to have drilled that level of fear into them.

"Caius told you to find me?" That Echo managed to formulate the question coherently was nothing short of a small miracle. A steady mantra pounded through her mind: *He's alive. He's alive, he's alive, he's alive.*

The woman nodded, though she had flinched at the sound of Caius's name so casually invoked. Once a Drakharin was elected to the throne of the Dragon Prince, their names were consigned to memory, and eventually forgotten. Their names were shed like the lives they'd lived before, so that all that remained was a person wholly devoted to a life in service of their people. When Echo had asked Caius how the Drakharin referred to Dragon Princes of eras past, he'd laughed and said, "With great difficulty." They were given titles after their deaths based on significant events during their reigns, but there was little consensus on which events were deemed most worthy of remembrance.

"How is he? Is he okay? What's Tanith doing to him?" The questions tumbled from Echo faster than the woman could answer them.

"Echo," Rowan prodded. "What are we going to do about *them*?" The last word was punctuated with a dismissive tilt of his head toward the ragtag group.

"Right," Echo said. They couldn't just leave them there. The next Avicen scouts to find them might not be as cautious as the one who had reported to the Ala. And if humans stumbled upon them . . . Well, that sentence was best left unfinished. She turned back to the woman, who seemed significantly less cowed by their presence after Echo's display of concern for the true Dragon Prince. That must have earned her some brownie points. "Does everyone here speak English?"

The woman shook her head.

"Can you translate?"

A nod.

Echo addressed the Drakharin, pausing every now and then to give the woman time to translate. "There's a safe place we can bring you. There are wards—strong ones—that will protect you. Not even Tanith can get through them." Echo recalled laying the ward with her strength and feeling her magic seep into the land. "Trust me. I built them myself."

The Drakharin shared a dubious look, none of them appearing convinced that leaving the relative safety of their hideout with an Avicen and public enemy number one was a grand idea.

"It's an island," Echo continued. "With a castle. It's very nice."

"Avalon?" Rowan's voice was flat and disbelieving. He spoke slowly, as if she had just said something very, very stupid. "You can't seriously mean to suggest we bring them to Avalon. That's insane. *You're* insane."

Echo grabbed hold of Rowan's sleeve and dug her nails into his arm as sharply as she could. He scowled and tried to tug his arm free, but she held on.

"Rowan," Echo said through gritted teeth. "Sidebar."

She guided him to the far corner of the room. The Drakharin could still see them and they could see the Drakharin, but if she pitched her voice low enough, she might not be overheard.

"Look at them," said Echo. The Drakharin were a sorry sight, but it was the children who tugged at her heartstrings the strongest. They were so young. Too young for the hardship they faced. And their parents didn't deserve to see their children suffer while they tried to find a better life for them. "They obviously need help. And think about the little ones, Rowan. They're just kids. We don't hurt kids."

"I'm not suggesting we hurt them," Rowan said, seemingly horrified that Echo would dare to accuse him of such a thing.

"No, you're just suggesting we don't help them, which is pretty much the same thing as hurting them," Echo said.

Rowan did not appear entirely convinced, but his shoulders had relaxed somewhat, and Echo could tell from the softening of his expression that he needed only the tiniest of nudges to come around. She laid a hand on his bicep. "You know this is the right thing to do."

He sighed. "I know, I know. It's just"—he looked back at the Drakharin—"it's not going to be easy persuading the council to open their doors to the Drakharin. Even refugees."

"And that's why you're going to win their hearts and minds," Echo said. "People like you. They respect you. They saw how you stepped up after the attack on the Nest, and they trust you and your judgment." She gave his arm a little squeeze. "They can't keep carrying on the way they always have. Somebody has to bridge the divide between the Avicen and the Drakharin. They need you to help show them a better way. The best way to fight hatred is with kindness. Be their example."

Rowan narrowed his eyes at her, but a soft smile played at the corners of his lips. "That's a mighty fine pep talk."

Echo gave his arm a little punch. "I learned from the best."

"I can't believe I'm saying this," Rowan said, "but what about Caius? And Dorian and Jasper?"

Echo squared her shoulders. "I'll go back to the cabin and wait for them. You lead these people to safety." At Rowan's dubious expression, she added, "Can't you handle a pack of Drakharin refugees on your own?"

He sighed. She saw the scales tipping within him. He didn't want to. He *really* didn't want to. But he would. Because it was the right thing to do. Because he was good in a way so few people were. After an interminable moment of Echo projecting a psychic *Say yes!* at him, Rowan rolled his eyes and said, "Yes. Fine. Go enjoy my stir-fry without me. I'll bring them to New York."

"I can't enjoy the stir-fry," Echo said. "You burned it, remember?"

Rowan shrugged. "So pick up some shawarma on the way back."

"I will."

"Fine."

"Fine." Rowan stuck his tongue out at her.

Echo rolled her eyes and turned back to the Drakharin, a warm smile on her face. "Pack your bags. This nice man here is taking you to Avalon."

CHAPTER ELEVEN

Autumn in Edinburgh was lovely. Or it would have been lovely if not for Jasper's dour mood. Instead of appreciating the turn of leaves from green to gold, all he saw was decay and the inevitable mess as the leaves fell from the branches to become soggy mulch on the pavement during Scotland's perpetual rainy season. He tapped one foot impatiently as he waited in line to order something warm to drink. Maybe if he ingested enough sugar, it would grant him a false sense of happiness.

Dorian had been in a rotten mood for weeks—understandably, but still—and it had proven contagious. Their last real conversation in the training yard hadn't done much to lift either of their spirits.

The café was bright and cheerful, and the girl who took Jasper's order offered him a wide smile he didn't bother returning. He tugged his hat down over his ears. He hated hats. It galled him to have to hide his feathers—they were *magnificent*—and it would be hell to unflatten them later. As he waited for the barista to prepare his and Dorian's drinks, he considered the patrons in the little café, nestled in a narrow side street in Edinburgh's Old Town but close enough to the tourist center that the number of people provided Jasper and Dorian a modicum of anonymity. Jasper's brown skin didn't stand out quite so much, and no one looked too hard at the concealer caked over Dorian's scales.

Jasper hoped Dorian's contact would reach them soon. He wanted this business to be over with. Not only for Caius's sake—he could admit to himself that he wasn't nearly that altruistic—but also for his own. Once Dorian was happy, then *Jasper* could go on being happy. That this was the way of things made him cringe internally.

The barista finished making their drinks, topping Jasper's with a generous helping of whipped cream and a drizzle of chocolate sauce. He might have separated himself from the Avicen by attitude and distance, but he shared the sweet tooth so common among his kind. He paid, tipped the girl well but not too well, as both stinginess and excessive generosity were bound to attract attention, and made his way to the table near the back of the café where Dorian was currently staring a hole into the wall opposite his seat.

"Yoo-hoo, earth to Dorian."

Jasper waved his elbow in front of Dorian's face, ripping him from his guilt-ridden reverie. Jasper stood beside the table they'd occupied in the Edinburgh café since that morning. Dorian eyed the two steaming mugs of cocoa in Jasper's hands with suspicion that lessened only somewhat when Jasper placed the plain one in front of Dorian and kept the sugary monstrosity for himself.

"The Avicen sweet tooth is a great and terrible thing," Dorian said. He gave his drink a dubious sniff, then crinkled his nose in distaste. "I asked for coffee." It was petulant, even for Dorian.

Rolling his eyes, Jasper slid into the seat opposite Dorian. He began spooning up the whipped cream and shoveling it into his mouth. He had to eat it before he could get to the liquid. Whipped cream facial hair wasn't cute past the age of five. "Trust me, Dorian, caffeine is the last thing you need. You're strung so tightly I'm expecting you to snap like a worn rubber band at any minute."

"I've been awake for the better part of forty-one hours," Dorian said, scrubbing a hand over his face. He did look tired. Dark smudges had appeared beneath his eyes, and his mouth was carved into a seemingly permanent frown. "And if I don't ingest something caffeinated soon, I'm likely to pass out, face-first, into this hot cocoa."

"Drink it," Jasper said, his tone softening. "The sugar will help keep you awake. And the soul-cleansing embrace of chocolate might make you slightly less gloomy."

With a grudging sigh, Dorian lifted the mug to his lips and took a tentative sip. Jasper had made sure it wasn't as excruciatingly sweet as his own. Dorian didn't appreciate the beauty of sugar the way he did. It probably would have damaged Dorian's street cred if all that world-weary stoicism enjoyed a doughnut every once in a while. Jasper blew on his own cocoa. It was a touch too hot to drink. But Dorian ignored the way the cocoa must have scalded his tongue.

Perhaps his guilt was making him feel self-destructive, as if he deserved the pain.

Jasper's amber eyes narrowed. "That cocoa is approximately eight million degrees. Let it cool down first."

Dorian took another sip.

Idiot, Jasper thought.

He watched Dorian drink in stubborn silence, his brow wrinkling in contemplation. Jasper was more perceptive than most people thought—raging narcissism was a mask he hid behind so that no one ever suspected how closely he was watching them—especially where it concerned Dorian. Especially since that night at Avalon, before Dorian had found out about Caius's abduction. Jasper knew that Dorian felt as though he'd truly failed the one person he'd sworn to protect. It had been a wonderful, joyous night, and in the weeks since then, Dorian had been acting as if he deserved neither joy nor wonder in his life.

"Didn't we talk about you punishing yourself?" Jasper asked.

"I'm not punishing myself," Dorian lied.

Jasper was kind enough not to call him on it.

Outside, an insistent autumn rain pounded against the sidewalk, painting the city in shades of gray.

Jasper cradled the mug in his hands, leaning down to blow gently on it again. His cocoa was still this side of scalding; it needed a few minutes before it was drinkable.

Silence—as complete a silence as one of the busiest cafés in the middle of Edinburgh ever saw, anyway—descended on the table he shared with the man who was potentially, possibly, definitely-not-but-definitely-maybe his boyfriend. They hadn't had that conversation yet, and judging by the storm clouds that perpetually flitted across his maybe-boyfriend's eye as his maybe-boyfriend contemplated the fate of a man who was *not* Jasper, it wasn't a conversation they'd be having anytime soon. Bigger fish to fry and so on. Jasper sipped his cocoa and burned his tongue.

Dorian drummed his fingers on the worn wooden table-top. In the past few hours, he'd already fidgeted with the salt and pepper shakers, peeled the label off a defenseless bottle of Heinz ketchup, and ripped no fewer than five napkins to shreds. His hands refused to be idle. Jasper knew they itched to reach for a blade—sharp, deadly things were comforting to Dorian in a way that Jasper should not have found quite so appealing—but stillness had been forced upon them while Dorian waited to hear back from his contact within Wyvern's Keep. Nothing to do but wait, and in the meantime, destroy the table settings. The silence stretched.

Jasper ached to reach across the table and take Dorian's agitated hands in his own, to stroke the scars and calluses on them until the tension bled from them, but he knew it would do no good. Dorian had turned down Jasper's offers of comfort at every turn. Gently, of course. He was always so gentle with Jasper, as if sensing that gentleness was the sort of thing with which Jasper was desperately unfamiliar, but there was no amount of softness that could take the sting out of his refusals. Jasper kept his hands wrapped firmly around the warm ceramic of his mug and ignored the hair-line fractures forming in his heart as he watched Dorian tear himself to pieces.

"You know," Jasper said, "this is probably the worst date I've ever been on."

Dorian grunted in response, his eye drifting to the door,

as it had been throughout the hours they'd been sitting there. His contact was late. Two hours and twenty-seven minutes late to be exact, but who was counting? Certainly not Jasper.

An abrupt stillness fell over Dorian, his one good eye riveted to the door. Jasper swiveled in his seat to see what had caused Dorian's shift, but all he saw was a twentysomething hipster entering the café, newsboy cap pulled low to protect his eyes from the drizzle that had been constant since their arrival in Edinburgh. The man fit the description Dorian had given Jasper before they'd left their nondescript little hostel—dark hair, thick eyebrows, strong jaw, prominent nose—but he was human. Not their guy. Jasper watched as the man bantered with the girl behind the counter before placing his order. With a sigh, he turned back to face Dorian just in time to see the Drakharin's shoulders droop. He looked deflated, as if the surge of expectancy had taken something vital out of him.

Jasper opened his mouth to reassure Dorian that everything was going to be okay—a saccharine platitude that he wasn't sure he could deliver with a straight face—when the bell above the door tinkled again. A stillness passed over Dorian as his one eye tracked someone approaching their table. Jasper chanced a look over his shoulder. A young man neared, his slate-gray eyes resting on Dorian.

He walked past their table and went into the men's room. Curious.

They waited in silence for a few minutes. Dorian said nothing. He simply sipped his cocoa with what would have looked like nonchalance to anyone but Jasper. Soon enough, the man exited the bathroom and walked right out of the café.

Without a word, Dorian got up and entered the bathroom.

A dead drop. Jasper smiled into his cocoa. In the loo. How clandestine.

When Dorian reemerged, there was a small, vial-shaped bump in the front pocket of his trousers. He sank back into his seat and picked up his mug.

"We should wait a few minutes before leaving," Dorian said quietly.

"Do you think we're being watched?" Jasper had scouted the café before they'd chosen it for their rendezvous. He hadn't noticed anything or anyone suspicious, but it was possible he had missed something, even with eyes as keen as his.

Dorian shrugged. "Probably not," he said. "But I find it's always best to assume the worst and be pleasantly surprised when it fails to come to pass."

Jasper snorted into his cocoa. "That's remarkably optimistic coming from you."

A smile ghosted across Dorian's lips. Jasper's heart gave an embarrassing lurch at the sight of it. "What can I say?" Dorian's tone was casual, but one hand rested on his pocket and its precious cargo. "Our day just got a whole lot brighter."

CHAPTER TWELVE

If there was one thing Echo had learned about magic in her seventeen years of existence, it was that ritual was of the utmost importance.

What made magic work wasn't the specific accoutrements each individual spell called for—it wasn't the cloying incense or the softly glowing candles or the particular arrangement of herbs and flowers around an altar. Each and every item served its purpose, but that purpose wasn't the mechanism of the magical event. Magic was powered by will. That was the most fundamental tenet of spell work. One had to believe that they possessed not only the ability to perform a spell but also the strength, energy, and focus. Doubt was the surest way to self-sabotage, and a lack of concentration was just as deadly to a spell's success as a lack of confidence. The supplies themselves worked no magic—they were there to serve the needs of the caster. In this case, Echo.

It was all an elaborate process to get one's head in the game. *In the zone,* Echo thought. This spell was more complex than what she was used to. Anything that reached across distance required a great deal of power and therefore a great deal of focus. She lit a bundle of sage with one of the candles that cast a warm, buttery glow on the cabin's walls. The scent reminded her of the healing chambers at the Nest. Sage was said to keep away negativity, and it was used as an all-purpose cleanser for rituals. It was sort of like the Windex of magic. The smell brought back memories: her first trip to the healer, cradling a broken arm, the Ala a warm, comforting presence at her back as magic stitched together the splintered bone quicker than her human body would accomplish on its own. Visiting Ivy during her apprenticeship. The smell had clung to Ivy for weeks as the senior healers had kept the apprentices busy with quotidian injuries too minor for their attention: burns, fractures, headaches, upset stomachs. The Avicen were a hardy lot; they rarely fell ill, but they weren't indestructible. They got hurt as easily as anyone else, a fact Echo could not afford to forget. All those fragile lives cradled in her hands, as delicate as spun sugar, and as easily crushed.

The scented smoke filled the small room, and Echo set the sage aside in a small metal bowl, where it would continue to burn on its own. She drew in a deep breath, then another, letting the sage work its unique magic, relaxing her, opening up her mind.

One by one, the voices in her head fell silent. As she had grown used to their presence, the sound of the previous vessels had faded into the background, like chatter heard between radio stations. The white noise had filled the gaps she hadn't known were there. Now the quiet was unnerving—Echo thought she would feel relieved for the voices to be gone, at least for a little while, but her mind felt curiously empty, as if the presence of the vessels had left her irreparably changed. Without the soft murmur of those voices, she didn't feel quite whole. And that was more unnerving than she cared to admit.

Echo poured water into the silver bowl pilfered from Perrin's shop. The spell in the book she had consulted called for water taken directly from the source—clean, unsullied by pollution—but since they didn't have enough shadow dust to gallivant about the globe, a bottle of Poland Spring would have to do. It had *spring* in the name; as far as Echo was concerned, that meant it pretty much came from Mother Nature herself.

She was vaguely aware of the presence of other people in the room. Dorian had not even needed to insist on being there. The fact that he would be was a given, and Echo was grateful, even if his smoldering unease was hard to ignore. The spell warned that the images the caster would see might be incoherent or disjointed. The firebird gave her a little extra—*a lot* extra—power to push the spell harder and further, but Echo was no Seer. It took a very particular skill to make sense of magical visions, a skill Echo had never needed to develop. Dorian might recognize things Echo would not if Caius was being held someplace familiar.

Jasper sat beside Dorian, his perfect stillness in stark contrast to Dorian's restlessness. Another given: that Jasper would not leave Dorian's side when he was quite so fragile. Not that either of them would ever admit that out loud.

Maybe not even to each other. Not in so many words, anyway. Their relationship still did not entirely make sense to Echo, but that was not the mystery she was preparing to solve.

Echo paused, her hands hovering over the implements gathered on her makeshift altar. She had read the spell a dozen times to memorize it and then a dozen more just to be sure, but still . . . It was so quiet in her head. It would be nice to have another voice ground her.

"Tell me again what I'm supposed to do," Echo said. "I didn't forget, I just . . ."

Dorian seemed to understand exactly what she needed. He spoke softly so as not to disturb the quiet atmosphere of the room primed and ready for magic. "You're going to say the chant. Then you're going to take the vial"—he indicated the small glass bottle beside Echo's right hand with a nod—"and you're going to pour it into the bowl. Then you repeat the chant. Focus on Caius. Think of him and only him. Clear your mind of anything else. The blood should start to form shapes if the spell is working. And then . . ." He trailed off, his words laced through with fear and longing.

Echo finished the sentence for him: "And then we wait."

What remained unspoken: the possibility that Echo would see nothing, that the blood would swirl in the water, imbued with no magic, take no form. The spell only worked on the living, after all, and if Caius was . . .

No.

It didn't bear considering.

Echo reached for the glass vial containing Caius's blood. Silver vines adorned with miniature flowers wrapped around it. The flowers were so perfectly carved that Echo was sure it had to have been done by magic. No hands could craft something so delicate so immaculately. A deep emerald-green wax sealed the stopper. A crest had been pressed into the wax—Caius's heraldry. Echo had seen it on the tunics of the guards at Wyvern's Keep and on the locket Caius had gifted to Rose a century ago. Now it hung from Echo's neck, tucked beneath her shirt. She hadn't taken it off since Caius was kidnapped. Not even to shower. It remained, a weight around her neck, a pressure against her heart, and it would remain there until she found him. It was not a matter of if, only of when. She refused to accept anything else.

"Jasper," Echo said. "The incantation."

A book slid into her line of sight, open to a page covered in painfully small script. It would have been illegible to any-one who hadn't spent years deciphering the Ala's atrocious handwriting.

The words were in Avicet, but they rolled off Echo's tongue with practiced ease. Months ago, pronouncing the incomprehensible phonemes of the language would have been impossible, but now she spoke it as fluently as if it were her first language. Even though it wasn't her mother tongue, it was Rose's. And what Rose knew, Echo knew. She clutched the vial tightly and let her mind retreat, allowing Rose's consciousness to pierce her waking brain further than she ever had before.

When she reached the part of the spell that called for a piece of the missing, she broke the wax with the tip of her dagger. The stopper slid free with an audible pop. Echo tipped the contents of the vial into the silver bowl. Blood spread through the clear water like scarlet clouds.

Echo watched the water stain crimson and repeated the

words of the Avicet chant. The blood didn't settle. It swirled and eddied in the bowl as if it had a life of its own, dancing with the rhythm of Echo's voice. There was a sound of other voices whispering, feminine voices. Not Dorian or Jasper. Echo almost looked up from the silver bowl, but her connection to the magic was only just building. If she looked away now, it would snap, like a too-thin rope trying to keep a boulder from rolling downhill. The voices joined hers in a susurration of ghostly chanting. As they rose and fell with the intonation of her voice, Echo realized what they were: the vessels, lending whatever traces of magical strength they had to her. The thought warmed her and did what the vessels wanted: it made her stronger.

With the added force of the vessels' chanting, Echo let her own words fly from her lips on autopilot. In order for the spell to work, she had to focus on the object of her desire.

Caius.

Desire was the most critical impetus behind all magic. It was the most basic form of willpower. A desire strong enough could move mountains, heal wounds, inflict pain; could summon fire and ice and wind and all the forces of nature. Desire could turn a human girl into a being of flame and fury until all there was left in her wake was ash and smoke.

She thought of Caius, flitting from one memory to the other, refusing to fall into any single one lest that throw the spell off course. It wasn't enough to simply remember with perfect clarity the line of his jaw or the sound of his laugh or the wrinkle that formed between his brows when he was mad. Her vision of Caius needed to encompass the totality of him, not merely be a snapshot of his existence.

She started from the beginning: the first time she had

ever seen him, his face bathed in moonlight and shadow. They had stood on the opposite sides of a war begun long before either of them had been born. She had gone to steal something from a museum and he had followed her there. He, a prince in disguise. She, a thief with a penchant for trouble. They had fit together like two pieces of a puzzle, though neither one had known it at the time. She had needed him to show her to her destiny, just as he had needed her to help him find his own.

They had not remained locked in those two identities for long. Echo had become an ally—however reluctant—and Caius had fallen from his throne. Both of them had been set adrift, unmoored from the truths they had taken as absolute.

She remembered the way his hands felt wrapped around her wrists the first time she kissed him. His thumbs had rubbed circles into her skin, tracing the lines of her veins. His lips had been warm, and softer than she had expected. The kiss had been slow. So painfully slow. And brief.

Not like this, he had said.

She hadn't understood it then, but she did now.

Caius hadn't been ready. Neither had she. Echo hadn't possessed the foresight to know it then, but he had seen it in her. He had known. And he had pushed her away. Despite how badly starved he was for touch, for even the most basic expressions of affection, he had pushed her away. He had denied himself for her benefit. But he had let her take her comfort from him. Had allowed her to fall asleep safe in the circle of his arms on the forest floor, the two of them entwined together against an uncertain future.

And then she had stumbled into the Oracle's lair and learned the truth of Caius's identity, and then into the room in which the Oracle had said Echo would find the firebird. In it, she had found only herself.

From memory, she conjured the sight of Caius in battle, his face speckled with the blood of the foes he had slain. He was most himself in the middle of a fight. He didn't relish it the way Tanith did, but it was as if the part of him he held tightly on a leash was unchained and let free. He fought like a dancer, all lithe grace and sinuous muscle.

Echo remembered the way he had kissed her after that. Soft and tentative, an exploratory gesture.

She indulged in the sense memory of his hand in hers as they walked down a crowded London street. A perfect moment, and one easily shattered but never lost.

She called forth the smell of his skin during a time she had sought solace in his embrace. Woodsmoke and apples and something indefinable and otherworldly. Something magical. A scent uniquely his own.

The blood in the bowl began to boil violently.

Echo's focus sharpened. She grabbed at memories of Caius as they flew by, a child snatching butterflies out of the air.

The huff of a quiet chuckle when he was trying not to laugh.

The little groan of ecstasy when he bit into something sinfully delicious.

The dance of his fingers over a blade as he tended to it with a whetstone and an oiled rag.

The crinkles at the corners of his eyes when he looked at her.

The low timbre of his voice when he spoke to her of myths and legends and stories passed down from generation to generation. Tales of dragons arcing through the sky on majestic wings. Of gods and nightmares and dreams of peace.

She thought of all the things that made him—as a person, not a prince—all the secret hopes and fears he had shared with her on sleepless nights. Of the way he said her name when there was no one else around.

A ruby glow began to emanate from the silver bowl as the clouds in its contents shrank and expanded and took shape.

A figure kneeling at another's feet. Head bowed, either in pain or supplication. Another shift of the blood in the water, another image, this one clearer than the last.

An unconscious man shackled with heavy manacles, his head lolling on his shoulders. One of his legs was bent at an unnatural angle. Someone stood over him, a healer perhaps, maybe even a mage, holding his hands out to the man's many wounds, closing them. Setting the broken bone.

Another figure, this one clad in shining armor, opening the wounds anew. Delighting in the spill of Caius's blood. A curling black wisp snaked across the surface of the blood. In the blink of an eye, it was gone.

The image writhed into nonsense and then began to solidify. Echo could see the shape of Caius's body, trussed up in chains in a cavernous room.

He was in pain. He was suffering and there was nothing Echo could do about it. The tether of magic tying her to the vision in the bowl wavered as anger and hopelessness warred for her attention.

A hand gripped her shoulder, a solid, comforting weight. Though Echo kept her gaze locked on the silver bowl, she felt herself buttressed by the strength in that hand.

"We need to expand the spell to see where he is," Dorian said. "It'll require more power. Take from me what you need."

Jasper cut in, his voice low and worried. "Dorian, I don't think—"

"There's no other way," Dorian said.

The act of sharing magic was not one to be undertaken lightly, especially when there was an imbalance of power between participants. Echo was human, but she contained a force that made Dorian's magic pale in comparison. It would be so easy to take his magic now that it was being so kindly offered, and to keep taking it. She could drink him dry. The firebird roiled inside her, aching to tap into that well of magic right in front of it like a starving woman falling upon a sumptuous feast.

But Echo was not ruled by her beast and its urges. She could—she *would*—fight it.

Echo placed her hand above Dorian's. The moment her skin touched his, power flared up between them, raw and vibrant. The firebird burned brightly inside her, but Dorian's magic had another feel to it altogether. His was gently rolling waves and the deepest fathoms of the sea. His was the coursing river and the drizzling rain. The beast inside Echo rolled around in all that magic, luxuriating in its warmth. She took only what she needed and not one drop more.

Echo repeated the final phrase of the chant, the one that focused on the location of that which was lost. The image in the blood grew smaller as the range of the spell widened beyond the room with its shadows and chains and captive prince.

The blood congealed into shapes: winged statues and

soaring columns and an altar set onto a dais. It was a church or a temple or some other place of worship. The ceiling had caved in in places, and beams of light fell on the frieze behind the altar. It depicted a dragon standing atop a heap of bones and swords and flags. One clawed foot crushed a skull; another bent a sword in its grip.

"I know where he is," Dorian said, breathless, as if he couldn't quite believe it. His hand squeezed Echo's shoulder once before severing their connection. Echo felt it snap like a rubber band, a sharp discomfort, and then nothing but the memory of sensation.

Her elation was powerful enough to disrupt the spell. She lost the rhythm of her chanting and suddenly the bowl was just a bowl and the blood was just blood, diluted in water.

A wave of dizziness hit her when the magic dissipated. She would mostly likely suffer for it later. A headache, probably. Maybe even some nausea. But right now she couldn't be bothered by the limitations of her aching human body.

"Where is he?" Echo said. "What was that place?"

"It's an old ruin," Dorian said. His eye was still on the scrying bowl, reluctant to let go of the image of his prince, wounded and chained but *alive*. "It was a Drakharin temple, centuries out of use. Caius and I went there once a few years after I entered his service. It's rumored to be haunted. Young men go there to prove how unafraid they are and come back uniformly terrified."

"Oh, this'll be fun," Jasper said. Echo had nearly forgotten he was there.

Ghosts didn't frighten her. She lived with them, every day, in the confines of her head. A haunted ruin was nothing in the face of her desire to find Caius and break him free of those chains. "Do you remember how to get there?"

"Of course." Dorian sounded offended she'd even felt the need to ask.

"Then we leave at dawn," Echo said. "Bring weapons. I have a feeling we're going to need them."

CHAPTER THIRTEEN

Ivy hated hospitals.

Hospitals, it would seem, hated Ivy in return. She'd never been inside one as a patient—the Avicen took care of their own, not to mention that it would be something of a colossal disaster for Ivy to be dissected because a human doctor had discovered her and decided to find out how she ticked. She'd avoided them at all costs, knowing that nothing good lay within. Human medicine seemed barbaric to her; how they made do without the aid of magic was a mystery.

She stared up at the imposing bulk of Lenox Hill Hospital—where, according to the evening news, the survivors of the attack on Grand Central had been transferred after their condition had stabilized—and wished that she'd paid more attention to Echo's particular brand of deviancy. Turns out, only half watching someone else pick a pocket didn't actually teach one how to do it oneself. Until that morning, Ivy had been perfectly content to allow Echo to be the resident criminal mastermind in their little group of friends, but now she would have given her left arm—or at the very least, a kidney—to have Echo by her side.

It wasn't the first time Ivy had found herself missing Echo since her best friend had departed New York on a mission to find Caius . . . if there was anything left of him to find. Ivy kept that thought to herself. The fragile hope she'd seen in Echo's and Dorian's eyes had been too delicate for her to shatter with pessimism. This time, though, the pang of Echo's absence was less sentimental and more pragmatic. There was a pickpocket-shaped hole in Ivy's life, and she felt it keenly as she watched doctors and nurses and security guards walk in and out of the hospital's main lobby, ID cards dangling from lanyards, pockets, and lapels. If she could only get her hands on one of those, she wouldn't need to worry about finding an alternative way to get inside. Echo had it right: being an upstanding citizen was a giant waste of time.

As it stood, Ivy had vials of bloodweed elixir burning a hole in her bag and she needed to get into that hospital. And the only way she could think of to sneak past the guards, and the nurses, and the patients, and the patients' families, and the people who were basically everywhere, all the damn time, was to go to a place she had absolutely zero desire to visit. It would be far less glamorous than using an ancient spell to break into the Louvre, that was for sure.

Movement in Ivy's peripheral vision attracted her attention. Beside her, Helios fidgeted in his borrowed clothes—a charcoal wool sweater and a pair of black jeans—although "borrowed" was perhaps a bit of a stretch. Ivy doubted that Rowan would have voluntarily loaned his clothing to a

Drakharin, even one as nice as Helios, so she had cut Rowan from the equation. Helios needed something to wear besides the armor he had left Wyvern's Keep in.

Helios had fidgeted all the way to the hospital, occasionally scratching his arms and squirming in his seat. Ivy had assumed at first that the wool was itchy and hadn't thought much more about it. But when Helios had slid his sunglasses down to read the subway map, Ivy caught sight of an expression she'd grown familiar with in the first few months of living in Jasper's London hideout. The stiffness of his shoulders, the darted glances searching for threats that weren't there. Dorian had been like that, living in the middle of London. Caius, too, to a lesser extent. Helios's fidgeting had worsened in the crush of bodies on the southbound 6 train, confirming Ivy's suspicions. He was trying valiantly not to show his discomfort, but it was written in the tense lines of his body, in the way he flinched from the jostling elbows and knees as the subway rumbled over the tracks. In the wake of the attack on Grand Central and the shuttering of the Agora, shadow dust reserves were strictly rationed. The Ala had requisitioned enough for Ivy to get into the hospital, but getting *to* the hospital had called for a slightly more mundane method of transportation. Hence the subway and Helios's unseasonal sweating.

The Avicen had lived in close proximity to humans for centuries, but the Drakharin were an insular race. They secluded themselves in remote areas, buried themselves beneath layers upon layers of protective wards, and let the inexorable march of modernity pass them by. Human invention was treated by the Drakharin with a carefully cultivated disdain that was equal parts superiority and superstition.

Why invent a microwave to pop corn kernels when you could toast some with magical flame summoned with a flick of the wrist? The Avicen tended to shy away from human technology, but only on a surface level. Just about everyone Ivy knew had their own little vices, from radios to hot pots and even the occasional cell phone. But the Drakharin were fastidious in their avoidance. Humans, with their technological shortcuts and their short, fleeting lives, were *other* and to be dealt with only when doing so became absolutely unavoidable. Being a lower-ranked Firedrake prior to his defection, Helios had likely never spent much time around humans. Now he'd been thrown into one of the most populous cities in the world. The belly of the beast, as it were.

Ivy sympathized. She'd seen how long it had taken Dorian to acclimatize to life in London, and she didn't want Helios to put himself through any unnecessary stress—gods only knew their lives were stressful enough as it was—but her insistence that he didn't need to accompany her to the hospital had fallen on deaf ears. He seemed determined to be her knight in shining armor, minus the armor, even if the majority of their trip involved her subtly watching him for signs of an imminent panic attack on public transport and him pretending that he didn't need to be subtly watched for signs of an imminent panic attack. So far, everyone had played their roles admirably, if Ivy did say so herself.

No one went out alone. That was the rule Caius had laid down in London, and that was still the rule. That was why Rowan, despite the little regard he held for the Drakharin, had accompanied Echo on her hunt for Caius. And why Ivy and Helios stood on the sidewalk across the street from Lenox Hill Hospital's main entrance, close enough to a hot dog stand to look like they were innocently waiting for food. Ivy knew every minute she stood on that sidewalk was a minute lost, but she really, really, really didn't want to break into the hospital via the morgue. Honestly, what had her life come to?

"Why do we need to be here?" Helios asked. He was eyeing the hot dog vendor with a curious stare. She wondered if he'd never seen a hot dog before. Did the Drakharin not have street meat? Maybe Ivy would buy him one if their plan succeeded. Provided he still had an appetite after the morgue. She knew she wouldn't.

Ivy patted the vials of bloodweed elixir in the side pocket of her messenger bag. "To save people," she said. "We're the good guys. It's what we do."

It was something Echo liked to say often. She was not wrong.

Helios tore his gaze away from the hot dog stand to make a face at Ivy as if she'd said something distasteful. Even more distasteful than processed meat stewing in dirty water on a sidewalk in Manhattan. "But they're human," he said, as if that explained everything, and to him, perhaps it did.

"Yes," Ivy said, fighting the urge to roll her eyes. He probably wouldn't notice on account of her sunglasses, but she would know. And she'd probably feel bad about it later. "But they're people."

"Human people."

"Still people."

He grunted, not quite acquiescing to her point, but apparently unwilling to argue it any further. It would take longer than a few weeks to cross that cultural divide.

"They may be human, Helios, but it's sort of our fault

they're in the hospital," Ivy said. *Our* being the Avicen, the Drakharin, and their associated monstrosity: the kuçedra. "From a purely strategic standpoint, we're not entirely sure how the kuçedra operates, but we think it's drawing power from the people it puts into comas, using them as a sort of battery. If we cut off its tie to those people, then maybe it won't grow quite as fast, which would make it easier for us to kill it . . . you know, when we figure out how." And if such a thing was even possible, but Ivy didn't feel the need to speak that thought aloud. It was entirely too fatalistic for her liking. She patted the vials again. Touching them was a comfort. So far, the elixir's creation was one of the few victories they'd earned, and Ivy had played no small part in it. "What's more important, avoiding humans or severing the kuçedra from a potential power source?"

Helios sucked his bottom lip between his teeth, another nervous tic Ivy had noticed. She didn't quite mind this one. Helios had a very nice mouth. "Severing the kuçedra from a potential power source," he said.

"That's right. If we administer the elixir, hopefully those humans will wake up and the kuçedra will be short a few meals. And if we can do that while helping a bunch of people whose only crime was being caught in the cross fire of *our* war, then everybody wins. Well, everybody except the bad guys. Let's not help them win."

"Fair enough," Helios said. He looked away from Ivy, turning his head toward the hospital. Through the revolving doors, Ivy could make out at least two guards and a dizzying array of hospital staff and patients, all standing between them and their objective. "But how are we going to get in?" he asked.

Ivy grimaced. "I have an idea," she said, pulling the small pouch of shadow dust from her jacket pocket. She'd spotted a supply closet on the subway platform they could use to access the in-between. From rats to corpses. Lovely. "But you're probably not going to like it."

CHAPTER FOURTEEN

"Why does it always have to be ruins?" Jasper grumbled, shaking the dust off his hair-feathers. Clouds of it cascaded from the ceiling, jolted free by the presence of living things disturbing the stale air. "Why can't we ever look for something at, like, an amusement park?"

His question went unanswered as Dorian helped Echo over a precarious pile of fallen stones. They had been climbing through the ruin for what felt like hours but had probably only been forty-five minutes. Echo's legs were significantly shorter than Dorian's and Jasper's, and her calves were beginning to ache with ferocity.

Echo paused, hefting her backpack higher on her shoulders. It contained everything she thought she might possibly need: the silver bowl, the glass vial half full of Caius's blood, her dagger, water, a flashlight, snacks. Echo didn't know what Tanith had been feeding Caius this whole time, but she was willing to bet it was terrible.

The temple was majestic in its own way, but it was very much ruined, very much forgotten. Broken statues lay in fragments at their feet; aggressive vines wound their way through holes in the cracked paving stones; the air was thick with the pungent scents of moss and decay. Every now and then, Echo heard a distant noise that was either the sound of an animal in distress or wind cutting through the rubble at just the right frequency to sound like a wailing ghost. She sincerely hoped it was the latter.

"What was this place?" she asked. Once Dorian had identified the location where Caius was being held, Echo had gone into overdrive, preparing for their departure and steeling herself for whatever they might find. It hadn't occurred to her to ask which ancient Drakharin god the temple had been dedicated to or what rituals had been performed there.

Dorian broke his tense silence to answer her question. "There was a time when every god in our pantheon had a specific place of worship."

"Before humans spread across practically every available inch of this planet like a plague?" Jasper interjected. "No offense," he added for Echo's sake.

"None taken." Not only did her humanity feel like a thing of the past, but when you're right, you're right.

"Yes, quite," Dorian said. He peered up at one of the statues that was still mostly standing, save for a left arm that had been knocked off at some point over the centuries. The stone figure was relatively humanoid. Two arms (in theory), two legs, one head. But then there were the wings. A set of them jutted forth from the statue's shoulder blades, creating a wingspan of at least twenty feet. They reminded Echo a bit of bat wings.

"Like the Avicen," Dorian continued, "our gods don't have names. We referred to them by their attributes." He laid a reverent hand on one of the outspread wings. "This temple was built for the god of battle." He inclined his head to the statues flanking the winged figure. "Those were probably minor gods. They embodied different aspects of the god—bloodlust, justice, mercy. Their places among the pantheon have largely been lost to time." With a look back at the god of battle, he said, "We only remember the major gods now. So much has been lost."

Jasper snorted as he sidled up next to Dorian. "God of battle. Really sneaky hiding place you picked here, Tanith."

Dorian cracked a short-lived grin. "She always was dramatic like that."

"Bet she's one of those bad guys who likes to monologue their big evil plan," Jasper said.

An involuntary and wholly inappropriate giggle burst from Echo's lips. "Yeah, she is."

The laughter died as abruptly as it had begun, because it was impossible to remember the new Dragon Prince's penchant for theatrical verbosity without remembering the death and destruction that came in its wake. Tanith did talk a big game, and her follow-up had a body count. Echo trudged forward, determined to push the memory of smoke and ash and screams from her mind. She picked up her pace, relishing the burn of her muscles as her legs plaintively begged her to slow down.

Jasper kept up a steady stream of chatter. Silence, particularly when it was heavy with sadness, made him uneasy, though Echo had no doubt the litany of questions and voiced thoughts was as much for Dorian's sake as his own.

If Dorian was focused on replying to Jasper's questions, then he couldn't use the entirety of his brainpower to agonize over what condition Caius would be in if—when—they found him. Especially if that condition was anything other than "alive and well."

"Did the Drakharin perform any nefarious rituals here?" Jasper asked. "You know, sacrificing cute, fluffy animals or dancing naked under the light of the full moon?" He waggled his eyebrows suggestively. "Magic orgies? That sort of thing? If you have any sordid tales of ancient Drakharin debauchery, I am all ears."

"Sacrifice has always been a cornerstone of the way we worship," said Dorian, "though not all the gods desired one. You jest, but ritual intimacy was not uncommon, especially during the harvest—"

"Stop." Echo held up a hand, motioning for the others to halt.

"But he was just about to tell us about the orgies," Jasper said, exasperated. "What could be more important than that?"

Wordlessly, Echo pointed to the statue in front of them. It was shorter than the winged figure—a minor deity. A red smear painted the face of whatever forgotten god it had represented. Against the bleached marble of stone flesh, the brownish-red stain stood out in lurid contrast. The blood flaked away at Echo's touch. It was old, but not very. Old enough to dry, but recent enough to have withstood erasure by the elements and the passage of time. Five smaller smudges orbited the bulk of the blood.

"A handprint," Echo said. "And I don't think it's been here very long."

Dorian drew closer, his hand reaching for the sword at his hip. He didn't draw it, but he let his palm rest on the pommel, ready for anything. Leaning forward, he inspected the bloodstain, scrunching his brow in thought.

"The shape is unclear, but the size is right," he said.

"Do you think Caius left this?" Hope and fear surged in Echo's heart. If Caius had smeared his blood across the statue's face, then hopefully they were not far from where he was. But it also meant that he had been bleeding profusely enough to have left a mark of that size.

Dorian nodded, his jaw clenching visibly. "I think so. I hope so." He pressed a finger to the center of the stain. Flecks of blood broke away from the marble, fluttering to the ground like paper ashes. "It's been here a week or so, I would wager."

"So we're on the right track," Jasper said. "Though I can't say I'm overly pleased to be following a trail of blood. Couldn't he have left bread crumbs like a normal kidnap victim?"

"Do you have to turn everything into a joke?" Dorian snapped.

Jasper didn't flinch, though Echo noticed the tightening of his eyes. His expression shuttered, like a window being slammed shut. She had seen him do that countless times. He clammed up when he slipped his mask on. When he was afraid his face would betray what he was truly feeling.

"Just trying to keep the mood light," said Jasper. "Between you and Echo, I'm getting a bit sick of the doom and gloom."

With a displeased grunt, Dorian turned away, toward the passage that the trail of blood seemed to indicate. Jasper caught his arm, his mask slipping just enough for Echo to see the way his eyes softened. Dorian paused but didn't turn around.

"He's going to be fine," Jasper said to Dorian's back. "We're going to drag him out of here and patch him up, and then you can mother-hen over him to your heart's content."

"I hope you're right," Echo said. She stepped around the two of them, taking the lead again. Dorian would likely take point at any sign of danger, but the sight of Caius's blood had made her own run cold, and putting one foot in front of the other quelled the unease she felt, if only slightly. They needed to find him. Now. Before there was nothing left of him to find.

They walked in tense silence through the dilapidated temple. Broken statues littered their path, strewn about like victims of a long-ago battle. Chunks of masonry had fallen from the walls, parts of a frieze depicting Drakharin gods and goddesses at war. Echo tried to piece together the story, but there were too many missing fragments for it to make much sense. A great tangle of roots had worked its way through the cracks in the paving stones as nature fought to reclaim the earth upon which the temple sat.

Echo's curiosity warred with her inclination to leave Dorian alone. She wanted, desperately, to ask him if he was familiar with the tale carved into the marble walls, but there was a purpose in his stride and a tension in the set of his shoulders that made her think he had no desire to satisfy her curiosity.

Jasper had no such reticence.

"I wonder what it all means," he said, stepping carefully over a particularly large segment of the shattered frieze.

To Echo's surprise, Dorian answered Jasper's non-question. "It's the same nonsense for which all monuments are built: we fought, we bled, we died, and all in the name of glory. And so we perpetuate the legend that all that fighting and bleeding and dying is worth something so that future generations can go on repeating the sins of the past while expecting it to result in anything besides more fighting and bleeding and dying."

It was by far the most poetic thing Echo had ever heard him say.

It wasn't difficult to imagine how beautiful the temple must have once been. High above their heads soared a barrel vault ceiling, the mortar tiles of which were flecked with bits of peeling paint. The support columns—which were mercifully in far better condition than the statues—were adorned with a curling form of Drakhar script that wound around each column like decorative ribbon. The writing bore some similarity to the Drakhar runes Echo had seen, but it seemed older. Ancient. Certain figures reminded her of the soft, curving lines of Avicet script. The Avicen and Drakharin had a shared past, though both sides behaved as though they would like nothing less than to remember it. But the words engraved in the marble columns betrayed the lie. Language knew. Language remembered.

Echo craned her neck to get a better look at the carvings high up on the walls. Her foot snagged on a root and, with a muffled curse, she went down, hands braced to break her fall. When she looked up, she found herself staring into the eyes of a dragon.

She may have screamed. She would never, ever admit to doing so.

"It's just a statue," Jasper said, resting his foot on the thing's severed head. He exhibited as much respect for the gods of the Drakharin as he did for the Avicen pantheon, which was none. Echo wanted to punch the smirk off his face. "Scaredy-cat."

The dragon's eyes were unseeing alabaster pools, though the delicate lines of its face had been hewn with exceptional realism. An open maw, lined with two rows of sharp teeth, snarled with such eternal ferocity that Echo thought she might be able to feel its sour breath upon her face if she stared at it long enough.

Jasper offered her a hand to help her stand, but that damnable smirk was still plastered on his face.

"I may be a scaredy-cat but at least I'm not—"

"Hush," said Dorian. He held one hand up in the universal gesture of "shut up." He cocked his head to the side, listening.

Echo hushed, silently grateful for his intervention, because she was sorely lacking in clever comebacks. She'd probably come up with one later. *L'esprit de l'escalier,* as the French liked to say.

"What is it?" Echo asked. She brushed her dirty hands against her jeans, but even that noise felt too loud in the silence. "What did you hear?"

"Nothing," said Dorian. "And that's the problem."

He was right, Echo realized. If Caius was here, then there should have been guards. Or at the very least some signs of life. But the ruins were undisturbed, as if no one had set foot in this forgotten place for years and years.

From everything Caius had said, Echo knew his sister to be a master strategist. She could be bold to the point where weaker men would have called it foolishness, but there was always a reason behind her actions, some clever tactic that at times only she could see. It was difficult to reconcile the idea of that person with someone who would go through the trouble of kidnapping a very powerful foe, only to abandon him in a run-down temple without the slightest security.

"Something's up," Echo said.

To that, Dorian nodded. He unsheathed his sword. "Be on your guard."

Without another word, he resumed their trek through the corridor, sidestepping fallen idols. Echo and Jasper followed, giving him a wide berth so that if he swung his sword, they'd be well out of his way. Jasper had a long, wicked-looking knife strapped to his back, and Echo had her magpie dagger tucked into her boot, but she knew drawing it in a fight would be a waste. Stabbing an enemy would be simple enough, but her real weapon was not wrought of steel, it was in her. She focused, feeling the current of magic that flowed through her veins as naturally as her own blood. Her body felt warmer as the magic responded to her. With each passing day, she was feeling more and more attuned to it. Using it still caused her pain, but so long as she inflicted some in turn on the Drakharin who had taken Caius, she could deal with it. A little pain for a lot of power seemed like a fair trade.

The trail of blood led them to an imposing slab of blue stone at the end of the passageway. White veins branched across its surface like a spider's web. At its center a single Drakhar rune was engraved in the same flowing script as the words they had encountered on the path.

"This doesn't seem good," Jasper said. "The last time

Echo went through a stone door into a mysterious inner chamber, she stabbed herself in the chest like the drama queen she is."

"I am not a drama queen," Echo said absently. She reached out her hand to the rune, but Dorian grabbed her wrist before her fingertips could touch it.

His single eye was trained on the symbol, his brow pinched.

"What does it say?" Echo asked, extracting her hand from his grasp.

"'Wind,'" Dorian replied. "Or 'air.'"

Dorian nudged Echo aside as he inspected the door more closely. There was no blood on its surface, but a few drops had spattered the ground. Caius had come through here. Or had been dragged through. An unpleasant thought.

"How do we open it?" Jasper asked. "I can pick just about any lock, but I don't see one."

Some doors, Echo knew, didn't require a key to open. Or at least, not a key in the traditional sense of the word. It was her turn to grab Dorian by the wrist. He frowned, but he let her pull his hand forward.

"Touch it," she said.

He did.

The moment Dorian's fingers brushed the carved lines, the rune began to glow a bright white that eclipsed the veins running through the marble. The light flared for an instant and then went out. The slab swung away from Dorian's touch, revealing a cavernous room and the soft babbling of a distant stream.

"Magic door," Echo said. "It's always a magic door. And

this being a Drakharin temple, I'm guessing it only responds to someone with Drakharin blood."

Dorian huffed, as if impressed against his will. He fell back into his stoic silence as he walked through said magic door, single-minded in his quest to rescue the prince to whom he had sworn himself, body and soul.

Jasper followed him, with considerably less aplomb. "Magic doors and trails of blood." He shot Echo a look over his shoulder. "For once, it might be nice to go on a normal adventure."

CHAPTER FIFTEEN

"**W**hy isn't it working?"

Ivy watched the patient on the hospital bed, unease stirring in her gut. The elixir had proven effective on the first three people she had administered it to, but the elderly man she had just dosed showed no sign of improvement. The black veins stood out on his rail-thin arms just as prominently as they had ten minutes ago. Machines beeped a steady rhythm, tracking the man's vital signs. No change there, either.

Helios spared her a glance from the door to the quarantine ward where he stood watch. Every fifteen minutes a nurse came by to check on the patients, recording vitals and making sure the equipment keeping them alive was functioning optimally.

Ivy and Helios had had to hide from her twice already, huddling behind a large cabinet shoved in a corner of the room to open up more space for beds. But the nurse's rounds had seemed more perfunctory than anything else. She hadn't noticed the subtle changes in her patients, nor was she likely to for a few days, when the elixir's magic would heal them enough for non-magical eyes to see the difference.

Ivy could feel the change, slight as it was. Even humans had a magical trace to them, an aura. It was difficult to detect, since most humans went through their lives blissfully ignorant of their own magical potential, rendering their metaphysical presence all but inert, but Ivy had been taught to scan the aura of all living creatures for signs of illness or injury. The kuçedra changed the fundamental nature of one's aura, altering it the way a stubborn stain affected carpet fiber. The bloodweed elixir removed that stain. So far.

"Did you give him enough?" Helios asked.

Ivy shot him a withering look. "Yes, I gave him enough. I know what I'm doing."

Helios held up his hands in surrender. "I meant no insult. I'm only trying to help."

"Sorry," Ivy said. "I know . . . I just . . ."

Don't actually know what I'm doing.

"Could there be a reason for him to be resistant?" Helios checked his watch—an antique pocket watch on a chain that Ivy had lifted from Echo's stash of treasures in the library. Echo hadn't gone back, but Ivy had. All her clothes had been lost at the Nest, and she and Echo were roughly the same size. Echo hadn't said a word when she saw her own clothing appear in the room they shared at Avalon, but Ivy had seen the shift in her friend's stance.

A relaxing. Subtle, but there. A little something familiar went a long way when it felt like nothing in the world made sense.

"I don't know," Ivy admitted. "I guess it's possible. Human bodies don't all process human medications the same way, so maybe this is no different."

Helios cast a glance down the corridor. It was empty. They had precious few minutes before the nurse came back, but they hadn't seen another soul. Ivy assumed no one was eager to spend unnecessary time in the quarantined area. The medical mystery behind the condition the kuçedra had left these people in had unsettled even the doctors sent by the CDC. Ivy had read about it in the paper she'd picked up at a newsstand after her last foray into the city.

"We're running out of time," Helios called in a hushed whisper. He abandoned his post by the door with a last searching glance and came to join her by the old man's bedside. He slipped the sunglasses down his nose and peered at the man over the top of the frames. His yellow eyes had a greenish cast to them in the ward's fluorescent lighting. He made a noise that sounded like he was considering the man's condition. Ivy suspected it was mostly for show. He didn't know the first thing about the healing arts. Ivy might be out of her depth, but she was confident she knew more than he did. For what that was worth, which was evidently not much at all. Helios picked up the patient's chart from the slot that held it at the foot of the bed and read, half mumbling medical jargon to himself.

"I don't understand," Ivy said. "He was affected at the same time and the same place as everyone else. The circumstances of his infection were identical. I already checked his chart. There's no preexisting disease or condition that might—"

"Did you look at his date of birth?" A puzzled frown pulled at Helios's mouth as his gaze bounced from the chart to the elderly man on the bed.

"No," Ivy replied. "I didn't think it was relevant."

Helios handed her the chart. "I admit, I'm not great at predicting human ages—they live and die so fast—but this gentleman"—he waved a hand at the man's wrinkled countenance—"doesn't look twenty-three to me."

"Wait, what?" Ivy scanned the chart. "He can't possibly be . . ."

Her questioning gaze found his date of birth, sandwiched between his name and gender. March 21. Nineteen ninety-four.

"What the flapjacks?"

"What's a flapjack?" Helios asked absently. He had removed his sunglasses and was leaning in to study the man's face closely. His nose scrunched as if he smelled something rotten.

"A pancake," Ivy replied. She flipped through the pages of the chart. Attached to the final page with a paper clip was a photograph of a smiling young man, face ruddy from the sun, standing on what looked like a mountaintop. White-capped peaks dotted the horizon behind him. A golden retriever sat at his feet. Ivy glanced at the man on the bed—withered with age and looking closer to seventy than twenty—and the man in the photo. The bone structure was the same. Identical strong eyebrow ridges. The broad jawline. The wide cheekbones. "How . . . ? Why . . . ?"

"Do you feel that?" Helios asked. He motioned her

closer to the man's bedside. Ivy stepped toward him and leaned over the bed's plastic guardrail. The closer she got to the man, the stronger that sickly sensation clogging his aura became. It hadn't been nearly as powerful with the other victims.

"Is it . . . ," Helios pondered aloud. "Could it be . . . ?"

"It's feeding on him," Ivy said, her speculation solidifying into certainty as she spoke the thought out loud.

"I thought it was feeding on all of them," Helios said with a dubious look. "Why is this man worse off than the others?"

"I don't know." Ivy shook her head. "It's possible the kuçedra doesn't deplete them all at the same pace. Maybe this is what it looks like when it's nearly sucked someone dry." This was something she would need to discuss with the Ala. From their previous conversations about the Ala's own experience under the influence of the kuçedra's toxic malevolence, it seemed a plausible enough explanation, though how the man had managed to age so rapidly without dying was an even bigger question.

Footsteps sounded from the corridor, the nurse's rubber-soled sneakers squeaking in the hazmat suit she donned every time she entered the ward.

"That's our cue," Helios said, tugging Ivy behind the cabinet. There was a very real chance they were going to be caught one of these days; Ivy hoped it wasn't today. She huddled against Helios's chest, closing her eyes as she held her breath, listening to the night nurse's steps as she puttered around the room. The smiling face in the photo ghosted behind Ivy's closed eyelids. Michael Ian Hunt. Born March 21, 1994. Age twenty-three. Hiker. Dog owner. Geriatric.

A shudder ran down Ivy's spine. A warm hand pressed against her lower back. Helios, trying to offer her what silent comfort he could.

If poor Michael Ian Hunt was getting weaker, it meant only one thing: the kuçedra was getting stronger.

CHAPTER SIXTEEN

I t was a moat.

Dorian thought calling it such was a generous description for the pungent waters that greeted them when they passed through the enchanted door. No one had tended to the moat for quite some time, judging by the thick layer of pond scum that coated its surface.

"Shouldn't the moat be outside the temple?" Echo asked, voice distorted as she pinched her nostrils.

"It isn't meant to keep people away from the temple," Dorian replied. He tried breathing through his nose, but it made the stench worse when he could taste it. "It's meant to keep people from exploring any farther."

Reeds swayed in a nonexistent breeze, reacting perhaps to the faint hum of magic Dorian could feel in the air. He and Echo stood on a narrow, muddy shore. Before them was a rickety bridge, half submerged in the black water and partially grown over with horsetails and cheerful water poppies.

The slats of aging wood were held together with rotting rope. It didn't look like it would bear his weight, much less the weight of three fully grown individuals. The bridge—a rickety contraption hardly worthy of the name—stretched across the water to the other side.

"What is that smell?" Echo asked, voice muffled by the hand clapped over her mouth and nose.

"Rot," Dorian offered. "Decay." The moat filled the cavernous room from wall to wall. He spotted another door at the far end of the room. There were no other exits.

"Splendid," Jasper said in a tone that made it clear that it was anything but. He stepped toward the bridge, but Dorian blocked his path with an outstretched arm.

"Wait," said Dorian. It couldn't be as simple as crossing a bridge to get to the other side. There had to be something else. The Drakharin weren't known for making things easy, and Dorian had no doubt that his ancestors had left behind obstacles to stymie the progress of anyone who threatened to plunder the temple, even after they were all dead and gone.

He scanned the waters for signs of life. The surface was still, but he suspected the calm was an illusion, one meant to lure an idiot into a false sense of security and then to strike when least expected. It's what Dorian would have done if he had designed a treacherous moat as a defense mechanism.

A shadow passed beneath the surface, almost imperceptible in the inky waters. Almost. Dorian tracked its movement and caught what looked like the flick of a tail. A very large tail. The thing stopped, as if it could feel his gaze on it, and Dorian saw a pale flash of skin before it dove deeper into the water.

"These waters are guarded," Dorian said. He pointed at

a pile of bones on the pebbled shore. "By nix, to be specific. That's probably what became of the last person who tried to cross. I'd wager they left the remains as a warning to the next fools stupid enough to try."

"Like us," Jasper said. He sounded as enthused by the idea of crossing the ominous waters as Dorian felt.

"Indeed."

Dorian scanned the surface of the moat again. It was still, eerily so. He could hear water babbling somewhere far away, perhaps from whatever larger body of water fed this one.

"And what, pray tell, are nix?" Echo asked.

"Mermaids," Dorian replied.

"Mermaids?" Echo asked flatly. Dorian occasionally forgot that she was human, for all she was integrated with the Avicen. Mermaids were probably not something she had encountered in her travels.

"Mermaids," he repeated. "I've never had the pleasure of making one's acquaintance, but it's said they have a taste for the dishonest."

At that, Jasper took several healthy steps back.

"What does that mean?" Echo asked, still observing the waters dubiously.

"It means if you're not true to yourself or others, the nix will know. Legend has it they can spot a lie in your heart before you even know it's there."

Dorian had more than two centuries of lying—to himself, to others, to his prince—in his ledger. All those fibs, great and small, would make for a tasty treat for the nix. He peered out over the water and hoped the nix were in a generous mood.

The moment was shattered by a loud splash and Echo's shout. "Jasper!"

Dorian's eye snapped to the shore just in time to see Jasper's multicolored feathers disappear beneath the surface of the water as pale, webbed fingers pulled him under.

Dorian was in the water before he'd even given it thought. As he broke the surface, his heart sang with the feel of water against his skin. He had always been more at home in rivers and seas than on dry land, and this time, when the moat's water called to him, he answered. He could hear Echo shouting after him. Dorian hoped good sense prevented her from doing something stupid, like jumping in after him. He could only save so many drowning fools at the same time.

The water was deeper than it looked from shore, and dark. The darkness muted Jasper's amethyst and gold feathers as he churned the water around him in his struggle. Pale bodies, propelled by muscular, fishlike tails, pulled Jasper farther into the moat's depths. Dorian swam toward him, cutting through the water as if he'd been born to swim rather than walk.

The nix had Jasper by the arms and legs, their sallow hands so bright in the inky blackness that they seemed to glow. Jasper's movements slowed, and the bubbles that rose as he tried to hold his breath petered out into a pathetic trickle. Dorian pushed himself even harder. He was nearly there; if Jasper could hold on for a few seconds more, they might both get out of this moat alive.

A single nix surged up to block his way, but it kept its hands—and, more important, the wicked spear it held—to itself. Dorian attempted to go around it, but it moved in front of him, keeping itself between Dorian and Jasper. The nix pointed toward Jasper with its spear before gesturing at Dorian with its free hand. When the nix spoke, it was not with words, but as a whisper in Dorian's mind.

We chose him. He is ours now.

Dorian may have been at home in the water, but speaking while submerged in it was a challenge, even for him. His garbled "What?" was more bubble than sound.

He—the nix jabbed its spear toward Jasper again—*belongs*—it punctuated the next words with two thuds of the blunt side of the spear against Dorian's chest—*to us.*

I don't understand, Dorian thought, hoping the nix's telepathic speech was a two-way street.

We demand a gift in exchange for safe passage, the nix said. *We have chosen him.*

Dorian had forgotten about that part of nix behavior. There was always a godsdamn sacrifice. His chest tightened in a way that had nothing to do with his rapidly depleting supply of oxygen.

The nix's voice boomed in Dorian's head. *Unless there is something else you would like to offer us?*

Jasper had gone limp in the nix's hands, feathers swaying as he drifted deeper into the moat. Dorian couldn't leave Jasper to them. He had been kind when Dorian had been cruel. He had reminded Dorian what it was like to be loved. To love.

Take me, Dorian thought. *Spare him.*

The nix's lips stretched over rows of viciously sharp teeth, sloppy with bits of meat and bone, in a gleeful snarl.

No, the nix said. It spun away from Dorian, swimming back toward Jasper.

Wait. Dorian pushed the thought toward the retreating nix.

The nix paused, slowly turning back toward Dorian. His chest burned. He had to surface soon, but he would not leave this moat without Jasper. There was no alternative. If the nix wouldn't take him, then they both died here and Echo would go on without them. She could save Caius; she had magic that Dorian did not.

I'll give you whatever you want, Dorian thought desperately. *Just tell me what you want.*

The nix unleashed its gruesome grin again. *Something that costs you dearly. Something you aren't eager to give up. Something precious. Give me a truth. One you don't want to admit, even to yourself. The truth is far more precious than gold and jewels.*

Dorian's lungs screamed for air. *I don't want to lose him.*

The nix angled its head to one side. *Is that all?*

Jasper was going to die if Dorian didn't reach him soon, but the nix was right. The truth came at a steep price. Dorian had held on to his hate for so long that admitting that Jasper—an Avicen—mattered to him had felt like losing a part of himself. But he remembered the kiss, their first one, that they'd shared at Avalon. He remembered how it felt to pull away from Jasper after Caius was taken. It had felt like an amputation, a severing of something that had been critical to his existence.

I care about him, he thought. *I didn't want to, but he's . . . different. Special.*

The nix seemed to measure Dorian's response for a moment. Dorian's lungs burned. *Not good enough,* said the creature. Without another word, it gave a powerful heave of its tail and turned, following its brethren deeper into the water.

Dorian opened his mouth to shout, but all that escaped him were bubbles. Panic rose, heady and hot, in his chest, supplanting even the desperate need for air. *Stop.* He propelled himself after the nix, oxygen-deprived muscles aching.

Stop! Dorian cried as loud as he could with his mind's voice. His vision blackened at the edges. His body was losing the fight for consciousness. But he couldn't leave without Jasper. He wouldn't.

The nix didn't stop.

Dorian sagged, limbs heavy, body leaden.

I love him.

The nix with whom he'd spoken flicked its tail and slowed.

But that wasn't all. Love wasn't what frightened Dorian. It was everything that came with it, the vulnerability, the helplessness. But love wasn't love without those things. *I need him.*

Tail churning water, the nix turned with the leisure of a creature that didn't need air to survive.

Dorian felt as though he was slipping to a place beyond pain. His lungs still burned, but it was a distant ache, like it was happening to someone else. *He makes me better. Before him, I wasn't . . . good. I was governed by hate and fear and pain, but he saw me. He saw me even when I couldn't see myself. I was a fool and I blinded myself to it, but I know now. He is mine and I am his and you cannot have him.*

The nix's lips pulled into a grotesque grin. *That cost you much to say.* It waved the spear at its brethren. As one, they released their hold on Jasper. Dorian swam around the nix to catch Jasper before he sank any deeper. He linked his arms around Jasper's chest and kicked with all his might, straining to swim as his oxygen-starved muscles resisted movement.

When they broke the moat's surface, Dorian's chest heaved with deep, greedy breaths that burned all the way down. Jasper was limp in his arms, and Dorian tried not to consider the possibility that he might be dead.

Echo ran down the shore to meet them. She hauled Dorian out of the water with a strength he hadn't known she possessed.

"Help him," Dorian said, pushing Jasper's unmoving body toward her. Jasper needed air; Dorian had none to give.

Echo nodded, brisk and efficient, but when she tried to pry Jasper from Dorian's arms, he lurched, clutching at Dorian with desperate hands. Jasper coughed up water on both of them.

He shook violently between bouts of heaving gasps and hacking coughs. Echo asked him if he was hurt, but he either didn't hear her or he wasn't interested in sharing. Dorian bit the inside of his cheek hard enough to taste blood. Jasper clung to him with weak hands, taking short, shallow breaths.

Jasper's shirt clung to his chest, and for the first time, Dorian noticed how slender he had become in recent weeks. He felt like he could wrap his arms around Jasper twice. He carded his fingers through the feathers on Jasper's head, smoothing them down, almost without thinking. He snatched his hand away when Jasper's golden eyes opened. There was a tiny, flickering spark in them. Then Jasper slipped his mask back into place, piece by piece. It was rather like watching a master craftsman at work.

"You're cute, Echo," Jasper croaked, voice raw and pained. "But I think I'd rather have the mouth-to-mouth from Dorian if you don't mind."

Dorian's strangled laugh was filled with more relief than he would ever admit to.

"Good to see you're feeling better," he said. Echo watched them with raised eyebrows. Her hands were trembling, but she curled them into fists when she noticed Dorian noticing.

Jasper managed a weak smile before spasms of coughing seized his body once more. Dorian held him as he calmed, tremors dying down to a more manageable shiver. Echo hovered beside the two of them, but Dorian ignored her.

Jasper peered up at him, droplets of water clinging to his blue and purple lashes. "My hero," he whispered.

And then he winked.

Not even a near-death experience, it seemed, would prohibit Jasper from making light of just about everything.

Dorian choked out a small laugh. His chest still burned. Despite the direness of their situation—Caius was still here, still waiting to be found, or so Dorian hoped—he couldn't fight the giddy feeling that bubbled up inside him. Half of him wanted to attribute it to the recent lack of air, but the other half—the smarter half—knew it for what it was: pure, unadulterated joy, made stronger in the face of unfavorable odds.

He couldn't help it. He didn't want to.

He kissed Jasper, selfishly stealing the breath from his lungs once more.

And unbelievably, Jasper kissed him back.

For weeks, Dorian had been an absolute wretch, tormenting himself with guilt and overwhelmed by his sense of duty to his lost prince. But Jasper kissed him as if none of it mattered. As if he had already been forgiven. A hand came up, ran through Dorian's hair, catching in the wet strands. It was divine.

He had never kissed Jasper in front of anyone else before. Had never shown him even the slightest crumb of affection when others might see. There was a tangle of reasons, centuries in the making, for his reticence, but now not a single one mattered. Dorian pulled back just far enough to rest his forehead against Jasper's. Damp feathers tickled his skin, and he sighed as he felt Jasper relax into him.

None of it mattered, because Jasper was his and he was Jasper's.

And today—on this miserable excuse for a day—that was enough to save them both.

CHAPTER SEVENTEEN

Nothing else troubled them as they crossed the moat via the rickety wooden bridge that should not have held the weight of three people but somehow did. Jasper suspected it was a magic bridge. It was always magic. Nothing in their lives was ever mundane.

The bridge led them to an equally decrepit wooden door set into moss-covered stone, which deposited them in a small antechamber. Damp seeped through the cold stone walls, settling into Jasper's already-wet skin. He shivered and Dorian pulled him close, rubbing warmth into his trembling arms. Echo politely looked anywhere but at them.

Jasper curled into Dorian, luxuriating in the warmth he radiated. The memory of their kiss played in his mind on a loop. It wasn't their first, and provided they both got through this temple alive, it wouldn't be their last. Not if Jasper had anything to say about it. But this kiss had been different, though no less monumental than the first, shared in a musty wine cellar deep in the belly of Avalon Castle. It was as though every strand of artifice had been stripped away, made flimsy by the urgency of the moment. Contained in that kiss were all the things Dorian never said, all the things Jasper never let himself believe. And to think, it had taken a gaggle of man-eating mermaids to bring that about. When he thought about it, he could still feel the frigid water closing around him, the unfathomable strength of the nix as they carried him down, deeper into the abyss, the burning of his lungs as he tried to hold his breath, the searing pain of water rushing into them when he failed.

Jasper had nearly died.

Not for the first time, and probably not for the last. But on the short list of maladies and disasters Jasper feared, drowning surpassed them all. He had never learned how to swim, his fear of drowning had been so great and so deeply ingrained. He and water simply did not get along, and so long as he kept his feet firmly planted on dry land, it wasn't a problem.

Right up until it was.

As if sensing the course of Jasper's thoughts, Dorian tightened one arm around his shoulders while his other hand kept rubbing soothing lines up and down Jasper's bare arm.

"Are you all right?" Dorian asked, the timbre of his voice low and soft, meant only for Jasper despite Echo's presence. She was valiantly trying to make herself as unobtrusive as possible as she studied the stone slab opposite the door through which they had entered the antechamber. Another room full of nasty surprises, Jasper guessed. They'd catch their breath and then move on, but Jasper was nothing if not a selfish creature, and in that moment, all he wanted, all he cared about, was basking in the feel of Dorian's arm around him and the wonderful, radiant heat he produced.

Jasper rubbed his cheek into the coarse fabric of Dorian's shirt. He turned his head so that he could rub his cold nose against the warm skin of Dorian's throat. The touch elicited a squirm that was sinfully delightful.

"I'm okay," Jasper said. "That would have been an ignominious end." He tried to make light of what had just happened, but he couldn't suppress the shudder that ran through him at the thought.

Dorian tilted his head so his cheek rested against Jasper's. When he spoke, his breath ruffled the fine feathers on the side of Jasper's head. "Anyone who means you harm is going to have to go through me. I've already lost Caius. I won't lose you, too."

A lump formed in Jasper's throat and he struggled to swallow. He buried his face in the crook of Dorian's neck so he could pretend, for just a little while longer, that they were anywhere else. That it was just the two of them. That they had all the time and comfort in the world to explore this fragile thing growing between them. Jasper had never been good at relationships. Echo had been his only real friend—and even then, they had barely trusted each other with anything of any great significance until she had burst into his home carting a half-dead Dorian. Relationships were an entirely different category of incomprehensibility as far as Jasper was concerned. But somehow, despite the overwhelming odds, he had managed not to mess this up. Yet. Dorian wanted him alive. Dorian wanted him safe.

Dorian wanted *him*.

Jasper splayed his hands across Dorian's back. The

sodden shirt clung to Dorian like a second skin, but he seemed unbothered by the wetness or the cold, as if they were inconveniences so minor they barely warranted notice. Jasper pulled away, still in the circle of Dorian's arm, just enough to meet that perfect blue eye. Dorian's pupil was dilated in the dim light—where the light came from Jasper hadn't a clue, and he was willing to chalk it up to magic, because why the hell not.

It would have been the perfect moment for a kiss. Another one. Slower. Less frantic. Not fueled by a daring escape from the claws of death. Jasper brought one hand up to trace the filigree of scarring on Dorian's left cheek. Dorian flushed.

Echo chose that moment to clear her throat, reminding them of her presence.

Dorian blinked and pulled away just enough to shoot her a look.

"This is a really beautiful moment," Echo said, "and I'm honored to be a part of it—"

"You're not," Jasper interjected.

"—*however*, we have work to do."

She was right. As much as Jasper wished she weren't.

Echo stepped away from the door she had been studying and gestured for Dorian to approach. This one was carved out of blood-red marble shot through with veins of gold. A rune was carved into the center in the same ancient script as the one they had encountered earlier.

"What does this one mean?" Echo asked.

Dorian stepped away from Jasper's embrace, and Jasper didn't think he was imagining the reluctance as the Drakharin put a modest distance between them. Dorian approached the door and canted his head to the side as he considered the rune. His hand hovered over the elegantly wrought lines.

"I've never seen it before," Dorian said. "It's most likely a dialect that died along with the people who worshiped at and tended this temple."

"Well, what's your best guess? I'm assuming it'll open the door the same way the other one did, but I'm getting cautious in my old age," said Echo. Jasper doubted that very much. "I'd like to know what we're walking into before we walk into it."

Dorian traced the curves and lines of the rune in the air with a finger, his features arranged in a scowl that shouldn't have been at all attractive but was. *You've got it bad,* Jasper thought.

"This part here"—Dorian indicated the left half of the rune, made up of two downward strokes bisected with an undulating line—"is similar to the symbol for 'fire.' Or maybe 'smoke.' Or 'eating utensil,' but I don't think it's that one."

"If there's something that wants to eat us behind that door, I swear to the gods, I will set this whole place ablaze," said Jasper.

Dorian continued, ignoring Jasper's threat. "And this part looks like the runic symbol for 'cat.'" His eye narrowed as he thought. "Or perhaps 'bird.'"

With a determined sigh, Echo tightened her ponytail. "Great. Well, at least we have some idea what to expect—a pyromaniac cat-bird."

"I'm fairly certain it's a reference to fire," Dorian muttered.

"If Caius is behind these doors," Echo continued, "then

I don't want to keep him waiting." She gestured to the rune. "Dorian, if you would be so kind?"

Dorian offered Jasper a sympathetic look. "Are you sure you're all right to proceed?"

Jasper might have appreciated the comfort Dorian had offered him moments ago, but he drew the line at coddling. "Right as rain. The sooner we get out of here, the better."

That earned a nod from Dorian and an "Amen" from Echo. Dorian raised his hand and moved it toward the center of the rune. Squaring his shoulders, he visibly gathered himself to face the next obstacle thrown in their path. They were so close to Caius, but one wrong move, one miscalculation, one error in judgment or fate, and their journey would come to an abrupt end. And now they were facing the one thing that made the loudest vessel in Echo's consciousness—Rose—quiver with fear and panic.

"Wait," Echo blurted.

Dorian's hand froze in midmotion, fingers inches from the smooth red stone. He angled his head so he could study Echo with his one eye. "Are you all right?"

Fire.

"Yes," Echo lied.

A single silver eyebrow raised, calling her bluff. Dorian didn't need words to communicate; his face said everything. He was probably terrible at poker.

"No," Echo admitted. "I'm not all right."

She looked back at the rune. Unlike the previous runes, all the lines of this symbol were angular and sharp—just like the harsh sound of Drakhar consonants.

Fire.

The word was laden with memory. It was fitting that their final—or so Echo hoped—obstacle was the element that plagued firebirds, past and present. Those jagged lines summoned images seared into Echo's brain: the crumbling white ash of burnt bark in the Black Forest; the golden flare of Tanith's power, setting the Oracle's sanctuary ablaze; the crackling timber of Rose's cottage after Tanith had ignited it. Echo took a deep breath. What she smelled was not the cool, earthy scent of the cavern beneath the temple, but smoke and ash. Ghosts of a life snuffed out in a fit of righteous anger.

"Whatever's behind that door . . . ," Echo began. She didn't finish her sentence. She didn't want to admit her weakness out loud. As irrational as she knew it was, she couldn't help but feel that voicing it would make it worse somehow.

"You can handle it," Jasper said. "I know you can."

"Not entirely sure I share your confidence," Echo said, "but I appreciate the sentiment."

Dorian had not lowered his hand, but he did draw back slightly. "Caius told me what happened," he said. "To Rose."

Echo shot him a puzzled look. "You didn't know?"

Dorian shook his head. "He didn't tell me when it happened. We weren't that close back then. I had only just joined the guard, and we were friends, but . . ."

"He didn't trust you," Echo said.

"Not in the way he came to. That took time. But he opened up to me eventually. It was killing him, keeping that secret to himself. It was too much for any one person to carry alone, even him." Dorian looked between Echo and the door as if weighing his options. After a moment, he seemed to reach a conclusion. He managed to sound both impatient and gentle when he spoke. He was in a hurry to get to the other side of that door, to find Caius, but in no hurry to cause Echo any harm. Perhaps it was the debt he felt he owed Caius; perhaps it was just simple friendship that propelled him to say "Whatever is behind that door, I can deal with it."

"I have no doubt that you can," Echo said. They were wasting precious time, but she couldn't bring herself to charge forward, not with the sense memory of charred skin and scorched air so powerfully and undeniably present.

"What I am saying," Dorian continued, "is that I can take it from here. You need not come with me. You can stay and I will scout ahead."

Relief, sudden and heady, rushed over Echo, followed by a pang of shame. She couldn't ask Dorian to face the next trial alone. That would be a level of cowardice to which she hoped never to ascend.

"I can't ask you to do that," Echo said. Her voice shook, but she said the words and she meant them and that was enough.

"You're not asking, I'm offering," said Dorian.

Oh, how tempting it was. But even in the face of fear, Echo knew she wouldn't take him up on it. She could not ask others to risk that which she would not, no matter what horrors dwelled in the labyrinth that was her shared memories.

She leveled her gaze at the carved rune. "No," she said. "We've come this far together, we keep going forward together. That's the only way we're going to make it through. All for one and one for all and all that jazz."

She didn't mean just getting through the temple. Or

finding Caius. Or getting out in one piece. She meant all of it. The war. The world outside. The great unknown. None of them would survive to see the end of it if they allowed themselves to splinter.

Dorian nodded, not in simple assent but as if he understood everything she did not say. "All right," he said. He held out a hand to her. She took it. Jasper held her other hand, and Dorian reached for the rune. His palm came to rest against the red stone, and beneath his touch, the carved lines began to glow a warm orange light that grew and grew until it was a blinding white, so bright Echo had to close her eyes against it.

"Together," Dorian said, perhaps sensing that Echo would be grateful for the comfort of his voice in the face of the oncoming trial. She was.

The door slid open under Dorian's hand, and together they stepped over the threshold and into the flames.

CHAPTER EIGHTEEN

It wasn't fire that Echo encountered when she followed Dorian through the red door.

It was lava.

Well, that's new.

One would have thought that a pit of molten lava would have warmed the antechamber they had just been in due to its proximity, but Echo hadn't felt the slightest hint of warmth radiating from the stone. The temperature had been as moderate as the rest of the temple, which was in itself strange, now that she thought about it.

A narrow stone bridge—wide enough for only one person to cross at a time—ran the length of the room, joining the landing on which they stood to an identical one on the other side. That landing had a door much like the one through which they had just entered. An array of figures and symbols had been carved into the walls. Echo recognized a few Drakharin runes here and there, peppered among drawings of dragons in flight.

On either side of the bridge were rectangular pools of bubbling magma. Every now and then, a jet of boiling fluid would shoot off like a small geyser, splashing the stones of the bridge. Anyone standing upon it would have been severely burned.

It said something about Echo's chronically perturbed state of mind that she found the presence of unthinkably hot magma more comforting than the fire she had expected.

The three of them stood on a stretch of stone tiles that ran the length of the wall they were all pressed against.

"So, who wants to go first?" Jasper asked. It was abundantly clear from his tone that he was not about to volunteer.

Before Dorian could indulge in more selfless heroics, Echo stepped onto the first tile of the bridge. It felt much narrower when she was standing on it, bracketed by those wicked pools of bubbling magma. The stone was so hot beneath her feet she could feel it through the soles of her boots. She hoped they didn't melt.

"Does anyone else feel like they're trapped inside a *Super Mario* game?" Jasper asked from his perch on the tiles by the door. He hadn't budged.

Dorian followed Echo onto the bridge. "Who is Mario and why is he super?"

"Oh, Dorian. I have so much to teach you," said Jasper. With extremely reluctant steps, he followed Dorian onto the bridge, eyes on the spurting lava to his left, the glow of the magma reflected in their yellow depths.

Their banter soothed Echo somewhat—as much as one could be soothed when there was a very real possibility of dying like Gollum clutching the ring of power in the fires of Mordor. At least it would make for an interesting obituary. *We regretfully announce the passing of Echo, no last name. She bit it in a pit of lava. It was excruciating, but she was comforted in her final moments by the thought of how badass it would make her obit sound.*

About halfway across the bridge, Echo felt the sudden spike of magic in the air. It crackled like static electricity, raising the hair on the back of her neck. She stopped.

"Something's up," she said.

"Is your spidey sense tingling?" Jasper asked. To Dorian, he added, "Spider-Man. I'll explain later."

The reference may have been meant in jest, but it wasn't too far from the truth.

She's here, whispered a voice at the back of Echo's mind. The spirits of the vessels—more like metaphysical fingerprints, according to the Ala—swirled around Echo's skull like a flock of agitated ghosts.

"Who?" Echo asked, ignoring the quizzical glances Dorian and Jasper directed her way.

The second the word left her lips, Echo realized what a hugely stupid question it was. There was only one *she* who could drive the spirits of firebirds past to that sort of frenzy, stirred up by Rose's fear. Her terror was a rich and heady thing. It made Echo's muscles freeze and joints lock like a deer caught in the lights of an oncoming car.

"What is it, Echo?" Dorian asked. "What do you see that we don't?"

Echo shook her head. "Nothing. There's nothing there, but I feel . . ."

She closed her eyes and extended her senses the same

way she had in the room that contained the moat that wasn't just a moat, attempting to detect something the room didn't want her to see. A swell of magic countered Echo's tentative exploration. It came at her with such force that she nearly lost her footing. If not for Dorian grabbing her arm tightly to steady her, she would have plummeted face-first into the magma.

"Tanith," Echo gasped. "She's here."

Dorian swore in rapid Drakhar and attempted to position himself in front of Echo, but the bridge was too narrow.

"Where is she?" asked Jasper. "I don't see anything, but I don't have your firebird sixth sense."

It was a good question. There was no one else in the chamber, nor was there a place for someone to hide. All around them was stone and lava. No obstructions. No alcoves. But there was the magic. And if magic could make solid ground look like a bottomless pit, then magic could hide a single Drakharin woman, especially one as powerful as Tanith was with the kuçedra tucked away inside her.

"If there's going to be a fight," Jasper said, "we're—how do I put this delicately—screwed." He had one hand on Dorian's forearm. His grip looked tight enough to hurt, but Dorian allowed it.

"Back up," said Dorian. "Get to the wall." He began to guide Jasper back to the landing with careful steps lest accident claim their lives before Tanith could.

"Echo?" Dorian called. She didn't follow them.

Jasper wasn't wrong. On the narrow bridge, there would be no room to maneuver. The stone landing by the door through which they'd entered was better but only marginally so. Echo felt Tanith's presence, mingled with the familiar sensation of the kuçedra's influence. Every person's magic had a unique aura, and Echo had felt Tanith's power months ago, in the Black Forest, and then again at Avalon. Only here it wasn't Tanith's aura alone.

A presence pulled at Echo, as if beckoning her to step forward, to keep walking the length of the bridge. It felt the way an oil slick looked, darkly beautiful but toxic. The power of the firebird thrummed in Echo's veins. It surged forward, as if yearning to be free of its mortal cage to pursue that dark force calling to it.

Opposites attract, Echo thought.

The kuçedra and the firebird. The dark and the light. Two sides of the same coin.

"You want my magic?" Echo let the energy slide outward from her core, down her arms, into her hands. It came easily. Painlessly. It wanted out, so she let it flow through her. "Come and get it."

"Now, now, little Firebird. Sheathe your claws."

Tanith's voice appeared before her body did. She materialized at the other end of the bridge, coalescing from a swirl of dark smoke. She looked at home amid the lava and the stone. Her hair fell free around her shoulders, wisps of it defying gravity to halo her face in a golden cloud. She wore a scarlet gown, as dark as freshly spilled blood. It had been a fine gown once, but the hem was in tatters. Her feet were bare, and her calves streaked with blackened veins. Her hands were so thoroughly coated in blood that at first glance Echo thought she was wearing gloves.

Tanith was a horror to behold, but it was her eyes that made a shiver run up Echo's spine. The irises were no longer crimson, but as black as coal.

Vermilion lips cracked into something too mad to be called a smile.

"I was wondering when you would show up, Firebird." Tanith took a step toward Echo, her bare feet leaving charred footprints on the stone. "I knew it wouldn't take long. Lay a little cheese in the trap and *snap*"—Tanith clapped loudly—"the mouse is caught."

Echo widened her stance, planting her boots as solidly on the precarious bridge as she could. "I forgot how much you love the sound of your own voice. I can't say I missed it."

Tanith blinked at Echo as if she had said something in ancient Greek. "My brother doesn't know what he has, does he? The love of one"—that smile widened—"no . . . not one . . . two, the love of two hearts so devoted."

"Look, can we just skip the half-crazed preamble and get on with it?" Echo let the fire in her hands crackle to life. "If we're gonna fight, then let's get to it. The less I have to look at your ugly mug, the better."

Tanith gazed at Echo with that uncomprehending stare. Slowly, the black bled out of her eyes. Her brows pinched and her lips turned down slightly. "I have no wish to fight you. Not now." She looked down at her hands as if confused by the presence of blood on them.

"It's a trick," said Dorian. Echo didn't risk glancing at him, but she was confident he was brandishing his sword, ready to fight.

Echo didn't buy it either.

"I never meant for this to happen," Tanith said distantly. Echo felt suddenly superfluous. "I wanted power, but not at such a cost. Not at the cost of his life. That was never my intention."

A mad laugh bubbled forth from Tanith's lips. "How strange that it has come to this."

Her attention returned to Echo. The black capillaries in her eyes had returned and were becoming more prominent. The red of her irises retreated from the encroaching darkness.

"Consider this a gift," said Tanith. "My first—and final— act of mercy. My goodwill will not last. Not with this beast inside me. It will not be denied. Not by me, not by you. There is only one way forward, and I have no doubt you will not appreciate it." She frowned again. "But there are some lines not even I will cross, no matter what the beast bids me to do. There may come a day when I claim my brother's life, but that day is not today."

With that, she disappeared.

One minute, Tanith was there. The next, she was gone. Not a swirl of smoke was left in her wake. Even the blackened footprints she had left upon the stone were gone. It was as if she had never been there. And maybe she hadn't.

Echo sent out a tendril of her own magic, feeling for the stain of the kuçedra's presence that she had sensed before. There was nothing besides the old, thrumming energy of the temple.

"Was that a hologram?" Echo asked. "Like, a magic hologram? Do those exist?"

"I don't know what a hologram is, but if you mean do magical projections exist, then yes," Dorian replied. Echo didn't take her eyes off the spot where Tanith had stood, but she heard the whisper of steel being slid into a sheath as Dorian put up his sword. There would be no fight today. One was brewing, inexorable and imminent, but it seemed they would have today as a reprieve.

Silently, Jasper came up behind Echo. "Did you notice that she didn't actually reply to anything you said?"

"Now that you mention it," Echo said, "yeah. It was almost like a recording."

"Magic voice mail," Jasper said.

Dorian approached. "That was unexpected. But if Tanith did leave some kind of projection, why would she leave it here?"

"Fire magic," Echo said. "That's what powers this chamber. Maybe she felt strongest here?"

Dorian nodded. "Perhaps she needed that connection to battle the pull of the kuçedra. She did say she was acting against its wishes."

"By leaving Caius here," Echo finished. She began walking toward the door Tanith—or her projection—had blocked. "And you know what? I don't really care how or why this is happening, but if she was telling the truth, then I'm not leaving Caius here a moment longer."

"Agreed," Dorian said, hot on her heels. When they got to the door, Dorian reached over Echo's shoulder to touch it. There was no rune, but the stone glowed faintly in the shape of his handprint and then slid open, revealing a dark chamber and another door—a plain wooden one, also free of runic inscriptions—set into the opposite wall.

"Let's go find him," Dorian said.

Tanith's perplexing presence opened up a whole host of questions that would need answering eventually, but right now Echo cared about only two: where was Caius, and what had his wretched sister done to him?

CHAPTER NINETEEN

The wooden door led to a spiraling stairwell that took them down, deeper and deeper into the belly of the temple. When they reached the bottom, they encountered another door made of the same nondescript wood as the first. Echo pushed it open, coughing as centuries of dust filtered down on her head. Inside, a soft amber glow emanated from the walls, illuminating a modest, round room.

Shelves lined the walls, carved out of the stone like long, shallow alcoves. Bits of ancient pottery sat in the depressions, hidden by layers of spiderwebs. There was another door set into the far wall, this one much less modest than the one through which they had just come.

A complex lock held the door shut. Echo approached, looking for a way to open it. Any lock could be picked, but this one just might be beyond her skills. The lock's exposed gears were made of a green metal. Flakes of rust had fallen off the teeth of the gears, and corroded metal peeked through heavy rust.

"What's all this for?" Jasper wondered aloud, peering at the earthenware pots. The ones Echo could see through the thick layer of white webbing that coated them were sealed with wax gone dark with age.

"Old potions and elixirs, I expect," Dorian replied as he, too, investigated the lock. "For healing. Or possibly killing."

Before Echo could touch the large gear in the middle of the lock, it started rotating. The smaller gears followed suit. More and more green flakes snowed upon the floor as the metal creaked and groaned, struggling to turn after countless years of neglect.

Echo could not see the inner workings of the mechanism that held the heavy door closed, but she could hear it turning, the tumblers of the giant lock clicking into place. Propelled by some unseen power, the door began to swing open with painful slowness, evidently deeming them worthy of entry for having survived the series of trials. A distant, detached part of Echo's brain noted the elaborate carvings hewn into the metal of the door: dragons, at least a dozen of them, flying in a spiraling formation, batlike wings spread wide, ferocious teeth bared in permanent snarls. It was hardly a welcoming image, but then, she supposed that was the point.

Echo was ready to step through the door as soon as there was room enough for her to slip by, but a hand on her shoulder wrenched her backward. Dorian shoved past her, and for a brief moment Echo wondered if he had seen something beyond the door that she had not, some threat or new trial, and was shielding her from it. But when she saw what lay within the chamber, she knew that it had not been altruism or a desire to defend her that had driven Dorian forward with such haste.

"Oh" was all she managed to utter. Behind her, Jasper let loose a curse in strangled Avicet.

The room on the other side of the elaborate door was massive. It wasn't a room so much as a cavern. The ceiling was high, and the ground opened up a few feet in front of them, revealing a pit that looked like it might actually be bottomless. The cavern walls were stone, and mottled with depressions where it looked as though the stone had been gouged out. A footbridge connected the landing to a round island in the center. And that was where he was.

Just as he had been in the vision provided to Echo by the scrying bowl, Caius was hanging limp from chains connected to the ceiling. Seeing him in person was far, far worse.

His head hung down, dark hair falling messily across his forehead and obscuring his eyes. If not for the shallow and too-quick rise and fall of his chest, Echo would have assumed he was dead. The mere thought of his being dead—and the sight of him so close to it—made her stomach clench. His chest was bare, and he was clad only in a pair of well-worn leather breeches. The clothes he'd had on the day he was abducted were nowhere to be seen. Indeed, there was nothing else in the room except for him—and the chains. A horrified gasp escaped Echo as she took in Caius's state. His torso was covered in dried blood. Welts marked his skin; it looked as though he'd been lashed with something thick and heavy, like a leather cord or a whip. The manacles around his wrists had rubbed his skin raw. The wounds were an angry shade of red and thickly encrusted with dried blood.

His fingers rested on the chain connected to his shackles, as if he were holding on to it to take some of the pressure off his shoulders, wrenched upward as they were. Gods, how long had he been standing like this, dangling like a slab of meat at the butcher's?

For all his haste to enter the room, Dorian was now as motionless as Echo. His expression was a rictus of pain, as if he himself were the one in chains, left to rot by his own sister.

"What are you waiting for?" Echo's voice broke halfway through the question as a choked sob threatened to escape her. "Get him down." Without waiting for Dorian to respond, she crossed the short footbridge to the island. She was mere feet from Caius when Dorian blocked her with an arm flung around her waist.

"I can't," he said bitterly. He jerked his chin at the ground.

Echo had been so transfixed by the horrific sight of Caius helpless and hurt that she hadn't noticed the ground surrounding him, but now she saw what had delayed Dorian.

A circle had been carved into the ground around Caius, with runes spaced evenly along its circumference. They were reminiscent of the protective runes Echo had seen Dorian and Caius use at Jasper's warehouse in London, though these were far more complex. The Drakhar script was sharp and jagged, and curiously well preserved, as if age could not touch them. There were additional runes drawn in straight lines from the outer edge of the circle and pointing toward its center. Toward Caius. A small moan escaped Caius—it was so quiet that Echo was half certain she had imagined it, but Dorian's hand tightened painfully where it held her. No, she hadn't imagined that pained sound.

Jasper drew even with them, slowly, seemingly reluctant to get too close to either Caius or the circle. "What is that?"

"It's a barrier glyph," Dorian replied. "Of ancient design, but the construction is similar to the ones we use in the Drakharin military." His voice was oddly cold. Perhaps he was trying to distance himself from the situation to be objective. Echo spared him a glance. Though his tone was detached, his expression was not. His already-pale face had gone ashen at the sight of Caius, and a slight tremor worked its way through his body.

The longer Echo looked at the circle—and it was easier to look at the circle than at Caius, though avoidance felt cowardly—the more she felt the magic emanating from it. The firebird allowed her to sense magic in the air, like currents. She could feel it. Taste it. She tilted her head to one side, looking askance at the runes. They shimmered with a sickly glow, like an oil slick in sunlight. A faint sense of unease seemed to radiate from the circle. Echo knew without being told that if she tried to cross it as it was, she might not survive the attempt. At least, not in one piece.

"Well," Jasper prompted, "how do we get through it?" He waved a hand at the chains holding Caius up by his bloodied wrists. "We can't just leave him like this."

Dorian whirled on Jasper, fists tightly clenched, and Echo worried that he was actually going to start throwing punches. "Don't you think I know that?"

To his credit, Jasper barely flinched. His eyes narrowed, but he was otherwise unperturbed. "Then do something."

Echo stepped between them.

"Dorian," she said, trying to keep her voice as level as possible. A presence fluttered anxiously at the back of her mind. Rose, drawn by Caius's suffering, no doubt. Echo pushed it down as best she could. "Is there anything we can do about the glyph?"

Dorian shook his head, not as though he were admitting defeat but as if he was adrift. Lost. His eye strayed to Caius, and Echo didn't miss the anguish in his gaze.

"There should be a way to break the glyph," Dorian said, voice thick with emotion, "even if this is the most complicated barrier spell I've ever seen."

"Anything that can be locked can be unlocked," Echo said. A peculiar quiet calm came over her. If she ignored the body hanging from chains, if she recast Caius as a puzzle to be solved, then she could focus on the problem at hand: how to free him.

With steady, careful steps, Echo walked around the circle, mindful of the barrier she could not cross. One of the first skills she had acquired as a runaway illicitly living in the shadows of one of the finest libraries in the world was the art of picking locks. It wasn't terribly hard once you knew what you were doing; it required patience and a bit of cleverness. Echo wasn't always brimming with the former, but she liked to think she had an abundance of the latter.

"Maybe if we . . ." The words died in her throat as she saw the ruin of Caius's back.

She remembered the landscape of his back, though not with her own memories—with hands that were not her own, lips that had never touched his skin. Faint scales dusted his shoulder blades, rounding the contours of bone and muscle to meet at the column of his spine, where they descended to the waistband of his pants. Echo knew how it would feel to trace that gentle arc of scales with the tips of her fingers. She knew the way the texture shifted beneath her touch, how the scales were slightly cooler than the skin around them. She knew that caressing the place where skin met scales would make Caius dissolve into laughter that was most unbecoming to a prince of the Drakharin.

She knew all that without ever having done any of it. The memory of how beautiful he had been made what had been done to him worse somehow.

Long angry welts crisscrossed flesh mottled by bruises, some old and yellow, others fresh and purple. Rivulets of dried blood caked Caius's scales, while split skin oozed thick, viscous crimson.

"Echo."

She started at the sound of her name. By the look on Dorian's face, it wasn't the first time he'd called it. His brow crinkled in confusion before he appeared to decide that her momentary lapse was not something he ought to be concerned about just then.

"There are two ways to break through a barrier glyph," Dorian said. "The first is with magic. If we had a skilled enough mage, they might be able to undo the spell work that created this one."

"Too bad we didn't think to bring one of those," Jasper muttered.

"And the second way?" Echo asked.

An expression that was too grim to be called a smile but too eager to be called anything else flitted across Dorian's face. "Good old-fashioned brute force."

Echo eyed the elaborate carvings on the stone floor. There was a faint vibration in the air, nearly imperceptible but noticeable if one paid very close attention. The glyph radiated with magic. Strong magic. A sense of foreboding flavored its energy, and each step Echo took closer to its outer circle filled her with the threat of malice. The spell work was beautiful in its complexity; it warned you off the closer you got to it, so that when you burned against its barrier you had no one to blame but yourself.

"So we just smash through it?" Echo could not help sounding dubious.

Dorian replied with a brief nod. "Yes."

"Is that wise?"

Dorian shook his head. "No. Probably not. But it's our only option to get him out of here before . . ." He let the words die in his throat, pain and sorrow etched across his face. "We need to help Caius before his wounds prove too much for even him to heal."

"The clock's a-ticking," Jasper said.

Echo nodded as she shrugged off her jacket. If she was going to use her power, she didn't want to singe the leather. "Then we better get to work."

Breaking the ground around the seal wouldn't work, Dorian assured them. The spell had been embedded into the carved inscriptions, but the magic would hold even after their destruction. So that plan was out.

So Echo did what was starting to feel like a natural response to situations that stymied her. She set the blasted thing on fire.

The magic inside her felt strained, but she reached for it all the same. Magic was not an infinite resource, and it did not come without a cost, but Echo would be more than willing to pay later in pain if she could only manage this one task. If she could perhaps burn the magic out of the glyph by overloading it with her own, like an outlet channeling too much electricity. It was a theory she prayed would work in practice.

"Are you sure this is going to do the trick?" Jasper asked.

"Nope," Echo replied.

She let the magic pour from her hands. There was a little pain, concentrated at the base of her skull, but there was also a strange sensation of relief. Like she had been carrying around a heavy weight that she was finally able to put down. The feeling didn't last long. The barrier tried to fight back, pushing against Echo's flames, driven by the only purpose it had: to keep Caius inside the circle and everyone else outside.

Echo threw everything she had into the flame, and when the well of magic ran dry, she dug deeper and found more. Her vision began to black out at the edges. She was vaguely aware of someone shouting her name, telling her to stop, but she could feel it—she was close. So, so close.

Pain blossomed into knife-sharp agony in her skull. But she couldn't stop. Wouldn't stop. She poured every ounce of power in her body into the barrier. Her legs gave out and she crashed to her knees, only distantly feeling the impact. It was nothing compared with the burning in her head and hands.

Echo summoned a last, desperate lurch of power before collapsing completely. Her forehead rested against the stone floor, blessedly cool against her feverish skin. If it weren't for the white-hot pain lancing through her, she would have thought she was dead. She couldn't even open her eyes.

"It worked." Dorian's voice floated to Echo through the haze of pain and fatigue that gripped her. Lying there, recovering, she listened as Dorian and Jasper worked to release Caius from his manacles. Echo allowed herself the barest of smiles when she finally heard the chains clatter to the floor.

Caius was free. And together, they were going home.

"I've got him," Dorian said. "Jasper, will you—"

A roar, sudden and viciously loud, consumed the remainder of Dorian's sentence. It reverberated through the floor, vibrating loose rocks against Echo's forehead. She pushed herself up to a sitting position, ignoring the aches in her muscles. They all fell silent and still, waiting.

"What the hell was that?" Jasper whispered.

Echo didn't supply him with an answer. She knew. They all knew, even if no one wanted to believe it.

"That's not possible," Dorian said under his breath.

But as the sound of leathery wings drifted up from below, Echo knew his disbelief was futile. The carvings on the walls of the lava room and around the doorframe they had passed through into this room had not been mere decorations; they were warnings to whoever was foolish enough to proceed beyond them.

Echo rose, her legs as shaky as a newborn foal's, and thought, *Here there be dragons.*

CHAPTER TWENTY

The ground rumbled beneath Echo's feet. The pit surrounding the island, previously dark with unrelieved shadows, began to emit an orange glow like the embers of a fire that stubbornly refuses to die. Another roar sounded from deep beneath the surface, so ferocious that the ground shook with it.

Dorian gently lowered the still-unconscious Caius to the ground. "It appears we have awoken the beast," he said.

"That room with the lava wasn't what the rune meant by fire," Echo said. Of course it hadn't been; that would have been far too easy. "This is pyromaniac cat-bird."

"It's Super Mario," Jasper whispered as he leaned over the edge, craning his neck for a better look. "I told you. That's Bowser, and Caius is Princess Peach."

"Who's Mario?" Echo asked, just as quietly.

"We're *all* Mario."

Echo reached for the reserves of magic within her, but

she felt empty, like a car out of gas. *Shit. Shit, shit, shit.* "So, what you're saying is, I have to slay a dragon to save the princess?"

"Prince," Dorian interjected.

"Whatever." A tongue of flame flickered to life in Echo's palm. Her exhaustion seemed to double with the conjuring, but she pushed it aside. She could rest when she was dead.

Dorian moved to stand beside Echo. His hand came up and pulled her behind him. A small, rebellious part of Echo wanted to protest, but a much larger and much saner part had little desire to be the first thing encountered by whatever was living deep within the bowels of the temple.

Even the beast below—which Echo was not entirely prepared to accept as a living, breathing dragon—held back its roar, as if giving its audience time to adjust to the impossibility of its existence.

The ground began to tremble again, this time with even more intensity. Echo imagined the great beast rising from its slumber, uncoiling a long, scaly body with slow, languorous movements. Gusts of wind rose from the pit, and the dragon—a real, live dragon—emerged from the shadowy depths. Echo's brain fought to process what she was seeing. Wings spread wide as the creature stretched, claws brushing the walls of its cave, its scales the pale color of moonlight on a clear night, its tail lashing this way and that. She had always wanted to see a dragon—as any child whose head was full of stories would—but these were not ideal circumstances.

Flashes of memory zipped through her mind. Caius tracing constellations of stars in the night sky, telling her the stories behind them, which gods and other figures from his culture's folklore they were meant to represent. Dorian regaling a bedridden Jasper with old Drakharin fairy tales, full of dragons guarding troves of priceless treasures and the intrepid young warriors who tamed such wild beasts. All those stories were as good as legend, taking place so far back in history that if there was any truth to them, it had been so thoroughly gilded over by time. The one thing all the tales had in common was that dragons had walked the earth once, but none had been seen for thousands and thousands of years. They were, Caius had explained, considered part of Drakharin history. None, he had insisted, were said to have survived the rise of human dominance.

"Caius told me your people believed dragons were extinct," Echo said, feeling oddly betrayed.

"We thought they were," Dorian said. His voice was full of marvel, like that of a little boy who has just learned that Santa is real.

"Does *that* look extinct to you?" Echo gestured, rather unnecessarily, to the dragon holding itself aloft with indolent flaps of its wings, sniffing the air with a long snout, nostrils flaring. A milky white film—cataracts, perhaps—covered its eyes, though it didn't appear to hinder the beast much. It could probably smell them.

Dorian shook his head in awestruck wonder. "It's incredible."

"Not the word I would have chosen for a thing that's about to kill us and then probably pick its teeth with our bones, but okay, sure, let's run with that." The dragon rolled its neck, a gesture that would have been comical considering just how long its neck was, but it was difficult to find anything attached to the creature the slightest bit humorous.

Never laugh at live dragons. The quote bubbled to the surface of Echo's brain. Probably Tolkien. *How fitting.*

The dragon snapped its jaws experimentally, as if testing its range of motion. It looked vaguely hungry. Echo didn't like that one bit. "How do we kill this bad boy?"

Dorian shot her an appalled glare. "We are not going to kill it," he hissed. "It is very likely the last of its kind. I will not be the Drakharin held responsible for rendering their species extinct."

"Okay," Echo said, keeping her eyes on the dragon. It dipped and twisted, flying around the island. It turned lazy circles, head swiveling to and fro as it rose, higher and higher, until its wings were brushing the roof of the cavern. A long forked tongue snaked out, rasping over lips peeled back from hideously sharp teeth. It was licking its chops.

It was *licking* its *chops.*

"Shit," Echo said, ever the soul of brevity.

The sound of her expletive made the dragon tick its head to the side. Those unnerving eyes narrowed into even more unnerving slits. It huffed and it puffed, raising itself as high as the cavernous ceiling would allow.

A sound rumbled from the depths of its chest, rather like that of a bellows. Gills that Echo hadn't noticed before opened at the sides of its neck.

But it wasn't underwater. Why on earth would it need gills?

It didn't take long for Echo to learn why.

The scales on its neck opened and closed, and through the narrow openings their movement revealed, Echo saw a glow, low and red. It was an angry glow, full of menace.

Echo had half a second to bask in the idea that dragons

really did breathe fire before the very real dragon breathed very real fire. Directly at her.

Her own fire responded without conscious instruction from her terrified brain. Her magic coursed through her body, driven by sheer instinct. She felt it spill not just from her hands, but from every inch of her exposed skin.

A wall of fire formed around her, brilliant white chasing away the shadows in the cavern. The dragon's blazing breath collided with Echo's own flames, and was overpowered by them. The fire was startlingly mundane, considering it had originated in a dragon's belly. Echo's, on the other hand, was pure magic.

The dragon's fire petered out and Echo felt hers fade in the absence of an immediate threat. Pain flared hot and bright at the base of her skull, so powerfully that in better circumstances, with fewer fire-breathing dragons, she might have vomited.

"Can we kill it if it tries to kill us first?" As it was so clearly trying to do. Echo kept her eyes on the dragon as she directed her question at Dorian. The creature seemed in no particular rush to lunge at her again, but one could never be sure. Most of the dragons she'd read about had been mercurial at best, acrimonious at worst. "Then can we kill it?"

"We are not going to kill it," Dorian hissed.

Before Echo could argue with him, the dragon roared and dropped its massive body into a dive. And that was when Caius woke up.

CHAPTER TWENTY-ONE

Death would have been a kindness.

Everything hurt. Every inch of skin, every fiber of muscle, every sliver of bone. Caius groaned, and that hurt too, his vocal cords stripped raw by his own screaming. Something hard abraded his cheek as he tried to turn his head. Something hard and solid, pockmarked and uneven. Like stone.

That was new.

He opened his eyes and the world shifted around him. The view was the same, but different. Same rounded cavern walls. Same lonely little door at the end of a narrow stone bridge. Same unrelieved monotony. But he looked at it all now from the vantage point of the floor. Days had passed since the iron shackles had locked around his wrists and he'd been strung up like a freshly butchered pig. He *felt* like a freshly butchered pig. The welts along his back that had started to heal widened with every movement, however minuscule, and his inflamed skin was feverishly hot compared to the cool stone beneath him.

Voices, familiar ones, drifted to him. With great difficulty, he turned his head toward them, noting the fractured lines of a broken circle in the stone. The glyph. It had been shattered. Thoroughly.

When he saw his friends, he would have wept had there been any tears left in him, had his sister not wrung him dry.

Hair the gleaming color of polished steel. A shock of vibrant feathers in a dozen different hues. Hair the rich brown of dark chocolate pulled back in a messy ponytail.

They had come. They had come for him.

Dorian. Jasper. Echo.

And a dragon.

Caius fought to find his voice, but it rattled around in his throat, scratching at its tender walls.

The dragon—oh, what a marvelous beast it was, with its alabaster scales and the soft golden tinge of its wings—dove toward Echo, who faced it with all the bravery of a knight out of a fairy tale. But unlike a knight, Echo was just a girl. Unarmed and unarmored. She didn't stand a chance.

With an earth-splitting roar, the dragon gnashed its teeth at Echo. A warning perhaps, or a promise. Wind gusted over Caius with each flap of the thing's powerful wings, abrading his broken skin. Fire blossomed in Echo's open palms like the first blooms of spring, pure white and blackest black dancing against her skin.

Stupid, Caius chastised himself. Echo didn't need a weapon. She *was* the weapon.

Dorian's sword was drawn, but Caius saw the reluctance in his stance. He didn't want to fight the dragon. To the

Drakharin, dragons were sacred. They were gods, on this earth but not of it. To harm a dragon was the gravest sin among their people, the highest and most unpardonable form of blasphemy. One who raised a weapon to a dragon would never find peace in the realms beyond this mortal life. They would be damned.

"Stop," he tried to say, his voice a shattered whisper.

They didn't hear him. Fire arced from Echo's hands, twirling through the air like ribbons of light and shadow. The dragon retreated from the flames, its milky eyes squinting against the onslaught of light.

Caius had heard the dragon shifting among the rocks as he'd hung there. There had been a soft quality to those movements, a mindless rustling, like a person in the throes of restless sleep. Caius had convinced himself he'd imagined the noise, that his desperate mind had concocted a creature out of shadows to keep him company so that he wouldn't die alone, but the dragon was beyond his wildest imaginings.

It would be a travesty to kill it. It had not done Caius harm; it would be poor recompense for his companions to cause it grievous injury.

"Stop," he said again, louder this time as his voice returned to him, shaken from its tortured slumber.

Echo's head snapped toward him, her brown eyes wide as she watched him struggle to stand. Her attention was only off the dragon for the barest of moments, but it was enough. The creature saw an opening and took it, dropping its clawed feet to the ground and lunging at her, jaws wide and dripping with saliva. Jasper barreled into Echo and they both went sprawling, missing the dragon's dagger-sharp teeth by inches.

A hand wrapped around Caius's forearm and helped him to his feet.

"My prince," Dorian said. The words were spoken in formal Drakhar, but Dorian's tone was chipped at the edges with emotion.

"My friend," Caius replied, letting his weight fall on Dorian. "There's a dragon," he added rather dumbly.

"Indeed."

"We can't kill it."

"No," Dorian agreed. "That would be a crime."

Caius tried to stand on his own, but gravity reminded him what a bad idea that was. He swayed back against Dorian's chest. "I have an idea. But I have to do it alone." He pushed away from Dorian again, unsteady on his feet but mostly upright.

"*Drakhanis,*" Caius said. The dragon's head swiveled toward him, its nostrils flaring as it sniffed the air. Perhaps it recognized Caius's scent—they had shared space for gods knew how many days—or perhaps it simply sensed the frailty of his abused body and didn't mark him as a threat. But either way, it did not attack. It cocked its head to one side, looking, a bit ridiculously, like a curious dog.

A single tentative step took Caius toward the beast. Then another. And another. Echo shouted his name, but Caius had eyes only for the dragon. He could smell its foul breath—a combination of burnt meat and brimstone—even from a distance.

The cavern was dark, but Caius could just make out the markings on the dragon's long body: mottled white-gold scales that reminded him somewhat of a spotted leopard. When its wings spread and lazily fanned the air, he noticed the underside was streaked with a dark pattern like the wings of a moth.

Caius approached the beast slowly, arms at his sides, his hands open to reveal that he was unarmed.

"I do not wish to harm you," Caius said in Drakhar. The tongue of the dragon, as it was known among his people. He prayed that the term was more than just a pretty phrase. The stories his tutors and governesses had told him in childhood burned fresh in his memory. All those tales emphasized that dragons admired strength and cunning and skill, but they demanded respect. Caius dropped to one knee and brought one fist up to his heart, a Drakharin sign of the utmost obeisance. Though every instinct in him screamed against it, he lowered his gaze deferentially. "I am your humble servant."

The others held their breath, a frozen audience, utterly silent. Not a single soul dared shatter the moment. Not even Echo.

With his gaze still fixed on the ground in front of him, Caius could not see the dragon step forward, but he felt it. The earth trembled with the force of its mass as it came forward in a four-legged crouch. It let loose an odiferous breath, huffing for all the world like a dog. A very large, very deadly dog.

Caius dared not raise his eyes, not even when he felt each lumbering step the creature took. Pebbles rumbled loose from the rocky ground, skittering away as if fleeing in terror. The dragon stopped when it was mere feet from Caius. Air gusted over him as the beast scented the area around him. Fat droplets of pinkish saliva dripped from the creature's bloodied maw. Caius tried very hard not to think of where—or whom—that gore had come from. He knew that several Firedrakes had accompanied Tanith when she'd deposited him here; he wasn't certain they'd all made it out alive. It would have been like her to offer one of her own as a sacrifice to the beast she'd left to watch her brother.

It inched closer, if something of such massive size could be said to inch.

Caius's heart hammered in his chest, beating out a staccato rhythm that screamed its desire to run far, far away.

But Caius held his ground, eyes still cast down and fixed on the loose pebbles that might very well be the last thing he ever saw. Forepaws with wickedly sharp talons tipped red with drying blood came into his range of sight.

A wet, hot breath gusted over the top of Caius's head, ruffling his hair. Something slightly damp snuffled at his head. A snout, he realized. The dragon was scenting him.

His skin prickled into goose bumps, but he allowed the inspection. Up close, the beast's breath made Caius's eyes water. He took shallow breaths through his mouth, which had gone frightfully dry.

Satisfied, the dragon stepped back and the claws disappeared from Caius's sight. With slow, incremental movements, Caius raised his eyes enough to see the creature. It sank gracefully to its knees in front of him, bending its enormous body forward in a gesture that looked remarkably like a bow. Its wings draped across the ground like a heavy blanket, spread as wide as the dragon was tall. It dipped its head low, vertical eyelids sliding closed for a moment. When its eyes opened, they were peering at Caius in a way that made him think the dragon was not nearly as blind as it appeared.

Caius met its milky, pearlescent gaze, unafraid.

With exaggerated slowness, he stood. Those unsettling eyes tracked his movements. He raised a hand toward the beast's head. When it didn't withdraw, he rested his palm against the ridge of its brow. The scales were warm to the touch, like the embers of a forgotten fire. He'd expected the texture to be rough, but the dragon's scales were as smooth as his own. The creature twitched, bumping its head against Caius's palm as if asking to be stroked. Caius slid his hand over its head, tracing the ridges of its skull. Its eyes drifted shut, and it huffed out a satisfied breath.

"It won't harm us," Caius said, petting the dragon's head. A faint rumbling, almost like the satisfied purr of a cat, bubbled up from deep within its chest. As the adrenaline rush dwindled, darkness began to creep in at the edges of Caius's vision. His wounds ached with renewed vigor, as if affronted that he had dared to ignore them for just a few moments. He wouldn't last long. Not with blood loss and hunger and dehydration ravaging him from within.

"As kenan, nes kenan," Dorian said.

Come in peace, leave in peace. It was an old Drakhar saying, one uttered both upon meeting and parting. Their people had an affinity for war, and valued strength above all other qualities, but they recognized peace even if they didn't always treat it as an ideal worth striving for.

"Holy shit," Echo breathed. "You're like Snow White, but with dragons."

Caius tried to summon a witty retort—he was no slumbering princess in need of rescuing, except perhaps he *was*—but the shadows overwhelmed him and his body succumbed to the blissful oblivion of darkness.

CHAPTER TWENTY-TWO

Their return to the cabin was a blur of action. Dorian and Jasper held Caius suspended between them while Echo navigated the unpredictable path through the in-between, bouncing from country to country to muddle their tracks. She felt the darkness tug at her as she traversed the void between doorways, as though it were hungry for her to become lost in its fathomless depths. The sensation reminded her of a book she had read about mountaineering disasters that described, in vivid detail, what it felt like to succumb to the siren song of hypothermia. It would've been so easy to let herself go, to sink into that velvety blackness. But she pushed onward, leaving smears of shadow dust and blood in her wake. She didn't trust Tanith's sudden change of heart. If a battalion of Firedrakes tracked them through the in-between, metaphorical guns blazing, Echo would not have been the least bit surprised. They had to get away, and fast.

Echo laid her palm against the door of a utility closet in a

Nairobi railway station. When the door swung open, instead of disused Cairo Metro track, they were greeted by heaps of snow—not something one encountered often in Egypt in autumn. There were train tracks half visible through the snow, though they stood not on the platform but on the solid-white-blanketed ground that stretched as far as the eye could see.

"Where the hell are we?" Jasper said. He had one of Caius's arms looped around his shoulders as he helped Dorian support the unconscious Drakharin.

Echo looked around wildly for any marker or sign that would inform her of their location. Perhaps if she could recognize the language, she would have a better idea of where they were. But even without a sign—of which there were none—Echo had a general idea of which part of the globe they were currently standing on.

The sky seemed to hang lower than it did in New York or Edinburgh. Above their heads ribbons of green and blue light danced against a dusky backdrop.

"Are those the northern lights?" Jasper asked. Dorian had been silent since they carried Caius from the temple ruins.

Despite the urgency of their situation, Echo found herself momentarily mesmerized by the unexpected sight. "Yep."

"That's fascinating," Jasper said, "but we need to get out of here." He looked around for some indication of how this patch of land operated as a gateway to the in-between. "How did we even get here in the first place?"

A very fine question.

Echo started kicking at the snow around her feet to clear it away. The toe of her boot connected with something hard, and she dropped to her knees to dig it out. The snow was bitterly cold against her bare skin, but she kept digging until her efforts revealed a signpost that had fallen to the ground and been buried during a storm. She worked her way along the metal post until she reached the sign at the end of it.

KIRKENES—BJØRNEVATNBANEN.

"We're in Norway," Echo said. "This must be an abandoned stop on this line."

"Great," Jasper said. "I've always wanted to visit an abandoned Norwegian train station. Now that I've done so, I can check it off my bucket list." Jasper hefted Caius up a little bit higher; he had begun to sag in their arms. "Can you get us out of here? He's a lot heavier than he looks."

Without answering, Echo pulled the pouch of shadow dust out of her pocket. The bag was distressingly light. If they ran out of shadow dust before reaching the cabin, they would be in deep trouble. Caius's condition was worsening with every trip through the in-between. Every breath he drew seemed to be shallower than the last. There was a very real possibility he would die propped up between Dorian and Jasper.

Echo had never tried to access the in-between in the middle of a train line, without a doorway to aid her, but if the magic along the railway was strong enough to bring them there, then maybe it was strong enough to get them out.

She dipped her fingers into the pouch, and they came away stained black with dust. It was a minuscule amount, but hopefully enough for the next leg of their journey. With a silent prayer, Echo dragged her fingers along the cold steel track and pictured the nearest gateway to the cabin they'd been able to find: a ring of tall oak trees, humming with magic older than any railroad station. She didn't want to waste any time jumping from gateway to gateway, not with the condition Caius was in. They'd taken a circuitous route back from the temple, but with the in-between as volatile as it had been lately, it was unlikely anyone—no matter how strong his or her magic—would be able to track their progress through it.

Black smoke slithered from the snow, like the first stubborn spring blossoms sprouting up through a layer of frost. Power shivered up Echo's arm, from her fingers, which grew cold against the rail, to her shoulder. It was a weak thread. Tentative. But it was enough if they worked together.

"The trees," Echo said, grasping the thin stream of magic curling outward from the in-between. "The ones near the cabin. Focus on them."

She hoped Dorian and Jasper did as they were told. With three minds envisioning the same destination, perhaps the in-between would be less likely to lead them astray again.

Echo stumbled into a copse of trees, stomach roiling with nausea. Travel through the in-between didn't bother her as much as it had before becoming the firebird, but struggling to resist the ceaseless pull of the void wore on her more than she had realized. She wanted to stand still just for a moment, to let her legs appreciate solid ground beneath both feet, to give her stomach a chance to stop bubbling threateningly. But they didn't have the time. Caius didn't have the time. She could tell from the way Jasper and Dorian struggled to keep Caius balanced between them that they, too, were feeling the effects of too much travel through an inhospi-table in-between.

With no small amount of difficulty, the three of them wrestled Caius out of the woods and into the cabin. Echo was once again grateful for its isolation. How they would explain carting a bruised, bloodied unconscious man, body decorated with whip marks and scales, should some hapless passerby stumble upon them, Echo hadn't the faintest clue.

Once they were inside the cabin, she felt something loosen in her chest. They had done it. They had saved Caius and brought him back to safety. The hardest part was behind them. All they had to do now was patch him up.

"On the bed," Echo said as she pushed open the bed-room door.

Dorian and Jasper deposited Caius on the mattress with as much gentleness as they could muster, which was not much at all. Caius's head lolled on the pillow and one arm dropped off the side of the bed. It was hard to tell through the blood and the bruises, but Echo thought she saw a spi-der's web of black veins near his wrists.

"That wasn't there when we found him, right?" Echo pointed at the darkened patch of skin, careful not to touch it. "Am I losing it? Did I just not notice before?"

Dorian stepped closer. He reached out as if to lay his hand on the raw skin of Caius's wrist, but then thought bet-ter of it. "No, that was certainly not there when we found him."

"This is bad," Jasper said unhelpfully.

"Very bad," Echo agreed. Caius hadn't shown signs of the kuçedra's taint in the temple. That they were appearing now was very bad indeed.

Dorian rummaged through Echo's bag. It took her a minute to realize what he was looking for.

"The elixir," Dorian said, holding up a glass vial of viscous red liquid.

"Okay," Jasper said. "Maybe this isn't so bad."

As much as Echo wanted to agree with him, she couldn't help the surge of dread she felt as Dorian approached with the bloodweed elixir. "Do you think that'll work?"

They all knew the elixir's success rate was not one hundred percent. The longer a person had been exposed to the kuçedra's blight, the less likely they were to respond to treatment. But for the moment, a silent consensus had been reached: they would not mention the likelihood of failure. What else could they do?

Dorian's hands trembled as he uncorked the vial. The pungent scent made Echo's nostrils burn, but she stayed close to the bedside—close but not touching—as Dorian tipped the elixir into Caius's partially open mouth. Echo realized then that she hadn't thought to pack some of the syringes she'd seen Ivy use to administer the elixir intravenously. *Stupid.*

Silence descended upon the room as they waited. Echo knew from observation that the elixir did not always work immediately, but none of them was eager to shatter the fragile bubble of hope and fear that enveloped them. It would be so easy to tip the scales to one side or the other.

A sudden shiver worked its way down Caius's body. Echo reached for him, but Dorian held her back. "Look," he said.

The dark veins on Caius's arm were not improving. They were spreading. Echo watched with growing horror as black lines marched across Caius's skin, branching out from his wrists to crawl up his arms and over his shoulders. They snaked across his collarbones as a powerful seizure racked his body. An alarming gurgling noise rose from his throat, swiftly followed by a red liquid tinged with black. For a moment, Echo thought it was blood, but once the acrid smell of the elixir hit the air, she understood what was happening.

"His body's rejecting it," Dorian said, sounding more hopeless than Echo had ever heard him.

A ragged scream tore its way from Caius's throat. He sounded like he was being burned alive.

"It isn't working." Echo fought against Dorian's grip, but it was like trying to break through iron bands. "It's killing him."

Jasper swore and left the room. Echo was ready to shout at him for his cowardice, but then he returned, wearing an absolutely absurd pair of bright-pink rubber gloves. The gloves had been under the sink when Echo and Jasper first arrived at the cabin, most likely left by its previous inhabitants.

"What are you doing?" Echo asked as Jasper turned a struggling Caius onto his side with brisk efficiency.

"I had a friend swallow a few too many pills once." Jasper held Caius's jaw open with one hand and reached into his mouth with two fingers. "It's not the first time I've had to make somebody puke."

It wasn't pretty.

Caius retched and Dorian let go of Echo to retrieve a bucket from beneath the sink. Jasper held Caius in his gloved hands, coaxing the elixir out of him. When it seemed as though most of it had been purged from his system, Caius sagged against Jasper, who rearranged himself so that his skin wasn't in danger of coming in contact with Caius's.

"What do we do now?" Echo's voice was as thin and helpless as a reed battered by a strong wind.

After disposing of the bucket's contents, Dorian sank to his knees beside the bed. "I don't know."

The black continued to spread, though more slowly. Every now and then, a thickened vein would throb and the darkness would pulse outward, as if propelled by the beating of Caius's heart.

"He's going to die, isn't he." Jasper didn't make it sound like a question but rather a statement of fact. They all knew it.

Dorian buried his face in his hands, as though he couldn't bring himself to look at his prince, to face his failure. His shoulders shook and though he made no noise, Echo knew he was crying.

Not like this, whispered a voice at the back of her mind. *Please, not like this.*

"I want to try something," Echo said, hoping she sounded more confident than she felt.

Dorian peered at her with a red-rimmed eye. "The elixir is the only thing we've found that helps fight the kuçedra's toxin. The circle Tanith had him in must have had some spell worked into it to halt its spread. When we removed him from it, we broke the spell. What can you possibly do?" There was an accusation in his words: *If not for you, we wouldn't be here. If not for you, he never would have been taken.* Echo didn't think Dorian was wrong, but recriminations would have to wait.

"I think he's right," Jasper said softly. He'd removed the gloves and slid off the bed. He wasn't touching Dorian, but it was painfully obvious he wanted to. "We're lucky we got this far. What's left for us to try?"

"Good old-fashioned brute force." Tongues of flame tickled Echo's palms. A deep soreness had settled into her muscles after burning the barrier and fleeing through the in-between. But rest would have to wait a bit longer.

Dorian and Jasper stood between Echo and the bed. Caius's already-shallow breaths were accompanied by a wet, rattling noise coming from deep inside his chest.

"What are you going to do to him?" It was Dorian's turn to hover and feel useless. Echo didn't envy him in the slightest.

"I'm going to burn the poison out of him," she said.

A resounding silence met her statement. A nice, long, stunned silence.

"You're going to do what?" Jasper asked.

"I'm going to burn the—"

He waved away the rest of her sentence. "Yes, I heard you the first time. But I don't understand you. Let me re-phrase: why the devil do you think you'd be able to do something like that?"

Echo shrugged.

"Are you mad?" Dorian blurted.

"Probably," Echo replied. "But unless you'd rather watch him fade away while that monster uses him as a living, breathing battery until there's nothing left, I suggest you get out of my way and let me try."

Dorian hesitated, still uncertain.

"What have we got to lose?" Echo said softly. "If we do nothing, then we lose him for sure. But there's a chance I can save him."

"How?" Dorian asked. He looked over his shoulder at Caius, at the whip marks and the burns and the black veins covering his body. "Try to explain it to me. Please." His voice broke. "I'm supposed to protect him."

Echo struggled to find the words to describe the feeling she had in her gut. "The kuçedra is supposed to be the counterpart to the firebird, right?"

Dorian nodded slowly, like he was trying to follow the ramblings of a crazy person. He probably was. "Right."

"Well, if you have a positive and a negative, they'll cancel each other out." Echo neglected to mention the growing patch of black on her own chest. Her logic was even less sound than they knew, but she was desperate, clutching at whatever half-formed straws she could find.

"I don't think dealing with cosmic forces is similar to doing basic arithmetic," Jasper said.

"No, but we know that the fire doesn't always hurt. In the Black Forest, it passed over my friends—over you—because I didn't want to harm you."

Their expressions remained firmly skeptical.

"The prophecy," Echo said. "The firebird prophecy. It said it was—I am—supposed to be able to change things for good. The firebird's power is not simply a destructive force. What if—and I honestly believe this is true—what if I could be the opposite of destructive? What if I could help heal him?"

Jasper threw his hands in the air and stepped away from the bed. "Fine. Do whatever it is you're going to do. He's as good as dead anyway. Even if you wind up killing him faster, then it would probably be an act of mercy."

Dorian flinched at the words. He was the one Echo had to persuade, not Jasper. She wouldn't be able to accomplish much of anything if Dorian insisted on fighting her every step of the way.

"A positive and a negative," said Dorian, as if he was measuring the idea, testing it for holes. There were plenty to find, but until a miracle solution presented itself, it was the best they had.

"The light and the dark," Echo said. "Two sides of the same coin. I can fight this. I have to believe that I can fight this." If she couldn't do it for herself, maybe, just maybe, she could do it for him. "And I have to at least try."

After a long moment, Dorian stepped aside. "Help him," he said. It was an order, not a request.

"I will."

And that was a promise.

Despite her outward confidence, Echo had no idea what she was doing. Since that was not a particularly unusual state of affairs for her, she did not let it deter her from the task at hand.

"Hold him down," she said with more authority than she felt.

Dorian shot her another skeptical look, but he kept his mouth shut and directed Jasper to take hold of one of Caius's arms while he held the other. They'd both donned gloves—the last thing they needed was another victim for the kuçedra to consume.

Caius's head lolled about on the pillow like a rag doll's. His skin had taken on an increasingly sickly pallor. Every minute that passed was one minute lost; if Echo did not figure out a way to save him now, they wouldn't have another chance.

Okay, Echo addressed the other vessels, whose voices, with the exception of Rose and her plaintive plea, had been blessedly silent for days. *If any of you have any ideas about where to start, I'm listening.*

The silence in her head grew even more profound.

Then, when Echo had all but given up hope of receiving an answer, a single small voice spoke up, one she had not heard before.

Touch him, whispered the voice.

Echo raked her gaze over the blackened veins that covered most of Caius's torso.

Are you sure that's a good idea? Like, really, really, really sure?

A familiar voice cut in. *Oh, for the love of the gods, Echo, just do it,* Rose all but shouted in Echo's skull. Phantom voice or not, it reverberated through Echo's head, rattling her bones.

"Okay, fine. I'm doing it!"

Echo didn't realize she'd spoken aloud until Jasper shot her a quizzical glance and inquired, "Who are you talking to?"

"No one," said Echo. Now was not the time for that conversation. She stepped closer to the bed, focusing on the sensation of magic coursing through her blood. It was always there, humming faintly like the rumble of a subway far below a city. It had been distracting at first, but one got used to it eventually.

Jasper didn't look like he believed her, but any other questions he might have had were interrupted by Caius's sudden thrashing.

It can feel you approaching, said the unidentified vessel. *It knows what you intend to do.*

The kuçedra. It may not have been in the room with them, but it knew. It had a presence, and all because of the blight besieging Caius. The Ala had told Echo that she believed the kuçedra was using its victims as a power source, as a way to charge its own magic. It fed on them, but Echo had not believed that the infection was sentient. If the voice speaking to Echo now was correct, then there was far more going on beneath the surface of Caius's skin than any of them had realized.

The closer Echo got, the more Caius struggled. He fought Dorian and Jasper, thrashing against their braced arms with all his might. He was not simply infected; he was a man possessed.

The last of Echo's reluctance fled at the sight of Caius's panicked frenzy. There was nothing she would not do to save him from the hell in which he was ensnared.

Unlike Jasper's and Dorian's, her hands were bare. She crawled onto the bed, dodging wild kicks from Caius's flailing legs. A few blows landed on Echo's shins. She would have impressive bruises to show for it later.

The moment her hands connected with Caius's chest, she felt the kuçedra dancing below the surface of his skin. Though Caius was sweating and flushed, he was not feverish; his skin was cool to the touch. Dangerously so. Echo knew what he should have felt like: pleasantly warmer than average. But his flesh was clammy and cold beneath her fingers, and it bruised immediately, no matter how light her touch. A pained utterance escaped Caius's lips.

No, not bruised. Burned. Echo yanked her hands back as Caius's skin began to blister.

"You're hurting him," Dorian said, voice strained as he wrestled down Caius, who had half risen in an attempt to buck Echo off.

The blistered flesh smoothed the second she ceased touching him. His skin was unmarred, save for the dark swollen veins crisscrossing his torso.

It's a ruse, said the voice in Echo's head. *It wants you to stop. It wants you to give up and go away. You mustn't.*

That was all Echo needed to hear. She pushed down on Caius's chest as firmly as she could, using her legs to leverage her weight as he continued to struggle against the three people holding him.

The veins stopped spreading.

"Was that you?" Jasper asked, as awestruck as he ever allowed himself to sound.

"I think so," Echo said.

But there was already so much darkness in Caius. She felt the power circulating in her own blood rise to the surface. A positive force and a negative force, attracted to one another as the laws of the universe dictated. There was a patch of dense blackness on Caius's chest, just north of his left pectoral muscle. It was right above his heart. Echo zeroed in on it.

Out, damned spot.

Just as she had done in the Black Forest and then again at Avalon, Echo let the magic flow through her as it wished.

She was a vessel. A conduit. The magic of the firebird was a river running over her, through her, from her. It wanted to be let out, and so she released it in a great, rushing wave.

She thought not of heat and fire and blinding light, but of warmth. Of purity. Of the gentle shining of the sun at dawn and starlight on the surface of the ocean. She thought of the songs sung by birds at the break of day and the crisp, clear scent of an autumn breeze. In her mind, she crafted an image that stood in absolute opposition to the stain she felt pulsating in Caius's heart.

Out, damn you.

Echo took everything she felt and pushed it into Caius. A sharp stab of pain flared at the base of her skull, right where she always felt the physical cost of magic first. The agony crested to a skull-splitting roar, but she forced herself to maintain the stream of light and magic emanating from her palms and soaking into Caius's skin.

He screamed, and she echoed it. They were both burning from within, but still, she did not stop. She could not—would not—stop until she had cleansed him of the kuçedra's venomous influence.

She held on and burned with him until there was nothing left.

CHAPTER TWENTY-THREE

The cabin's modest living room was disappointingly empty. What Jasper would've given for a distraction, any distraction, so long as it got his mind off Dorian. As it stood, the only company Jasper had to keep from wallowing in self-pity were two ancient armchairs upholstered in a fabric that would have made a grandmother weep, a grandfather clock so loud and annoying he was ready to pull out its gears, and a rotund black cat that hissed with astonishing viciousness when Jasper dared approach it. He didn't know where the cat had come from. It had just wandered in through the kitchen window like it owned the place. Jasper slumped onto the slightly less hideous sofa in the middle of the room and stared into the fire crackling cheerfully in the hearth. Dorian and Echo were still fawning over Caius, who seemed the worse for wear and would require the attention of a proper healer soon.

Jasper considered making a break for it. Not permanently,

just long enough to have some distance, some perspective. Emotions were messy. That was why he usually preferred not to traffic with them, but this time his own messy emotions had refused to be denied. He felt powerless to stop the swell of jealousy he felt when Dorian had so tenderly reached for Caius, when that blue eye had softened and then filled with tears, tears Dorian had not been too proud to shed at the way Caius had unself-consciously reached to lay a hand on the back of Dorian's head and muttered something in soft Drakhar to him that Jasper did not understand. The moment had belonged to them, filled with the years worth of history to which Jasper was not privy.

The sound of a door creaking open pulled Jasper from his thoughts. He angled his head to see who was coming, sure to keep his expression neutral. Dorian, however, did no such thing. He looked haggard, his shoulders sagging with something Jasper suspected was relief. It was a noticeable change from his demeanor of the past several weeks, which had been marked with tension so strong that Jasper had thought Dorian might snap at any moment.

For his part, Dorian did not even look at Jasper as he entered the room. He made straight for the ancient bar tucked in the corner, popped open a decanter of what looked like whiskey, and poured a generous amount into a glass. He downed the entire thing in one smooth motion. He grimaced at the burn of alcohol down his throat before pouring himself another glass. "Want one?" Dorian asked.

The offer was tempting, but the last thing Jasper wanted or needed was to have alcohol loosen his tongue and give it license to spill every embarrassing thought in his head. "Nah, I'm good."

Dorian grunted. Drink in hand, he made his way to the sofa and slumped onto the cushion beside Jasper. He sipped at his drink, staring listlessly into the fire. With his free hand he rubbed at the scarred skin beneath his eye patch. Dorian may have been relieved to have found Caius, but that little gesture told Jasper something was still bothering him. Dorian had his tells just like anybody else, and Jasper had always excelled at reading tells.

The silence wasn't awkward—not exactly—but Jasper still felt the need to fill it. "How is he?"

Dorian heaved a weary sigh. "He is . . . unwell."

"That's putting it mildly," Jasper said. He wondered if Dorian would look like this should something happen to *him*. It was not a generous thought, and not one Jasper was proud of, but he couldn't help but wonder.

"I never liked Tanith," Dorian said. "I can't say I was surprised when she betrayed Caius for the throne or when she tried to have us tossed in the dungeon, but I never truly believed that she would do him harm. Not like that." Another sigh, this one even wearier than the first. "Her own brother. Her own blood."

And just like that Jasper's horrible, petty thoughts seemed even pettier, even more horrible. He would have felt ashamed if shame were something he ever bothered to waste time on. Even so, a tiny inkling of it escaped his otherwise sturdy defenses.

"What I want to know is how Echo kept him from falling into a coma like everyone else who's come into contact with the kuçedra's poison or venom or whatever the hell it is," said Jasper.

Talking about this was so much easier than dealing with

the riot of emotions that assaulted Jasper when left to his own devices.

Dorian shook his head, looking just as perplexed by Caius's condition as Jasper felt. "She figured out a way to counteract that effect, but it drained him even more, as if his body was fighting a battle on two fronts. None of the afflicted who responded to the elixir at Avalon appeared quite so . . ."

"Mostly dead?" Tact had never been Jasper's strong suit.

Dorian winced, and Jasper immediately felt apologetic. Emotions were sloppy, Jasper reminded himself, and they made you do stupid things and say even stupider ones.

"Bluntly stated," said Dorian, "but not incorrect." He ran a hand through his silver hair, tousling it even more than it already was. Unkempt was a good look on him. "He'll need the attentions of a true healer soon. We've done all we can, but I'm afraid it's not enough."

Jasper watched Dorian in silence for a few moments. "And you? How are you holding up?" He tried to keep his tone light, and failed spectacularly.

"I'm fine," Dorian said into his drink, voice muffled by the glass.

"Liar." Jasper reached over to pluck the glass from Dorian's unresisting hand. Why was it that dealing with someone else's emotions was so much easier than dealing with your own? "I think that's enough for now, don't you?"

"You're right," Dorian said. "We may have found Caius, but that doesn't mean I can afford to let my guard down. There's always the possibility that we were followed and that someone is going to burst through that door, sword in hand, eager to take him back to that monster's clutches." He made as if to stand up, but Jasper placed a firm hand on Dorian's knee.

Obtuse, thy name is Dorian.

"That isn't what I meant," said Jasper. "I just don't think drowning your sorrows ever really works."

"You sound like you're speaking from personal experience," Dorian said.

Jasper realized then that he had been lying to himself when he imagined himself as a stranger to shame. He was indeed speaking from personal experience, but those were not experiences he wanted to share with Dorian. Despite a storied history of disdaining the good opinion of others, Jasper found himself wanting Dorian to believe the best of him, in the face of all evidence to the contrary. A strong and undeniable longing unfurled in Jasper's stomach. He wanted so strongly for Dorian to look at him like he had hung the moon, wanted it in a way that manifested itself as an almost physical ache. More than anything, he wanted to be worthy of that look.

Jasper hadn't become one of the most notorious contacts in Echo's roster of criminally inclined individuals by making admirable life decisions.

"After Quinn . . ." The glass of whiskey was suddenly heavy in Jasper's hand. He thought about downing what was left in it, but that would have been the height of hypocrisy. He set the glass down on the rickety end table and started again. "After I left Quinn, I was a bit of a mess."

Dorian's hand twitched where it rested on his own thigh, as if he were considering reaching out to touch Jasper, to offer some form of physical comfort, but the hand did not move any farther. And, oh, what torture that was. A memory came to Jasper, rendered in Technicolor clarity, of a kiss shared in the darkness of the wine cellar, of those hands in his hair-feathers, of those hands soft and reverent against his skin. One night was all they had had before the world came crashing down around them, and Jasper had played that series of moments over and over and over again in his mind to the point where he half suspected them to be the product of a painfully realistic fever dream.

"You were so young then," Dorian said softly. "You are still so young. You're allowed to be a little messy."

Jasper let out a mirthless little laugh. "I was *a lot* messy. It's kind of what happens after someone completely destroys your sense of self." Another pang of shame. "But we're not talking about me now, we're talking about you. Don't think I didn't notice that you avoided answering the question." Jasper asked again, just for good measure: "How are you doing? And no deflecting this time. I won't stand for it."

Dorian made a noise that was almost a chuckle but was too soft, too quiet to qualify as one. "Has anyone ever told you that you're infuriatingly perceptive?"

"Yes, shockingly enough, more than once, but it didn't take any Holmesian levels of deduction to see that you are very much not okay right now," Jasper said. "And correct me if I'm mistaken, but I think you're used to no one asking you if you're all right. And I think maybe that question flummoxed you a little bit."

Dorian rubbed his scars again, fingers lingering on the raised flesh as if that touch could ground him. "I just . . ." A frustrated grumble ate the rest of his words. "I don't know how to talk about this. About him."

About Caius, Jasper thought. But he didn't push. He

didn't prod. This conversation had to happen at Dorian's pace or it wouldn't happen at all.

"It's very easy," Dorian said, "to grow accustomed to silence. If you deny yourself something long enough, you can start to ignore it, but it never really goes away. It's just something you've seen so many times that you become almost blind to it. Until suddenly, something happens, and you can't not see it. It is there, and it is undeniable, and there is no escaping the truth of it. And try as you might, you can't hide from it. Even if you stubbornly refuse to name it, it's there, with you, and you realize then that you were its hostage all along."

This was getting far more introspective than Jasper had anticipated.

"You love him," Jasper said, his voice soft in the dimly lit stillness.

The silence that followed that simple statement was complete and unyielding. The grandfather clock ticked away seconds that felt like hours. And then, the unexpected. A laugh bubbled up from deep within Dorian's chest, a wild thing that careened into the quiet, shattering it.

"You know," Dorian said, "I don't think I've ever said that out loud."

"Technically, you still haven't," Jasper said.

A strange resolve seemed to come over Dorian then. He kept his gaze forward, eye trained on the slowly dying fire as he spoke. "I loved him."

Loved? The past tense did not escape Jasper's notice.

"I still love him," Dorian said.

And just like that, the fragile hope blossoming in Jasper's

chest began to shrivel up like a potted plant someone had forgotten to water. Without pausing to consider that maybe inebriation was not the best of plans, Jasper picked up the discarded glass of whiskey and knocked it back, refusing to wince as the alcohol burned his throat all the way down. He was not stone. If you pricked him, he would bleed. And Dorian had just wielded the blade guaranteed to cut the deepest.

Jasper was ready to flee, muscles in his legs tensing, his brain plotting the quickest escape route, when Dorian appeared to sense the shift in his mood. With aching slowness, the hand that had refused to reach out to Jasper earlier made its move. Now it was Dorian's turn to pluck the glass from Jasper's hand and place it to the side. His fingers rested against Jasper's knuckles as if unsure of their welcome. Slowly, ever so slowly, Jasper turned his hand over so that their fingers interlocked.

"I still love him," Dorian repeated. "But not the way I used to."

CHAPTER TWENTY-FOUR

Caius had spent enough time alone—more than enough, quite frankly—to begin to catalog different types of silence. There were myriad varieties, each possessing unique qualities. A tormented silence had filled his most recent days, full of the echoes of his own screams and the memory of fresh suffering.

He had found no comfort in that silence. It had been a way to mark time, between one agony and the next, as he waited. Waited for his sister's madness to abate—an unlikely scenario, he knew, but one he could not stop hoping for, as if the very act of hope had become intrinsic to his survival. Waited for Tanith to return, pale skin marred by blackened veins, crimson eyes stained dark with corruption. A heavy coil of dread wound its way around him as he remembered the silence that heralded her return. Even the quiet murmur of the guards outside his door had died, voices hidden like woodland creatures waiting for a predator to pass by.

That silence had invariably been followed by the most exquisite pain imaginable. The feeling of his power— something he'd always believed was uniquely his, a notion proved tragically incorrect—being leached from his body like blood being drawn from a vein. But unlike freshly drawn blood, his power—that ineffable force that connected him to the in-between—did not want to leave his body. Tanith drew it out against its will, if it could be said to have one. The magic knew Caius. His body was its home. It had always been there, coursing through him like a subtle current. But Tanith—or whatever force was staring out of her eyes— had found a way to break the tether holding Caius and his magic together using brute force and enthusiastic beatings. Every second of separation was a study in torment. Every moment of silence between one leaching and the next was almost as bad. Tanith had waited for the well within Caius to refill itself, slowly, painfully, before returning to take more and more until he was sure it would run dry, leaving nothing for her to steal.

The silence that surrounded him now held none of the promise of malice to which he had become accustomed. There was a softness to this silence. Not to say that it was free of pain; it wasn't. A steady ache lingered in his bones, the kind so deeply rooted it felt as though it would be there forever, and his throat felt raw and shredded from screaming. His memory of the hours after his rescue was a patchwork mess of images and sensations, but he remembered the most salient points: Dorian bursting through the door, Echo and Jasper hot on his heels, all of them looking more than a little worse for wear; the feeling of hands on him, not the phantom touches his dreams tormented him with, but hands made of flesh and bone; the searing flare of Echo's magic burning the tainted blood from his body.

There was a safety to the silence. The quiet was not complete. Caius could hear branches scraping against glass—there was a window in the room. That alone was enough to make him want to succumb to a paroxysm of joy; more than anything else it signaled his freedom from the wretched ruin in which Tanith had ensconced him. Outside, little nocturnal animals chittered among themselves. In the distance, an owl hooted, followed by the flap of wings, as if the bird had spotted a succulent mouse upon which to descend.

Within the room, the silence was punctuated by the soft sound of someone breathing. Caius turned his head to the side as far as he was able, which was not very far considering the violent protest of pain that sang through his muscles. Even in the dim moonlight that came through that blessed window, Caius was able to make out a familiar head of messy brown hair. Echo's chest rose and fell with steady breaths; she was asleep. Her heroics had probably exhausted her as much as they had him. A blanket was tucked up under her chin, held close in a white-knuckled grip. She was curled in on herself, and her limbs twitched under the covers. An unintelligible noise escaped her lips. Caius couldn't understand the words she spoke in her slumber, but he didn't need to. Her distress was clear enough. She was in the thrall of some nightmare, held captive by her own desperate need for rest.

He tried to speak her name, to call out to her, but his voice was little more than a suggestion of a whisper. The metallic taste of blood lingered at the back of his throat. He'd screamed himself hoarse enough to make himself bleed. There was a glass of water on the nightstand, but the thought of reaching for it and holding it steady enough to drink from was laughable. Despite his body's vociferous protests, Caius rolled onto his side, his muscles spasming in pain. An alarm clock also sat on the nightstand; with one clumsy hand, he knocked it over, the little bell on top clattering as the clock hit the floor.

Echo awoke with a start. She pushed away the blankets, untangling herself from her cocoon in a blind panic. Her gaze darted around the room, looking for the source of the noise. When her eyes alighted on Caius, his hand still dangling limply off the edge of the bed, she froze.

"Wake up," he managed to croak.

It took Echo a few moments to gather her wits. Caius watched as she shook off the remnants of her dream like a fly-stung horse. She attempted to sort out the tangle of her hair but gave up after a few aborted strokes of her fingers through it. It seemed to dawn on her that Caius being conscious was nothing short of a minor miracle. Echo got to her feet and approached his bed slowly, as though wary of spooking him.

Caius attempted to sit up—to greet her while horizontal seemed astonishingly rude considering he owed her his life—but his head barely made it an inch off the pillow before he collapsed, driven back to the mattress by a racking cough and a wave of pain. Echo hurried to him, taking the glass of water from his bedside table and holding it to his lips. Caius felt ridiculous, like a helpless child, but the moment the water touched his dry lips, the relief was great enough to wash away his feelings of inadequacy.

Echo brushed hair off his forehead, her skin cool against his. He desperately wanted to pretend that he hadn't arched into it like a touch-starved cat, but he had. Shameful, he thought, not feeling an ounce of shame.

"Are you all right?" Echo's voice was a welcome change to the silence. He'd heard it in his head countless times during his captivity, but now he was appalled that he had ever mistaken those fever dreams for anything but. There was a roundness to her voice, a softness, that no hallucination could replicate. This was real. She was real.

He had to try twice before the words came out, but eventually he managed to say, "I'm fine."

Echo frowned. "You don't look fine."

Now that his throat had been marginally soothed, words came easier to Caius, even if they did scratch on the way out. "Couldn't even let me have that small lie to spare my dignity?"

Echo offered him a smile. "Someone's got to keep you honest."

She sank to her knees beside the bed, her chin coming to rest on the coverlet. One hand returned the glass of water to the nightstand, while the other splayed on the mattress beside her face. Caius remembered with sudden clarity a night that felt so long ago, when Echo had been ensconced in a pile of blankets, and he had been the one to watch over her fitful sleep. Then, her slumber had been haunted by the memory of blood freshly spilled, of a life taken in defense of his. The Avicen girl, Ruby, had been a gifted warrior, even at such a young age, but her worthiness as an adversary made her death no less tragic. One more life snuffed out before its time. One more death added to a sea of losses.

The distance between them became unbearable to Caius in that moment. Without giving himself time to consider why, exactly, what he was about to do was a bad idea, he did it.

"Come here," he whispered, so quietly that if Echo had been any farther away she would not have heard him.

She did not move, not at first. Those soft brown eyes bored into his, searching for something he could not name. Perhaps trying to determine if this was some kind of a trick or the mumblings of an addled mind. The fingers of her left hand tightened on the coverlet, as though she were bracing herself to either walk away or heed his plea.

He would not beg. Though a small, fragmented part of him wanted to. In all his life, Caius had never, ever felt quite so wretched. His eyes drifted shut, and he told himself it was because he was terribly, viciously tired, and not because he could not bear to watch Echo retreat to her side of the room.

The mattress dipped as she sat on it.

"I'm not sure this is a good idea," said Echo, wise beyond her years.

"Oh, I'm certain it's a terrible idea," Caius said. As if that had ever stopped them before.

The comforting silence returned, warmer now that she was next to him. Caius kept his eyes closed and drifted on the border between wakefulness and sleep. He was halfway gone when Echo spoke again, her voice pulling him back from the cliff's edge of slumber.

"Is it me you want? Or her?"

The *her* required no specification.

For so long he had kept memories of Rose at a distance, as though careful avoidance could blunt their sharpened points. Only in dreams had her specter visited him, and even then, the event of her death—her murder at the hands of Tanith—loomed larger than any other memory. It eclipsed everything else. Decades had passed since that awful day, and Caius had rarely allowed himself to remember Rose as anything but the victim of his sister's wrath.

Now, with his eyes closed and Echo beside him, he let himself remember.

The scent of her hair-feathers. Pears, it had always reminded him of. Rose had detested pears, and yet the smell of them clung to her like a stubborn perfume. He wondered how that had come about. Maybe it was an ingredient in the cleansing oil she used. He hadn't let a single pear pass through the kitchens of Wyvern's Keep during his reign. No one had questioned it. Every Dragon Prince had his or her peculiar quirks, and if the worst of Caius's was an aversion to pears, well, the nobility saw fit to offer no complaints.

He remembered the way those feathers had felt slipping through his fingers, as soft as silk and surprisingly smooth. He'd expected them to feel coarser. He had touched Avicen before Rose, but only in the heat of battle. Never with tenderness. Never with a desire to touch more.

He remembered her voice, as clear as a bell and as lovely. She'd liked to sing. He would often tell her that she should have become a singer instead of a spy, and she would chuckle and claim to have no great talent for the former and an abundance for the latter. He'd found this a dubious claim, considering how terribly awry her final mission had gone. Although, since her final mission had involved seducing him, perhaps it had gone better than he'd given her credit for at the time, though he was sure that falling in love with him negated her success on that front.

Is it me you want? Or her?

Echo's question had been laced through with insecurity that she hadn't bothered to mask. Rose's ghost may have visited Caius in his dreams for the better part of a century. But Echo had to live with it every day, with no reprieve on the horizon. He could understand her worry. He wondered if he would be as magnanimous if he were in her position. Probably not. But then, Echo had always been the best of them. He had known that almost immediately. Divine providence, perhaps. Or a fool's penchant for loving impossible women.

"You," Caius said simply. "Just you."

He knew the words were true as he spoke them. He hadn't been sure, not entirely, but once the proclamation had been made, it was as clear to him as a simple fact of the universe, like the sky being blue or the sun setting in the west. He had loved Rose, that was undeniable. But he had lost her. And then he had mourned her. And now, finally, after all these long years, he gave himself permission to lay her to rest.

A hand gently prodded him in the side. He opened his eyes and saw Echo gazing down at him. Her eyes shone with telltale wetness that he was too kind to point out, though he did reach up to cup her cheek, his thumb rubbing the slope of her cheekbone. She angled her head so that her lips rested on his palm. It wasn't a kiss, but the contact sent a shiver through him.

"Scooch," she said, lips dragging over his palm, the sensation unspeakably intimate.

Caius didn't know what the word "scooch" meant, but he gathered that she wanted him to make room for her. And so he did, in more ways than one. Echo slid under the sheets, her legs brushing against Caius's. Her arm wrapped around his stomach, gently, without too much pressure put on his bruises. The pain was nothing compared with the comfort of having her near. Caius drifted off to sleep, only half hearing Echo hum the melody of a lullaby he'd fallen in love with long ago.

CHAPTER TWENTY-FIVE

Dorian was no blushing innocent.

Though he had never been one to participate in the bawdy gossip that ran rampant in the barracks, he was no stranger to the physical intimacies that the other soldiers discussed with such careless abandon. He had simply kept his exploits to himself. He saw no reason to brag about filling a basic biological need any more than he would have gloated about satisfying his hunger with a hearty meal.

That was part of it. There was another dimension to Dorian's silence that had nothing to do with modesty, one that he never discussed with another soul, much less the men and women of the guard who had long since grown accustomed to his stony silence when conversation turned to topics more salacious than drills and weaponry.

He had never been with the person his heart desired. Sex and love were unrelated as far as Dorian was concerned. Every encounter he'd had, from his first clumsy tumble with a stable boy in a hayloft in the barn outside the keep to the more sophisticated experiences he'd shared with men who valued discretion as much as he did, had been marked by disappointment.

Until now.

He turned over, slowly, carefully. He didn't want to disturb the person next to him, but he wanted to look. To remind himself that this was real, that this had happened.

Jasper was enchanting, even in sleep. The early-dawn light subdued the riotous color of his feathers into softer shades of indigo and gold. Dorian felt—insanely, he thought—bereft of the sight of Jasper's amber gaze. He quelled the urge to reach out and gently wake Jasper just so he could watch him blink the sleep from his eyes. It was a deeply selfish impulse, but Dorian couldn't find it in himself to be ashamed of it.

Shame had haunted him for years, but not the same kind of shame that plagued humans who desired partners of the same sex. Among the Drakharin—and, he assumed, the Avicen—there was nothing deviant about love between two men or two women. They were a long-lived race, and it made little sense for them to frame sex as useful only for procreation as so many humans did. If Drakharin reproduced at the same rate as humans did, they'd overrun the planet in short order.

Dorian's shame was of a different sort. It was the shame of someone who had yearned for something he could not have with someone out of his reach. Caius had known, perhaps longer than even Dorian himself, that the love Dorian had harbored for him extended far beyond the loyalty and affection common between guard and prince. Caius had known and, out of kindness, had not mentioned it. He could have sent Dorian away, assuming that such a love would cloud Dorian's judgment and impair his ability to perform his duties, but he hadn't. He had kept Dorian by his side, as a guard and as a friend. For Dorian, it had been a special kind of torture, to feel so close and yet so far from the one person in the world he wanted most.

He had grown so accustomed to never getting what he wanted that he was afraid to close his eye and surrender to sleep the way Jasper had so readily. He feared that if he did, he would awake later to find that it had all been an elaborate dream, coaxed from his subconscious by decades of loneliness. Though if he were honest with himself, he couldn't quite imagine that his own mind would have conjured up an Avicen to heal the wounds of his fractured heart.

But Dorian had been so scared. Scared of losing Caius. Scared of losing Jasper. Scared of losing himself if he lost all of his people. There was only one thing to do that made sense. He would love the people he had while he had them.

And so he had kissed Jasper downstairs, and it hadn't taken long for that kiss to evolve into something more. Jasper had kissed Dorian like he had something to prove. Maybe he did. Maybe they both did.

The wall Dorian had carefully constructed between them in the wake of Caius's abduction came crashing down. For the first time in as long as he could remember, Dorian let himself want with abandon. Gone was the not-so-secret shame of unrequited love. Gone was the oppressive guilt that had hounded him in the weeks after Caius had been taken. In place of those things was a feeling so strange that Dorian had trouble naming it at first. The last bastion of resistance in him put up a fight against verbalizing the one fact he knew was completely and thoroughly undeniable. He wanted to say it. He ached to say it. But he couldn't. Not yet.

Instead, he spoke with his lips and his hands, returning Jasper's insistent kisses with equal fervor. Those feathers were softer than they looked. He had forgotten how soft they were, and once he'd sunk his hands into them, he couldn't stop touching them. Jasper hadn't seemed to mind.

They'd moved to the second bedroom eventually. Dorian would never live it down if Echo caught him kissing Jasper on the sofa like an overeager adolescent. He still had his pride, after all.

What followed was quite possibly the most transcendent experience of Dorian's life.

After, Jasper had fallen asleep with a smile gracing his kiss-bruised lips. Dorian had tried to stay awake as long as he could, determined to etch every detail of Jasper's sleeping form into his memory. But inevitably, sleep had claimed him. He'd awoken to the sound of the forest coming alive outside the cabin. Birds sang as the sun inched upward, and Dorian found himself watching Jasper once more. It felt deliciously indulgent.

A knock pulled him from his thoughts. Jasper grumbled something in his sleep and wound his arm tighter around Dorian's torso. Getting up was evidently not an option. The person who'd knocked didn't wait for an answer before opening the door. Dorian sighed. They were all going to need to sit down and have a very frank discussion about boundaries.

Echo poked her head through the open door. A single eyebrow quirked upward at the sight of one perfectly made, undisturbed bed. Dorian flushed scarlet. The embarrassment he felt at being caught in bed, hair likely a mess, a slumbering Avicen tucked under his arm, was multiplied by the feeling of Jasper burrowing closer, burying his nose in Dorian's pectoral muscle as if he were seeking out every bit of heat he could find. With as much dignity as he could muster, Dorian said, "May I help you?"

Echo wisely did not comment on the position in which she found Dorian, a kindness for which he was absurdly grateful. He wasn't ashamed of what he felt for Jasper or of what they had shared, but he preferred not to be caught with his pants down. Literally and metaphorically.

"Caius is awake," Echo said. "And you're gonna want to hear what he has to say."

CHAPTER TWENTY-SIX

Ivy slid the empty vial into her bag, its glass stained red from the bloodweed she'd just administered to the man in the hospital bed before her. The machines that kept him alive and breathing continued their steady beating, tracking his vital signs. She couldn't afford to dally, but she stayed by his bedside as long as she dared to see if the elixir took. It was the last dosage she had. Already, she had given it to a dozen patients in the restricted ward, and all of them had responded favorably. If the man on the bed showed signs of pulling through, Ivy's day would be a rousing success.

"Is it working?" Helios asked in a hushed whisper. He stood by the door, keeping watch. If anyone came through the doors at the end of the hallway, he would see them and they would hide. So far, the day had graced them with a fantastic run of luck. Not even a close call. Yet.

"I don't know." Ivy watched the man's face. Infected humans didn't always wake up right away. Sometimes the reaction was almost instantaneous; other times, it took hours. The man's eyes darted beneath his lids, but that wasn't unusual. Those who had survived bouts with the kuçedra's toxic influence had told Ivy later that it was like being trapped in an endless nightmare, tailored to their specific fears. The thought of it sent a shudder through Ivy. She hoped the man's torment was nearly at an end. The preternaturally aged Michael Ian Hunt had shown no improvement since their last visit, but he hadn't gotten any worse, either. It was a frail silver lining, but Ivy counted it as one nonetheless.

Ivy had nearly given up hope for the afflicted man before her when a tiny movement caught her attention. She looked away from the man's face and searched the rest of his body for signs of life.

His finger twitched.

He was waking up.

Ivy broke into a grin. *Thank the gods.* "It's working," she told Helios.

He matched her smile with one of his own. "That's wonderful." Suddenly, his gaze cut to the right, toward the door at the end of the hallway. "Someone's coming."

He left his post and pulled Ivy behind the tall cabinet at the back of the room. It was a tight squeeze.

Footsteps sounded in the hallway, an unhurried tread approaching the quarantine room. Ivy had made sure to come to the hospital after hours—not that a hospital of this size ever really settled down for the night—and so far they had managed to avoid detection. But no streak of good luck was infinite, and Ivy began to worry that theirs may have just run out.

Her back was pressed tightly against the wall. Helios had one hand propped beside her head, the other rested lightly on her hip. It was an innocent touch, perfectly innocuous in its practicality. It was where he had touched her when he had pushed her—gently—behind the cabinet, but Ivy could focus on little else besides the warmth radiating from his palm through her light sweater.

The door to the room opened, and Ivy held her breath. Without making the slightest sound, Helios pressed closer. He bent his head so that he would not be seen over the top of the cabinet. Ivy's hands settled on his chest. It was right there. She couldn't think where else she was supposed to put them.

Helios had tucked the sunglasses he used to hide his yellow eyes into his back pocket when he had taken up watch by the door, and Ivy had similarly shed her own so she would be able to work with ease. Now nothing stood between Ivy and that piercing sunshine gaze. His eyes met hers as they both listened to the person who had entered the room. They were standing so close that if Ivy wanted to, she could count his eyelashes one by one. She flushed.

The sound of a clipboard being removed from the slot at the foot of the bed broke their connection. A nurse, then, Ivy mused. She listened as the nurse recorded patients' vitals, removing and replacing clipboards with efficiency. Helios drew in a quiet breath, and Ivy's fingertips sank into the wool of his sweater.

After an interminable amount of time, the nurse departed and the door slid shut behind her. Ivy thanked every single god she could think of that the nurse had been too lazy to do a thorough check of the black-veined skin of her patients. The bloodweed had already begun to work its magic—literally—on some of them, and Ivy had noticed a few of the dark, swollen veins diminishing in size and intensity.

Helios did not move. Ivy did not complain.

She waited a few more seconds, listening to the nurse's footsteps retreat down the hallway and out of the quarantine wing.

"She's gone," Helios said.

"Yeah," Ivy agreed.

Another moment passed before Helios stepped away. A small smile flashed across his face, as if he, too, had realized that there had been plenty of other places for Ivy's hands to rest besides his chest. But he didn't say anything to make the heat in her cheeks elevate to dangerous levels. If she blushed any harder, she would probably pass out. And then Helios would have to cart her unconscious body back home. And then she would never be able to look him in the eye again.

Ivy stepped out of the hiding spot and straightened clothing unnecessarily.

"We should probably get out of here," she said.

Helios nodded, and with a knowing backward glance, he made his way to the door. "Let me make sure the coast is clear."

Slowly, he opened the door and peered into the hallway. Ivy waited, standing a respectable three feet behind him. Satisfied that they were unlikely to run into anyone, he opened the door all the way and waved Ivy forward.

"All clear," he said in a soft voice, entirely too intimate for the sterile surroundings.

Ivy mumbled her thanks and followed him out. Heads down, they slunk through corridors, past the watchful eyes of nurses and the less watchful eyes of doctors, faces buried in clipboards. Getting out was always easier than getting in. They snuck out of the hospital the same way they'd entered—through the morgue—and despite the covered cadaver lying on a slab in the middle of the room, not once did that small smile flee Helios's face.

Adrenaline hummed in Ivy's veins. She was beginning to understand why Echo relished the act of breaking and entering. There was no thrill quite like slipping through the shadows of a place where you didn't belong. The pleasure of successfully evading watching eyes had a certain addictive appeal. Combined with the knowledge of a job well done— and several victims of the kuçedra healed—the feeling sparkled in Ivy's chest like celebratory fireworks.

Helios held the door open for her as they exited the in-between via a utility closet on the far end of a subway platform near the hospital. Not one soul paid them the least bit of attention.

"Are you hungry?" Helios asked.

"I would murder someone for a cupcake," said Ivy. Crime, she found, made her hungry. Maybe that was why nearly everything Echo ate was stolen; it was like feeding an addiction.

"Personally, I prefer my cake without bloodshed, but I'm sure we can find something to your liking," he said as they skirted a small crowd on the platform. They went up the stairs, through the turnstiles, and out into the world. "Lead the way."

There were few places open, so Ivy opted for a nearby

coffee shop that kept absurd hours, catering to the constant flow of traffic to and from the hospital. Human eateries were still something of a marvel for Helios, and Ivy relished the chance to watch him ogle the display cases full of decadent desserts and puzzle at the menu of incomprehensible beverages.

"What do you want?" Ivy asked.

The café was quiet at this time of night—as quiet as one near a major hospital ever got, which was not very quiet at all. But the crowd wasn't large enough to cause Helios any undue trauma, which relieved Ivy. He was growing more and more accustomed to being around humans, but large groups of them remained problematic. Ivy sympathized. She pulled the scarf around her head tighter, her feathers hidden under the silk.

She knew what she was getting. Something gigantic and full of sugar. With extra whipped cream. And maybe a cupcake. Or a doughnut. No, both.

Helios peered up at the sign, squinting at the names of drinks scribbled in chalk as if trying to puzzle out the meaning of ancient hieroglyphs. "I don't know what any of this means. What's a skinny mocha latte? How do you make coffee skinny?"

"You use skim milk instead of cream," Ivy replied, suppressing a smile. This was delightful.

"What's skim milk?"

"Milk that isn't whole."

He looked at her over the dark lenses of his sunglasses. It always surprised Ivy how few stares she and Helios attracted when they wore sunglasses at night; people probably just thought they were pretentious.

"How strange," Helios said, pushing up the sunglasses before anyone spotted his unusual golden eyes. "I understand each individual word coming out of your mouth, but when you string them together like that, they cease to have any meaning."

"Do you want me to order for you?" Ivy asked.

He shot her a look so deadly it pierced the tinted lenses. But confusion overpowered his pride and very, very grudgingly he said, "Yes, please."

He didn't have the sweet tooth Ivy did, so she opted for something simple. Coffee. A splash of whole milk. One sugar. Ivy didn't know how non-Avicen taste buds operated, but that seemed reasonable to her. She didn't know how someone could choke down bitter bean juice without at least eight packets of sugar, three pumps of syrup, and a generous swirl of whipped cream, but that wasn't any of her business.

Their fingers brushed when she handed him the cup and that awful blush returned, this time with even greater zeal. Ivy hid her face behind her cup as she took a scalding sip. Gods, it burned. She accepted her change with all the grace of a socially inept buffalo and buried her mortification in an unseemly generous bite of cupcake. Vanilla, with lemon buttercream frosting. Bliss.

Drinks—and doughnut and cupcake—in hand, they made their way to the subway station at Seventy-Seventh Street. Helios, seemingly determined to assuage Ivy's obvious embarrassment, asked her questions about things he spotted on the way. Unusual architecture. Poems written on the sidewalk in multicolored chalk. A dog wearing a sweater and walking down the street, sans owner. Ivy couldn't explain that last one.

The cell phone in Ivy's pocket rang, startling her. No one ever called it. Only three people had the number, and if it was one of them, then she was about to get either very good news or very bad news. She thrust her hot chocolate into Helios's hands and fumbled for the phone. Once it was in her hand, she looked at the caller ID flashing on the screen.

Echo.

Ivy swiped the screen with her thumb. "Echo?" Her voice came out in a rush. "What happened? What is it? Are you okay?"

"We found him."

Relief cascaded through Ivy in a powerful flood. She had lived each day since Echo's departure dreading the worst: that her best friend would be hurt or that someone she had come to care about would be lost to them forever, ensnared in a madwoman's trap, that one or more of their party would fail to return home.

As if sensing Ivy's need for reassurance, Echo added, "We're all okay. We'll be heading back to Avalon in mostly one piece once Caius wakes up."

Ivy frowned. "Mostly?"

A weary sigh hissed through the phone. "Tanith took a few chunks out of Caius's back with a whip. And there's a constellation of bruises and scars on the rest of his body."

"Holy shit."

Helios arched an eyebrow in question, no doubt puzzled by the half of the conversation to which he was privy.

"Yeah," Echo said. "That about sums it up."

"But you're okay, right?" Ivy asked. "Like, really okay?"

"I'm fine," Echo assured her. "I'll see you soon. Just wanted to let you know. I know how you worry."

Ivy thought she could hear the tired smile in Echo's voice when she said that.

The news made Ivy feel lighter. Perhaps there was a sliver of a chance of things looking up. Maybe they'd be able to fight the bad guy, save the day, and have all their lives go back to whatever normal meant for them now. After everything.

A thought occurred to Ivy suddenly. "We missed your birthday," she blurted before Echo could hang up. "We should do something when you get back. Celebrate. I've always wanted to throw a *Great Gatsby* party."

Echo laughed, and it sounded more genuine than any of her laughs over the past few months. "Did you even read that book?"

"No, I just think I'd look cute in a flapper dress."

"I don't want a birthday party where someone dies in the pool at the end."

"Fine, fine. Have it your way. But I'm still going to wear a flapper dress. Maybe a fascinator." Ivy squeezed her eyes shut. "Just come back in one piece, okay? Then you can spoil *The Great Gatsby* for me, 'kay?"

"Okay," Echo said. "But I'm still going to make you read the book and not just watch the movie."

They said their goodbyes and Ivy slid the phone back into her pocket. Helios offered her cup.

"Everything all right?" he asked.

"Yeah." A knot of anxiety that Ivy hadn't even realized had formed at the base of her neck began to loosen. "They found Caius. He's okay. Echo's okay. Everybody's okay."

Helios tapped her cocoa with his coffee, a travel cup toast. "Good," he said. "The day has been kind to us." He offered her his arm as they descended the steps to the train that would take them north, toward Avalon. The city had worked hard to get the trains up and running again after the attack on Grand Central, but the 6 didn't go any farther south than this. Ivy pushed the thought away. Much better to focus on the good. The day had been kind, and Ivy prayed their run of luck would last just a little bit longer.

The problem with prayers was that sometimes, no one was listening.

CHAPTER TWENTY-SEVEN

Echo watched in fascination as Caius shoveled another forkful of pancakes into his mouth. It was his eighth or ninth so far. The first words he'd spoken upon waking were "We have to talk about Tanith." The next were "But not before I eat something." His stomach had emphasized the sentiment with a well-timed growl. Fair enough. Echo had neither the desire nor the energy to dive headfirst into a discussion of the machinations of his insane sister on an empty stomach either. It was bad for digestion. It had to be.

And so she had found herself on breakfast duty, cobbling together a respectable meal out of the meager supplies in the cabin's pantry. She didn't mind. Cooking gave her hands something to do and her mind something on which to focus that wasn't related to kidnappings, malevolent shadow monsters, the voices in her head, or the possible end of the world. It was a nice reprieve. She was glad they had enough flour, sugar, and milk to make it happen.

Dorian had pushed aside the plate Echo offered to him. Once Caius had finished his first serving, he'd taken Dorian's and devoured that, too. When it was clear that his time in captivity had left him with a hunger that would not be satisfied until he'd eaten everything that wasn't nailed down, Echo offered him her pancakes as well. Jasper, being Jasper, didn't share his.

Tidying up the mess she'd made of the kitchen gave Echo a moment to think about the previous night. Something had changed between her and Caius. Something about *her* had changed. She was no longer the Echo who had been Rowan's girlfriend. Rowan belonged to a part of her life that was now so foreign to Echo, it felt like it had happened to someone else. Rowan looked at her and saw the girl she used to be.

But Caius saw her as she was: an amalgamation of disastrous events, a mess of a human being whose head was occupied by ghosts. He didn't expect her to be anything other than what she was. There was no pressure for her to be the same Echo whose chief concern was picking enough pockets for the money to buy a slice from the pizzeria on the corner of St. Marks and Avenue A when her hands had been clumsy and untried. He understood the complexity of her life. He was living it with her. And that was why it had been so easy to give in, to let him slide his arms around her waist and pull her close, to luxuriate in the feel of his warm breath against her neck as he slept, wrapped around her like she was the only thing keeping him afloat. They had slept like that, twined around each other. It had been too warm under the layers of blankets, but Echo hadn't felt the slightest desire to move. It had felt right, lying next to Caius. It had felt like where she was supposed to be.

Not even the sight of him scarfing down pancakes like there was no tomorrow was enough to dissuade her of that notion.

"When was the last time you ate?" Echo asked, picking up the cooling mug of coffee she'd left beside the sink. She sipped it, taking a strange pleasure in watching Caius eat. If his appetite was this ravenous, then it must mean that he was all right. She didn't have much of one herself. Now that she'd washed the flour off her hands and left the pan to soak, she found herself thinking once again about kidnappings and shadow monsters and how bad things would turn out if Tanith was left to rampage unchecked.

"What day is it?" Caius said.

"Wednesday."

"I don't know why I even asked. I don't remember."

Dorian's eye narrowed. "As if kidnapping you wasn't bad enough. She couldn't even be bothered with feeding you."

Caius set his fork down on his empty plate. He looked around, as if scouting for more food. There was none. "To be honest, I'm not sure there's anything left of my sister to speak of. What she's become . . . what the kuçedra has made her . . ."

"There's no excuse," Dorian said. "Not for what she did to you or for what she's going to do."

"I know that," said Caius. "I just . . . every time I looked at her, I couldn't help but try to find some semblance of the woman she was, of the person I knew. And there was nothing." He sighed. "Do we have any fruit?"

"Only some sad overripe bananas. I'll go get them," Jasper said. He was in a much better mood after the night he'd spent with Dorian. Echo assumed they'd worked out . . . whatever it was between them, if the state she'd found them in that morning was any indication. She hid her smile behind her coffee mug. Today was far less dire than yesterday. Caius was safe and eating them out of house and home. Jasper and Dorian had cuddled. Echo had managed to use her powers for something besides raining death and destruction down on her enemies. Things were looking up.

As Caius ate, he told them what he knew: Tanith had a plan. A well-organized one. Her endgame was a mystery to him, but once Echo had informed him of the increasing instability of the in-between, he began to put the pieces of the puzzle together.

"I think she's attempting to destroy the in-between," Caius said. He frowned, then amended his statement. "Actually, not the in-between, but the veil between this world and the in-between. That's what she's trying to unmake."

"What?" Echo choked on a mouthful of coffee. She had suspected Tanith was involved in the disturbances to the in-between, but this was beyond what even she had thought possible. With the firebird and the kuçedra entering the physical plane of existence, there were bound to be repercussions on a larger scale—that much magic didn't come into the world without tipping the scales somehow—but Echo hadn't believed that a single person could affect the in-between to such a degree. Why would Tanith want to, mad or not? "Why?"

"My sister isn't thinking clearly," Caius said around a mouthful of banana. He chewed, then swallowed. "She's always been ruthless, but there was, without fail, a method to her madness. A rationality. Reasoning. I saw none of that in her eyes when she . . ." His expression darkened. ". . . when she ordered me flogged so that I would be too weak to fight back."

Dorian pushed himself to his feet and began to pace the room. The blue of his eye had gone an almost storm gray. "Why would she do that? Just to make you suffer?"

Caius put the remains of the banana down, as though he couldn't bear to stomach one more bite as he remembered what Tanith had done. "She was using me as a conduit. A battery, if you will. Most of the time, she left me somewhere under guard—close enough to where she would be but far enough away and hidden so that I would not be able to get a bearing on my surroundings. She took me with her once, to a tomb. Inside, there was a seal. I could feel the hum of the in-between through it. It was like the veil was thinner there than in other places, even stronger gateways. Tanith had Drakharin mages with her, but it was my power she used to break the seal. She had done some damage to it already, but she leached my power to deliver the blow that cracked it open. I believe the mages were there to contain the overflow of the in-between until we were clear of the broken seal."

Dorian stilled his restless pacing. "But why have you beaten and whipped? She was already torturing you by draining you of your power. The Drakharin have a long history of considering themselves above the common rules of engagement, but that's one thing we've never done, especially not to each other."

"Tanith bled the magic out of me," said Caius. "It was easier to steal when I was wounded and vulnerable."

A pall fell over the room. After a few moments of silence, Jasper said, "Your sister's a real bitch."

That pulled a startled laugh from Caius. "I . . . yes. Yes, she is."

"But why screw with the in-between?" Echo asked. It didn't add up. "What is she hoping to accomplish?"

With a shake of his head, Caius started in on the last banana. "If I had to hazard a guess, I would say she's trying to sow as much chaos as possible. The kuçedra seems to thrive on it. She mentioned creating a new world from the ashes of the old, but I haven't the foggiest idea if she means that literally. I don't see how it would be possible."

"Well, it seems like an awfully elaborate plan just to create a little chaos," Dorian said. "What does tampering with the in-between accomplish? Why seek to destroy it?"

He wasn't wrong. There had to be something they weren't seeing. Some hidden cog in the machine that would make it all fit together. Echo drummed her fingers against her thigh. *Think. Think, think, think.* They were missing something— some crucial detail that, when revealed, would illuminate Tanith's endgame. From everything Caius had told her about Tanith when they had spent months hiding in Jasper's London warehouse, Echo knew his sister to be a cunning commander: strong on the battlefield and sly at the war table as she designed plans that lesser minds could never have dreamed up. Caius had been the youngest Dragon Prince elected in the history of the Drakharin people, and Tanith had been the youngest commander of their armies. Her elevation had nothing to do with her brother's position; she had earned it entirely on her own merit. But the kuçedra had changed her. Echo hadn't accounted for that. The firebird hadn't changed *her*. At least, not in any way she had noticed. Beyond the obvious. The fundamentals of Echo—of who she was as a person—were the same. But the kuçedra was different; it could not be tamed or controlled. Tanith was not its vessel—she was its slave. The calculating commander would never have set in motion a series of events that might result in nothing but wild, chaotic destruction. The kuçedra craved such a thing. Tanith wouldn't. But if there was any part of her left, as Caius so desperately hoped, then perhaps she was trying to steer that unbiddable beast in a direction not too far off from her own aims. Glory for the Drakharin. Victory against their enemies.

Zugzwang, Echo thought. *German. A situation that arises in a game of chess when a player has to make a move that would harm their own position.* It was not impossible to win a game once maneuvered into such a position, but it was difficult. That was where Tanith must have found herself once she'd realized what, exactly, she had let into herself. A skilled tactician could theoretically turn the tide of a game in her favor after landing in *zugzwang,* but the kuçedra cared not for tactics. Echo had looked into its swirling depths after it had torn through Grand Central. Caius was right. It did want chaos. It was a mad horse, champing at the bit; Tanith was its rider, attempting to rein it in. She might not be able to direct the pieces in this chess game to a neat victory, but there was one move left to her: flipping the damn board.

"It's not the in-between she wants to destroy," Echo said. The conversation had continued, but the others went silent at her words. She knew they were true as she spoke them, with a great, ringing clarity. The chorus of voices in the back of her mind swelled from their relative silence, words blurring together so they sounded like trees rustling in a breeze.

"Then what?" Dorian asked. "What is she trying to destroy if not the in-between?"

Echo met that single, sharp eye and said, "Everything else."

CHAPTER TWENTY-EIGHT

T he air smelled wrong.

Not the normal wrong of New York City subways, a unique pungency composed of a mixture of noxious aromas—sweltering trash, old urine, and something unidentifiable that made Ivy think of rat sweat. Not that she had ever had the opportunity to smell a particularly sweaty rat, but she imagined that was what one would smell like.

This was a different sort of wrong, hard to put a finger on. It was the nasal equivalent of staring at two nearly identical images full of nonsensical clutter and trying to find the slight variations—the discrepancies difficult to find at first, but once the eye saw them, they couldn't be unseen.

Or, in this case, unsmelled.

The cocoa in Ivy's hand grew less and less appetizing the more she tried to puzzle out exactly what was off about their surroundings. The subway platform was as quotidian as ever. She and Helios had migrated to the far end, where they were least likely to draw attention to themselves. That left the entirety of the station open to her inquisitive gaze. The crowd was of the usual sort: professionals coming home from a long day at the office; a cluster of high school students wearing blue blazers and khakis, probably only just leaving whatever fancy academy they attended after practicing some sport or studying for whatever standardized test plagued their existence. Ivy didn't know what went on at human schools, but from all she had gathered, it was unpleasant. There was an artist with a large rectangular portfolio hanging over her shoulder, reeking of something that smelled like skunk but probably wasn't. A woman taking a nap surrounded by worn shopping bags, an empty coffee cup sitting in front of her with a few coins in it. An elderly man muttering to himself as he worked his way through a book of crossword puzzles. More than a few souls still wearing scrubs, which made sense this close to the hospital.

None of them seemed perturbed by the wrongness of the air. None but Helios, who was scrunching his nose as he peered over the top of his sunglasses and looked up and down the tracks.

"Do you feel that too?" Ivy asked.

He nodded. A mostly empty coffee cup dangled from his fingertips. She wondered if he'd also lost his appetite.

"What is it?" Ivy took a step toward him, closing the distance between them until only a few inches separated the fabric of their sleeves. The air felt slightly less wrong this close to him, as if the magic innate to his presence counteracted whatever was causing the disturbance they both felt.

"I'm not sure," said Helios. "It feels like . . ."

The remainder of his sentence was cut off by the

rumbling of a train entering the station at their end of the platform, the wind in its wake sending the ends of Ivy's scarf fluttering about her neck. She held the scarf in place with one hand. A weird vibe in the air would be the least of her problems if she were unmasked and her feathers revealed to a platform full of humans.

The feeling of wrong swelled suddenly, stealing the breath from Ivy's lungs. She dropped her cup of cocoa. Her knees went wobbly and she reached for Helios just as he was reaching for her. Instinct made him push Ivy behind him, to protect her from whatever onslaught was about to occur, but none came.

The wrongness coalesced into something she recognized, as if it was rearranging itself into a semblance of order for a few frenzied seconds.

The in-between. Its acrid ozone scent sizzled around them, stronger than Ivy had ever felt it before. The air shuddered with the force of it.

Ivy peered around Helios's torso just in time to see the train barrel through a gash of ink-black darkness that had sliced right through the tracks. As suddenly as it appeared, the tear in the in-between disappeared. And that was exactly what it was: a tear. A rip along a seam that never should have been there.

All was silent for a long, horrible moment.

Then one person screamed, and another. Some people stared dumbly at the tracks, at the space where a train—a train full of living, breathing people—had just been, their minds refusing to process what their eyes had just seen. Others stampeded toward the stairs leading to the street. The artist dropped her portfolio and ran. The woman with the bags and the cup of coins blinked at the now-empty tracks, shrugged, and went back to her nap.

The train was gone. The entire length of it. Every single car. Swallowed up by a gash in the in-between that had opened of its own accord. It was impossible. It *should have been* impossible. And yet.

A tremor worked its way through Ivy's body, starting at the top of her head and moving down to her toes. Her entire body shook and her stomach roiled, threatening to expel its contents. She thought she might be in shock, but the notion was a distant one, as if her brain couldn't quite grasp the enormity of what had just occurred.

Helios was as still as stone, his gaze fixed on the point where the train had disappeared.

He said Ivy's name twice before she reacted.

Slowly, she raised her face to look at him. She felt as though she were moving underwater, her body oddly weightless.

The wrongness in the air began to dissipate until it was little more than a memory. Helios had removed his sunglasses and was peering at Ivy with eyes a touch too wide, just this side of terrified.

"We have to go," he said, one hand coming up to cup her elbow. Already, the booted feet of police officers were clomping down the stairs at the other end of the platform. One of the people who'd fled the station must have found them, alerting them to the fact that something had just gone drastically awry. When the police hit the platform, they slowed. There were two of them, and they wore matching expressions of bewilderment. Ivy wondered what they'd heard from the mouths of frightened commuters or what they'd expected to find. An explosion maybe. Or some other disaster that would align with the idea of a train disappearing.

But they found nothing, for there was nothing for them to see.

"Ivy," Helios said, tugging on her arm. His sunglasses were still off. Weird yellow eyes were probably less suspicious in that moment than two people wearing shades underground and at night.

The first step Ivy took felt like she was pulling her feet free from clinging muck. Each subsequent step was easier as the primitive part of her brain screamed at her to flee in the face of danger. A solid instinct.

Helios ushered her past the befuddled police officers, who were muttering something about drug-induced hallucinations. A mad giggle clawed its way up Ivy's throat, but she swallowed it before it could escape. The last thing she and Helios needed was to draw attention to themselves. The stage makeup Ivy had plastered over Helios's scales before they left Avalon was enough to fool a casual glance, but it wouldn't hold up under intense scrutiny, which they were sure to experience if the cops saw a laughing madwoman fleeing the scene of a potential crime.

The woman with the shopping bags woke with a start when Ivy passed her. Their eyes met and Ivy's steps floundered. The woman looked at her as though she could see right through Ivy's tinted sunglasses and her silk scarf to the distinctly avian eyes and feathers that marked her as decidedly inhuman. A gap-toothed grin cracked across the woman's lips.

"It's breaking apart," said the woman. "Breaking down."

"What is?" Ivy asked, ignoring Helios's impatient tug on her arm.

The woman raised her hands and spread her fingers wide in an all-encompassing gesture. "The world," she said in a conspiratorial whisper. Then she clapped her hands over her eyes and began muttering to herself in a language that seemed to be made up of nothing but garbled nonsense.

Before Ivy could ask any more questions, Helios dragged her away, past the police officers who were starting to question the people still on the platform. Their dubious expressions indicated they didn't believe what they were hearing—and why would they?—but the obvious distress of the people they spoke to merited an investigation, even if just an obligatory one.

Ivy stumbled as Helios all but hauled her up the steps. The woman's words rang in her head and she spared a glance over her shoulder, trusting Helios to make sure she didn't plummet down the stairs. The woman had uncovered her eyes and met Ivy's gaze with a piercing look. She smiled that gap-toothed grin again and mimicked an explosion with her hands. She laughed, then fell into a fit of coughing. One of the officers looked at her for a second, then shrugged and turned away, evidently writing her off as just another questionably sane itinerant.

Madness and magic were not so distant from one another. In humans, the former was often a sign of sensitivity to the latter. It was as though the human mind was incapable of adapting to the presence of magic in other races, ones whose life's blood was full of it, like Ivy's kind. The woman knew something. And it was driving her mad.

Before Ivy knew it, she and Helios had reached the surface. Never had Ivy been so glad to gulp down stale city air. Compared with the stifling wrongness of the subway platform and the sickening sensation of the in-between tearing itself open and slamming itself closed, the city air felt as fresh as a meadow.

Helios guided her a block and a half away and she let him, glad not to have to think beyond the simple act of putting one foot in front of the other. She was still trying to come to terms with what they had just seen.

The in-between wasn't supposed to open on its own. That was why they needed shadow dust. It was a key. That door wasn't supposed to open without one.

And yet.

And yet.

Their frantic pace slowed. Helios released his hold on Ivy's arm reluctantly, like he didn't want to lose her solidity. He looked back in the direction they had come. A crowd was beginning to gather around the station entrance, drawn by curiosity like moths to a flame.

"What just happened?" It didn't sound like Helios was asking Ivy specifically. There was an awestruck quality to his question that made it seem like it was simply something he needed to vocalize for the sake of his own sanity. After all, it wasn't like Ivy understood any better than he did.

The in-between had been acting strangely recently, but this . . . this was something else entirely. It was the difference between taking the wrong exit off the highway, and ending up in a bottomless abyss.

All those people. Ivy clamped down on the thought. If she went there, she wouldn't be able to come back. It was too horrible to consider. Hundreds of people, lost to the void. *No. Don't think about it.*

"I don't know," Ivy said helplessly. The woman's words echoed in her ears.

It's breaking apart. Breaking down.

The problem of the in-between was larger than any of them had ever dreamed.

"We have to tell the Ala," Ivy said. It was the only thing that made sense. The Ala would know what to do; she always knew what to do. Ivy felt the need to cling to the Ala's skirts in a way she hadn't done since childhood. The Ala would know. The Ala would help. "Come on." Now it was her turn to tug on Helios's arm. "We have to go home."

Helios stayed rooted to the spot. He peered at Ivy with a look of such supreme puzzlement, she would have laughed if not for the horror threatening to choke her. His voice was plaintive and deadly serious when he asked, "How?"

Ivy lost the battle against the hysterical laughter that had been threatening to spill out. It tumbled from her lips in a crazed cackle.

How?

They'd been taking the train because the in-between had been acting too unpredictable, and now *this*.

Ivy doubled over, clutching her gut, unsure whether the tears tracking down her face were from laughter or sadness, and not quite sure whether it mattered.

Madness and magic. Not far from each other indeed.

CHAPTER TWENTY-NINE

"The world is falling apart at the seams," said the Ala.

Echo paused, a doughnut halfway to her mouth. She didn't know what kind and generous soul had delivered the box of assorted doughnuts to the library at Avalon, but she knew that she loved them and would gladly take a bullet for them if need be. She, Rowan, and Caius were the only ones eating. Ivy and Helios were still rattled from what they'd seen while waiting for the train the day before. Dorian was too stoic to enjoy the miracle of fried dough covered in eight kinds of sugar. And Jasper didn't like eating things that were messy. His loss.

"Come again?" Echo said. Ivy wrapped her arm around Echo's and rested her head on Echo's shoulder. Ivy was shaking like a leaf. Echo brushed off the powdered sugar that had landed on Ivy's feathers when Echo had reached over her for a doughnut. At least the sugar blended in with her feathers.

"The rift Ivy and Helios witnessed open on the subway tracks," the Ala said. "The mysterious seals Caius saw that Tanith used his power to help break open. The increasing instability of the in-between. They're all connected."

"What exactly are the seals?" Rowan asked.

The Ala pulled books off her shelves so quickly that Echo doubted she'd stopped to give the titles even a cursory glance. Most of them were bound in earth-toned leather that was worn with age and use, dark in places from oil from readers' skin. These were well-loved books. Well-read books. The Ala probably knew every groove and indentation in their spines. "The seals have existed for as long as anyone can remember," the Ala said.

"Kind of like the war that has raged for as long as anyone can remember?" Echo was beginning to tire of things older than memory.

"They are even older than that. Little is known about their creation." The Ala scanned the pages of one book before snorting in disgust and tossing it over her shoulder. Echo winced as it hit the ground, covers spread like wings, spine cracked. "Most of it has been lost to time. What we do know we've managed to glean from fragments of memory passed down through generations, though it's been considerably gilded by myth over the years. The seals are as much legend as the firebird was."

Echo spread her arms wide, jostling Ivy. "And yet here I am."

That earned her a tight smile. The Ala began arranging the books on her desk in an order that made sense only to her. "Indeed. And as the firebird is every bit as real as you, the seals are every bit as real. And from what the young prince told me, centuries—no, millennia—of neglect have rendered them disastrously vulnerable."

"Well," Rowan said, "what *do* we know?"

The Ala sighed. Her feathers shivered with the rise and fall of her chest. "We know that they were created thousands upon thousands of years ago by a tribe that predates our modern notions of Avicen and Drakharin."

Echo recalled the Oracle she had met in that cave hidden deep within the Black Forest. The feathers that had adorned her arms. The scales that had graced the back of her hands, dusted across her knuckles. She had not been one or the other; she had been both and neither. The Oracle had been something ancient and almost forgotten. A link to their past that had been cruelly severed before Echo had even begun to scratch the surface of her mysteries. Like the seals, the Oracle predated the division that had torn their ancestors asunder. Perhaps she had been the sole survivor of a time when hatred and mistrust had not so clearly delineated the battle lines. But since Tanith had brought the ancient creature's long life to an end, they would never know. All they had was supposition.

"There are several variations of the story of how that one tribe split into two," the Ala continued. "But there are a few consistencies that crop up in different tellings of the tale, which leads me to believe there is a kernel of truth hiding in them."

"The Drakharin claim the war began when the Avicen stole their magic," said Caius, brushing the powdered sugar off his hands. He was still ravenous. "I never put much stock in the story myself. It always seemed like a convenient tale to pass down to perpetuate the cycle of hate and mistrust. But perhaps there's something to it, as much as I am loath to admit it."

The Ala nodded thoughtfully, considering his words. "It is possible," she mused. "But I think there is more to the story than that. Far more." She pulled another book off the shelf and flipped through it with speedy efficiency. "The seals Tanith used Caius's power to break were part of a vast network of structures all over the globe that stabilize the in-between and fortify the barrier separating the world in which we live from the abyss. It's how we're able to travel through it without being lost to the void or torn apart by its magic. I visited one or two a few centuries ago, but they were never of particular interest to me, so I never pursued a study of them. But now I find them *fascinating*. Their creation would have consumed a great deal of power. Infinitely more than any one mage could wield, or even a group of mages working in tandem. A magical working like that would drain their reserves of energy, leaving them nothing more than lifeless husks once it was through. And even then, that amount of magic would hardly be enough for a spell of that magnitude. To maintain the spell, to keep it in place long after its original caster, or casters, had died would require something more permanent, a lasting solution that would survive the passage of time."

"Our magic," said Caius. He pushed away from his seat by the window wearing the expression Echo had come to know as his thinking face. "They used it to lock the seals." He started pacing, engulfed by the enormity of such a revelation. "It makes sense, when you consider it. Magic is generational. It's genetic, passed from mother to child through the ages. They must have found a way to isolate it and then to harness it for some greater purpose. The level of skill that would have taken is tremendous."

The Ala nodded. "It's possible Tanith can undo this magic—which should not be able to be undone—because the kuçedra is linked to it. The seals held back the dark from this world and the kuçedra is a creature born of that darkness. It has fed on conflict and pain and woe for millennia and that has made it strong, but it originated long before we ever took up arms and started hacking away at each other. Its evolution into the being we've encountered—and the ritual employed to lock it away forever—was the catalyst for the war that made it grow fat on our pain."

Echo rested her cheek on Ivy's head. All that suffering. All that hatred. The only thing it had accomplished was creating more suffering, more hatred. "Is there anything we can do about the seals?" Echo asked. "Is there some kind of magical tape we can smack on them to hold things together until we find a permanent solution?"

"I'll send a team of mages to one of the seals we know is broken." The Ala turned to Caius. "Do you think you would be able to locate the places Tanith brought you to?"

With a chagrined expression, Caius shook his head. "I can try, but I was blindfolded and mostly unconscious during transport."

"Any details you remember will be helpful: whether you were underground or aboveground, the color of the stone or the smell of the soil." The Ala began sorting through her papers again. She pulled out a slender leather-bound notebook. "I have noticed a pattern of irregularities in the natural ebb and flow of magical energies—"

"Is that Seer-speak?" Echo asked.

The Ala looked at her as if it was unreasonable that she didn't know all about the natural ebb and flow of magical energies. "Yes." With that out of the way, the Ala continued. "With your help, Caius, I believe we can locate the specific seals Tanith has already compromised."

"I'll do everything I can to help," said Caius. "My sister wouldn't have been able to break them without me. I can't help but feel at least somewhat responsible."

"It's not your fault, Caius," said Echo. She doubted he would believe her, but it merited mentioning regardless. He had that look about him, the one that told her he was so deep into self-abasement that there was little chance of her pulling him out of it with a few kind words.

His black moods are never so easily dispelled, Rose whispered.

"Oh my god, shut up." Echo hadn't realized she had spoken aloud until she noticed every pair of eyes in the room on her.

The Ala must have realized who Echo was speaking to. A heavy tome slid from her hands and landed on the table with a loud thunk, drawing all those inquisitive gazes away from Echo. She mouthed a silent *Thank you* at the Ala, who acknowledged it with a wink. "Oh, how clumsy of me," said the Ala, who in all the years Echo had known her had not been prone to clumsiness.

The only person who had not fallen for the Ala's distraction was Caius. That green gaze remained on Echo, so intently she felt her skin itch. He raised his eyebrows in a silent question, but she responded with only a very slight shake of her head. *Not now,* she tried to telegraph. And not ever. He was the last person she wanted to confide in on this particular point. It would make things exceptionally awkward if he knew that his long-dead lover was sharing personal insights into his character with Echo.

The conversation continued without Echo's active participation. She heard fragments of it: the Ala would work through the night, helping Caius recover his memories and craft a map by morning to lead them to the broken seals; the mages would concoct a spell to help close the seals. Echo let the familiar sound of her friends' voices wash over her. The bubble of elation that followed Caius's rescue hadn't taken long to pop. She had known it would be a short-lived joy, but had hoped, foolishly, that it would last longer than this.

But now the enormity of what they were facing threatened to overwhelm her. The very fabric of the world was beginning to unravel, and few beyond the walls of Avalon Castle even knew it was happening.

CHAPTER THIRTY

The refugees were exactly where Caius had been told he would find them on Avalon's grounds. He watched the small cluster from beneath an archway leading to the ruined courtyard, hidden enough in the shadows that he would not be noticed.

The refugees were mostly servants from the keep. Caius recognized one of the cooks who had worked in the kitchens for as long as he could remember. She was a portly woman who used to sneak him treats whenever he sought solace in the warmth of the kitchen, hiding from his tutors or his weapons instructor, or even the father he barely remembered but whose lectures on the soaring expectations he had for Caius and his sister had left an indelible imprint on his memory. The cook—Helena, that was her name—had never chided Caius for hiding behind the oak barrels or for stealing the spice cakes that had been his favorite. She had been one of the few people to treat him like a child, to direct indulgent smiles his way when he showed up covered in mud, his fine clothes a fright, looking as much a mess as any boy would at that age. She had been kind to him, but after he had grown into the role for which he had been bred—despite the fact that no Dragon Prince's ascension to the throne was a certainty—he had barely spared her a thought. But to see her now, alive and well, made the ever-present worry in his chest decrease, if only by a few degrees. His people were not lost, not entirely. And now he was in a position to help them.

Caius hung back, unsure of his welcome. What would they see when they looked at him? A disgraced prince who had failed them once before? Or someone worth putting their faith in again, after he had proven so undeserving of it the first time? He hadn't protected them from Tanith. He should have. It was his most solemn duty to protect them, and he had not done so. His role, his purpose, was not to lead the Drakharin to an "age of glory," words that were often bandied about among nobles deep in their cups at great feasts. The Dragon Prince was a guardian. A guide. And he had led his people, through his own willful ignorance, to ruin.

Helena looked up just then and caught Caius's eye. Never one to quail before nobility, she raised a hand to beckon him over. He hesitated for a moment, and her expression resolved into the fierce stare that had haunted his childhood. No one questioned that glare, not even a prince.

Cautious steps led Caius to the small group huddled around the fire. Helena's eyes lingered on the limp he couldn't hide, try as he might. He stood—rather awkwardly—off to the side. Every set of eyes save Helena's dropped respectfully. It was a gesture that marked the difference between them. They were all of the common class, even the soldiers who had guided them during their long and arduous flight from the keep. Caius was not one of them and never had been. Self-consciousness struck him as he realized he had no idea how to act. He was not their prince any longer, but their habits—and his—were harder to shake than he cared to admit.

"Hello," he said, for lack of anything better.

"Sit down, boy," Helena said gruffly, shifting to make room for him.

Boy. She hadn't called him that in centuries, literally. Caius realized then that he had no idea how old she was. She had been the same for as long as he could remember. Old, cranky, kindhearted Helena. As eternal as the rising and setting of the sun.

With as much grace as he could muster, Caius sank into the seat she had vacated for him.

"Leg bothering you?" Helena asked. A cast-iron pan of something fragrant was cooking over the open flames.

"My leg and everything else," Caius admitted. There seemed little reason to keep up appearances around Helena. Doing so would have been disingenuous, and she would see through him anyway. Perhaps it was time for his people to see him as he truly was, flaws and all. Caius sniffed at the scent of sizzling meat. Chunks of meat had been cut up and sautéed with root vegetables. Whatever the creature had been while alive was difficult to ascertain. "Please tell me you didn't cook a bird," Caius said. "The Avicen might kick us off the island for insulting their feathered friends."

Helena barked out a sharp laugh. "I won't say it didn't

cross my mind, but rest easy, my boy. This here is scraps of rabbit and squirrel and whatever else we could get our hands on. The Avicen may have provided a roof over our heads, but I don't fancy they'd take too kindly to us depleting their stores of food." She glanced at the guards who were lounging stiffly at the edges of the courtyard designated for Drakharin use. They were looking more than a little gaunt. "Doesn't look like they've got much to spare."

Caius nodded. It was no easy task, feeding a small island full of people without arousing suspicion. The Avicen had emergency stores, but they were burning through them fast.

"How have you settled in?" Caius asked Helena. It was a vague enough question, but from the slight sigh that escaped her, he thought she grasped the nuance. She heard the things he didn't ask.

"As well as can be expected," she said. After a moment of grudging consideration, she amended her statement. "Better than we expected. The Avicen . . . they have not been unkind to us. They offered us shelter when we had none and they had no reason to give it. The young one, the boy who brought us here . . . he spoke for us. Made our case to the others. Persuaded them to let us stay."

The boy. Rowan. The tiniest flame of jealousy licked at Caius, but he doused it as soon as he recognized the emotion. Rowan was a good person. After all, Echo was an excellent judge of character. She wouldn't waste time on anyone unworthy.

"The world is changing," Caius said. "And we must change with it."

Nodding, Helena scooped up a heaping mound of stew

with a wooden spoon and began distributing it into chipped porcelain bowls that had seen far better days. "Are you hungry?" She studied Caius with her piercing brown eyes. "You look like you could use a good meal or ten."

"That bad?" he asked.

"Worse."

That earned a small laugh from Caius. "You were never one to mince words, Helena."

"Well, I won't have no prince of mine going hungry." Helena shoved a bowl into his hands, her expression daring him to argue with her.

Shaking his head, Caius accepted the bowl. He reached for a spoon and stirred the stew a bit. It smelled divine. "I have no claim to that title. Not anymore."

Helena dropped a hunk of hard bread in his lap. "You know what else I won't have? Self-pity."

Caius blinked at her. "Excuse me?"

"Oh, I know you nobles like to think you're bound by the rules you lot made up, but frankly, anyone who's done what that tyrant has doesn't deserve my obedience or my respect." She brandished the wooden spoon at Caius when he failed to eat with the alacrity she expected. "Those things are earned. And she hasn't earned them from me." A somber look passed over her face. "Shame, that. She was always such a bright child."

"That she was," Caius said softly.

One of the young Drakharin inched closer to Helena, wide blue eyes fixed on Caius, as if unsure whether approaching was a wise strategy. He winked at the child and tossed her his bread. She caught it with dirt-smudged hands and smiled, two dimples forming in her cheeks. She buried her face in Helena's skirt as she chewed, her eyes never leaving Caius.

"You weren't perfect," Helena said. "No prince is. I've lived long enough to see more than one rise and fall, but you"—she poked him with her spoon—"you cared. About us. About all the people who didn't matter."

"Of course you matter," Caius said with a frown.

"That attitude is what sets you apart," Helena said, pleased that Caius had seen fit to prove her point immediately after she'd made it. "That's what we need. Not some tyrant who grabs at power for the sake of having it."

Caius looked around at the group of weary Drakharin. They had given up the pretense of polite disinterest and were now staring at him openly, waiting to hear what he would say. A great deal hung on his next words. Their anticipation coiled around him, an insistent pressure that would not be relieved until he found just the right assortment of words to reassure them.

The little girl noisily chewed the hunk of bread, blinking up at Caius with wide eyes. When he caught her gaze, she pulled at Helena's skirt to hide her face. They had traveled so far from their homes. His people were an insular lot. For them to have sacrificed so much, to have wandered away from the only safety they had ever experienced into the unknown, was nothing short of astonishing. It spoke to their need for change.

"I lost my title," Caius said. He would not lie to them or pretend to be anything other than what he was, no matter how badly they wanted him to be their savior. "It was not taken from me. I let it go because I was not strong enough to keep it."

Helena hummed in consideration. "I suppose that is the way of it," she said with a tired sigh. There was defeat in her voice and, even worse, disappointment. That, Caius could not stand. These people had been through much, but they were not broken. And neither was he.

"I was not strong enough to keep it," Caius repeated. He met each of their gazes in turn and saw the steel in his own eyes reflected in theirs. "But I can promise you that I will be strong enough to take it back."

Caius left the Drakharin to their meal. He was still exhausted, and he could practically feel the softness of a bed beneath him, so powerful was his desire for sleep. As he was walking back to his quarters, he spotted the familiar head of silver hair, half hidden by a column near the courtyard entrance.

Dorian was leaning against the column, waiting for him. His hair had grown longer than he normally kept it, and stray strands fluttered against his cheeks in the breeze. He had a long, cloth-wrapped parcel tucked under one arm. "The Ala is confident we can finish the map by dawn," he said. "We leave for the first seal tomorrow."

Caius nodded. His head felt heavy, as if it weighed too much for his neck to support. The thought that they would be departing come morning was enough to make him weep. He wouldn't. But he wanted to. "No rest for the wicked, I suppose."

Dorian responded with a noncommittal noise. After a moment, he said, "I was watching you just now. You were good with them."

"Was I?" Caius leaned against the column next to Dorian. It wasn't quite wide enough for both of them, but Caius found a certain comfort in the feel of Dorian's shoulder pressed against his. Dorian was a constant in his life. A welcome reprieve after the brutal solitude of Tanith's care. Dorian was home.

"You were," said Dorian. "But what's all this about taking back the throne? I thought you were done with that."

Caius let his head fall back against the cool stone. His eyes drifted shut. "I thought I was. No Dragon Prince has ever lost his crown and lived to win it back. But I cannot leave them at my sister's mercy. I owe them to at least try."

He felt Dorian shift his weight from one foot to the other. Dorian sometimes fidgeted when he was nervous or treading into territory of which he felt unsure. Caius wasn't sure his friend even realized he did it. Everyone had their tells, even his stalwart guard.

"Do you think you can?" Dorian asked.

It was a good question, and not one to which Caius had a satisfactory answer. Helena might have put her faith in him, but there were others who would not look so kindly on a lost prince's return. "I don't know," he said honestly. "But I have to try."

Somewhere in the distance, a bird sang a warbling lullaby. The sun continued its westward dip below the horizon. A voice called out, beckoning the children to come in for their supper. Life went on for all these people, no matter how many disasters befell them.

Dorian was silent, giving Caius the space he needed to form his thoughts into something resembling coherence.

"We have always been ruled by the will of the people," he said. "We have forgotten that, especially among the noble classes. But it wasn't always the nobility that elected the Dragon Prince. Once, the leader of our people was chosen by the people, not an insular sect that deemed themselves superior to the common man. One had to earn the respect, the love, and even the fear, of the people he was to rule before he was allowed to call himself the ruler."

Dorian inclined his head in the direction of the small group of refugees. They seemed less huddled on themselves now than they had moments ago. "Is that what happened just now?"

"I suppose so." The weight of that responsibility was settling gradually on Caius's shoulders, but it was not an unwelcome weight. It was one he would bear gladly. And hopefully he would do so with more wisdom this time than he had displayed during his reign.

A furrow formed between Dorian's brows as he considered the implications of what he had witnessed. Abruptly he asked, "Did you just start a civil war?"

"Yes."

Dorian seemed to consider this information, then shrugged. "All right, then. I just thought I'd check before I gave you this." He hefted the package in his arms and presented it to Caius.

"What's this?" Caius asked. The bundle was heavier than it looked.

"Just open it."

Caius unwrapped the parcel, revealing the loveliest set

of long knives he had ever seen. The hilts were wrapped in soft leather, easily molded to the hands, and the pommels studded with jade. The bronze wrist guards gleamed in the light of the setting sun. The blades shone so brightly that Caius was sure he'd be able to see his reflection in them.

"Jasper helped me acquire them," Dorian said. "Can't have you heading into battle unarmed."

"No, we cannot." Caius reverently examined the knives in his hands. They were perfectly balanced. "They're incredible."

Dorian flushed. "Stop fondling them. This is getting obscene."

Caius met Dorian's gaze. "Thank you. I shall try to be worthy of such a gift." He bumped his shoulder against Dorian's. "You know, you're taking the idea of a coup rather well."

Dorian shrugged. "Whatever your play," he said, "I'll back it. As I've always said, you are my prince, and I will follow you anywhere." He pushed away from the column, pivoting so he was walking toward the castle backward. "Besides, I plan on taking great delight in watching Tanith get her just deserts. I never liked her."

Caius laughed, and it felt as though a great weight had been lifted. With Dorian at his side, the impossible seemed merely improbable.

When Dorian reached the archway leading to the kitchens, he gestured for Caius to follow him. "In other news, a little birdie told me there was pie."

Caius's stomach growled at the thought of pie, loud enough for Dorian to hear. Caius looped an arm around

Dorian's shoulders, tugging him toward the delicious smell. "Was this little birdie named Echo, by chance?"

"Possibly." Dorian's lips quirked into a small smile. "But you know what they say: a revolution without pie is a revolution not worth having."

Caius chuckled. "I don't think anyone says that."

"Well, they should," Dorian replied. "Because it's true." He angled his head to scan Caius with his one good eye. "Now let's get some food into you. Helena was right—you look absolutely terrible."

CHAPTER THIRTY-ONE

Something pricked at Echo's arm. She slapped at the offending sensation, but it was too late. The mosquito had already bitten her, adding to the constellation of bug bites on her exposed arms. It was the first time Echo had visited the rain forest of Puerto Rico, and with luck, it would also be the last. The human family she had left as a child had been of Puerto Rican descent, but that part of her felt distant, like it belonged to someone else. She had memories of cuddling a stuffed coqui, the tiny frog native to the island, but her human ethnicity hadn't mattered so much to the Avicen, and for the most part, Echo hadn't given it much thought since the Ala had taken her in. Though she sometimes felt a faraway sadness for the heritage she knew so little about, she was finding it hard to appreciate Puerto Rico's natural beauty at the moment. As picturesque as El Yunque National Forest was, Echo was too much of a city girl for all this greenery. And the mosquitoes. Good gods, the mosquitoes.

"I told you to wear long sleeves." Rowan didn't even bother trying to hide the smugness in his voice. While Echo couldn't deny the satisfaction of an appropriately timed *I told you so,* she vastly preferred to be the one delivering it.

She shot him a scowl as they tramped through the undergrowth, mindful of the chaotic network of vines and roots that threatened to trip them with every step. They walked in single file—Sage and a few Warhawks in the lead; Echo in the center; Caius, Violet, and several Avicen mages behind her, with Dorian bringing up the rear—as it was easier to navigate the jungle that way. Echo had no idea where they were going, but she trusted Sage not to get them lost. An Avicen settlement was nestled deep in the jungle, seemingly as far from the cosmopolitan nest as one could possibly get, and conveniently located close to one of the seals on the map the Ala had made. Echo knew that such settlements existed, but she had never seen one herself; the Ala had told her of them in her youth when explaining the complex path of Avicen history. Most Avicen opted to live in human cities—the center of power was in New York, as it had been for centuries—but there were a few holdouts who preferred a life of solitude and isolation to the bustle and boisterousness of city life, even if said city provided a teeming mass of humanity to act as a shield against possible Drakharin aggression. Although, Echo thought as she surveyed the riotously colorful wilderness around them, perhaps isolation was its own protection. After all, the city had provided little deterrent when an attack had finally come, and the warning Sage had sternly delivered before they'd stepped through the gateway she and her mages held open ricocheted through Echo's mind: *Stay on the path. Do not stray. The jungle is filled with traps you won't see until it's too late. I'm not bringing any corpses back with me if you're stupid enough to go off on your own.*

Sage really did have a way with words.

In response to Echo's vitriolic scowl, Rowan tossed a sweetly innocent smile at her over his shoulder. Which meant he wasn't looking where he was going. Echo replied with a saccharine smile of her own as Rowan, blissfully ignorant of the dangers Echo saw fit *not* to warn him about, walked smack into a low-hanging tangle of vines and branches.

Echo stepped around Rowan as he struggled to free himself from the grasping vines.

"I do believe Sage told you to watch your step," she said breezily.

Rowan swore in two languages—English and Avicet—as his shirt snagged on a thorn. With the animals scurrying to and fro, the cries of exotic birds, and the rustle of foliage, the jungle was far from quiet, but the sound of cotton ripping as Rowan struggled was loud enough to bring a smile to Echo's lips. She could do smug just as well as—no, better than—Rowan ever could.

The Ala had sent them on their journey to the jungle settlement with a litany of instructions they were to follow to the letter, lest they risk being strung up from one of the towering canopy trees by their own intestines. Echo had started to say something flippant about the threat, but a pointed look from the Ala had said loud and clear that it was not mere hyperbole.

These are not like the Avicen you have come to know, the Ala had warned. *They will not take kindly to a human in their midst. And they may even see an approach from their northern brethren as an unwelcome incursion into the territory they have so fiercely guarded.*

A cheerful thought. Echo replayed the Ala's instructions in her mind as she walked. Anything to distract her from the sweat beading on her brow and the ache in her muscles as she hiked through the jungle's uneven, inhospitable terrain. El Toro, the forest's highest mountain peak, was occasionally visible through the canopy. Like the rest of the rain forest, it was lovely, from afar. Echo slapped at another mosquito on her forearm, cursing it and its entire family.

The Ala's first instruction: *Get close to the camp, but let them find you. Do not enter their gates without an explicit invitation.*

Echo had inquired as to what might happen should they simply walk through the settlement's front door.

Their archers will strike you down before you've taken a single step over the threshold, the Ala had said. *So don't do it.* Echo thought that last bit was specifically meant for her.

The second instruction: *Be respectful. Show deference.* And then, to Echo, she added: *For the love of the gods, keep your mouth shut and let Sage do the talking.*

Echo had bristled at that. Her smart mouth had gotten her out of as many scrapes as it had gotten her into, but the steely look in the Ala's eyes made her think that, perhaps just this once, discretion would be the better part of valor.

The third instruction: *Deliver this*—the Ala had handed Echo a small package wrapped in plain brown paper— *unopened to the head of the clan.*

Echo had been on her best behavior and had not opened the package despite her burning curiosity. When the Ala had placed it in her hands for safekeeping, Echo had given the package a good shake, but no sound provided a clue as to the nature of its contents. When she had asked what it contained, the Ala brushed off her question and said simply, *Something their leader greatly desires.*

Cryptic, but so long as the package wasn't ticking, Echo could live with mystery for a few more hours.

The package rested in her backpack, carefully arranged on top of her other belongings so that it didn't get crushed. That had been the Ala's final instruction to Echo: *Do not damage this package. Your life may depend on it.*

All in a day's work. Echo would have felt downright bereft if she'd been packed off to the middle of the jungle without a single ominous warning. She was growing accustomed to them. Ominous warnings were a part of her routine now.

They trudged through the rain forest, brushing aside low-hanging vines and stumbling over roots hidden by the thick carpet of fallen leaves that squelched beneath their feet. It could have been two hours, or ten. Time ceased to have meaning. It passed in a haze of sweat and buzzing mosquitoes and the occasional screech of some unseen bird hopping around the network of entwined branches overhead.

Echo was just about ready to lie down and pray for the sweet oblivion of death's embrace when Sage came to an abrupt stop.

The chatter down the line, which had been the only thing keeping Echo awake, grew quiet. The birds and beasts held their tongues. Even the drooping ferns ceased their susurrations. It was as if the jungle was holding its breath, waiting for something. Or someone.

Echo's skin prickled at the nape of her neck. She could

have sworn she felt a penetrating gaze marching along her flesh.

A sound broke the stillness as a figure materialized out of the indigo shadows. Footfalls, deliberately placed to snap dead twigs. Echo realized a moment too late that the approach was a distraction. Something sharp and solid pressed against the soft skin behind her ear. Like the head of an arrow, nocked and ready to sink into the vulnerable flesh of her throat. They'd all been so busy looking straight ahead they hadn't bothered to check behind them.

Stupid, Echo thought.

Tired, her body reminded her.

Dorian swore in rapid Drakhar and the arrow pressed harder against Echo's neck.

The person wielding the bow and arrow spoke in low, unhurried Avicet right into Echo's ear but the dialect was unfamiliar to her. Without turning her head, she swiveled her gaze to Rowan, who was in much the same position, though the weapon held to his jugular was a wickedly curved blade. "Translation?"

Rowan swallowed, and then looked like he regretted the motion as the knife's blade pressed deeper into his flesh. "She said, 'We don't take kindly to strangers in our land, even if they come wearing feathers.'"

Lovely. They were off to a fantastic start.

Sage and the person holding the arrow to Echo's throat exchanged words in Avicet, and after a few tense minutes, the arrow retreated and Echo could breathe again. Someone prodded her in the back, ushering her forward.

"They're taking us to their camp," Sage called down the line. "Everyone be on your best behavior."

"I'm always on my best behavior," Echo said. She couldn't help it.

Rowan snorted, Sage sighed, and the person behind Echo poked her even harder in the back. They trudged through the rain forest and into the settlement. Echo hoped whatever was in the package was enough to guarantee that they made it out alive.

An Avicen with the greenest feathers Echo had ever seen was sitting in the center of what she could only describe as a tree house. Or maybe a tree mansion. The Avicen of the rain forest didn't live in huts on the ground, but in wood structures built into the trees like miniature palaces. Winding staircases wrapped around ancient trunks, and bridges made of rope and smooth wooden slats connected the dwellings, forming a complex network high above the ground.

The team of scouts they'd encountered in the wild had led them here, to the most elaborate of the dwellings, located in the center of the village. One of the scouts must have gone ahead to alert the Avicen of their return, because a party had been waiting for them, resplendent in armor suitable for hot, humid jungle terrain and with weapons polished to perfection: spears topped with wickedly curved blades, bows made of gleaming dark wood, more daggers than Echo could count.

In the center of it all was the green-feathered Avicen—the group's matriarch, judging from the deference the others showed her. She studied Echo with eyes as black and as sharp as the Ala's. When she spoke, her voice held all the authority of a queen comfortable with her power. "You dare bring a human into our home?" With a disdainful look at Caius, she added, "And two Drakharin?"

"The Ala has decreed that these Drakharin are our allies," Sage replied. "At least for the time being. What could have possessed the Ala to bring them into the fold the gods only know, but I have no interest in breaking her oath of allegiance. She can be most fearsome when she wants to be." Sage motioned Echo forward. "She is no mere human. She is the firebird, the one prophesied to bring an end to our troubles."

An explosion of hushed whispers arose from the assembled Avicen, but the green-feathered one silenced them with an upraised hand. "I have heard speak of the one you claim is the firebird. Come here, child. Let me see you."

Echo glanced at Sage, who offered a shrug that wasn't particularly comforting. Gripping the package, Echo approached the clan's matriarch. As soon as she was close enough, the Avicen's hand shot out to grasp her chin. Echo held still as the woman tilted her face from side to side, examining her.

Whatever she saw must have met with approval, because a pleased smile flashed across her face like a whip. "And here I thought the Ala was spouting nonsense." She let go of Echo's chin and looked down at the package. "Tribute, I assume?"

Echo nodded mutely and held out the package.

The Avicen accepted the package and delicately opened the taped seams. When Echo saw what it was, she wanted to scream. "You've got to be kidding me," she said.

It was a box of Twinkies. A box of goddamn Twinkies.

With a grin, the Avicen handed the box to one of her

subordinates, a member of the scouting party that had led them to the camp. She nodded at Sage. "Your tribute is accepted and we offer you our hospitality," she said. "You may call me Reina."

Spanish for "queen." It said a great deal about her, as the Avicen tended to choose their own names. *Humble,* Echo thought.

Sage responded with a short bow. "We have come about the seal. The Ala said you sent word that it had been compromised."

Just like that, Reina's smile vanished. "Compromised," she said, her tone somber. "That is one way of putting it. Come, I will show you the seal myself." She stood, and Echo noticed for the first time how tall she was. The top of her feathered head nearly brushed the ceiling. She had a warrior's body, with long limbs and graceful strength. "The seal is indeed compromised, but I am afraid that is only half the problem."

CHAPTER THIRTY-TWO

Reina led them to a cave half a day's walk from the settlement. Echo lost count of how many mosquitoes had feasted on her flesh.

"The seal is through this cave," Reina said. "It goes deep into the mountains. Our mages have been holding the seal together as well as they can, but I fear it is only a matter of time before they can contain it no longer. Perhaps the Ala's mages will be able to help, though I am not hopeful. But first, I will show you what happened to the guards we had stationed here before the Dragon Prince gifted us with the broken seal's chaos."

"Tanith must have come here after Echo rescued me," Caius said. "I've never seen this place before. She must have siphoned enough magic from me to break the seal on her own."

A round space near the front of the cave served as a makeshift infirmary. Mages wearing the same lightweight armor as Reina's scouts moved among their patients, brandishing bundles of cloying incense and various potions in colorful glass vials.

Two Avicen lay on pallets on the cave floor. Their skin was waxen and pale, and a thin wheezing sound rose from one with every indrawn breath, as if the continued act of living was proving far too much for him to handle. The other dozed, eyes moving wildly under closed lids, head twitching infinitesimally, as if he was lost in the throes of a terrible nightmare.

Echo drew closer, squinting in the dim light.

The wheezing one cracked his eyes open at her approach. His eyes rolled madly, trying to focus, but they were covered in a milky bluish film. Cataracts. He croaked out an inquiry in a hoarse, tired voice. One of the mages answered in that unfamiliar dialect. Echo recognized the Avicet words for "fire" and "bird."

Wrinkled, flaking skin stretched over a once-proud bone structure. The Avicen's eyes were sunken, and his hair hung in graying clumps, exposing patches of bald, pockmarked skin.

Echo had never seen an elderly Avicen before. It wasn't that they didn't grow old; they aged, but incredibly slowly. As children, they developed at the same pace humans did, but once they reached full physical maturity, their bodies slowed. The Ala had tried to explain it to Echo once—something about magic counteracting the process of cellular degeneration—but Rowan had shown up with a bag of potato chips and a stack of bootleg Disney DVDs and Echo had been thoroughly distracted. She remembered enough, though, to know that *this* never should have been possible.

"Their magic was leached from their bodies," said Reina. "Our people are not kept alive by the simple beating of a heart. Magic sustains us. Without it, we wither like leaves fallen off the tree."

"It's like the man Ivy saw at the hospital," Echo said. At Reina's questioning look, Echo shared all Ivy had related to her. The twenty-three-year-old aged well beyond his years. The sickly feeling of his tainted aura. The presence of the kuçedra lingering like a noxious cloud around him.

Reina's expression darkened. "The Dragon Prince feeds on them to make herself stronger. Perhaps it is not only magic she craves but life itself."

"That about sums it up," Echo said, looking back down at the stricken Avicen. "These two were unlucky enough to get in her way."

"They were tasked with protecting the seal. Our tribe has always done so. It is one of the reasons we stayed here." Reina knelt beside the pallets and said a short prayer in Avicet. "They gave their lives for their sacred duty. Now follow me, and I will show you just what they were protecting."

The seal could hardly be called such anymore. A dozen Avicen mages formed a circle around the rift. Torches stuck in the ground illuminated the cavern but failed to pierce the darkest depths of the broken seal. Writhing black tendrils of the in-between lashed at the barrier the mages had constructed around the broken seal, as if testing the limitations of their magic. Violet and the other mages who had accompanied Echo's group from New York had already joined the circle, adding their power to the barrier.

Reina prevented them from going more than a few feet into the space. Caius pushed to the front of the group, a grim expression on his face. The Avicen of the rain forest had barely given him a second glance, and now Echo understood why. The threat they faced in the heart of their own territory was far more frightening than a single Drakharin in their midst.

Echo could feel the hot pulse of the in-between beating at the shimmering field, aching to be set free. The scar on her chest throbbed in time with the rift, as if the shadows peeking through the hole in the universe were calling to it, beckoning it to join them. Echo gritted her teeth against the sensation. "It looks like it's about to burst at any moment."

And she did not want to be near the broken seal when that happened.

"This is the best we've been able to do." An incongruous growl of frustration escaped through Violet's clenched teeth. Her pink and lavender feathers, which normally fell in soft waves around her shoulders like a candy-colored cloak, were mussed, with strands sticking up as if agitated hands had run through them and pulled them. Echo had seen her often in the Agora, a smile a seemingly permanent fixture on her softly angular face, and at Warhawk training when Echo had gone to spy on Rowan after he first joined their ranks. Yet never had she seen Violet look quite so disheveled. "It won't hold," Violet said.

Reina shook her head. "Why tamper with the seals?" She looked down at Echo. "You have faced her in combat. What do you suspect?"

"Tanith is a grade A psychopath," Echo said. "She wants to build a new world, to remake it in her image. But first she has to tear this one down."

Reina made a disgusted noise. "And she thinks she can build a world atop the chaos she has unleashed? Fool."

Caius approached the circle. Reina didn't try to stop him. He crouched, studying the Avicet runes carved into the dirt. They were slightly darker than the soil.

"You sealed them with blood," Caius observed.

Reina nodded. "It was the only way to hold the barrier together, but it is a temporary measure. We can hold the in-between back, but we cannot close the seal altogether."

Violet said something in Avicet to the mage next to her. "They think Tanith's blood might be able to close it," she then said to Caius, "but I take it you're not walking around with any of that."

"Sadly, no," Caius replied. He stood. "But what about my blood? Tanith is my twin. Our blood is identical."

"It *was* identical," Violet replied. One of the mages who had accompanied Reina and Echo's group tapped Violet on the shoulder. Violet dropped her arms and stepped back, and the mage took her place. "Tanith's blood has been tainted," Violet said. "Altered. Irreparably, I'm guessing."

A look flickered over Caius's face, there and gone before anyone could see it. Except for Echo. His features hardened into an implacable mask, showing no hint of the emotions that lay beneath, but Echo had seen them—the grief, the loss—written on his face as though Tanith had carved them there. It was so easy to forget that their enemy had been a person once. Not a good person—not in Echo's reckoning—but Caius had loved her. He probably still did. The bonds of family were not so easily severed.

Altered. Irreparably.

It was a succinct way of saying there was no hope for Tanith, that she was beyond saving. Echo watched Caius's hope sputter and die in that one fleeting expression. Then it was shelved wherever he put all his other inconvenient emotions. Echo had thought she was good at compartmentalizing, but Caius had perfected it, made it an art form.

"It's worth trying," Caius insisted. He rolled up one shirtsleeve, not waiting for Violet to object. "Do it."

She did it.

The blade sliced through the skin of his forearm with ease, so sharp it took a second for the blood to well. Scars stood out along his arm, pale and shiny against the tan skin. Violet led Caius by his bleeding arm around the circle, fortifying the Avicet runes with his blood. The barrier shimmered so brightly it became nearly opaque. Echo felt the grasping energy of the in-between recede.

"I don't believe it," Violet said, gazing at the circle with awe. She let go of Caius's arm. "It actually worked." She reached a hand toward the shining barrier and closed her eyes. After a moment, she said, "It'll hold. For now, at least. We'll need Tanith's blood to close it for good."

Caius was pale when he rejoined the group. Reina studied him with an appraising look, as if taking his measure. She made a gruff sound of approval. "I suppose you have your uses after all," she said.

Caius offered her a tight smile in response and looked at Echo. "How many broken seals are on that map?"

Echo fished the map out of her backpack and unfolded

it. A dozen Xs were scattered across every habitable continent. "Eleven more."

Reina clapped Caius on the shoulder, with enough force that he nearly staggered under her hand. "Rest up, Dragon. You've got a lot of bleeding to do."

CHAPTER THIRTY-THREE

Caius's blood was not an infinite resource.

They had made it to one more seal on the Ala's map, this one located in Iceland, before Sage sized him up and prescribed a period of rest long enough for his blood to replenish itself. It wouldn't do to have Caius die of exsanguination before they'd gotten to all the seals. Sage had also insisted on making camp near the mended seal in order to conserve their dwindling supply of shadow dust. Ever the pragmatist, that one.

And so Echo found herself staring up at the glittering blue-green lights of the aurora borealis while standing at the center of what appeared to be an abandoned camp somewhere in the middle of miles and miles of Icelandic nothing. Perhaps not *nothing*. The landscape surrounding the camp was quite possibly one of the most gorgeous sights Echo had ever laid eyes on. Long stretches of rolling green hills were capped with a dusting of the season's first snowfall.

The camp itself was situated near a magnificent fjord that stretched toward the sea like a blanket of deep-blue velvet.

It was hard to tell where the water ended and the sky began. One bled into the other until all the eye could see was the soft indigo darkness sliced through with ribbons of light. Echo hadn't had time to appreciate the sight when she last saw it. Caius had been too near death, their situation too desperate. She had been too scared. But now she could gaze upward and wallow in a sense of cosmic insignificance. It was strangely comforting. If not for the sound of voices as people wandered about setting up camp and lighting fires, she would have been able to pretend that she was all alone. A tiny speck in a vast wilderness.

Stjerneklart, she thought. Norwegian for "a night illuminated only by starlight." Echo turned the word over in her head, savoring the rightness of it.

Behind her, footsteps crunched over the frosted grass. When she turned, she saw Caius standing there, watching her watch the sky.

His hair had grown long enough to have a slight wave to it. A gentle breeze sent a lock of it tumbling over his forehead, which he promptly brushed away with an irritated sigh. A vain attempt at a smirk accompanied his words when he spoke. "If it gets any longer, Dorian's going to be at me with the scissors again."

"He likes to fuss over you," Echo said, matching the forced lightness of his tone. "Like a mother hen."

Caius's smile failed to reach his eyes. They were nearly black in the darkness, but every now and then, a bit of green glimmered like an emerald, reflecting the shining lights dancing in the nighttime sky. The scales on his cheekbones refracted the light, highlighting the planes of his face and making it abundantly obvious when he flinched at a far-away shout. He wasn't hunched, exactly—his spine was straight and his shoulders proudly squared—but there was a stiffness to him that seemed altogether alien to Echo. She had grown so used to the casual grace with which Caius moved that its absence was startling, though imperceptible to those who hadn't spent a great deal of time looking at him. Echo had.

"The others are waiting inside," Caius said. He inclined his head in the direction of one of the larger buildings at the center of the encampment. Chipped red paint coated its exterior, and its roof sagged in the middle. It had probably served as a meeting hall when the settlement had been up and running. The Avicen used it as an outpost between their territory in the Americas and the Drakharin's in the British Isles. And now it was their temporary home. There were enough buildings to house the mages and warriors without anyone having to share a room. After the cramped conditions at Avalon, the arrangements were positively luxurious.

"Ivy and Helios have arrived, along with some reinforcements from Avalon," Caius said.

"I know," Echo said. "I just . . ."

"Needed some air?" Caius offered.

She nodded.

"As did I," he said. An inscrutable expression flitted across his face. Then he shook himself, as if trying to knock loose the grip of a spitefully stubborn memory.

Echo wanted to ask him if he'd been allowed outside during his captivity, if he'd felt the warmth of daylight on his skin or if he'd seen the sky, but she kept her queries to herself. If there was anything Caius felt obliged to share with her, he would share it in his own time.

"How are you holding up?" she asked. General questions seemed safe.

He heaved a weary sigh before answering. "Well enough. Violet healed most of the cuts on my arms. The blade was plain steel. Unenchanted. That helped. Wounds inflicted with magic are harder to heal."

Well enough to get through today and maybe even tomorrow. Well enough to stand on his own two feet and do what needed to be done, like a good soldier.

"So, terrible, then," Echo said.

This time, Caius's grin had some life. There was a ghost of his true smile in it. "Am I so transparent?"

"Only to me."

The moment stretched between them in a thick, meaningful silence. Something in Caius began to loosen, as if the earlier stiffness Echo had noticed was working its way out of his system. He didn't have to pretend around her. She knew too much. She and Rose.

Neither Echo nor Caius acknowledged this revelation. It didn't need to be said. It was simply the truth, and it allowed Caius to let go of the tension he held so tightly.

"We should go back," he said. "Before they send out a search party."

"Mother Hen would be most displeased," said Echo. She wanted so badly to see that smile again, to know that he was wounded but not broken.

It flashed across his face for the briefest moment before he schooled his features into something more staid. "Come," he said, offering her his hand. His skin felt feverish to the touch, but Echo knew that was his normal temperature. "They're updating the map and managing to work together without killing each other. It's all very impressive, but I don't know how long it'll last."

It lasted longer than Echo would have thought possible. Though the alliance was heavily skewed toward the Avicen, most of them had come around to having the Drakharin present. Echo thought it was hard for them to hold on to their animosities after they had watched Caius spill his blood to protect them. Dorian had carved a niche for himself when he'd been at Avalon and earned the Avicens' grudging respect. Echo had had precious little time with Helios, but if Ivy trusted him, that was good enough for her.

With a frustrated sigh, Echo knocked her head against the wooden backrest of the chair she'd claimed at the table. Across the table's surface lay a larger, more detailed version of the map she had carried in her backpack. Black markers had been placed on the two seals they'd managed to close, while ten red markers remained dispersed across the continents. The sheer amount of work ahead of them— coupled with the ever-present danger of travel through the in-between—was enough to make her head throb. Even if mages closed the seals with vials of Caius's blood, there was nothing stopping Tanith from tearing open more. She didn't seem to need Caius to do so anymore. Either she'd siphoned enough of Caius's magic, as he suspected, or the kuçedra was strong enough to open the seals on its own. Neither possibility filled Echo with much hope. Closing the seals was a losing battle, but at the moment, options were less than abundant.

Sage had led the meeting, with Violet and Caius taking point. They'd discussed additional guards for the mended seals and the unbroken ones Tanith either hadn't discovered or simply hadn't gotten around to breaking yet. Ivy brought news of more Avicen refugees filling the halls of Avalon Castle. Word of its wards had spread far and wide, and anyone with a shred of sense knew there was a clash brewing, a game-ending battle between the firebird and the kuçedra. Everyone wanted to be behind those wards when it happened. Dorian updated the group on the progress of his agents working to undermine Tanith's power base at Wyvern's Keep and the likelihood of Drakharin reinforcements. Barring some kind of miracle, they were unlikely to arrive anytime soon. Echo had drifted in and out of consciousness, lulled into a half-dozing state by listening to plans she couldn't help but find tedious.

The black mark on her chest itched. She rubbed at it through her sweater, but that only made it worse. Ivy shot her a curious look across the table. "Mosquito bite," Echo whispered. A small white lie to mask a big black scar.

"That about covers it," Sage said, resting her hands on the table. Even she was beginning to show signs of exhaustion. Violet rubbed soothing circles into her back. "We set out for the next seal tomorrow. Our scouts will report back with any unusual activity near their assigned seals, but if we're lucky, Tanith will take a night off. Gods know we could use one. There's dinner near the fire at the center of camp. Eat well and rest up. We have a long day ahead of us tomorrow."

One by one, they left, until only Echo, Ivy, and Caius remained. "You coming?" Ivy asked.

"I'll catch up," Echo said. "I need a minute."

Ivy shrugged. "Suit yourself. I'll save you some food. Those Warhawks eat like wild dogs." She left without a second glance.

Caius lingered. "Is everything all right?"

Echo smiled, hoping her expression didn't betray her. The black mark felt hot. She had snuck a peek down the front of her sweater after leaving the second seal. Either she was hallucinating or the mark had grown larger. She needed to double-check. Not that there was anything she could do about it. Still, their lives were hard enough without this hanging over their heads.

"I'm fine," Echo insisted. Another lie. Soon she'd be buried under a mountain of them. "Go eat. You need it."

Caius nodded, not like he was convinced but like he was giving in. "Find me later," he said.

"I will," Echo replied. "I promise."

As soon as he was gone, Echo claimed one of the lanterns holding down a corner of the map and found a room with a half-broken mirror mounted over a rusted metal sink. There was no lock on the door, so she shoved a chair under the knob.

She stripped to the waist and stood before the mirror. Black veins branched away from the mark over her heart, snaking around her rib cage and reaching nearly to her stomach. If they spread a few inches upward, they would reach her clavicle and be visible above the neckline of her sweater.

"Shit," she said, tracing the thin black lines with an unsteady hand.

The mark had nearly doubled in size since it first appeared, after she fought Tanith at Avalon. The growth hadn't been immediate. Only in the past few days, since the first seal, in the rain forest, had it changed.

Tell someone, came Rose's voice.

"I can't," Echo told her reflection.

She pulled her sweater back on, shoved her arms through the sleeves of her leather jacket, and left the mirror and its unwelcome truth behind.

The sight that greeted her at the center of camp was one she would have thought impossible just months ago. Avicen and Drakharin working together. Both accepting her as one of their own. Ivy called Echo over and handed her a plate heaped with roasted meat and vegetables. Echo accepted it with a smile, ignoring the inquisitive glance Caius shot her. She would tell him. Soon. Eventually. Maybe. But not now.

Now they needed her to be a hero. To be the firebird. To be the one thing around which they found the strength to rally. The image of the prayer beads around Sage's wrist flitted through her mind. She couldn't let them down. No matter what it cost her.

CHAPTER THIRTY-FOUR

Sweat trickled down Ivy's back, making the thin cotton shirt stick to her skin. Autumn in Iceland was colder than she had expected, and relentlessly dark. Blink and you miss the sunlight, Echo had said. But here, in this room, there was nothing but the overbearing heat of the fire and the foreign weight of the blade in Ivy's hand. She tightened her grip on the hilt and stared down the blade at Helios's grinning face. A stray feather escaped from the loose ponytail she had put her hair-feathers into, but she wouldn't risk bringing her free hand up to push it from her forehead. One wrong move and Helios would exploit the distraction and bring her down. She would not let him disarm her. Not again.

His grin turned feral and he leaped at her. His movements were so quick, so efficient—not a single one was telegraphed. He was in one place and then, all of a sudden, he was someplace else. Ivy barely had time to react. She pivoted on the balls of her feet, keeping her weight light, remembering everything Helios had taught her about balance. A hand shot out to grab the wrist of her knife hand, but she twisted away just in time. Fingers brushed against her skin without finding purchase. She basked in a brief moment of elation before realizing the move hadn't been an honest attempt at disarming her. It was a feint.

Her back collided with a broad chest as arms came up to encircle her, pinning both her arms to her sides. She still had a firm grasp on the knife, but it was useless. She fought against the hold, but she might as well have been trying to break free from a cage of solid steel, for all Helios budged. Warm breath ghosted over her ear as he chuckled, low and dangerous, his chest rumbling with laughter.

"Got you," he said. "Again."

Ivy spat a curse in the most wicked Avicet she knew. It didn't have a direct English translation, it was so vile. Helios laughed again. "Such language," he said. "Wouldn't have expected something so filthy from the mouth of a dove."

That's it.

Ivy slammed her heel down on his instep. His arms loosened but didn't release her. It was just enough slack for her to maneuver one arm forward and drive her elbow, with all the force as she could muster, into his solar plexus. She felt as much as heard the air rush out of Helios. In the fraction of a second it took for him to recover, Ivy had dropped down, knees bent, and slipped out of the prison of his arms.

Momentum propelled her around to face him. She rose, the knife in her hand pointing up, up, up until she felt the tip of it press against his sternum. One good hard push would plunge it through his flesh and into a vital organ.

Helios stilled. They stood frozen like that, the only movement the rise and fall of their chests. His golden eyes locked on Ivy's, warm with pride.

"Very good," he said. "You could have killed me had you wanted to."

Ivy kept her blade pressed to his sternum. It took some effort to keep her voice as free of strain as his; he was a trained fighter and in much better shape than she was. "You goaded me on purpose, didn't you?"

His smile widened. "Maybe." He raised his eyebrows and dropped his gaze to the hand holding the knife. "Do you plan to eviscerate me?"

"Not today." Ivy lowered the weapon and took two very deliberate steps back. She felt more confident in her footing than she had the day before. It was progress, certainly, but though she was loath to admit it, she knew there was no way she had bested a Firedrake in fair combat. "You let me win."

"I did no such thing," Helios said. With a flick of his wrist, he pushed the hair off his forehead. He'd barely broken a sweat. Ivy tried not to hate him for it.

She gave him her best dubious glare.

His expression turned momentarily bashful. "All right, I may have gone a little easy on you."

"I'm never going to learn how to defend myself if you don't take this seriously."

"I do." He held out one hand and, after a brief staring contest, Ivy placed the knife in his upturned palm hilt-first. It disappeared into the sheath on his belt with practiced ease. "But you also wouldn't learn if I trounced you every time. You need to know what it feels like to succeed." Helios winked at her, and despite her annoyance, it sent her heart aflutter. "Even if I have to help you along sometimes."

"Not that I don't appreciate the sentiment," Ivy said, "but is that really the best way to impart your wisdom? Cheating?"

"It isn't cheating. I'm teaching you a valuable skill. I'm not trying to break your spirit."

Ivy remained unconvinced. It must have shown on her face—which was probably an embarrassing shade of red from exertion—because Helios's expression softened. He toyed with the chain at his neck as if it was bothering him. Maybe sweat was making it chafe. "Do you trust me?" he asked.

Her answer came without a pause. "Of course I do."

"Then accept that I know what I'm doing. You're not the first person I've trained. I used to work with fresh recruits, and trust me, you're a far better pupil than a great many of them." He offered her his hand just as he did at the end of every lesson. "Good fight."

His skin was unbelievably warm against her own. Echo had mentioned that increased body heat was a Drakharin thing—a biological quirk, nothing more—but the heat of Helios's hand in Ivy's made her cheeks flush. Hopefully, the blush blended with the exercise-induced one already staining her skin. She had logged several shameful defeats during their lesson—excepting her most recent, assisted victory—and quite frankly, she didn't need any more humiliation in her life.

"Thanks." Ivy extricated her hand from his and made her way to the corner of the room, where she'd left two water bottles. She handed one to Helios and downed the other in short order. The camp had no electric light, so they relied strictly on lanterns and fireplaces for illumination. It would have been cozy if she hadn't spent the past hour sweating her brains out.

She caught her breath while she watched Helios carefully put away the weapons they'd been using. In the absence of proper training equipment, he'd gone straight for the real deal. There were no blunted tips on the swords and knives available at the camp. They had to travel light, and that meant bringing only what was essential. Practice weapons didn't make the cut. At first, Ivy had been wary of handling a blade sharp enough to kill, but she soon realized the only way she would ever land a fatal blow on Helios was if he let her.

"Thanks," she said when he'd finished tidying up. There was a small stack of steel blades in one corner. The room had been designated as a training area, but Ivy hadn't seen anyone use it besides Helios and herself. She probably needed more practice than anyone. Avicen healers rarely fought. While they would wade into battle alongside their warrior counterparts, they carried no weapons, only the tools of their vocation. Some had rudimentary combat training, but most eschewed such things in favor of pursuing further knowledge of their craft. Ivy had never truly entertained the idea of learning to fight—not until she knew what it felt like to be helpless. She didn't relish the thought of feeling that way again. Ivy didn't know what awaited them at the location of the next seal on the map. It could be nothing. It could be a very dangerous something. All she knew was that if someone wanted to hurt her, she would make them earn it.

"It's no trouble." Helios raked a hand through his black

hair. He didn't appear to be as out of breath as Ivy, but she enjoyed the fact that she'd managed to make him look at least a little disheveled. "Training you is the least I can do. I have much to make up for, after all."

Ivy went to take another sip from her water bottle before remembering she'd finished it. Helios offered her his. She accepted it. "Thanks," she said. "But what do you mean, you've got a lot to make up for?"

An inscrutable look flickered across his face. "I pledged my loyalty to Tanith, even though I knew what she was capable of. The Dragon Prince—Caius—wasn't always popular with the nobility, but I knew why they elected him. He's a good man. Tanith . . . well, no one ever said anything like that about Tanith. And still, I followed her."

Ivy reached for him without thinking. Touching while sparring was one thing. Casual touch was something else altogether. Helios's gaze bounced from the hand she'd placed on his arm to her face. Whatever he saw in her expression made him smile, but it didn't quite reach his eyes. "But you're here now," Ivy said. "Whatever you did before—whatever you were before—none of that matters. Your past doesn't define you."

"If only that were true," he said sadly. "Not that I don't appreciate the sentiment." He smiled again as he delivered her own words back to her. "It's just . . . being around people like Dorian and Caius has reminded me of what we should be, of what the Drakharin could be. For so long, we've prided ourselves on being strong and ruthless and vicious, and where has that gotten us? We live on an isolated patch of land in the middle of nowhere, and the ones not lucky enough to be granted residency at Wyvern's Keep or any of our other strongholds live like rats scurrying away whenever humans get too close."

"You're starting to sound like Tanith," said Ivy. She regretted it when Helios's expression turned sour. "I didn't mean—"

"No," he interjected. "You're right. A part of me—a very small part—understands her motivation, but I don't agree with what she's doing." His brow furrowed. "It's important to me that you know that."

Ivy gave his arm a gentle squeeze. "I do. And it's important to me that you know that you're a good person, too. I don't like watching my friends beat themselves up."

Helios canted his head to the side, studying her. "Is that what we are? Friends?"

The question disarmed Ivy as effectively as Helios did during their lessons. Of course they were friends. They hadn't known each other very long, but extraordinary circumstances such as theirs had a tendency to bring people together. When life-and-death situations trimmed the fat off one's interactions, friendships had a way of forging themselves in the fire.

"Yes," Ivy said with absolute certainty.

Helios huffed a little laugh. "Well then, I will try my utmost to be worthy of your friendship."

Ivy started to draw back the hand that still rested on Helios's arm, but he caught it with both of his own. His gaze dropped. Dark lashes fanned across his cheeks, a stark contrast to his pale skin. It was not quite as white as Ivy's, which could be described without hyperbole as snowy, but almost human-pale. Even his scales were faint, practically invisible against his slightly flushed cheeks. Maybe she'd given him a better workout than she realized.

"It means more to me than you know," Helios said, "that you offer someone like me your friendship so readily. Especially when I don't deserve it."

Ivy didn't know where this bout of self-flagellation was coming from, but she'd heard enough. "Hey, you saved my life. If it hadn't been for you, I never would have made it out of Wyvern's Keep alive. Tanith would have burned me at the stake and roasted marshmallows on my smoking corpse."

Helios grimaced. "Not a visual I needed."

Ivy forged on. "I believe in you. Even if you don't, I do."

He didn't look comforted, but a little lost, as if her words had unmoored him. With her free hand, Ivy reached up to cup his cheek. Her touch startled him out of his daze, and his eyes shot up to meet hers. Ivy didn't remember stepping closer, into his space, but she must have. Helios breathed in deeply and his chest brushed hers ever so slightly.

"Why?" His voice was soft, the word more breath than sound.

Ivy shrugged. "I just do."

He shook his head, covering her hand with one of his. "I never thought I'd meet someone like you."

"And I never thought I'd have a Drakharin teaching me how to fight with knives."

Helios smiled, his tongue darting out to lick his bottom lip. The fire dried out the air, chapping his lips in the process. Ivy was riveted by the sight. Her brain felt sluggish in a way that was not even remotely related to her physical fatigue.

They were so close. Close enough to kiss.

Ivy had never kissed a boy before. Or a girl. Well, Echo, once, but that was more of a peck, and it was during a game of spin the bottle, so she wasn't sure that really counted.

Helios was looking at her lips. Perhaps he had noticed her looking at his and was reacting accordingly. Perhaps she had something on her face and he was looking at that. A dozen possibilities to explain the way he was gazing at Ivy flurried through her mind.

Maybe he wanted to kiss her. Maybe this was a good moment. Maybe the more she stood there, silent and still, the further away the moment got. Ivy knew, distantly, that something in her brain had short-circuited.

"We shouldn't," Helios said, making absolutely no attempt to move away. Ivy's heart didn't plummet, it only sank a little.

"Yeah," she agreed, not meaning it at all. "Probably not."

With painful slowness, Helios began extricating himself from her. She tightened her grip on his hand as she spoke. "Except . . ."

"Yes?"

"We could die tomorrow."

He nodded. "Very true."

Ivy swallowed. Her throat was very dry. As if she hadn't just drunk one and a half bottles of water. "Please."

Another nod. "As you wish."

Helios inclined his head as Ivy rose up on her toes. He brought their clasped hands up between them so that he was supporting her weight against his chest. When his lips brushed hers, she thought she might explode in a fury of feathers and flame.

Ivy had always wondered what the big deal was. Now she knew.

Kissing Helios was nothing like what she had imagined. And, oh, how she had imagined it. It wasn't passionate and demanding, as it had been in her fantasies. It was sweet. And soft. And she never, ever wanted it to stop.

His hands came to rest on her hips, tentatively, as if unsure of their welcome. She took a tiny step forward, closing the already slim distance between their bodies. Helios was warm, like the comforting heat of a roaring fire.

Ivy didn't know what to do with her hands. They fluttered at her sides before moving of their own accord, first to skim the fine bones of Helios's wrists, then over the corded muscles of his forearms, around the curves of his elbows. Her hands paused on the swell of his biceps. That was a fine place to leave them.

His mouth slid away from hers. He placed a light kiss against the corner of her lips, then another one on her cheek, right below her eye. When she blinked, she could feel her eyelashes brushing against his skin. She had never been more aware of her body than at that moment.

Teeth scraped her bottom lip, and all rational thought fled.

Far too soon, Helios pulled away, his golden eyes glazed over.

"Thank you," he said.

"You're welcome," Ivy replied, blinking away her stupor.

So that was what all the fuss was about.

He smiled, and it was such a lovely smile Ivy wanted to smack it off his face. No one should smile like that. It should be illegal.

"I'm going to go find a shower," he said.

Oh. That wasn't a visual she was going to complain about. Ever.

She watched him leave, her heart drumming an irregular beat inside her chest. She was finally beginning to understand why people got so stupid around people they liked. Wiping the sweat from her brow, she left the room, pointedly choosing the opposite direction from the one Helios had taken. If she followed him, she couldn't trust what she might do. If they lived through this, there would be time enough for that nonsense. *If* they lived through this. It was a sobering thought, but not even the notion that death might find them tomorrow was enough to dispel the effervescent cloud of joy that enveloped Ivy all the way to her room.

CHAPTER THIRTY-FIVE

Echo rolled the tin of healing balm Ivy had given her between her palms. The metal was cold against her skin, and its contents would remain solid until her body heat warmed them up. She felt her cheeks redden as she remembered the conspiratorial look on Ivy's face when she had pressed the tin into Echo's hands and said, "For the wounds on his back. You'll enjoy applying it more than I would."

And that was why Echo found herself standing in front of the door to the room that Caius had claimed for himself. She had just raised her fist to knock when she heard an indistinct curse come from the other side of the door. She didn't know what exactly Caius had said, but she knew that it was in Drakhar and that he sounded like he was in pain.

Echo pushed open the door and poked her head inside. "Everything all right?"

Laughter bubbled up in her throat at what she saw.

Caius was trapped inside his sweater.

His raised arms were held captive by the sleeves, and his voice was muffled by a layer of wool over the lower half of his face. "Everything is perfectly fine."

That he managed to deliver such a statement with unflagging dignity was impressive in its own right. He turned away from Echo as he attempted to extract himself from the sweater, and her laughter came to an abrupt halt.

She understood then how he had become entangled in his own clothing. The angry welts on his back had scabbed over, but the scabbing had tightened the skin. Caius's movements were restricted lest he open the healing wounds and start them bleeding anew.

He paused when he noticed Echo's silence. "Is it that bad?"

Echo nodded before realizing he couldn't see it. "Yeah," she said. "It looks even worse now than it did when . . ."

When she had found Caius, chained up and left for dead by Tanith. The remainder of her sentence went unspoken. Some things didn't bear repeating, not when the wounds were—literally—so fresh.

"Let me help you," said Echo. That was why she had come to find him, after all.

Caius did not protest as she gently liberated his arms from their woolen prison. As carefully as she could, she slipped the sweater over his head, wincing in sympathy as he let out another string of Drakhar curses. She understood a few of them from the handful of profane phrases Dorian had taught her during their time in hiding. Some of them were truly filthy.

"I'm shocked and appalled to find a prince with such a

deplorable potty mouth," she said, feeling neither shocked nor appalled.

His laugh was laced with a twinge of lingering pain. "I was a soldier before I was elected prince," he said. "You learn all the best turns of phrase in the barracks, I assure you."

He stood before her, bare-chested, without the slightest hint of self-consciousness. It wasn't until he cleared his throat that Echo realized she had been staring.

Heat crept up the back of her neck as she pulled her gaze away from the expanse of tanned skin in front of her. She looked up and found Caius looking back at her, his green eyes dark. A slight but undeniable smirk danced at the corners of his lips. She wanted to insist that it wasn't simply his physique that had overwhelmed her. The long red scars that crisscrossed his torso were hypnotic in their awfulness. But her momentary lapse seemed to amuse him, and it would have been unkind to tell him she was gawking at the evidence of his sister's cruelty. That was what Echo told herself as she held up the tin of healing balm like a shield between them.

"I got this from Ivy," she said. "It's for your back." *And your front.*

Caius plucked the tin from her hands and opened it. He sniffed the gelatinous goo inside. "Not bad," he said. "These things tend to have a rather unappealing odor about them."

"It's the crushed mint," Echo supplied. "Ivy uses it to mask the stench."

Caius hummed in agreement. "Will you help me put it on?"

Oh, gods have mercy.

"Yes." Echo was proud of the fact that she managed to speak the word like a sane human being instead of squeaking it. And she was even prouder that she hadn't said "Please."

He's in pain, she reminded herself. *You unbelievable letch.*

Caius sat on the edge of the bed, one leg dangling off the side, the other folded in front of him. Echo settled behind him, keenly aware of the crumpled blankets and the closed door and the overall coziness of the room. A fire burned merrily in the small hearth set into the far wall, bathing the space in a soft amber glow.

Echo placed the open tin on the sheets beside her. She scooped up a generous glob with one hand. The balm was still cool, so she rubbed it between her palms to warm it. Caius's silence amplified the intimacy of the moment. Rarely did he allow himself to appear vulnerable in front of an audience, but he had shown no reluctance to bare his wounds to her eyes. Maybe it was because she had seen them before, and with him in a far worse state than he was in now. Or perhaps there was no artifice between them anymore. Once, he'd hid behind a mask, pretended to be someone he wasn't to trick Echo into trusting him. It had worked, for a time, but masks fell. They always did. The truth outed itself. The walls dividing them had crumbled, slowly, gradually. He knew that Echo possessed knowledge of him she shouldn't have—Rose's memories supplied her enough detail to fill in the gaps in her understanding of him—but there was something else there, something beyond her access to the firebird's vessels that had opened a channel between her and Caius. He had let her in. He'd let her see the parts of himself he'd kept hidden for so long, and in turn, she had opened up herself—through conversations shared under starlit skies and chaste touches that offered more comfort than she could possibly express. With Caius, Echo could be herself, not a symbol or a savior or a soldier. And with her, he didn't need to be a leader or a prince or a beacon of hope for his people. This room, with its messy bedding and crackling fire, was perhaps the only place in the world where the two of them could just *be*.

She brought her hands, shiny with balm, to his back. He flinched when she touched him, even though she was careful to place her fingers on a spot of unblemished skin first; then he relaxed with visible effort.

"Okay?" Echo asked. Her hands still rested on the curve of his shoulders on either side of his neck. She could feel the tension in his muscles even as he fought against it.

He nodded. "Okay."

She kept her touch light as she spread the balm over the worst of his wounds. Her fingers traced the abraded skin as if following a road map, starting from his shoulder blades and wandering down the column of his spine to the slight dip of his lower back.

It didn't take long for whatever herbs Ivy had mixed into the balm to work their magic. Caius's head drooped forward, and every now and then he exhaled soft sighs of relief.

Echo was only halfway done when he spoke. "Thank you."

Don't say any time. *Do* not *say* any time.

"Any time," she said.

A quiet chuckle made the muscles in his back twitch beneath her hands.

"Sorry." She winced. "That was crass."

He turned his head slightly so he could meet her eyes

over his shoulder. "Don't you dare apologize. I'm not made of stone. It's nice to feel appreciated."

Echo groaned. "You're enjoying this, aren't you?"

"Should I not be?"

"No," she grumbled, working the salve into a particularly nasty cut.

A tightening of his eyes was the only sign of discomfort he allowed himself. "Then I shall endeavor to behave in a more suitably somber fashion if it pleases the lady."

"Lady." Echo snorted. "You can take the urchin out of the street, but you can't take the street out of the urchin."

Another soft chuckle. "I'm sure we can make a proper lady of you yet. All we need is a nice frilly dress, a parasol, maybe a fan. A goat to sacrifice to the gods."

She slapped his unharmed shoulder as he laughed. A tiny snort might have escaped her.

"Make that two goats," Caius added.

"Shut up and let me work," Echo said. A lightness blossomed in her chest as the tension seeped out of the room. The warmth was pleasant, as was the company. It felt unbearably good to remember that not everything was war and death and loss. Echo wanted to bottle the moment and carry it with her so she could remind herself of that comforting truth when she needed it most.

Caius's head rolled forward as Echo dug her thumbs into a knot of muscle low on his back. Her efforts were rewarded with a grunt of pleasure as the knot loosened under her touch. A different kind of heat flared in her cheeks, this one having nothing to do with embarrassment.

"I knew you would come for me."

Caius's voice was so quiet she had to lean in to hear him. Her hands still against his back, the skin tingling from the salve. They were so close that the hairs at the nape of his neck stirred with her breath.

"No matter what Tanith did or where she took me, I knew you would find me."

Echo inhaled and exhaled slowly, mesmerized by the way his skin twitched as her breath hit it. "I was afraid I wouldn't," she said. "Or that I'd be too late and you would already be . . ."

Dead. She couldn't bring herself to say that. They had lost so much between the two of them that the mere thought of adding his name to the growing list of the fallen was too much to bear.

With careful movements, Caius turned to face her. She wondered if her expression mirrored his. It was open. Raw. His pupils were dilated, perhaps because of the dim light. Or perhaps they'd been like that because she'd been touching him. His eyes hid nothing from her. He reached for her hand, unbothered by the slippery balm coating her skin. His thumb worked circles into her palm, an echo of what she had done to the stiff muscles of his back.

This close, she could smell his skin, even with the thick, cloying scent of the balm. Oil, the kind she knew Dorian used to clean his weapons. A faint whiff of woodsmoke, probably from tending the fire in the hearth. Beneath that, the slightest hint of apples. She never knew where it came from, but it was always there.

Takuminarsivalliajuq, she thought. An Inuit word to describe a person who becomes more beautiful over time.

Nothing about Caius had changed intrinsically, but as Echo looked at him now, it was as if all the other times she'd looked at him didn't really count. He was different now. *She* was different.

From this distance, she could see each individual scale on his cheekbones. She could have counted them if she wanted to. They caught the light from the fire, glistening in a way that reminded her of stars dappling the surface of a lake. His lips parted on a long exhalation, drawing her eye.

"Caius . . ."

His eyes closed lazily when she said his name. He leaned in, his forehead coming to rest against hers. It would have been easy for him to close the space between them, to press his lips against hers. She wouldn't have resisted if he did. But he didn't.

Echo's heart beat so loudly in the quiet that she thought Caius could probably hear it.

"Thank you," he said again.

She knew he wasn't talking about the healing balm. He meant *Thank you for saving me. For not leaving me alone. For caring enough to come for me.*

How easy it would be to tell him. To pull back the curtain on the last secret she had: the mark with its branching shadows slithering beneath her skin. Unlike the other occurrences of the kuçedra's poison, this one did not transfer through touch. She had touched and been touched since then and no one had suffered for it. No one but her. It would be such a simple thing to lay herself bare before him now, when all artifice and armor had been stripped away.

She felt the mark pulsing with every beat of her heart.

She and Caius were both scarred, in their own ways. Echo recognized it in him because she knew what it felt like to feel cold inside. To be cut off from things other people took for granted: compassion, empathy, love. She knew the harsh bite of neglect. And she knew what it felt like to discover those things, to come to know, without a doubt, that there were people in the world who cared. Who loved her. Caius hadn't been truly alone, but a part of him had withered after Rose, like a garden without a soul to tend it.

For a while, they simply sat like that, breathing the same air. He wouldn't push. Wouldn't make demands. If the gap between them was to be closed, she would have to be the one to close it.

So she did.

Her lips brushed his softly, a tentative exploration. He stayed still, allowing her to angle her head just so, letting her direct the intensity of the kiss. She kept it light. He sighed, the feel of it tickling the sensitive skin of her mouth. His thumb continued to rub small circles on her palm, a counterbalance to the soft pressure of the kiss.

Echo had expected a spectral interruption in the form of Rose's presence at the back of her mind, but none came. She was alone in her head.

She pulled away, just enough to break the contact of their lips. When Caius leaned back, his movements a mirror of her own, her hand snaked up to rest on the back of his neck, keeping him close. He tensed, but didn't retreat another inch. Echo stroked the baby-fine hairs at the nape of his neck and felt him relax into her touch. His lashes fanned out against his cheeks, dark against his too-pale skin.

"Is this okay?" he asked softly.

"This is okay," she replied.

He let out a slow breath as he leaned into her. They held each other up like that for a while. Echo would have been perfectly content to stay that way. Or, better yet, to let her tired body tip to the side and sleep there, face to face, knee to knee. She remembered the way he had rolled into her side when she'd crawled into his bed the night they had rescued him from the ruined temple. After weeks—months—of danger and gut-churning terror, it had been the first bit of peace she'd known. She wanted to feel that again. She wanted *Caius* to feel that again.

She pressed her lips to his, deepening the kiss. His hands found her waist, pulling her closer. With a shaky exhalation, he broke the kiss. His lips trailed over her cheekbone, along the curve of her jaw. They found her neck and the fluttering pulse there. She spared a moment's thought for the black mark hidden beneath her shirt, but she couldn't bring herself to care.

BANG.

The sound of the door crashing open had them both jumping away from each other, like guilty children caught with their hands in the cookie jar.

Dorian stared at the two of them in dismay. A feathered head poked over his shoulder.

"I knew it," Jasper hissed. "You owe me five bucks."

"Can I help you?" Caius asked, remarkably casual, considering where his lips had just been.

Echo flushed scarlet.

"It's Tanith," Dorian said, finding his composure. In his hand he cradled a pendant, one side a mirrored surface, covered in smeared blood. "Our contacts at the keep have sent a call for help. Caius, she's massacring them. We have to go back. Now." Dorian started to exit, but then turned back. "If you want to try to get her blood, this is the best chance we're going to get."

CHAPTER THIRTY-SIX

Caius stepped through the massive archway in the center of Wyvern's Keep, and his chest seized up. He had the barest of moments to appreciate the arch's soaring architecture—the two iron dragons with upraised heads meeting in the center, bellies burning with crackling braziers—before the guards registered his presence. They stared at him dumbly for a handful of seconds before one of them had the wits enough to press the edge of his sword to Caius's throat. It was remarkably sloppy. He'd have to remember to see them properly chastised for their sluggish reaction time later. When the dust settled. And if he was still alive.

A smirk stole across Caius's lips as he remembered explaining his plan to Echo.

"I'm not going to storm the keep," he'd told her. "Those walls have withstood countless assaults for a thousand years, and they're not about to fall to a ragged force of Avicen and

Drakharin who can only just barely work together without falling at each other's throats."

"Then how do you plan to get in?" she asked.

"The front door," Caius said, as if it weren't an insane thing to say.

"You're just going to walk in like you own the place?"

At that, Caius smiled, sharp and wicked. "Indeed. Technically, I do own the place. It *is* the Dragon Prince's official residence, after all."

When in doubt, Echo liked to say, bravado. It was a lesson Caius had absorbed well.

Their numbers were small, but if Caius couldn't pull off what he was about to attempt on his own, then it wouldn't matter if he showed up with an army at his back. Dorian's presence was a given. Echo's was a bonus—how marvelous it would be to sweep into his old home, the one that had been stolen from him, with the firebird at his back—but Ivy's insistence on accompanying them was a surprise.

"After your previous experiences with Drakharin hospitality, I didn't think you'd ever want to set foot within those walls again," Caius had said, the pouch of shadow dust heavy in his hand.

Ivy had tipped her chin in Echo's direction. "Where she goes, I go."

And that was that. The four of them had escaped the keep all those months ago, and now they were waltzing right back into it. There was a beautiful symmetry to it, rounding out the madness of Caius's plan.

Caius stood, his hands at his sides. The knives Dorian had given him were strapped to his back, but they remained sheathed. The guards were startled enough; it wouldn't do to start a fight before he'd even set foot through the door. That would vastly complicate his plan to get to the great hall—and the throne it contained—with minimal bloodshed.

"Halt," said the guard in Drakhar. She wasn't wearing Firedrake armor, which was a minor blessing. If she had been one of Tanith's, then Caius likely wouldn't have lived long enough to see her cast a look over his shoulder, where Dorian and Echo stood, the former with his sword drawn, ready to fight. Anything less would not have befitted the captain of his guard.

"I've halted," Caius said, in Drakhar for the guards' benefit. "Though I can say this is a warmer welcome than I expected. Much appreciated."

The second guard circled to Caius's left side, where Dorian stood. Neither one of them would have been much of a match for Caius or Dorian alone, but they were Drakharin soldiers, and they would do what they had been trained to do. If Caius started slashing, they would stand their ground or die trying. Perhaps they weren't as hopeless as their initial bewilderment suggested. Fortunately for them, Caius had no intention of decorating the chamber's tiles with their blood. Not if he could help it.

The sharp steel against his throat was a steady presence, neither pressing down nor retreating. "I . . . You . . . What . . . ?" The guard's sword was steady, but her words were not.

"Let me guess," Caius said. "Your new Dragon Prince didn't give you specific orders about what to do if I sauntered through the keep's front door as if I didn't have a care in the world?"

The guards shared a look. It was clear the answer was no.

"Caius," Dorian breathed behind him. "We have to keep moving. Let's dispatch them and go. The longer we remain here, the more likely it is we'll be discovered by—"

Caius held up a hand and Dorian fell silent. The sword at his throat quivered. He met the eyes of the guard before him, and her brow furrowed. The blade steadied, but her expression betrayed her. Every ounce of indecision she felt was written across her face as plain as day.

"Tell me, soldier." Caius pitched his voice low and even. "Do you plan to slit my throat?"

The guard swallowed. She was young and untried and hadn't been in armor long, judging by the metal's distinct lack of scuffs or dents. Even the most lovingly maintained armor showed wear as time went on. Hers gleamed brilliantly in the light of the braziers.

"I've watched you in the training yard," Caius continued when she didn't answer. "You drop your right shoulder when you lunge. It leaves you open."

"Is that a threat?" asked the second guard. He was a burly fellow, much larger than his partner but just as young and inexperienced.

"Hardly," Caius replied. "Consider it a bit of helpful advice. If we're going to fight here and now, I want you at your best."

The first guard shook her head, perplexed. "Standing orders are to detain you if you're sighted." She nodded at Echo. "Same with her."

Echo's willingness to remain silent reached its limit. "What did Tanith say about me? Tell me. Was it mean? Is she talking smack?"

"Her orders are to capture you," Caius explained. "And me."

"Oh, I'd like to see her try," Echo said.

"I'm sure you would." Caius chanced a look at Echo, willing her to put away her claws. "But I don't think that will be necessary." He turned back to the guard. "And what of Dorian?" he asked, mostly out of curiosity. "What was to be his fate?"

"Standard kill order. No detainment. No interrogation."

Naturally. He heard Dorian scoff behind him.

"Then we are at a crossroads, are we not?" Caius held his hands out in front of him, wrists pressed together. "Clap me in irons." He let a whisper of a smile dance across his lips. "If you can."

Again, the guard shot a helpless look at her partner. She licked her lips nervously. "We heard about the dragon," she said.

Just as he had hoped. Dorian had made sure to spread the word to their contacts within the keep. The gossip mill worked overtime in a world as insular as theirs. Even the simplest stories could grow to be myths, given enough time.

"What exactly have you heard?" he asked.

"That you tamed it," the guard said. "That it listened to you."

"Ah, that sounds like the stuff of legends, does it not?"

She nodded. Her blade lowered an inch so it was hovering closer to Caius's collarbone than his jugular vein. A marked improvement.

"It's said the princes of old called dragons to do their bidding," said the guard. "That they used to be chosen by the dragons to rule."

"Divine mandate from a dragon god," said Caius. "What a thing that would be."

Another nod. Slowly, the blade lowered until it was pointing at the floor.

"What are you doing?" hissed the second guard. He took his eyes off Dorian to glare at his partner. It was a mistake he would make only once.

Dorian was on the man before he had time to react. A standard-issue longsword clattered to the floor as the man's knees thudded to the ground, the sound of armor hitting marble cacophonous in the high-ceilinged chamber. Dorian had his own sword to the man's throat, cutting off the shout of protest before it fully left his mouth.

Caius tsked.

"I'm not going to fight my prince," the first guard told her partner. "The dragon chose him, Amon. I'm not stupid enough to ignore that."

"It's just a story, Kora."

"I suppose," Caius interrupted, "you have to ask yourself how much stock you put in the old stories. And how much faith you put in me. Or in Tanith."

At that, even the second guard quailed.

"You have seen her," Caius said. "You know what she has done. And what she's doing right now."

The first guard—Kora—nodded. There was a haunted look in her eyes, as if she'd seen some of Tanith's more grue-some acts closer than she ever wanted to. Perhaps she had exiled herself to gateway guard duty, the farthest from the throne one could get while remaining in the keep.

"You have a choice," Caius said. "Let me pass, or die fighting for a prince you never elected and don't respect."

Kora took a tentative step back, but she didn't put up her sword. It remained in her white-knuckled grip. "She'll kill me if she finds out."

Of that, Caius had no doubt. His sister had had little capacity for forgiveness even before she'd bound herself, body and soul, to a beast of shadow and suffering.

"If you fail," the guard continued, "we die."

Caius took a few brisk steps toward the chamber's exit. Neither guard made a move to stop him. He gestured for Dorian and Echo and Ivy to follow. When he reached the door, he turned and met the guard's gaze. "Then I will not fail."

The guard inclined her head in a shallow nod of acknowledgment. Almost as an afterthought, she clapped her right fist to her heart. It was an old gesture, rarely used among the Drakharin but known to all of them. It was a salute. A sign of recognition, of respect. Of fealty. Of faith.

Caius accepted it with a nod. As he threw open the heavy wooden doors leading deeper into the keep, he prayed to the gods that he would be worthy of all that gesture meant.

CHAPTER THIRTY-SEVEN

Caius knew the halls of Wyvern's Keep as intimately as if a map of the fortress had been etched into his bones. He had come to know its labyrinthine corridors as a child, chasing his sister and being chased in return. He had carved his name into the foundation, like so many young nobles before him, hoping to steal for himself a slice of its timeless strength, its eternal solidity.

That knowledge served him well now as he slunk through the keep's halls, silent as a mouse, danger humming through his veins.

"That was easy," Echo said, trotting to keep up with Caius's long strides. The corridor leading from the central gateway was empty, but their run of luck would not be infinite.

"It won't be, going forward," Caius said. "If they'd been Firedrakes, they would have sounded an alarm and put up a fight. We were lucky. Astonishingly so."

"And we won't be for much longer," Dorian said. He stopped and tilted his head, listening. "Boots. Three pairs. Heavy armor."

Firedrakes.

Caius drew his knives and strained to listen. He could hear them now, approaching from one of the service corridors branching off the main hallway. They were walking slowly, in no great hurry, unaware that the most wanted Drakharin in all the land was yards away. They would be in for an unpleasant surprise. "Echo, Ivy, stay out of the fight if you can."

His words were met with an unladylike snort. "Yeah, okay," Echo said. "Sure. No problem. I'll just pull up a chair and watch you slice and dice your way through the keep. Maybe make some popcorn. You don't happen to have a microwave in this musty castle, do you?"

She was rambling. She did that when she was scared. Caius wasn't sure she even realized it.

"Defend yourself if you must," said Caius, "but leave the fighting to us."

Echo opened her mouth to protest—as he knew she would—but he silenced her with his best stern look. He was only a little surprised it actually worked to quell her indignation.

"I've seen you in battle, Echo," Caius said. "I do not doubt your abilities, but I didn't bring you here to shed Drakharin blood. This has to be done a certain way."

It wouldn't do to have the firebird's formal introduction to his people involve her cutting them down with a magic they had believed was the stuff of fairy tales.

An unhappy frown stole across her face, but she nodded. "Got it. Consider this bird's wings temporarily clipped."

The trio of guards rounded the bend. Red cloaks. Golden armor. Firedrakes indeed. They charged, and Caius was ready.

They were disarmed easily enough. One fell beneath Caius's knives, the second succumbed to Dorian's brutal strikes, while the third threw down his sword and clasped his fist to his chest once he had seen Caius's face.

"She is in the throne room," the guard said in a quiet, tremulous voice. Fear flickered through his eyes. "Help us." And though begging was not the way of his people, the guard added, "Please."

Caius had simply nodded and accepted the man's surrender. With Dorian, Ivy, and Echo following close behind, Caius traversed the halls he knew so well, the guard's words an unnecessary guide.

Crumpled bodies—wizened with age and depleted of magic—lay strewn throughout the corridors and slumped over in stairwells. Servants and soldiers. Peasants and courtiers. His sister had not discriminated in her cruelty.

She had taken what she craved and left in her wake the empty husks of the people she should've protected.

Dorian whispered a prayer for the dead under his breath. Echo and Ivy fell into a sickened silence. Caius could only hope that when they reached their destination there would be someone left to save.

The throne room was awash with blood.

The bodies of the dead lay scattered about like a child's toys after a violent tantrum, while the living huddled against the walls, as far from the dais as they could get.

A trail of corpses led from the door to the gilded throne upon which Tanith sat, her bare arms crimson with blood, her smile as sharp as a blade. A figure knelt at her feet, its back to them. All Caius could see was a head of black hair and the red cloak of a Firedrake. Tanith raked her nails through the kneeling man's hair, the way one would absently pet a dog. A dozen Firedrakes stood at the foot of the dais, their faces hidden behind golden helmets.

"Hello, Brother," she said. It wasn't Tanith's voice. Something lurked behind it, something dark and awful. "Fancy seeing you here." She threw her arms wide. "Do you like what I've done with the place? I always thought it needed a splash of color." She canted her head to the side, her smile ticking farther up. "And you've brought friends. How lovely." She waggled her fingers in a mock wave. "Hello, little dove. Did you miss me so terribly that you simply had to come back?"

To her credit, Ivy didn't shrink from Tanith's unnerving gaze. Shadows shifted in Tanith's eyes, overwhelming the red of her irises. The monster within was chipping away the last vestiges of Caius's sister; it wouldn't stop until there was nothing left. Soon, Tanith would be as much of a husk as the broken bodies she'd left around the keep.

Tanith stood, sweeping her scarlet cloak to the side as she descended the dais steps. The hem was darker red than the rest of the cloak, and damp. Blood, probably. The Tanith Caius knew wouldn't have been caught dead in soiled armor off the battlefield. But now she was unkempt. Her hair was a tangled mess of bloody blond curls, her armor scuffed and stained. "How heroic you must feel, Caius. Coming to the rescue of this lot like some valiant prince straight out of a children's story." She stepped over the crumpled form of their former treasurer, Oeric. The medal of office still hung from his neck, resting against the fur lining of his tunic. They'd been a pair once, Tanith and Oeric. Now she moved around his body—Caius couldn't tell if the man was dead or just close—as if he meant nothing to her. "I had a feeling you might come."

"Is that so?" Caius tightened his grip on his knives. His magic had been returning slowly, but he was nowhere near fully recovered.

"Indeed." Tanith toed Oeric's boot. His foot flopped limply to the ground. "I knew there were holes. Places where information leaked. Spots where it filtered in, like an annoying drip that won't stop drip, drip, dripping. I tried to find out who our traitor was, but no one wanted to talk." She gazed at the mess she had made in the hall, at the lives she had ended in a fit of pique. "And I tried so hard to be persuasive. Fortunately, I had help."

She continued her approach and Caius stood his ground. The crowd behind Caius shifted in expectation. Anticipation clogged the air like a heady scent. When Tanith was about fifteen feet from him, she stopped, her brow furrowing. "It was a mistake to leave you there. To let you be found. Weak. Weak, weak, weak."

She turned away, raking her hands through her unruly hair. "But I couldn't do it. Wouldn't do it. Shouldn't do it. But it must be done. My last distraction. The final thread. The anchor. Not right. Wrong, all wrong."

"She's not talking to us, is she?" Dorian wondered aloud.

Caius shook his head. "Tanith!" he called.

Her head snapped around and she blinked, as if she'd forgotten they were there. Her eyes narrowed.

"Come here, pet," she said, snapping her fingers. A gold chain dangled from her other hand, a pendant swinging slightly with every movement she made. The kneeling figure, who had remained by the throne when Tanith had risen, stood and turned to face them.

Dorian let loose a string of curses in Drakhar, vicious enough to scald. Helios kept his eyes lowered, but there was no mistaking him. There he stood, in full Firedrake regalia. Those proud shoulders slumped in shame, and he refused to meet Caius's gaze. In the rush to leave for the keep, Caius hadn't given much thought to Helios's absence. There had been other things to consider, far more important than the whereabouts of a single soldier. When had Helios departed? How had no one noticed?

The same way you didn't, Caius's mind supplied. *You thought he was insignificant.*

"Helios?" Ivy's voice was so small, she doubted it carried far enough for him to hear her, but his head bowed, eyes closed, as if he had. "Tell me it's not true."

Helios opened his eyes and raised them to meet Ivy's. The guilt in his expression was unmistakable. His mouth opened and closed, but no sound emerged, as if he was too much of a coward to offer a response.

That unbelievable bastard.

"I trusted you," Ivy spat.

A cruel laugh erupted from Tanith. "That was rather the whole point," she said, her sharp voice slicing through the heavy pall of betrayal that had settled over Caius. "Do you think I was stupid enough to simply let you waltz out of my fortress with nary a scar to show for it? Did you honestly believe I was that startlingly incompetent?"

Tanith turned to Helios. A black-veined hand stroked his hair as if he were a well-behaved dog that had just performed an impressive trick. "You must have done an even better job than I anticipated. I had made it through only half the courtiers when he showed up, fresh from the little Icelandic hideout you thought I didn't know about, and told me everything." She held up the small pendant Dorian had sent Ivy into the keep with all those weeks before, one side mirrored and smeared with blood. "He even used this trinket that the little dove smuggled in to send you that message." She cupped Helios's cheek with one hand, her nails digging into his flesh. "Perhaps I was wrong to doubt you."

"No," said Helios, shaking his head. He shuddered at her touch, and even from a distance, Caius could see the resolve harden his yellow eyes. "You weren't."

Caius saw only the briefest flash of steel in the dim light before a knife plunged into the vulnerable sliver of exposed throat above the collar of Tanith's armor. Helios held on to the blade even after it sank to the hilt.

CHAPTER THIRTY-EIGHT

Tanith did not bleed.

Echo waited to see blood pooling around the wound, but none came.

Helios stared at the dagger as if it had betrayed him. He let go of it and stumbled back a step. Tanith wrapped her hand around the hilt and yanked the blade free, her breath gusting out in a relieved sigh, as if being stabbed were nothing more than a minor inconvenience.

The wound gaped. Something thick and viscous oozed from it, but it was not blood. Rivulets of black sludge pulsed from the tear in her skin, behaving nothing like blood from a fresh wound.

"What the fuck?" Echo whispered softly but with great feeling.

Caius shifted beside her, gripping his knives even tighter, for all the good they would do him. "My thoughts exactly."

Tanith flung the offending weapon away with a look

of disdain etched upon her fine features. "Little fox," she drawled, her blackened eyes seeking out Helios. "Has being my fox in the henhouse made you brave?"

Thick plumes of black smoke punched up from the ground around Helios, winding around his ankles and up his calves, holding him in place while Tanith advanced with measured steps. She flicked her hand, and the dark tendrils yanked him to his knees with a thud. Red-tipped fingers tapped his chin, angling his face up to meet Tanith's piercing gaze. Her hand ghosted gently over Helios's cheek before tangling in his hair and yanking his head back, baring the pale, vulnerable column of his throat.

"Betrayal. Betrayal everywhere I look." Tanith's eyes slid from Helios to Caius. "And this, too, will be washed away in blood and shadow. An end for a new beginning."

With that, she pulled Helios to his feet. "Enough of you." Her free hand balled into a fist and slammed into his breastplate, sending him flying into the far wall with a jangle of metal and the thick thud of flesh and bone against stone. He crumpled to the ground, limbs limp. Lifeless. Another broken doll in Tanith's collection.

Wiping her hands on her soiled cloak, Tanith turned back to face the others. Her brow pinched in thought and her head tilted to the side, as if she were listening to a song only she could hear.

"Caius," Echo whispered. "This isn't good."

He pushed her behind him, jaw clenched. "Stay back."

Echo tried to protest, but Dorian obeyed his prince and maneuvered Echo and Ivy behind him, keeping his own body between them and the watching Drakharin. An Avicen and a human running amok was perhaps too much additional excitement for them. "No." Dorian shook his head. "Not yet. Not unless he needs us."

"Are you insane?" Echo said. Tanith was stronger than they'd anticipated. Stronger than Echo, even with the power of the firebird flowing in her veins. They couldn't let Caius face her alone.

"He has to do this on his own," Dorian hissed.

Tanith shook her head. "And his story must reach its end, but I will not—*cannot*—be the one to end it. Better things to do. Bigger castles to crumble." She looked to her Firedrakes, still arrayed in an arc around the throne, as still as statues.

"Show my brother the mercy he deserves," said Tanith, her voice sounding more like her own than it had just minutes ago. The taint had receded from it, infinitesimally.

She turned her eyes—redder now, but no less vicious—to Caius.

"Kill him."

The words were a cruel taunt. An echo of something Caius had said months earlier, when faced with two Avicen prisoners at his mercy while his sister watched. The bloodlust had been strong in her even then, before the kuçedra had brought out the worst in her, watering her venom like a diligent gardener so that it could grow stronger than ever before.

In a swirl of scarlet wool and black smoke acrid with the stench of the in-between, Tanith was gone, whisked away to gods only knew where, while her hounds obeyed her command.

Show my brother the mercy he deserves.

Caius had half a second to appreciate the irony of being on the receiving end of those words before the Firedrakes rushed him, a solid wall of gold and crimson closing in, swords brandished.

His body moved before his mind had time to formulate a strategy, instinctively dropping into a defensive stance to steel himself against the first battering blows. There were a dozen of them, but they couldn't all come at him at once, blocked by each other's bodies as they were.

The gaze of the court beat down on him, brimming more with anticipation than fear now that Tanith was gone, an undeniable and unavoidable audience. But he didn't want to avoid them. He wanted them to watch. He wanted them to see what he was made of, to measure his mettle against those who would strike him down.

His knives found flesh, slipping between plates of armor, seeking out the weaknesses he knew he would find. An unprotected armpit. The bend at the back of a knee. The sliver of neck between breastplate and helm.

One fell. Then another. And another.

Three down, nine to go.

Caius's muscles sang with the effort of the dance. Despite the spider's web of old scars and new bruises traced across his body, he felt more alive than he had in weeks. Wondrously, marvelously *alive*. Sweat trickled down his spine and gathered at his temples, but it was nothing compared with how he made the Firedrakes work, transitioning them seamlessly from offense to defense as he hurled himself through the air, sliding beneath swinging swords and leaping over kicking legs. With his back to the wall, it was hard for them to surround him, and they bottlenecked in their approach, putting themselves at a disadvantage as Caius turned himself into a whirlwind of sharpened steel. He didn't need to think. Didn't need to plan. He simply needed to do what he had done so well for so many years.

Two centuries' worth of combat had honed him into something more than a man, more like a weapon. He spun the hilt of his dagger in his palm, bringing the pommel down on the head of the nearest Firedrake, who folded beneath the blow in a clatter of golden armor.

Four down.

The Firedrake collapsed against the legs of one of his compatriots, startling the man—he was too tall and broad of shoulder to be any of the women Caius knew to take up Tanith's banner—and that moment's break in focus was all Caius needed. He kicked the man's knee and was rewarded with a scream, which he silenced with a whisper of steel against the man's throat. Blood poured over the gilded breastplate, a richer red than the crimson of the Firedrake's cloak.

Five down.

Two of the Firedrakes broke away from the pack, trying to find a way to circle Caius. He dove as one of the remaining five found courage enough to attempt a head-on attack. Wood splintered behind him as the Firedrake's sword buried itself in one of the long tables that had been pushed to the side, no doubt to make room for Tanith's spectacle of depravity as she'd drained the magic from her own courtiers one by one. A Firedrake tripped over a corpse, cursing as he lost his footing and landed in the path of Caius's dagger.

Six down.

Halfway there.

Dorian was right. This was one battle Caius had to fight alone. Only he could prove to the people he had failed that he was worthy of their choice. That he was strong enough to keep them safe. They had known that once, but they had forgotten. And Caius had let them forget. Now was his chance to remind them.

Caius came up behind the Firedrake struggling to free his sword. His armor gaped beneath his arms and Caius buried his dagger there, slipping it free as the guard fell.

Seven down.

There was a place beyond pain, beyond sweat and blood, and that was where Caius pushed himself, deaf to the scream of his own muscles, of his body begging him to slow, to rest, to lay down his arms. His focus sharpened to a razor's edge as the crowd fell away, leaving only himself and his foes.

Lunge, parry, strike.

Dodge, dive, pivot.

Slash, stab, repeat.

Caius knew the steps of this dance by heart. Had fought against worse odds and triumphed. Certainty was a balm to his wounds, his sore limbs, his fevered skin, his aching lungs.

Another down. And another.

A pause as the remaining three Firedrakes withdrew, searching for a momentary respite and hoping Caius wouldn't follow. He saw their gazes rake across their fallen comrades, over the blood pooling around burnished armor. Red and gold, just like Tanith's colors. He wondered if they resented her for what she'd done. For leaving them here to die. He wondered if he cared.

There was no space left in him for mercy. He let them catch their breath while he caught his, but defeat was written in every inch of their bodies. Their stances were sloppy. Their swords were clean. He hadn't let them close enough to make even the tiniest nick, and he hadn't even worn proper plate. His armor was soft, made of leather supple enough to allow for unrestricted movement at the cost of protection. But Caius had not needed anything more than his wits and his skill. The asymmetry, he had no doubt, was not lost on their captive audience.

The Firedrakes never stood a chance.

Not against Caius.

Not against the rightful Dragon Prince.

Two of them darted forward, but the third dropped his weapon and fell to his knees in surrender. Caius would deal with him later.

Dispatching them was far less difficult than it should have been. Tanith—the true Tanith, not the poisoned monstrosity she had become—would have been so disappointed. They were tired and it showed. Evading them was easy. Caius barely had to sidestep their blows. Their swords glanced off his daggers, sparks rising off the clashing steel. His own blades found their weaknesses and exploited them with ease.

Within minutes, it was done. Their bodies lay at Caius's feet, as still as their fellows'.

The last Firedrake had remained on his knees as Caius had cut down his brothers. His head was bowed low, accepting of his fate.

Caius approached the kneeling Firedrake, stepping over bodies, both freshly fallen ones and desiccated husks.

He stood before the man, chest heaving. Now that his body wasn't in constant motion, the fight was beginning to take its toll. But he had to stay on his feet just a little longer.

"Remove your helmet," he ordered, his voice ringing across the hall's stones.

The Firedrake did as he was told, his hands steady. Admirable, in the face of death. He set the golden helmet on the ground beside him and waited.

"Give me your sword." Caius sheathed his own daggers despite the blood on their blades.

Again, the Firedrake obeyed Caius's command.

The sword was far heavier than Caius's own long knives, but it was much better suited to the task at hand.

There was only one way to deal with surrender among the Drakharin.

Caius hefted the broadsword, the muscles in his back burning with the effort. Gravity did half the work as Caius swung the blade down, severing the Firedrake's neck in a single clean swipe.

It was a quick death. A merciful death.

The sword clattered to the ground as it slipped from Caius's numb fingers. Exhaustion was catching up to him, and fast.

Just a little longer.

He turned to the assembled nobles. No longer were they huddled against the walls in fear of their prince. One by one, they dropped to their knees as his gaze raked over them. His eyes landed on Echo. Neither she nor Ivy knelt, which was fine. He wasn't their prince. Ivy's fair skin had a sallow tint to it, as if she was about to be sick. Echo's expression was inscrutable. If she disapproved of what she had just witnessed, she didn't show it.

Caius turned from them and let his feet carry him toward the throne. When he reached the dais steps, a movement off to the side caught his eye.

Helios.

He was alive, then. Not for much longer.

Caius withdrew one of the daggers from its sheath and approached Helios's prone form. He had moved, perhaps reflexively, but he was still now, his yellow eyes open and resting on Caius. Blood trickled from a laceration on his head, probably where his temple had struck the stone wall.

"Ivy!" Dorian called, but he was too late to stop her. She ran toward Caius, falling to her knees beside Helios.

The tip of Caius's knife tilted Helios's chin up, despite the pained whimper the motion caused. There was a commotion somewhere behind them.

Ivy swore and moved as if to grab the blade with her bare hand, but she thought better of it before touching the sharp edge of the knife. She settled for leveling a glare at Caius, which he ignored. Mercy was wasted on traitors. They had allowed this one into their lives, had trusted him. Helios had earned his pain.

"You know what has to happen." Caius modulated his tone carefully. He sounded dispassionate. Impartial. He felt anything but. It was, however, not a prince's place to show weakness in the face of treason. That would only invite more of it.

The blood was bright against Helios's fair skin, even in the dim light of the fire in the hall's sconces. Golden eyes stared up at Caius, tight with pain. Helios coughed, his spittle crimson. "I know what I did," he said once his voice returned to him. "And I know what you have to do."

It took Ivy a few seconds to put the pieces of their exchange together, but Caius saw the moment realization dawned. Her face fell and she shook her head, too rapidly. "No," she said. "You can't."

Oh, he could. And he would. "He betrayed me. He betrayed *us*. The punishment for such betrayal is death." He should have done it then, drawing the blade against the vulnerable triangle of skin that showed over Helios's armor at his neck. It would have been so easy. But there was something Caius needed to know first. "Why did you do it? Why spy for her?"

A sharp, aborted laugh spilled from Helios's blood-flecked lips. "Does it matter?"

"I suppose not," Caius replied. One swift flick of his wrist was all it would take. He tightened his grip on the hilt and prepared to strike.

A hand shot out, wrapping around the wrist of Caius's knife arm. "No," she said again. Her eyes, wide and watery, met his, and his resolve faltered. "Please. Not like this."

Ivy's phrasing was deliberate. She wanted Caius to feel like she was giving him an out. But there was nothing to be done. The boy had to die. His life in exchange for his honor. It was the Drakharin way. It always had been.

Ivy shook her head, tears falling freely now. A shaky hand reached up to wipe them from her cheek, but all Helios managed to do was smear his blood on her face. It looked like a gash on her cheek.

"Please, Caius." Her fingers trembled against his wrist,

but her grip stayed firm. "Please don't make me watch you kill him."

Caius looked between her pleading gaze and Helios's wilting one.

"Do it," Helios choked out in Drakhar. So Ivy wouldn't understand, Caius realized. "Don't drag this out any longer."

"He betrayed you most of all," Caius said to Ivy. "Why do you want me to spare him?"

She shook her head, pulling her bottom lip between her teeth as she fought to find her answer. "I don't want him to die" was all she said.

Helios coughed again, blood bubbling up from his ruined lungs, choking him. Tanith's strike must have broken a rib or three. One of them had probably pierced a lung. He was dying already. A knife across the throat would be a mercy. More than he deserved. But Caius relaxed his hold on his blade as he watched Helios's gaze slide from him to Ivy. The boy was no coward; he would face his death, knowing it was just, but he wanted one last look at Ivy before he went.

And it *was* the Drakharin way. But perhaps, Caius thought as he looked at Ivy, on her knees, begging for the life of someone who had brought her such pain, it didn't have to be. Perhaps there was another path, and he could be the one to forge it. He withdrew his knife, and Ivy sagged as her hand fell from his wrist.

"Thank you," she gasped.

Caius wanted to tell her it was more than a stay of execution, but the words stuck in his throat. It was too close to a lie. He was uncertain—not a feeling he relished. Showing mercy would compromise the position he had only just regained. He was within his rights to claim Helios's life here and now, but Drakharin law allowed for a trial to determine the matter of his guilt, as indubitable as it was. There would be voices among his own people to see the traitor delivered to a swift and final end. Helios's death might still loom in the not-too-distant future. But it would not come today.

Today, he was safe.

Caius hoped the boy knew Ivy had just saved his worthless life.

He left her to tend to Helios's wounds as he ascended the dais and stood before the throne he had lost.

And now he had reclaimed it.

He turned to face his people. They had voted against him once, either out of genuine belief in his sister or out of fear. None of that mattered now.

Now they knelt before him. The Dragon Prince once more.

He sank down onto the throne, hoping his fatigue didn't look as glaringly obvious as it felt.

The hall was a disaster. Blood and bodies everywhere. He couldn't undo the damage Tanith had done, but he could right the path she had put his people on.

Dorian stepped forward and spoke the words that would make Caius's ascension official.

"Does any among you object?"

Silence.

Dorian met Caius's gaze and nodded. It was done.

Caius leaned forward, elbows on his knees. He needed to rest. Soon. But he had one order of business that could not wait.

"By royal decree," he said, his voice resounding but still rough as gravel in his throat, "I hereby call an end to the war against the Avicen." A titter rose among the gathered nobles. Already they were complaining. Some things never changed. And some things had to, if any of them were to move forward. "The Avicen are not our enemies. Not any longer. It is a far greater threat we face." He met Echo's gaze across the room. Her features were indistinct from such a distance, but he didn't think he was imagining her small, proud smile. "And the only way we can defeat it is if we face it together."

CHAPTER THIRTY-NINE

In a quiet room, set apart from the main living quarters of Wyvern's Keep, Ivy sat by Helios's bedside and remembered a time, not too long ago, when she had tended to another Drakharin's wounds. She and Dorian had not been friends then; they had been something only slightly less than enemies. Circumstance had positioned them on the same side, but time and effort had allowed Ivy to see another side of him. It would not have been possible if he had not been willing to grow beyond the limitations of his hatred. He'd shed his well-worn prejudices like snakeskin. He had become someone Ivy could trust.

But trusting one Drakharin was not the same as trusting them all. She had let herself forget that they were enemies. Not just to her—in the great scheme she was not an individual, but rather a stand-in for a people, an idea—but to all the Avicen. Months of friendship with one would not—could not—overcome centuries of hatred. Only a fool would have thought so. A naive, optimistic fool.

Her hands went through the motions of checking the bandages on Helios's head. The force with which Tanith had struck him had sent him careening into a wall of solid stone. There was probably a Helios-shaped hole in the throne room now.

"Serves you right," Ivy muttered. Even so, her hands were gentle. Once the white-hot flare of her anger had subsided— she had trusted him—she found that she didn't want to hurt him. With Dorian, the fear and mistrust had come first— when he frightened her, hurt her, she had wanted to hurt him right back—but Helios . . . Helios had been kind to her from the moment their eyes met across the courtyard of Wyvern's Keep, when a backstabbing warlock had delivered her right into Tanith's waiting claws. He brought her food. He helped her escape. He told her to be brave.

And then he turned on her. On all of them. They had welcomed him into their home. He had tended their garden. He had stood beside Ivy in the kitchen, sweating over a steaming cauldron of boiled bloodweed, assisting her as she distilled its putrid essence into an elixir that would save the very same lives he was planning to jeopardize.

And still, Ivy did not want to hurt him.

She stared at him. His face was motionless, eyes still hidden beneath their lids, too deep in his pained slumber to be plagued by dreams. His pale skin was even lighter than it normally was; Ivy could see the blue lines of his veins beneath the surface. Bruises blossomed along one cheek; the line of them extended across his jaw, down his neck, and along his collarbone (likely fractured).

"That doesn't sound like the Ivy I know."

Ivy turned from her study of Helios's many wounds to look at Dorian. He was leaning against the doorframe. The battle had left him with but one injury: a gash across the knuckles of his right hand. One of the other healers had wrapped it with gauze after applying a salve. Ivy could smell the witch hazel from where she sat. He'd been watching her work in silence. No one was to be alone with the prisoner, according to Caius, enthroned once more as Dragon Prince. Dorian had silently volunteered to act as guard, though Ivy didn't think an unconscious Helios was much of a threat. Not anymore.

"Really?" She arched a brow, but she wasn't nearly as good at doing so as Dorian was. "Because I'm such a saint?"

That pulled a tired smile from Dorian's lips. "Not saintly, no. Just kind."

Ivy snorted. "Right. Kind." She turned her attention back to Helios. His chest rose and fell with deep, even breaths. Her gaze stayed resolutely attached to the slope of his collarbone. She didn't know what her expression betrayed; she had never had much of a poker face, and she didn't feel like having Dorian—or anyone—dissect the thoughts she opted not to voice. "That's probably what makes me such an easy target."

She didn't see Dorian approach the bed, but she heard the scrape of chair legs as he pulled up the only other seat in the room. His movements were slow as he sank into it. Maybe the burn on his knuckles wasn't the only memento the fight had bestowed upon him.

"You're not an easy target," Dorian said. "Being kind is not a weakness. And that is not something I would have said a year ago."

Ivy huffed. She didn't want a pep talk. But then, she also didn't *not* want a pep talk. She didn't know what she wanted in that moment, but it was easier, somehow, with Dorian beside her. Even if he insisted on resorting to shallow platitudes as a clumsy attempt at consolation. "Maybe if I had been a little less kind, I wouldn't have played right into his hands."

"He had us all fooled," said Dorian. "Even me." He quirked a silver eyebrow at her. "Do I look like an easy target to you?"

Ivy did look at him, carefully, knowing full well that the words she didn't say were written on her face. She couldn't say that it felt like her heart was breaking. She couldn't say that she had let herself care about a boy she barely knew. She couldn't admit that she had been blinded by a pretty face and sunshine eyes and a kind smile. All she could say was "I trusted him."

Dorian's injured hand came to rest atop her own. "You saw the good in him. There is no shame in that."

"I brought him into our house." Truthfully, allowing Helios access to their home, their sanctuary, their secrets, had been a group effort, but Ivy could not fight the blame that seemed determined to rest on her shoulders. "How can you say that?"

"Because you saw the good in me."

He said it as if it were that simple. It wasn't. "That was different."

Dorian met her glare with a roll of his eye. "I punched you in the face, Ivy."

"And I forgave you."

"Well, maybe someday you can forgive him."

They stared at each other for a moment before Ivy buckled under his relentless onslaught of optimism. "When did you get so nice?"

"I had a very good teacher," he said, patting her hand with his injured one. She wondered if it hurt.

A movement from the bed drew Ivy's attention: the shifting of bedsheets. Helios's lips cracked open to release a soft groan, his hand—also bandaged—rising to inspect the gauze wrapped around his head.

Dorian stood, pushing his chair back and inserting himself as much between Ivy and the bed as he could. She tried to push him aside, but she might as well have tried rolling a boulder away. He stayed right where he was, one hand resting, not at all subtly, on the pommel of his sword. It was a threat, delivered with stone cold certainty. Try anything and say goodbye to your innards.

No, Ivy thought. *Not an easy target at all.*

It took a few seconds for Helios to blearily open his eyes. He blinked up at Dorian, a wrinkle forming between his brows. Ivy saw it dawn on him that he was alive and then, in quick succession, that he was in a great deal of trouble.

"Captain." Helios's voice tripped over the syllables, rusty from disuse and dehydration.

"Dorian," Ivy said. "Move." She shoved at his hip, and this time, he did move. Slowly and grudgingly, but he stepped aside to let her see the man lying helpless in bed.

At the sound of her voice, Helios's eyes, clouded and disoriented but still as brilliantly yellow as ever, cut to her. He swallowed thickly before speaking. "Ivy." Her name was a whisper on his lips.

Something critical to her structural integrity buckled

at the way he said it. Dorian misread her reaction and moved to stand between them again. "No. You don't get to talk to her."

Dorian's kindness was evidently not an infinite commodity.

"What was that you were saying about forgiveness?" It was easier for Ivy to talk to Dorian than it was to look at Helios.

"I said *you* might forgive him." His fingers drummed against the hilt of his sword, perhaps for no greater reason than to remind Helios that it was there and that Dorian had no qualms about using it. "I never said *I* would."

Before Ivy could conjure a suitable reply, a hacking cough erupted from Helios's throat. She responded without thinking, the sound of a person in distress flipping the switch inside her that activated her healer mode.

"Out of the way," she said to Dorian. Her tone held the authority of an order, making it abundantly clear that it was not a request. He got out of the way without protest.

Ivy took up the glass of water one of the other healers had left on the bedside table, intending it for Ivy when it became clear she had no intention of letting one of the others sit vigil as they waited for their prisoner to wake. She held the glass to Helios's lips, careful to tilt it just enough for him to take a shallow sip. He was propped up by enough pillows not to choke on it.

She was aware of Dorian watching warily from the sidelines, his gaze as sharp as an eagle's. If Helios made any sudden movements, he was likely to find himself short of a limb or two. Not that such a thing was likely to happen, since Ivy was fairly certain his skeleton was boasting more than its fair share of fractures.

Helios rested back against the pillows when he finished drinking. Wordlessly, Ivy set the glass back on the bedside table.

"Thank you," Helios said softly.

For lack of anything better to say, Ivy replied, "You're welcome."

A great, oppressive silence fell.

Helios's eyes flitted from Ivy to Dorian. "I don't have the right to ask . . ." He worried his chapped bottom lip between his teeth, his gaze settling behind Ivy. He couldn't look her in the eye, but his words were clearly meant for her. "But can I speak to you? Alone?"

Dorian's answer was quick and absolute. "No."

Ivy sighed. "Dorian . . ."

"I'm not leaving you alone with him. He's a traitor."

"And what could he possibly do to me?" Ivy gestured at the bandages swathing great expanses of Helios's body. "Stare at me vengefully? I may not be much of a warrior, but I'm pretty sure I can handle an invalid."

For a moment, Helios's expression turned mutinous, as if he wanted very much to argue her assessment of his physical capabilities. But when he tried to sit up, pain sent him flopping right back onto the pillows. "She's right," he said. "I'm not a threat in this state. The only person I'm capable of hurting is myself."

Words, Ivy thought, were sometimes better weapons than fists. But she kept her musing to herself. While a part of her had no interest in Helios's groveled apologies or flimsy excuses, she was too curious to ignore an opportunity to hear what he had to say for himself.

"I'll be fine, Dorian." That was probably a lie. "Just give us a minute."

Dorian hovered beside her, a silent sentinel, for so long that Ivy thought he was not going to move. But then he heaved a weary sigh and relented. "Fine." To Helios, he added, "But I'll be right outside that door. If Ivy calls, I will hear her and I will come back in. You don't want me to come back in, Helios."

A shallow, terse nod. "No, sir."

"If you say anything to upset her, I will gladly cut out your tongue."

That was a lovely visual. "Caius wants to interrogate him later," Ivy said, out of a sense of obligation.

Dorian shrugged. "He doesn't need a tongue for that. We can supply him with paper to write his answers down."

Helios, to his credit, seemed remarkably unperturbed by their glib discussion of his possible mutilation. "The last thing I want to do—the last thing I *ever* wanted to do—was hurt Ivy." His yellow eyes flicked to Ivy. "I'm sure you think the worst of me, but please . . . know that."

Dorian advanced on him. "You have the audacity—"

"Dorian." Ivy held up a hand.

He didn't wrest his glare from Helios when he spoke. "Right outside that door," he promised.

Helios nodded a fraction. "Understood."

Ivy watched Dorian leave. The door clicked shut behind him, and she kept her eyes on it because she wasn't sure what she would see or think or feel when it was just Helios in the room with her. It had been far simpler when he'd been unconscious.

"Ivy."

She turned back to face him, slowly. "What?"

Dorian thought she was kind, but she was more than that. Kindness wasn't a passive quality. It was a choice one had to make, and right then, Ivy didn't feel much like making it. The wound of Helios's betrayal was too raw for kindness. Maybe Dorian was right. Maybe one day, she would dig deep within her soul and find the capacity for forgiveness he was so certain she had. But today was not likely to be that day.

Helios closed his eyes, lashes dark against his sallow skin. She'd once found him obscenely handsome. She still did, if she was honest with herself.

"I'm sorry," he said, tensed as if expecting a blow.

"You're sorry," Ivy repeated, her voice hollow. "That's it? You're sorry."

He risked a glance at her. "Does anything else matter?"

The question caught Ivy off guard. She could not have said what she had expected, but it wasn't that. "I . . . don't know."

"I won't insult you by offering you excuses, but I wanted to say that to you first. I'm sorry. I mean it."

As much as Ivy wanted to doubt his sincerity, she found that she couldn't. "Helios . . ."

He shook his head even though the effort caused him obvious pain. "You don't have to say anything. I don't deserve your forgiveness. I did what I did and I will face the consequences. You just—you deserved to hear that. I never lied to you, Ivy. Not once. And I'm not lying now."

"Never lied to me? How can you say that?" Everything he'd ever told her had been a lie. Every moment since the first had been a lie. "When I asked you why you were helping me—helping us—you said you wanted to do the right thing. You said you couldn't stand by while Tanith ripped the world to shreds. You said you watched her cut down her own people and it made you sick. Did any of that even happen?"

Helios's mouth hardened into a grim frown. "It did."

"Then *why?*" Ivy was struck by how badly she needed to know. "Why did you keep working for her? You could have come clean; we could have helped you."

His expression shuttered, as if he were slamming down a window. "It doesn't matter why."

"It does," said Ivy. "To me. If she threatened you—"

"It wasn't me she was threatening." For a brief moment, his countenance faltered and his face was an open book. He tried to gather himself, with visible effort, but Ivy had peeked behind the mask and saw the truth he seemed so determined to hide.

"Who?"

Helios shook his head again. "It doesn't matter," he repeated. "Not anymore. He's probably already dead. After what I did . . ."

"Helios, please," said Ivy. "Tell me."

Despair flitted across his face, as plain as day. "My brother." Helios swallowed thickly. "She said if I didn't do as she commanded, she would kill him. And it would be slow. She gave me that locket with his picture in it to remind me. The one I showed you in the garden. I used it to send messages to her. The same way you used that pendant to communicate with Dorian when you were being held captive in the keep." He squeezed his eyes shut. "Our parents died when we were very young. It's always just been me and him. I couldn't . . ."

He trailed off, and Ivy felt a tug in her chest, the gentle pull of compassion that drove her to study the healing arts, that guided her hands as she worked.

"I'll see if I can find him," Ivy said.

Helios opened his eyes to study her. "Why? Why would you help me after what I've done to you?"

Because it's the right thing to do. But Ivy said nothing. She started packing up her supplies, her emotional reserves exhausted.

After a full minute passed in silence, save for the glass vials of salves and elixirs clinking as Ivy placed them back in her basket, Helios spoke again. "You should hate me."

Ivy gathered up the folded bandages and placed them in the basket. She looped the handle over her arm and stood. She didn't speak until she was at the door, one hand on the knob.

"I don't hate you, Helios. And I don't want to."

She turned the knob and opened the door. Dorian was right outside, leaning against the wall, arms crossed over his chest. His eyebrows rose when he saw her. She wanted him to hear what she had to say too.

When she turned back to Helios, she found those sad, bright eyes boring into hers. "Hate is a choice. And it's not one I'm interested in making."

CHAPTER FORTY

It was unbelievable to think that Echo could be here, walking these halls so freely, when everything she had ever been told dictated that this was a place where she would never be safe. Wyvern's Keep was the dragon's den. The seat of Drakharin power. She would never be Avicen, but she had always been their ally, and this was the place they feared most, home to the most fearsome figure of Drakharin lore: the Dragon Prince. Echo knew him to be real, to be flesh and blood, as she was, but to the Avicen he was a monster of mythical proportions. He was the bogeyman they told their children about to scare them into their best behavior. She had not known what Caius was when she had first met him. He had told her that he was a mercenary hired by the prince, and she had believed him. She'd had no reason to doubt him. But the truth had outed itself, as it was wont to do. She had come to know him for who he was. She had come to know the truth of him—not his title; titles could be won and lost—but the solid core of him. After all this time, she liked to think that she knew what made him tick. He was fearsome, that much was undeniable, but he was also kind and loyal, possessed of a wit she grudgingly admitted was as quick as hers, if not quicker. He held within himself layers that a dark, secret part of her wished she had the luxury to explore.

But time was not on their side. Caius had assigned Dorian the task of weeding out those soldiers still loyal to Tanith and remanding them to the keep's dungeons while Drakharin mages and scouts worked to track Tanith's location. Echo hadn't been given a task, and while she appreciated having a night off, she knew the reprieve would last only until morning.

She knew she should probably catch a few hours of rest, but her nerves were still electric, so she stalked the halls of the keep, relishing the free passage granted to her by the Dragon Prince himself. Within these walls his word was law, and while the guards she passed on her meandering journey glared at her with barely concealed suspicion, they would not raise their weapons to her or question her right to be there. Their rightful prince had spoken, and they would listen.

She was not sure where she was going. All she knew was that she needed time away from all the people crowding into the great hall—miraculously clean of blood, as if none had ever been shed—who were celebrating the return of their lost prince and his declaration of peace. As if they weren't the reason he had been driven from these walls. His sister might have stolen the throne out from under him, but they were the ones who had allowed it to happen.

Echo trailed her fingers along the embroidered tapestries

lining the walls. An aimless series of twists and turns had brought her to a quiet part of the keep. The voices of the celebration raging below had long since faded to silence. The corridor was dimly lit by sconces. The glimmer of firelight illuminated her path, undulating against the red runner that ran the length of the hallway.

At the other end of the corridor, a door stood ajar. Echo took one curious step forward, then another. That narrow opening glowed with a soft amber light that beckoned her forward. She was halfway to the door when a mournful tune drifted from the room. Someone was inside, coaxing sad notes from a piano's keys.

Her footsteps were quiet as she approached. She couldn't quite make out who was sitting at the piano; all she could see was a shadow falling across the plush red rug covering the stone floors, the vague impression of a person curved over the keys, the edges of their form flickering in the unsteady light of candles. Curiosity got the better of her, and she pushed the door open a little more.

The hinges squealed.

Abruptly, the music stopped.

Echo was already backing away. "Sorry, I just—"

"Echo?"

Caius's voice froze her to the spot.

"You can come in," he said, picking up where he'd left off in his playing. "No need to skulk about like a castle ghost. We have enough of those as it is."

Castle ghosts? She filed that away to ask about later.

Echo entered the room, pushing the door closed behind her, the thick wood meeting the doorjamb with a meaty thud. The silence felt complete, as if the door were more than just a physical barrier from the sounds of the party drifting through the halls of the keep.

She took a moment to drink her fill of the room's opulent decor. Thick carpeting covered nearly every inch of the stone floor, the same slate-gray as the rest of the fortress. Tapestries lined the walls, their silken threads shimmering in the amber glow of firelight. Candles sat at strategic positions around the room, illuminating the space just enough to grant it a sleepy, intimate warmth. Some had been placed in brass candleholders, but others had simply been wedged into the pools of wax left by their predecessors. The effect they created, combined with the plush furnishings and shelves packed to bursting with leather-bound books, reminded Echo a little of the Ala's chamber at the Nest. That had felt like home, and so did this.

It also felt undeniably like Caius.

A gleaming black piano sat in the far corner of the room, its polished surface reflecting the light of the candles and the silver moonlight that fell through the only open window. On the matching bench in front of the piano sat Caius, his fingers resting gently on the keys. He watched Echo approach through heavy-lidded eyes, his head tilted quizzically.

"I take it you also found yourself in need of a break from the festivities," he said as Echo drew nearer.

A sofa and two chairs sat at the center of the room in front of an unlit fireplace, and a daybed upholstered in rich emerald fabric was positioned near the open window, but there were no seats close to the piano. Echo went to stand next to it. She felt suddenly awkward, like a wallflower at a high school dance. Or how she imagined a wallflower at a high school dance would feel. She'd never attended one herself. Everything she knew about high schools she'd learned from *Gossip Girl*.

Wordlessly, Caius slid across the bench, making enough space for Echo to sit beside him. She sank down, the wood creaking slightly under the added weight.

"Your people know how to party," Echo said. "A little too well."

A faint smile whispered across his lips. "That they do. And they take great pride in it." His fingers plucked out a half-considered melody. "To the outside world, we're known for our passions on the battlefield. Our lust for action. Our desire for victory at all costs. Not many know that all that comes from a yearning to live life to its fullest. To savor each and every moment with zeal."

Hearing the words "passion," "lust," and "desire" in the dimly lit setting, with his thigh pressed against hers and their shoulders brushing, was a bit much. Caius arched an eyebrow at her. He knew exactly what he was doing. He had to. He was too smart not to.

Echo thought about putting an inch or two between them. She didn't. The pressure of his body against hers was nice. He was warm and solid, and she found she liked it very much. "That's a very poetic way of describing the shenanigans going on downstairs," she said. "I saw one guy puking into a vase made of solid gold."

He huffed out a small laugh. "Ah, my people do nothing by halves, that much is true."

"And what about you?" Echo nudged him with her shoulder. He nudged back. "Not in the partying mood?"

Caius shook his head, his dark bangs falling over his

forehead, long enough to brush the tops of his eyebrows. He shook his head like a shaggy dog to get them out of the way. The gesture was oddly endearing. "Not particularly." He dragged his fingers across the piano keys. Not enough pressure to make a sound, though they gave slightly under his touch. "I find myself in a rather contemplative mood."

Echo watched him consider the notes he could play. There were words left in him. She could practically feel him vibrating with their unspoken potential. "Do you want to talk about it?"

He was silent for a moment, fingertips resting on the keys. He pressed down on one and a single lonely note floated into the air. They listened to it soften, then fade.

"I'm going to have to kill my sister, aren't I?"

Echo turned her head to face him fully. His bangs had fallen forward again, masking his eyes. Save for the slow rise and fall of his chest, he was still.

It was an awful thing to contemplate. A truly horrific thing to consider, taking the life of someone one had loved, in the not-so-distant past. Probably. She had no siblings, not by blood, but Ivy was as close to a sister as Echo would ever have, and the notion of doing anything to cause her physical pain made her stomach turn. She couldn't imagine having to kill Ivy, to know with such wretched certainty that she would *have* to kill her. Couldn't even imagine Ivy doing anything to deserve it. Echo watched that great and terrible weight settle on Caius as he slouched on the bench, his shoulders curving over his hands, which still rested on the keys.

"Caius . . ."

She didn't know what to say. He wasn't wrong. There

was no disputing it. Tanith—and the monstrous thing riding her—had to be stopped. Permanently. And Echo wouldn't shed a tear over it. She sincerely doubted she'd lose a single wink of sleep over the death of someone who had caused so much pain, such intense and prolonged suffering. It wasn't like Ruby. Even if Echo had to sink her dagger into Tanith's heart herself, it would never be like Ruby, who had done nothing but follow the orders of a man she idolized. Killing Ruby had been a tragedy. Killing Tanith would be a triumph.

But it was hard to feel triumphant in the face of Caius's pain. Echo inched her hand closer to his, waiting for him to withdraw. He didn't. She twined her fingers with his and he turned his hand over to better grasp hers.

"I'm sorry," she said. And she meant it. She would not regret Tanith's death. But she would regret, for the rest of her days, the stain it would leave on Caius's soul, no matter how justified killing her might be.

He looked at her, his green eyes nearly black in the dim light. "Is it wrong to mourn her? After all she's done?"

Echo shook her head. "No."

His gaze dropped to their joined hands. "I'll be the only one who will."

Echo did not dispute that.

There was such profound sadness in his expression. For the sister he was about to lose. For the people he'd already lost. Echo leaned into him, resting her head on his shoulder. After a moment, she felt his cheek press against the top of her head as he let himself lean on her. His breath stirred the flyaway strands of hair near the crown of her head.

"What will you do?" Caius asked. "After?"

After they had saved the world from being torn to shreds by a madwoman's whimsy. After they had laid to rest gods knew how many of their friends. Echo pushed the thought away. Harsh realities could wait just one more day. Tonight, she wanted something different, something sweeter.

"Retire at the ripe old age of seventeen," Echo said. "Move someplace warm. Grow tomatoes."

Caius huffed a little laugh into her hair. A thought struck her suddenly. *Not* at the ripe old age of seventeen.

"What day is it?" she asked, raising her head.

"Tuesday," Caius replied.

"No, I mean the date."

"October twelfth. No. The thirteenth now. It's past midnight."

October thirteenth. Ten days past Echo's birthday.

"I'm eighteen," Echo said. She hadn't forgotten a birthday in years. Her biological family hadn't given her many fond memories, aside from a sad supermarket cake the year she turned six, but the Ala had seen fit to commemorate the occasion every year after taking Echo in. The Avicen didn't put much stock in birthdays, not once they'd reached full maturity, but the Ala knew it mattered to humans and therefore to Echo, and so it had mattered to the Ala. But with all the commotion of the past several weeks, Echo hadn't given much thought to the inexorable march of time.

"Since when?" Caius asked.

"Ten days ago." A sliver of a memory pressed at her. It felt like lifetimes ago when Ivy had jested about throwing Echo a party. She'd forgotten that, too. "Ivy wants to have a *Great Gatsby* party."

Caius's ghost of a smile transformed into a real one. Small and tender, but real. "Does she know how that book ends?"

"I'm surprised you do." It was human literature, after all.

Caius gestured to the walls of shelves, lined with hundreds of tomes. "I'm well-read."

"Touché." Echo sighed and rested her temple against his shoulder, finding comfort in the solidity of his presence. "For the record, *Tender Is the Night* is Fitzgerald's best book."

"Agreed." He angled his head to press his lips against her temple. The feel of his mouth against her skin sent a shudder of warmth through her body. "Happy birthday," he said softly. "And to think, I didn't even get you a gift."

Echo smiled into his shoulder. This was better, this comfortable back-and-forth. Far better than talk of death and dying and losses so great they were nearly impossible to comprehend. "How about a song?"

She felt Caius smile. "I think I can manage that."

Echo sat up so her head wasn't resting on his shoulder, but she didn't move away. Her thigh pressed against his in a warm line of contact, and she could feel the slight shifting of muscle as he worked the pedals. Music spilled from his fingertips, filling the room with a gentle tune that Echo knew as well as the beat of her own heart.

The magpie's lullaby. It had been Rose's song once, a long time ago. And then it was Echo's. And now it was theirs. With deft hands, Caius twisted and pulled the notes, rearranging them into something altogether different and achingly beautiful.

When the last note rang out, Echo looked up from watching Caius's hands dance over the keys, calloused from weaponry but no less elegant in their movements. He was looking back at her, his eyes gone even darker with what Echo recognized as longing.

"Kiss me," she said.

He did.

His hands came up to cradle her face, cupping her jaw as if she was something delicate, something worth treasuring. This time, there was none of the soft hesitance of the kiss they'd shared at the camp in Iceland. It was all firm pressure and confident insistence.

Echo brought her own hands up to trace the lines of his throat, along to the dip of his collarbone, down the ridge of his sternum, skating over the jumping muscles of his abdomen, around to the sides of his stomach. Her explorations brought a groan to his lips, muffled by the press of her mouth.

He broke away, breath stuttering, uneven. "Echo . . ."

Her lips tingled in the absence of his. "Do you want to stop?"

A rueful smile broke across his face. "That is the last thing in the world I want, but . . ."

"But what?"

He drew in a breath, as if preparing himself to pull away from her. "Maybe we should."

Oh, hell no.

Echo wrapped one hand around the back of his neck and brought him in close. "Caius. We could die tomorrow. And if we *do* die, I don't want to die regretting the things I haven't done."

Caius stared at her, his expression carefully shuttered. "I'm not certain that's the most solid foundation upon which to base one's decisions."

"Caius, I—"

He held up a hand, but his steady gaze faltered, as if even breaking that much contact with her caused him physical pain. "I do not want you rushing into something you aren't prepared for because you feel like you won't have other chances. You *will*, Echo."

Echo thought his confidence was rather optimistic, but she didn't argue. "I know myself, Caius. I know what I want and I know what I can handle."

His hand returned to its post on the curve of her hip, impossibly warm even through a layer of denim, hot as a burning brand. "And what if I can't?" he asked, voice whisper soft. "I haven't—not since Rose."

Oh. *Oh.*

Echo said the first thing that came to mind. A terrible habit, one she really ought to consider breaking. "Well, I don't think the mechanics of it have changed much in the past century."

That pulled a startled laugh from Caius. "You are yourself," he said, chuckling. "And no other." He inclined his head to press a kiss to the corner of her mouth. "And I would not have you any other way."

Echo swallowed thickly. He had said something to her, months earlier, before he'd been taken from her. Three small words that contained multitudes. She hadn't said it back then. Wasn't sure she could say it now. But she wanted to. Oh, how she wanted to.

Love was not as it was described in fairy tales. It was terrifying. Not in a giddy, heady way, like tumbling down the steepest slope of a roller coaster. It was terrifying in its enormity. It had the power to crush, to destroy, more thoroughly than any weapon. No one ever warned about the terrible cost of that ache, that need. It chipped away at one's defenses like a siege on a castle's walls, claiming ground until there was nothing left it had not touched.

It was a cliff one had to jump off to know the true depth of its valley.

And so she jumped.

"I love you," she said. Simply. Succinctly.

Something like pain, but not quite, flickered across Caius's face. "Truly?"

She nodded.

He kissed her, and they collided like stars.

Echo broke away just long enough to stand and tug him toward the daybed near the window. He followed, his hand warm in hers.

The backs of her knees hit the cushion and her legs, already wobbly, folded under her. She sank into the seat, pulling Caius after her. She thought it would be awkward, to be so entwined, but it wasn't. The parts of her that she found ungainly fit against his body as if that was where she was meant to, had always been meant to be.

His hands traveled up her waist, his face buried in the crook of her neck. Her body was alight. She was a supernova, filling the sky with light.

Her brain processed sensation in fragments. A kiss pressed to her jugular as if to calm its frantic pulsing. A hand tracing the side of her torso, from her hips. Up and up and up. He trailed his mouth against her skin, his nose pushing against the collar of her T-shirt.

So close. Too close. His breath ghosted over the cotton shielding the black mark from view, and though Echo knew the effect was all in her head, the scar seemed to shrink from his touch, chased back into the deepest recesses of her being by his warmth.

"Don't touch me," Echo said. Caius's response was immediate. He withdrew completely, sitting back on his haunches, hands upraised as if to suggest he meant no harm. She smiled to soften her words. "No, it's fine. Just . . . not there."

She tugged her shirt up. A frown creased his brow. She glanced down. A thin tendril of black had snaked upward, peeking over the collar of her shirt. It was hardly a millimeter, but it was enough.

"Echo," Caius breathed, voice low, as if he already knew the answer and was dreading it. "What is that?"

"It's nothing."

"Echo."

"Fine." She sat up and shrugged out of the leather jacket she was still, for some ungodly reason, wearing. The T-shirt followed it, leaving her in nothing more than her jeans and a black sports bra, but there was no self-consciousness in her disrobing. It wasn't longing that colored his stare, but concern.

He reached for her, his fingers falling short of the scar. She had told him not to touch it, and he respected that boundary.

"When did this happen?"

"At Avalon," Echo answered. "When Tanith attacked. I'm not even sure how." She looked down at the mark. "Lucky shot, I guess."

Caius tore his gaze away from the scar to meet her eyes. Without her jacket and her shirt and the warmth of Caius's own body heat, she was cold. A shiver skittered down her spine. Caius's gaze softened.

"May I?" he asked, gesturing to the scar.

Echo's shoulder hunched, as if that would make her seem smaller. "I don't know if it'll hurt you."

He shook his head. "I don't think it will."

"How can you be sure?"

He lifted one shoulder in a shallow shrug. "You burned the poison out of me once. You saved me. You protected me then. And I think your power is protecting you now."

After a moment's hesitation, Echo nodded.

His fingers brushed her skin, sending an entirely different kind of shiver dancing along her bones.

Nothing happened. The skin of his fingers remained the golden tan it always was. He traced the lines of the scar as if he were mapping the branches of a tree. As if it weren't a grotesque stain splashed across her flesh.

"You will fight this," he said softly, leaning back into her space. Already she felt warmer. "You will fight it and you will win."

"I'm not sure I can." Her words puffed against his skin.

He pressed his lips to hers, silencing her doubt. His hand splayed across the scar, covering it with his palm. She let herself collapse against him, lighter now that she was no longer carrying her secret alone.

He pulled away, close enough to touch her everywhere she wanted to be touched, but far enough for her to feel the force of his gaze, steady and full of love.

"You will," he said, his voice devoid of even the slightest doubt. "And there isn't a force in this world that will tear me from your side when you do."

A riotous mess of emotion bubbled up in Echo's chest, well beyond the capacity of words to describe. And so she abandoned them wholly and leaned in to kiss him again. And again. And again.

CHAPTER FORTY-ONE

Echo was roused from her slumber by the shrill sound of Stravinsky streaming from her phone. With a muffled curse, she blinked awake. The curtains were partially open, and sunlight fell in bright beams against the library floor. She had changed her ringtone countless times, but Jasper insisted on stealing her phone away to set it back to Stravinsky's *Firebird,* no matter how much the song grated on her. Every time the phone rang, the frantic strings wreaked havoc on her nerves.

Grumbling about shrill violins, she groped at the floor beside the daybed, where she had a vague recollection of depositing her jeans the night before. A warm, solid weight was thrown over her midriff, pinning her in place. As wakefulness replaced the slow stupidity of sleep, Echo remembered to feel embarrassed about the position she was in.

It wasn't the first time she'd woken up beside Caius. However, it was the first time she'd woken up beside Caius absent certain pieces of clothing. She had pulled on his sweater sometime in the night when the brisk evening had proven too cold, even with his body acting as her own personal furnace, but she was suddenly very aware of the way his skin felt against her bare legs.

Stravinsky looped as the phone continued to ring, starting the *Firebird* suite from the top. Echo tried to shove Caius's arm away, but her efforts met only with a string of incoherent grumbling in Drakhar, and his nose buried deeper in the crook of her shoulder. He hooked his ankle around hers, ensuring her captivity.

"Go back to sleep," he mumbled. He was awake, but he didn't bother opening his eyes as he burrowed closer.

"My phone," Echo said, though her conviction was wearing thin in the face of Caius and his strong arms and his sleepy drawl and his mussed hair. And his everything else.

"Let them leave a message." Caius's voice was muffled by her neck, his words warm puffs of air against the column of her throat.

Abruptly, the sound of Stravinsky fell silent.

"See?" Caius said. "They're leaving a message."

The phone rang again. Caius swore. Echo wasn't sure if it was her imagination playing tricks on her or if the strings seemed even more frantic than usual.

Groaning in frustration, she rolled as far as she could toward the pile of her clothes with Caius still holding her. She spotted her phone sticking out of a pocket of her crumpled jeans, the screen blinking with the caller ID. She reached for it, but it was just far enough to be out of reach of her wiggling fingers.

"It's Ivy," Echo said. Caius harrumphed something that

might have been acknowledgment. His arm loosened around her middle, his hand coming to rest on her hip. His thumb brushed the bare skin there. Echo flushed. The easy familiarity with which he touched her was strange, though not at all unwelcome. She shimmied out of his grasp, but not off the daybed completely, and grabbed her phone. With a swipe of her thumb, she silenced Stravinsky, making a note to delete the blasted ringtone from her phone once and for all. Jasper would probably just download it again. *Bastard.*

"Hey, Ivy," Echo said as she brought the phone up to her ear. "This had better be good."

"Oh, Firebird, I assure you. It is."

Echo's blood turned to ice. She sat up, her hand clutching the phone hard enough to make the plastic casing creak in protest. Caius looked at her, his brows raised in question. The hand on her hip stilled.

"Tanith." On Ivy's phone. Fury blazed through Echo; power sparked at her fingertips. The connection crackled with static as her grip on the phone tightened, her hand hot with magic. "What did you do to her?"

"Nothing," Tanith replied, her tone full of false sweetness. "Yet." Her voice went distant as she talked to someone on the other end. Echo couldn't make out the words, but they had the air of a sharply spoken command. She heard the sound of shuffling, as if the phone was being jostled.

The noise ceased, and a sobbing breath came through, loud and clear. "Echo?"

Relief slammed into Echo, hard enough to make her lose her grip on the phone. She caught it with her other hand and brought it up to her ear. "Ivy? Are you okay?"

"Echo, I'm here, I'm okay, but it's a trap, don't listen—"

The sound of flesh hitting flesh cut off Ivy's words. The impact had a meaty sound to it, like a punch. Fire flared up Echo's free hand, licking all the way to her elbow. All thought of control fled as she imagined Tanith striking Ivy.

I'm going to kill you, you piece of shit.

"Enough of that," came Tanith's voice. "The little dove is alive and well. For now."

"If you hurt Ivy—"

"You'll what? Set me on fire?" Tanith asked, breaking into a short, mad laugh. "Run me through with that little dagger of yours? We all saw how well that went when that sly little fox tried it. I'd even stand still to let you have a go if you wish. See if you can draw blood this time. That's what you wanted, isn't it? My blood. Come and get it, if you dare."

Echo pushed herself off the daybed and began fumbling for her clothes. She put the phone on speaker and tossed it onto the cushions as she attempted to pull her jeans on. Caius followed suit, dressing himself in haste. The tangle of denim proved a struggle for her trembling hands and she gave up on the jeans. "What do you want, Tanith? I'm so fucking sick of your games."

"Isn't it obvious? I want *you*, Firebird."

"Then leave Ivy out of it." Echo didn't trust that Tanith was telling the truth, that she hadn't harmed Ivy. The thought of her in that monster's clutches—*again*—sent Echo's stomach roiling with a wave of fearful nausea. "Let her go."

"Oh, I intend to," Tanith promised. "Once *you* come home."

CHAPTER FORTY-TWO

The line went dead. The world tilted and Echo's vision grayed around the edges. She closed her eyes and drew in a deep breath, begging her heart to steady itself. Caius had already taken off, summoning guards and raising the alarm. Echo was still wearing his shirt. Power simmered beneath her skin, itching to be let free. Her muscles trembled with strain. It would have felt so good to let it out, to watch the furniture catch flame. To set the curtains ablaze. The need for release surged so strongly, she almost gave in. A flurry of sparks cascaded to the floor, burning holes in the carpet.

Home.

Not the isolation of Avalon Castle, hidden by its layers of warding and protective spells sealed with Echo's blood. Not any of the places she had used as hideouts over the last few months in futile attempts to stay safe from the forces that wanted a piece of her.

Home meant only one thing to Echo: New York City. The streets on which she had raised herself. The library in which she had taken shelter. The place that called her back no matter how many times she left it for far-flung lands and exotic locales.

And Tanith was there.

Caius skidded back into the room, now fully clothed. Dorian was on his heels, buckling his sword belt around his waist.

"Echo?" Caius gave her a puzzled frown. She hadn't budged since he'd left. Every ounce of effort had gone into restraining herself from flying into a blind rage and burning the castle down around her.

Dorian's gaze slid down to her bare legs and hurriedly up again. He gave Caius a look. Jasper chose that moment to stroll into the room behind them, incongruously blasé. Some of the Avicen at the Icelandic camp had joined them at the keep after Caius's declaration of a formal cease-fire and Tanith's revelation that their secret base in Iceland had not been so secret after all. Jasper had been the first to arrive, and his presence at Dorian's side had caused quite the stir among the Drakharin. Hair-feathers askew from slumber, Jasper followed Dorian's line of sight. He turned to Caius and said, "Great minds." He nudged Dorian's shoulder in what would have been a playful gesture if not for the tightness in his eyes and the hard set of his jaw. His mask was good, but Echo knew him too well to be fooled by it. He was scared.

"Yeah," Echo said belatedly. The fog of anger thinned as she tried to get her bearings. Pants. She needed pants. And shoes. And a machete to hack Tanith's head off.

"We have to go," Caius said slowly, as if he wasn't sure Echo was entirely present in the moment. Which, she supposed, was fair enough, considering she was standing in the middle of the library on a cold autumn morning half dressed and raining monochrome sparks.

With a brisk nod, Echo pulled on her jeans, singeing them only slightly. Her boots fared slightly better, leather proving far more fire resistant than denim. Control was so distant a possibility it seemed like something she had read about in a book once. She knew it existed, but she wasn't capable of it. Not just then.

Unconcerned with her audience, Echo pulled off Caius's sweater and tugged her own shirt over her head. Her dagger had slid halfway across the room when she'd kicked her shoes off the night before. She retrieved it, secured it in its sheath, and tucked it into the back of her jeans. She pulled her hair back into a ponytail with a tie she scrounged up from the lint-ridden pocket of her jacket.

"Ready?" Caius asked. His green eyes were filled with worry. For Echo. For Ivy. Maybe even for his sister. Even after all Tanith had done to him, to them, he'd been harboring the hope that she could be saved, that there was enough left of his sister to salvage. Echo watched that hope die, fully and finally, in Caius's eyes when he saw the resolution in hers. Echo was not, under any circumstances, going to attempt to save Tanith's soul. She was going to stop her. For good.

Echo patted the hilt of the dagger to make sure it was secure. She grabbed her jacket and shoved her arms into the sleeves. And with that, the final piece of her armor slotted into place.

"Let's see if we can make this bitch bleed."

* * *

"Echo, wait!"

Caius grabbed Echo's arm, stopping her in her tracks. She quite liked where her tracks had been leading her—to revenge—and was not in the mood to be stopped in them. She shot Caius her most acidic look, but the grip he had on her forearm did not loosen in the slightest.

She spun around to face him, heedless of the scene they were making. Guards were streaming down the corridor, armor in various states of disarray. It was evening in New York. Tanith couldn't have chosen a better time to make trouble in the middle of Manhattan; the city would be abuzz with people living active, vibrant lives, blissfully unaware of the imminent peril that threatened them.

"Caius, your maniac sister has my best friend, and I can't even begin to think about what she's doing to her." Echo tried to wrench her arm free, but his grip was absolute. "Let me go. I have shit to do and people to kill."

"And that is exactly the mind-set Tanith wants you in when you face her." Despite Echo's continued and enthusiastic protestations, Caius managed to steer her into an alcove tucked into the corridor, getting them away from the bustle of activity overtaking the keep. Word had spread quickly, and the Drakharin were preparing to head into battle against the person they had hailed as their leader only hours earlier.

"What are you talking about?" Finally, Echo yanked her arm away from Caius, but the simmering intensity of his expression prevented her from going on her merry way to cut out his sister's heart with her dagger.

"Pain," Caius said. He pushed up one sleeve, exposing

the scars on his left arm. The bracelet of scarring around his wrist was healing—more rapidly than it would have had he been human—but the skin was still mottled an ugly yellow-green, discolored most strongly where the manacles had bit into his flesh. "That is what she wants to inflict, and you're playing right into her hands."

The sight of his wounds only added fuel to the fire burning in Echo's belly. Anyone who could do that to their family—to their own goddamn twin—needed to be stopped.

Perhaps sensing the direction of her thoughts, Caius plowed on, cupping her elbow with his other hand. "Do you remember what I told you about why Tanith had me whipped?"

Echo nodded impatiently. "Yeah. You said it made it easier for her to drain your magic so she could bust open the seals, but what does that have to—"

"What could possibly cause you more pain than targeting the people you love?" Caius interrupted. "What could possibly hurt worse than destroying the only home you've ever known right before your eyes?"

Oh.

It made a twisted sort of sense. "You think she wants to suck my magic dry," Echo said. She closed her eyes, thumping her head against the wall of the alcove with a soft thud.

"Think about it, Echo." Caius dropped his hand, the gesture oddly helpless. "She has Ivy, but we know she hasn't harmed her. Not yet. Not severely, anyway. She wants to make you watch when she does it. It's a solid strategy—force your enemy to play by your rules. She's chosen the field of engagement, set up the pieces to her advantage. If you charge in there like this"—he waved a hand in front of her, as if to indicate Echo's very being—"then you're meeting her on her terms. I know my sister. Playing by her rules is never a good idea."

"Then what do you suggest?" Echo spoke through gritted teeth. He wasn't wrong. But he wasn't right, either. "That I do nothing? That I sit this one out?"

"If I asked you to, would it do any good?"

Echo replied to his question with the answer it deserved. Dead silence.

Caius ran a hand through his hair and sighed. He had his two long knives strapped to his back, their gilded pommels gleaming in the torchlight emanating from the sconces lining the corridor. Dark circles stained the skin beneath his eyes, highlighted by the fan of his lashes as he let his eyes momentarily close.

"I can't lose you, too."

The words were spoken so quietly, Echo thought she had misheard him. But when he opened his eyes again, revealing the raw emotion in them, she knew she hadn't.

"I lost Rose." His voice was choked, as if he was struggling to get the words out. "And I have lost my sister. I cannot lose you, too." He shook his head, his hair, still messy from sleep, falling across his forehead.

"Caius—"

"This is your fight." His eyes bored into hers. "I know it is. But I just—"

Echo brought her hand up to the back of his neck and pulled him down into a bruising kiss. Their teeth clacked together gracelessly as she swallowed his small gasp of surprise. She broke the kiss and rested her forehead against his.

"You're not going to lose me," she said. "I meant what

I said last night. Every word. This war ends today. And after . . . Well, we have the rest of our lives to figure out what happens next. But one thing is certain: I won't let her win. We end this." She gave the back of his neck a gentle squeeze. "Together."

He nodded, his forehead nudging hers. "Together."

Furious Drakhar whispering sounded from the other end of the hallway. The firebird making out with the Dragon Prince was probably the most salacious bit of gossip the keep had seen in gods knew how long. Echo was about to pull away from Caius, but he stilled her with a hand on her waist. "Swear to me you'll be careful."

She stepped out of the alcove, straightening her jacket and securing the dagger tucked into her belt. "Careful is my middle name."

Someone called Caius over in Drakhar. Dorian, Echo saw, was waiting at the end of the corridor with a contingent of guards. All were fully armored. Caius spared them a glance before turning back to Echo, a grim smile in place. "That is the grandest lie you've ever told."

Echo shrugged and started down the hallway. She had no idea how they were going to subtly enter New York City and fight a potentially world-ending battle without alerting all of humanity to the existence of magical creatures among them, but she figured the logistics were best left to savvier minds than hers. She had bigger fish to fry. "True," she said. "But I swear, I'll be as careful as I always am."

Caius snorted, adjusting the crisscrossed straps that held the daggers in place. "That's exactly what I'm afraid of."

CHAPTER FORTY-THREE

"So much for subtlety," Echo said as she stared down the barrel of a gun. Floodlights surrounding the ruins of Grand Central backlit the group of soldiers who had the misfortune to find themselves standing directly where Echo and her company had emerged from the in-between. "We really should have seen this coming."

"Drop your weapons!"

The owner of the gun—a National Guardsman, judging from his pale fatigues—couldn't seem to decide where to direct his gaze. Wide eyes flicked between Echo and the group of assorted Avicen and Drakharin behind her. Compared to them, Echo was positively plain. Not a scale to ogle or a feather at which to marvel. Her own attention was divided between the rifle pointed squarely at her face and the gigantic tear in the sky, through which arcs of what looked like black smoke were shooting like the negative image of solar flares. An enormous gash in the in-between had opened up right above Midtown Manhattan, impossibly dark against the deep violet of the night sky. From her vantage point at the center of what remained of Grand Central's main concourse, she could see the long line of it, cutting across the heavens like a cruelly torn seam. Half a dozen Drakharin mages had lent their power to transporting them all here, and the reception was somewhat chillier than Echo had anticipated.

The National Guardsman shook free of his initial shock just enough to speak in a tremulous voice. "Who the hell are you and where the hell did you come from?"

"Umm." What did one say to such a query? *Hi, I'm the firebird, you may know me from folklore of various cultures all over the globe. And these are my friends, members of magical species you had no idea existed until twenty-seven seconds ago. We teleported here to fight evil!*

The in-between where they'd come through refused to close behind them, as it should have once the gateway was no longer in use. Instead, it remained, a gaping hole in the ground, as black as sin. A side effect of the world falling apart at the seams. Echo hoped nothing else came through besides them. It felt a bit like leaving the door to one's house unlocked. And it probably made them look even more fearsome to the trembling soldier in front of her. Echo wasn't quite sure how to explain any of it in a concise manner the man would believe. She was spared from having to figure it out by a familiar voice coming from behind her.

"Easy, soldier. They're with us."

The Ala glided into Echo's field of vision. She had traded her customary skirts for an ensemble of leather armor the likes of which Echo had never dreamed of seeing her wear. It was curiously stuffed and aged, as though it had seen some use, and the Ala wore it with ease, as comfortable in the outfit as she was in her flowing silk dresses. A broadsword Echo had never seen before was strapped to her back, snug in a bejeweled sheath that looked like it would be at home in a museum.

A handful of Warhawks followed her, along with a few Avicen who weren't fighters, not by nature or trade, but who were wielding swords and knives and bows all the same. It looked like whoever was able to carry a weapon had joined the fray. Echo scanned the group until she caught sight of a familiar head of tawny feathers. Rowan. He met her eyes with a shallow nod. His face was covered in soot, and a long, ugly gash ran from the outer edge of one eyebrow to the middle of his cheek. As fast as Echo had hurried here, it looked as though the fight had started without her. The Ala appeared wholly unperturbed by the array of guns and the human men who brandished them. As if literal millennia of hiding from humanity hadn't just imploded in spectacular fashion.

"Someone's been busy," Echo observed. The gun lowered and she exhaled a shaky breath, glad her brain wasn't about to be painted across the floor. Grand Central was enough of a mess as it was, with the debris only partially cleared away and cranes and scaffolding surrounding the pit in the center of the concourse.

The Ala made a gesture for the other guardsmen to lower their weapons. They did.

"What happened here?" Echo said, her hands still held out at her sides. The rifles were no longer aimed at their faces, but the men holding those rifles seemed as unsure of

Echo and her company as she was of them. The forehead of the man who had confronted her was beaded with sweat, and while he had obeyed the Ala's command with the rest of his men, he was still eyeballing the Ala as if he wasn't quite convinced she was real.

"These fine gentlemen and I have come to an agreement," said the Ala, her onyx eyes bearing down on the fidgety guardsman. "Nothing brings people together quite like a shared threat, wouldn't you agree?"

"So it would seem," Echo said. The unlikely band of allies standing at her back was proof enough of that.

"When the sky tore open right above our heads, we realized our time living in the shadows was at an end," said the Ala. She came to stand beside the guardsman in front of Echo. The soldier, who didn't appear to be a day over twenty-five, took a small, probably unconscious step away from the Ala. Not that Echo could blame him. Even disregarding the inhumanly black skin—as dark as a starless night sky—and the feathers, the Ala cut an imposing figure in her armor.

"Tanith has Ivy," Echo said. A more detailed explanation for the impossible logistics of what had transpired in her absence could wait. There were more pressing matters to attend to, and so long as she wouldn't have to dodge bullets while staging a rescue mission that was also an assassination, Echo found she didn't much care how it had come to pass that the Avicen were working alongside the human military.

A murderous look passed over the Ala's face. "I know. Ivy was at the hospital, tending to the sick, when Tanith appeared in the middle of the ward and absconded with her."

Rowan drew closer to the group, his eyes never quite

straying from the human soldiers surrounding them. Several of them stared openly at the knife Rowan held tightly in his right hand. The blade was bare, save for a coating of a red fluid that appeared too gelatinous to be blood. He wiped it off on his jeans before sliding it back into the sheath strapped to his forearm. "A nurse called the police to report what she had seen, but no one believed her. Not until monsters started falling from the sky."

Caius pushed to the front of the group. The Drakharin in their party seemed even more ill at ease with the presence of humans—and human weapons. Echo assumed he had been busy making sure none of them spooked and started a fight. *That* would be the last thing anyone needed. "Monsters?" he asked.

"Like the one that attacked the Nest," Rowan replied. He rolled his shoulders as if fending off an ache, jostling the bow he'd slung across his back. Echo had a vague recollection of him telling her he was much better at ranged weapons, much to his chagrin. He'd always thought swords looked cooler. "But smaller. A lot of them."

A shudder ran down Echo's spine at the mention of the vile creature that had decimated the Avicens' home and a good chunk of Grand Central. A nightmarish entity, formed of writhing shadows and screaming souls. Before Tanith had bound herself to the kuçedra, it had gone in search of its counterpart, sniffing out the firebird in the places where her presence was strongest. And Echo had led it right to the Avicens' doorstep.

Rowan pulled an arrow from his quiver, showing them the red-tinged head. "It's bloodweed," he said. "I thought if it could stave off the infection, or whatever was literally sucking people dry of their life force, then it would hurt those things. Nothing else did."

It was a clever solution, and Echo felt a brief swell of pride in Rowan for having thought of it. "But you beat them back?"

There wasn't a shadow beast in sight.

Rowan heaved a tired sigh. "For the moment, yeah. But they keep coming in waves." He jerked his head up at the breach in the sky. "They're falling through that thing."

Echo peered up at the rip in the in-between. It wasn't swallowing the clouds around it like a black hole the way she had imagined it might, but there was a void in its immediate vicinity that took her a moment to puzzle out. Starlight, faint through the dense smog that blanketed the city, peeked through the smattering of thin clouds everywhere but near the tear. "It looks like it's swallowing the light around it."

"Yeah," Rowan said. A layer of grime coated his clothes, along with patches of drying red that Echo hoped was not his blood.

A commotion drew their attention to the cluster of Drakharin behind them. Dorian's voice, sharp as a knife, cut through the crowd as he pushed his way forward. "What the hell is he doing here?"

Echo followed Dorian's vicious gaze.

Oh.

Among the Avicen stood a single warlock, who'd been hidden behind the bulk of their group. He had starlight eyes full of magic and mischief. Hair as black as night. Skin a burnished gold.

Quinn. He'd been a prisoner of the Avicen since he'd tried to betray Dorian (and Ivy and Jasper) months earlier, but someone had let him out of his cage.

The warlock held up his hands in a placating gesture, as if Dorian were a temperamental colt that needed calming. "Would you believe me if I said I'm here to help?"

"No," said Dorian and Jasper in unison. Dorian's sword dripped with the bloodweed elixir being passed around. Jasper's gaze dripped with disdain.

Quinn lowered his hands. "Then believe this: If that crazy bitch has her way, this world will crumble, taking every single one of us with it. Including me. I'm here to help myself. Helping the rest of you is just a fortunate by-product of my own self-interest."

"That's enough," the Ala said. "We can't afford to be precious about our allies."

Dorian looked ready to argue, and Echo didn't blame him. She wasn't sure about having the warlock at their back, even if his reasoning was grotesquely sound.

"We need all the help we can get," Rowan said decisively. That, however, was not what halted the words on Dorian's tongue. Echo felt it before she saw it: a growing malevolence. Rowan's expression mirrored her own. A frown spread across his features as he glanced upward. "Ah, crap," he uttered, more tired than surprised. He slung the bow off his shoulders and slotted the arrow into place. "Incoming."

The Ala looked toward the breach, uttered an incredibly descriptive curse in Avicet and drew her sword. The others followed suit, even the still-skittish Drakharin. Rifles swiveled upward. One of them caught the light just enough for

Echo to see that the tip of the barrel had been coated in the bloodweed concoction.

Echo gazed up at the gaping maw of the in-between. Shadows swirled from its unfathomable depths, taking form as they poured forth, solidifying into loosely defined beasts. Their amorphous forms shifted from one shape to another. The kuçedra had looked like a dragon when it had attacked the Nest, taking the form of that which the people in its immediate vicinity feared the most, but now every soul in New York City was watching the breach spew forth monsters made of Darkness, projecting their own fears onto them, forcing them to adopt forms too varied to truly congeal into coherence.

With her free hand, the Ala tossed a thick plastic bottle toward Echo, a wide-mouthed purple container emblazoned with the logo of New York University. She caught it, surprised by the warmth radiating from it. "For the rest of their weapons," said the Ala. Her arched eyebrows said the rest: *You are your weapon.*

Echo slid the dagger from her belt, unscrewed the bottle, and dipped the blade into the bloodweed mixture. The smell assaulted her nostrils while she held the open bottle in her hand, but the odor lessened once the liquid met steel. Fascinating. She passed the bottle to Caius, trusting he would distribute it among his troops—their troops, she supposed.

Be ready, Echo, whispered a voice at the back of Echo's mind. Rose's own fear slithered around inside Echo's skull. *Tanith will not fall without a fight.*

Rowan nocked an arrow and then let it fly. It pierced what passed for a hide on one of the creatures. A shrill, unnatural shriek sliced through the air. Echo clapped her hands over her ears, but Rowan seemed unaffected. Maybe he'd grown used to the sound of those things dying. "Echo, you either have the best timing . . . ," Rowan said as he retrieved another arrow from his quiver. There were a dozen left, maybe fewer. ". . . or the worst. Either way"—he let loose another arrow, his hazel eyes already seeking out his next target— "welcome home."

CHAPTER FORTY-FOUR

It should have been a five-minute walk, maximum, from Grand Central to the library on Fifth Avenue at a leisurely pace. Fifteen if Echo made her routine stop at the Sephora on Forty-Second Street for a little casual shoplifting—pricing lip gloss at sixty dollars a pop was the real crime—but now the streets were even less welcoming than they were at rush hour, and that was saying something.

A car—an entire car, airborne—whizzed past Echo's head a second before a hand clamped down on her arm and pulled her into the doorway of a bank, away from the things that were tearing apart the street with a grotesque, oddly childlike glee.

Echo looked up into the face of a National Guardsman, who stared back at her with wide blue eyes. She and the guard were pressed closely together, and the butt of his rifle dug into her shoulder. His hands were shaking so badly,

Echo would have been shocked if he managed to shoot anything he actually meant to shoot.

"Our training didn't cover this," he said with aplomb, despite the trembling of his voice. Echo's estimation of him went up several notches.

"Really? I thought magical monsters and the sky being ripped a new asshole would have been covered in basic." A storm still raged inside Echo, but quipping was reflexive. It grounded her. Helped her think beyond the blinding rage that urged her to tear her way through the ruins of Midtown Manhattan with as much mindless ferocity as the creatures wreaking havoc around them.

Echo peered around the young man's shoulder. And he was young. If he was a day over twenty, Echo would have bought a hat just for the sake of eating it.

The rifle shifted, grinding into Echo's shoulder. The soldier swallowed thickly before speaking. "What are those things?"

Those things continued their rampage up and down the street, tearing up slabs of sidewalk and wrapping their sinuous bodies around abandoned vehicles, seemingly for no greater purpose than the satisfaction of crushing them like boa constrictors in a frenzy of screaming metal. They looked like the shadow beast that had torn its way through the Nest searching for Echo all those months earlier. The monstrous entity that was responsible for the hole in the ground where Grand Central's main concourse used to be.

"Shadows," Echo said. "Scary shadows that can tear through you like tissue paper."

"Yeah, I got that, but *what* are they?"

There was no time for a lesson on the metaphysics of the

kuçedra and vessels and Tanith's homicidal tendencies, so Echo just shrugged and said, "Cover me."

Before the guardsman could stop her, she darted out from the alcove and ran the length of the street. She heard her name shouted behind her—by Caius, maybe—but the voice was swallowed by the sound of one of the shadow beasts screaming with what sounded like joy as it spotted her. The marble hulk of the library was just at the end of the block. Ivy was in there, somewhere, with Tanith, and Echo would be damned if some baby shadow-dragon thing was going to get in her way.

The shadows scrabbled toward her, tripping and tumbling over one another in their eagerness to be the first to rend her flesh wide open, to spill her blood, bright red and full of life, across the filthy city streets.

Echo was nearly at the intersection. The shadows converged, and through the cacophony, she heard a male voice ring out into the night.

"Get down!"

There. An overturned news van, its satellite cracked down the middle and pointing toward the asphalt. Echo dove behind it, her palms scraping hard against gravel, her boots churning dirt and dust as she took cover.

A hailstorm of gunfire erupted, bullets raining down right where she'd been standing, right where the shadow beasts had lunged for her. They broke apart like a fractured cloud, ink-black particles dispersing into the darkness of night.

For a handful of seconds, there was silence.

Echo peered around the side of the van and saw the guardsman who'd pulled her into the alcove wave at her. She tossed him a crooked salute. The remaining shadow monsters were drawn to the source of the gunfire and forgot her for a moment.

A moment was all she needed.

She got to her feet and kept going, toward the library—her library—stark white against the blackness of the night, a stone monument huddled beneath the hole in the sky.

CHAPTER FORTY-FIVE

Echo took the steps two at a time, white marble flying beneath her feet, heedless of the aching burn in her lungs and the protestations of her sore muscles. Her heart pounded high in her throat, a throbbing litany of fear and desperation that propelled her forward. Sparks cascaded from her fingertips. Power boiled in her veins, eager to be unleashed with the full force of her fury behind it.

"Echo, wait!"

Caius's voice rang up the steps after her, his words reverberating around the empty corridors.

Echo barreled through the entrance to one of the library's staff-only wings and then through a nondescript door that led to the stairs.

She didn't slow down. She didn't look back. Caius's footsteps sounded behind her as he followed her, boots pounding against stone, but waiting was not an option. A fresh shower of sparks singed a wooden plaque mounted on the wall as she passed. She could picture the knife scoring its way across Ivy's pale flesh. How red her blood would be against all that white. Echo put on an extra burst of speed as she climbed up the last flight of stairs to the roof.

The door had already been kicked open. The remains of the padlock that had held it shut—which Echo had picked hundreds of times—hung from the mangled backplate. Burned into the rusted metal of the door was a handprint. Tanith's, Echo assumed. Rubber marks lined the floor, the kind sneakers left on waxed floors. Maybe Ivy had struggled as Tanith had dragged her, throwing the weight of her body back with all her might, her strength nothing compared with Tanith's, refusing to be led like a lamb to the slaughter.

Echo flung the door open and stepped onto the roof. Wind whipped the loose strands of her hair around her face. Smells assaulted her once she was out in the open. Acrid smoke, throat-clogging ash, and the electric charge of the in-between, distinct and powerful even in the chaos of the battle raging below. Another scent cut through the olfactory clutter: the sharp, coppery tang of blood, freshly spilled. A gray haze crowded the edges of Echo's vision. If Ivy was dead, if she was too late . . .

"Echo, so glad you could join us."

Tanith emerged from behind a large air-conditioning unit, its sloping aluminum vent incongruous next to the battered gleam of her golden armor. Blackened veins branched across the angular beauty of her face. She looked worse than the psychic projection she had left in the Drakharin temple. The kuçedra was devouring her, slowly but surely. Echo understood with sickening clarity the emaciated corpses, the poor souls drained dry of life and magic. Stolen vitality was the only thing keeping Tanith alive. She held Ivy in front of her, one arm around Ivy's waist and arms, while her other hand held the knife to Ivy's throat at an angle that forced her head up and back, cruelly exposing the soft skin of her neck. Ivy's black eyes were wide with fear, and tears had made tracks through the dirt on her face, but she was alive. *She was alive.*

The door banged against the wall behind Echo as Caius finally caught up to her. He was panting, each breath accompanied by a wet rattling sound. It had been one fight after another, and he hadn't had the time to properly heal. Magic could only do so much for him when it was magic that had caused him so much pain.

"Oh, and you brought company," Tanith said, forcing Ivy to inch ahead in front of her. "Hello, Brother. Miss me already?"

The gash in the sky seemed even larger from this higher vantage point. There weren't any towering buildings to block Echo's view of it. It was bared to her in all its great and terrible glory.

"Let her go," Echo said. "You want to fight, we'll fight. But first you have to let her go."

Tanith let out a harsh, broken laugh. "I have to let her go?" She tightened her hold on Ivy, who gave a whimper of pain. Even without the kuçedra to aid her, Tanith was strong enough to break bones with her bare hands if she wanted. "I do not *have* to do anything. Such arrogance to make demands. I have always found that to be an especially odious hallmark of your species. And one of the many, many reasons I am going to take this world back from those who do not deserve it. I shall cleanse the world of those who have shown, time and again, that they do not appreciate what they have." She gesticulated with the knife, waving it at the New York skyline. "I will bring about a new era where my people can know peace—true peace—and prosper. All I seek to give them is a place where they can be proud. Where they do not have to live like rats hiding in the walls. We never should have let your kind have this world. Your fear became our shame, and I will bear it no longer."

"Save the supervillain speech for someone who cares," Echo said. "And let Ivy go."

Tanith paused, as if the interruption had been unexpected. And she thought Echo was arrogant. "No."

Echo made to lunge forward, to force the knife from Ivy's throat, but a hand on her forearm stopped her. Caius pulled her back. "Tanith, if any part of you is still in there, please, listen to me. You can fight this. This monster isn't you."

"Monster?" Tanith blinked owlishly at him. Her once-red eyes were awash with black as deep and dark as the abyss slicing through the sky above. "I am not so monstrous." The blade at Ivy's throat caressed her skin with deceptive gentleness. "I wanted to give the firebird a chance to say goodbye. Your pain will be such exquisite agony."

The pressure of the knife eased enough to allow Ivy to speak. "Echo, no matter what happens to me, fight her. Don't—" The knife returned, pressing deep enough to draw a thin rivulet of blood, red as the darkest rose against the snowy whiteness of Ivy's skin.

"That's enough, little dove." Tanith spoke to Ivy, but her eyes were for Echo. A vicious grin slashed across her face. "Say your farewells, Firebird."

Echo screamed as Tanith began to slowly pull the blade

across Ivy's throat. She lunged, and Caius didn't try to hold her back.

The knife never finished its journey. A roar so loud the air vibrated with the force of it sent Echo crashing to her knees, her hands clapped over her ears. Tanith started, her hold on Ivy loosening just enough to allow the girl to slither out of Tanith's grasp. Caius pushed Echo flat to the ground, shielding her with his body.

The gust of wind slammed into them before the cause of it came into view.

Two large pearlescent eyes gazed down at the rooftop as wings lifted the beast aloft, its long neck angled toward Caius in greeting. Even Tanith was momentarily stymied by its sudden appearance.

The dragon.

The dragon had followed them—followed Caius—to New York. As it approached the roof, a purr rolled from behind its closed jaws, sounding for all the world like the rumbling meow cats made when greeting their humans. It nudged Caius's shoulder with its snout, hard enough to knock him onto his rear. Caius placed a hand on its muzzle.

Echo had asked Caius once about all those stories of dragons and their hoards. Caius had smiled that soft half smile of his and told her, *Dragons are very possessive.*

No shit, Echo thought.

The gateway to the in-between hadn't closed behind them. And it had been large enough for a sizable group to pass through it all at once. Large enough for a dragon, if that dragon was crafty enough to take advantage of all the holes Tanith's madness had torn into the world.

"Hello," Caius said to the dragon in a perfectly modulated

voice, as if it weren't odd that a dragon was hovering with great flaps of its massive wings in the center of New York City. As if every camera in the vicinity weren't capturing that moment.

A body collided with Echo's side and she brought her hand up to strike before she realized it was Ivy. She curled her fingers into a fist before the sparks in her hand could blossom into a full fire. Ivy wrapped Echo in a fierce hug that lasted only a second or two before she pulled away.

"Are you okay?" Echo asked, trying to keep both Ivy and Tanith within her field of vision.

"Yeah," Ivy said. "I'm fine." She was trying very hard to make it look like she wasn't attempting to hide behind Echo and Caius. Echo spared her the indignation of having to make that choice for herself and yanked Ivy behind her. If Tanith wanted a piece of the Avicen, she was going to have to go through Echo.

Tanith glanced from the dragon to Caius as it came to rest beside him, its talons sinking into the roof's masonry as easily as if it were sand. Echo sincerely hoped the roof was strong enough to accommodate its weight; otherwise, they were all in for a great deal of pain.

"I see it's taken a liking to you," said Tanith. She brushed off her armor as if she hadn't a care in the world. "No accounting for taste, I suppose."

"Jealous?" Caius asked, one hand gripping a knife Echo hadn't seen him draw, the other resting protectively on the side of the dragon's neck.

Tanith scoffed and waved a dismissive hand, conjuring an undulating mass of black shadows. They grew larger with each lazy flick of her wrist, taking shapes that resembled smaller versions of the dragon. "I will not lie, it would have been grand to go into battle with a true dragon by my side, but I can make do with what's on hand just fine."

The shadow creatures expanded and solidified, landing a few yards away with audible thuds. They had weight and substance, even more so than the ones Echo had seen on the streets below.

Echo pushed Ivy toward the door. "Go," she said. "Get downstairs."

Ivy shook her head, her black eyes wide but certain. "Echo, I'm not leav—"

"There are wounded below. They need your help."

It was the only thing Echo could have possibly said to dissuade Ivy from throwing away her life to fight at Echo's side. She watched conflicts war in Ivy's expression, her brow pinching, her eyes sliding to the door, then back to Tanith.

"Ivy," Echo said. "Please. I can't fight her and protect you, too. Dorian and Jasper are down there. There are people who need you. Find them."

After a painful moment, Ivy finally—*finally*—nodded, her eyes bright and shiny with tears. "Don't let her win," she said, edging back toward the door, her gaze locked on Tanith.

Tanith smiled and waved a mocking goodbye. "Always a pleasure, little dove. But right now you are far more trouble than you're worth. More than one way to skin a cat and all."

As much as Echo wanted to watch Ivy's retreat, to make sure she reached the door and descended into the relative safety of the library—if any place in all of Manhattan could be said to be safe—she didn't. She kept her eyes on Tanith. But still, she made her promise to Ivy. "She won't. She'll have to kill me first."

Echo realized what a poor choice of words it had been the second they escaped her lips. Caius shot her a look that his dragon seemed to mirror.

"Oh, my sweet firebird," said Tanith, her voice oozing across the rooftop like an oil slick. "That can be arranged."

And then she and her shadow beasts attacked.

CHAPTER FORTY-SIX

Jasper was good in a fight. Better than most people expected. He had spent years carefully cultivating an air of languid indolence, projecting an ease that said to all who looked his way that he was more of a lover, not a fighter. That he preferred to keep his hands clean no matter how dirty his task. It was a ruse. A shadow of a lie that had served him well. Being underestimated was a weapon all its own, and one Jasper knew how to wield with skill.

But this was no fight.

This was chaos. This was the slam of one body into another, the sound of cloth and metal and flesh tearing, the fever pitch of shouts and wails and pleas. Smoke clogged the air, battling for dominance with the electric ozone scent of the in-between hovering above it all. Somewhere, gas was leaking, painting the atmosphere with its thick, sickly stench. Jasper thought that if he struck a match, the air itself would catch fire, burning them all in an orgiastic frenzy of violence and blood and death.

Metal screeched as a body landed atop the car behind which Jasper crouched. Shattered glass rained down from the ruined windows, scattering to the ground like chunks of hail. Dorian knelt to one side of Jasper, sword drawn, while Ivy huddled by the wheel on his other side, her already-pale skin even paler, her black eyes wide. Jasper had spotted her white feathers as she'd come running out of the library. Luck had drawn her eyes to them, and Jasper hoped that luck held on a little longer.

He peeked over the now-concave roof of the car. It was the body of an Avicen warrior—the bloodstained feathers protruding from its head confirmed that much—but whoever it was had parted with their face and what looked like half of their internal organs. Bile rose, quick and sour, in Jasper's throat as he ducked back down. Something dark and sinuous weaved between the nearby vehicles before disappearing from view.

"This is bad." Jasper usually tried to avoid stating the obvious, but the situation was so very bad it seemed worth mentioning. "They're being slaughtered, if our new friend here is anything to go by."

"Stay here," Dorian said, already leaning around the trunk of the van to gauge his next move. The sword sat so naturally in his hand that it might as well have been an extension of his arm. "Take care of Ivy."

Jasper seized hold of Dorian's sleeve before the other man could escape to throw himself boldly into the fray.

Dorian glanced down at Jasper's hand, then darted his

gaze up, his expression more than a little forlorn, dusted with a hint of desperation. "Jasper, I—"

Jasper stole the rest of Dorian's sentence with a kiss. There was no grace to it. Just a hard press of lips and teeth. It was over far too quickly. "I love you," Jasper said.

Dorian blinked, startled. "I love you, too." He said it reflexively, as if it wasn't something he needed to think about. Something deep inside Jasper lurched with glee.

"And if you think," Jasper continued, "that I'm going to let you die in a blaze of glory, you are sorely mistaken."

Jasper unsheathed the twin set of knives he'd strapped to his forearms before they'd left the keep in a whirlwind of steel and magic; then he reached into Dorian's pocket for the small vial of bloodweed elixir he'd seen Caius toss to Dorian before running after Echo toward the library. He slicked a coating of it over the two blades before Dorian had a chance to protest. Oh, the protest was coming. Jasper could see it forming on those perfectly plump, kiss-bruised lips. But Ivy—patron saint of perfect timing—swooped in with the save.

"I'm not staying here," she said. Her eyes were a hair too wide and her skin a touch too pale, but there was a determination in the set of her jaw that Jasper knew was reflected in his own expression. "I'm a healer, and there are people out there who need my help." Dorian frowned, and Jasper saw another protest trying to break free before Ivy cut him off. "I *can* help. And I will."

A scream cut through the air, accompanied by what sounded like bones cracking. Another screech—this one distinctly monstrous—rose above the cacophony. Jasper fought an involuntary shiver. Dorian's head twitched toward the source of the noise.

He closed his eye briefly. "There's nothing I can say to convince the two of you to find a nice, safe place to hide, is there?"

"No," said Jasper and Ivy at the same time.

"Fine," Dorian said through gritted teeth. He pulled Jasper in for another kiss, this one as vicious as the last.

Behind him, Jasper heard Ivy mumble, "Time and a place, guys." He flipped his middle finger at her, then immediately regretted it, as there was a very real possibility it would be the last thing he ever communicated to her.

Dorian pulled away just far enough to rest his forehead against Jasper's. "No unnecessary risks."

"Like getting run through by a sword meant for you?"

"Just like that, yes."

Jasper afforded Dorian a small smile and nodded. They both knew it was bullshit, but Dorian needed that promise, no matter how flimsy, and there was nothing Jasper would deny him. Besides, being impaled once was more than enough. No one needed a repeat of that. Especially Jasper.

"Stay close," Dorian said to them both.

The next instant, he was on his feet, rounding the corner and delving into the chaos, Jasper and Ivy one step behind.

Dorian's penchant for heroics might have been one of the things Jasper loved about him, but if Dorian got himself killed, Jasper was going to follow him to the afterlife and smack the pretty right out of him.

Jasper gripped his knives tighter and plunged into the fight, praying to gods he wasn't sure he'd ever believed in that they would all make it out of this mess alive.

*　*　*

Dorian's sword sank into the beast's hide with startling ease. The dark flesh moved and bunched as if there were muscles flexing beneath the skin, but there was little resistance as it parted beneath Dorian's blade. No catch of bone or gristle, no spill of blood across naked steel. A piercing cry sliced through the air, loud enough to make Dorian want to drop the sword and clap his hands over his ears. He didn't. But gods, it was loud.

He slid his sword free and the shadow creature—not an animal; animals bled—disintegrated, its particles spreading free like smoke on the wind.

A grunt sounded from behind him and he turned to find Jasper crouched low, one of his knives slicing through the neck of one of the blasted creatures while his other clattered to the ground. A tendril of liquid shadows had wrapped itself around his wrist, preventing him from plunging the second blade home. Dorian moved without thought; his legs ate up the distance between them, and within seconds, the beast met the same fate as its brethren.

Jasper wasted no time picking up his fallen weapon. His feathers had tumbled from their normal artful styling, and swooped across his sweaty brow. "Thanks," he breathed, pushing himself to his feet. He glanced around, and Dorian followed his gaze. The shadows were coalescing into other shapes, bigger and more monstrous. The things couldn't be killed. They could be slowed. Stopped, for a time. But not killed.

"Jasper," Dorian said, hefting his sword to meet the on-coming assault. "Do me a favor."

Jasper brushed the feathers off his forehead with the back of his hand before sinking into a fighting stance, his back to Dorian's. "Anything."

"Don't get yourself killed."

Ivy let Jasper and Dorian go on ahead, clearing a path. She spared the mangled Avicen's corpse a glance, ignoring the sickened roil of her stomach. It was, by far, the worst thing she had ever seen.

Dead, Ivy told herself, wrapping her hands around the straps of her borrowed backpack. It was Echo's. Ivy had stuffed it full of all the healing supplies she could get her hands on at Wyvern's Keep, before Tanith had taken her hostage, and it felt like the only thing grounding her in that moment. *Nothing you can do. Move.*

A soft moan drifted to where she stood.

She followed the sound to a recessed alcove tucked between two storefronts. There she found one of the human soldiers huddled, his limbs splayed and quivering, one arm wrapped around his bleeding midsection. His eyes widened as she approached, flicking between the feathers on her head and the eyes that were larger and blacker than any human's could ever be.

He began to mumble incoherently as she knelt down beside him, trying to back away despite the fact that there was nowhere for him to go.

"It's okay," Ivy said, her voice as soothing as she could make it. She set the backpack down and began removing the items she'd need from it: sterile bandages, a salve that tingled in her palm with the healing magic imbued in it, a potion to help with the pain and slow the bleeding. The soldier blinked too rapidly at the brisk movements of her hands, but the trembling in his limbs seemed to abate. "I'm here to help."

There are too godsdamn many of them.

Jasper had just enough time to form this thought before three of the shadow beasts fell upon him, black teeth flashing, death dripping from fangs that shouldn't exist.

Dorian's sword glinted in the too-bright lights mounted atop a nearby Humvee as it arced through the air, graceful and deadly as it sliced through the gathering shadows. But there were so many. So, so many.

Ivy pressed her hands into wounds that wouldn't close, willing the blood to weaken to a trickle between her fingers. Magic flared between torn flesh and her sullied palms. She had never been taught this skill, this healing by touch, but in the heat of battle, it came to her as naturally as breathing. She poured her magic into the cracks and hoped it was enough to hold the wounded together.

The sword was not Jasper's weapon of choice. He'd never felt the need to overcompensate. Smaller weapons, easily concealed—those he was good with. A whisper of steel in the night. Death sneaking in on little cat feet, on you before you even knew it was in the room.

But watching Dorian made Jasper reconsider everything

he'd ever thought about swords. Dorian held his the way Michelangelo held a paintbrush. It was art. And with it, he painted the streets black with the remnants of shadows.

Maybe we'll make it through this, Jasper thought. *Maybe we'll—*

They were falling faster than Ivy could fix them.

A weight slammed into Dorian's back, solid and heavy and full of malice. It disrupted his balance, made him lose the steps of the dance, faltering in his fleet-footed elegance. He brought up his sword, but the creature was too close and he was too late. He lashed out anyway, and his blade connected with something—not the monster on his back; one of its siblings, maybe. The blow shivered up his arm all the way to his shoulder, but it was wrong, all wrong. The thing on his back screeched and attacked, wrapping itself around him like a snake strangling a rabbit—

Talons, black as coal, raked across skin so deeply it took a moment for the pain to set in. Dorian's vision went red, then black. A scream tore its way up his throat as the world went dark.

Blood caked in white feathers, tears tracked down soot-covered cheeks as another one slipped through Ivy's fingers. For every one she patched up, another two were lost before she could even get to them. Cries of agony pierced the night.

Ivy packed a wound, then another, and another, eyes on each patient, on their skin, their feathers, their scales. Flesh torn apart and put back together, as fast as she could and still too slow.

Jasper watched Dorian collapse, knees crashing to the pavement as his legs folded beneath him as if he were a marionette with its strings cut. The air rushed from Jasper's lungs as Dorian slumped to the side, one hand cradling the right half of his face, fingers slick with blood. His sword hung limply from his other hand, tip scraping uselessly against the asphalt. A shadow beast dove toward Dorian, eager to finish what it had started, jaws open as it prepared to land a killing blow.

Jasper's knife flew straight and true, right into that gaping maw.

He felt something inside him shatter as he ran. Something deep and vital and beautiful splintering into ugliness. A high-pitched buzz scratched at his ears. His lips were moving as he pulled Dorian into his lap, but he wasn't aware of the words spilling from them, only of the way Dorian's eye patch dangled from his face, the string cut by those sweeping black talons, the mass of scar tissue clustered around his left eye socket, the mess of blood and thicker things clogging his right.

Jasper's heart hammered out a rhythmic plea as he shouted for help, for Ivy, for anyone.

No no no no no no—

* * *

Dorian could hear a heart beating against his ear, and he knew it to be Jasper's, but he couldn't see him. Darkness, more complete even than the one that had rendered him blind, threatened to engulf him. The last thought that drifted through his mind was that he was going to die without seeing that stupid beautiful face one last time.

A monstrous injustice, he thought, lucid somehow, even through the pain. But then the shadows swallowed him whole and he thought no more.

CHAPTER FORTY-SEVEN

"Caius!"

Echo's shout reached Caius at the same moment the shadow beasts slammed into him. They moved fast. Faster than any living creature should be able to.

The impact stole the breath from his lungs. Jaws lined with coal-black teeth snapped at his face, and he brought up his arm to block the onslaught. The leather of his gauntlets might as well have been butter. One of the creatures sliced through his armor with ease. Sharp stabs of pain lanced through him as the thing's teeth scraped against his flesh, raining down drops of Caius's blood onto his own face. The wounds burned, bright and immediate, as if acid had been splashed into them.

The dragon tumbled from the roof, brought down by several of the shadow beasts, clinging to its hide like lampreys. Caius could hear it roaring as it fell, its wings beating powerful gusts of wind as it struggled to keep itself aloft. He felt a momentary surge of fear for the dragon. But it could take care of itself. It would have to.

He kicked with all his might, dislodging the beast enough for him to roll away. A second creature was on him before he'd risen past his knees. It was like being struck by a boulder. They went down together, rolling across the roof in a tangle of limbs and gnashing teeth. An arm across the thing's throat kept its jaw away from Caius's face, but only barely. Black drops of something the vague consistency of saliva dripped onto Caius's cheek, scalding everywhere they touched. The beast braced its legs on Caius's, as if it had seen what he'd done to its brethren and was determined not to allow him to pull the same trick twice. The scabbard on Caius's back dug into his skin; the other knife was in his hand, but there was no way he could get the leverage to wield it with any sort of finesse.

It wasn't a fair fight, but the parade of instructors that had bestowed their knowledge upon Caius had not wasted time preparing him for fair fights. The trick to besting a bigger, stronger opponent was finding a way to use their own size and momentum against them. The creature had Caius's knife arm pinned, but he'd be a poor warrior indeed if that was enough to stop him. Caius angled the knife in his fist upward. The bloodweed-stained tip of the blade was inches away from the beast's flank.

If Caius couldn't bring the knife to the beast, then he would have to bring the beast to the knife.

He turned his head to the side and dropped his arm. Without it braced against its throat, the creature fell forward, teeth ripping at the air beside Caius's face. He felt the knife slide into the thing's soft belly until the guard stopped it from sinking any deeper.

It didn't bleed.

It went limp and then it went weightless.

The beast fractured into a writhing mass of black smoke.

Without its weight on him, Caius was free to draw his second long knife. Another creature leaped toward him, heedless of the naked blade in Caius's hand. He drove it straight into the thing's throat. Wisps of black swirled around the blade as the beast lost its corporeal form.

Already, the undulating dark masses were joining together, perhaps to create an even larger, deadlier mirror of themselves.

A crash drew his attention from the amorphous entity. He turned to see Echo crumpled at the base of an air-conditioning unit. The metal casing bore a dent the size of her body. Sparks showered wildly where she fell, as if she were no more in control of her fire than she was of her own breathing at that moment.

Tanith approached Echo, her scarlet cloak dragging against the gravel.

"Tanith!" His shout was nearly lost in the riot of noise surging up from the street. More and more of Tanith's shadow beasts were forming in the darkened corners between buildings. Some took the shapes of dragons, others of nameless creatures shifting from one form to another, with wicked teeth and lashing tails. The bloodweed seemed to slow them down, but only for a short while. They were an endless army. One that could not be killed. Only, with luck, stopped.

Tanith did not respond to the call of her name. She

advanced on Echo, who stared up at her with defiant eyes. Caius slashed at the shadow beast that was now surging toward him. It flinched from the touch of his blade, hesitant, as if it remembered the pain it had inflicted.

I hope they're not sentient, Caius thought. He ran toward Tanith. The monsters had driven him to the far edge of the roof during their tussle, and the space that separated them now seemed infinite.

Tanith's back was to him, but she must have heard the slap of his boots on the rooftop. She threw up a hand, keeping her predatory gaze fixed on Echo. Flames shivered to life around her hand in a tangle of orange, yellow, and deepest black. The blaze shot toward him, reaching with hungry tendrils of searing light. Caius ducked and rolled, sliding beneath the arc of fire. He righted himself just in time to see Echo push herself up and lunge—with the full weight of her body—against Tanith.

Together, they hit the rooftop. Echo's fist snapped into Tanith's face. She was yelling something at Tanith, but Caius didn't catch all the words. "You—won't let—hurt them—I swear to—"

Tanith's fire circled around Caius, correcting its course. A ring of flames erupted around him, trapping him. He had never seen it do that before. She shouldn't have been *able* to do that, not when she was so thoroughly distracted by Echo's artless but effective blows. Even magic, at least the kind he and Tanith and all his people wielded, had to obey the laws of the universe. Humanity had found explanations for certain aspects of the magical world and called it physics, but even that which they had not been able to explain away with modern science had an order to it. Magic was controlled. It was not a wild power. It obeyed the will of the person who cast it, but these flames seemed to have a mind of their own. Like the shadow beasts, the fire seemed to operate independently of Tanith's instruction.

His skin tingled with the memory of the fire against it. During those long weeks, lost to the darkness and the ceaseless fear that had dominated every waking moment, Tanith had found new and inventive ways to cause him pain.

Pain was her weapon of choice. It had made him tractable, weak. Vulnerable. She had used her fists. Cold, sharp steel. Lashing whips of corded leather. And fire.

She had held her hands against his as she'd summoned flames to her palms, holding him to prevent him from pulling away from the heat and the mind-shattering pain. The memory was so clear, so vivid, that now, staring into the blinding brightness of the blaze circling him, he thought he could smell his own flesh burning.

It's not real, he reminded himself. *Just a memory. And you are stronger than that.* He watched as his sister dislodged Echo and sent her flying halfway toward the roof's ledge with a single kick. She was stronger than she had been before the kuçedra had twisted her into something monstrous. Echo couldn't triumph against her if it came to trading blows. Not alone.

Caius tightened his grip on his knives and rushed forward through the flames.

A tendril of black nothingness struck out and wound itself around Caius's ankle. It lurched back, bringing him crashing to the ground, half his body still submerged in the flames.

It *burned.*

He flailed blindly at the circle of fire with his knife. The blackness receded, though the orange and gold flames remained unaffected. It was enough. Caius dragged himself forward, trying desperately to block out the agony of his burned legs. He had suffered worse attacks in battle, he reminded himself. *Get up, godsdammit.*

Echo needed him. He wouldn't fail her like he had Rose. He would not let Echo become another of his sister's victims. The cycle ended here.

He pushed himself to his feet. Tanith was standing yards away, staring down Echo, who was only now struggling to control the fire at her call. It blossomed around her balled fists like white and black petals of flame. It was lovely, but nothing compared to the strength of Tanith's blaze. He'd been right in his prediction; Tanith wasn't trying to kill Echo. If she had been, Echo would not have lived long enough to throw that first punch. Tanith was baiting her, goading her into expending her energy, like a cat playing with a mouse.

"Tanith!"

This time, she did turn to him. "What?" She sounded irritated, as if he had just disturbed her at her studies.

"This ends now." Caius willed himself to think past the burns, the new wounds freshly opened, the old ones crying in protest. He approached the edge of the roof, where his sister stood on steady feet.

Tanith stared at him for a beat. Then a wicked smile stretched across her lips. "Yes," she said. "It most certainly does."

She raised her arm high above her head. Echo chose that moment to unleash a burst of flame toward Tanith, but it was too small, too weak. Tanith brought her hand down in a slicing gesture, and the ground beneath Caius's feet split. The sound of rending cement cut through the air with a resounding crack. He had one last glimpse of Echo's screaming face before the rooftop collapsed in a cascade of stone and steel.

He was falling,
falling,
falling.

This is it, he thought. *This is how I die.*

And then he landed. On something soft. He thought splattering across the pavement of Fifth Avenue would have been more unpleasant. But there were sounds all around him: someone calling his name, someone else shouting in agony. Echoing explosions of gunfire and grenades. The roar of a waterfall of stone crashing to the ground.

He wasn't dead. He was, in fact, very much alive.

He rolled his head to the side to see what had saved him. There was a patch of grass beneath him, perhaps five feet from where he hovered.

"Hey!" The pink-haired Avicen mage who had accompanied them to Iceland stood not ten feet away, her hands extended and quivering with exertion. "You good?"

Violet. Her name was Violet. Her hands were streaked with blood and a cut had opened up just above her left eyebrow. Blood and dirt caked that side of her face, surely obscuring her vision. Caius nodded. "I can't move, but other than that, I'm good."

Suddenly, he fell, landing on the grass with an undignified *oof.*

Violet offered him a hand, which he gratefully accepted. She hauled him to his feet and he bent immediately to scoop up his knives, glad they hadn't fallen too far from him.

"Where's Echo?" he asked Violet. Pieces of masonry littered the ground around them. It looked like Tanith's strike—whatever it was and however she'd done it—had demolished half the building. Echo was nowhere in sight.

Violet shook her head. "I was hoping you could tell me." Her chest fell and rose in rapid, shallow breaths. "We're losing. There's too many of them."

An endless army, Caius thought. And all it had to do to win was outlast them.

CHAPTER FORTY-EIGHT

Screams rang through Echo's ears, and it took her a moment to realize they were coming from her.

The library's once-proud facade had crumbled, split down the middle as if sundered by a vengeful god. The remaining outer wall protruded like a row of broken teeth.

The head of a lion rolled to a stop by Echo's boot. Half its mane had been blown off, and its sightless stone eyes stared up at the wound in the sky. It was Patience, the guardian of the southern side of the library's entrance. Her sister, Fortitude, remained on her perch on the north side of the steps, her head angled toward Echo. It looked like she was surveying the destruction of her kingdom, knowing there wasn't a damn thing she could do to save it.

The library had been Echo's refuge. The first place in the world she had ever felt safe. The first place she had ever belonged. It was her *home*. And now it was destroyed, blown apart as easily as if it were a child's plaything, a castle built of hollow blocks, toppled with a finger.

Other voices came to Echo. Other screams. Not far from where she had landed, she saw a flash of vibrant feathers crouching over a still form, their colors as wild and lovely as those of a peacock. Jasper. In his lap he cradled a head of silvery hair, a pale face streaked with blood. Dorian. There was something wrong with his face, something desperately wrong. Even through the cacophony and the chaos, Echo could see Jasper's hand covering half of Dorian's face, trying in vain to stanch the bleeding. Then she realized why. Dorian's eye. Someone had cut it out. Jasper's body heaved with violent sobs as he begged in a medley of English, Avicet, and broken Drakhar for Dorian to please not die.

Bile rose in Echo's throat. Nothing had ever hurt like this. Not the dagger she had sunk into her own chest. Not the feeling of her own fire burning her from the inside out. Not the horror of finding the person she'd loved strung up like so much meat.

Your pain will be such exquisite agony.

A sob clawed its way from Echo's throat. Tears blurred her vision. The fight raged on all around her, but she could not take her eyes from the spectacle of senseless destruction in front of her. Flames flickered around Echo's fists, scorching the earth beneath her bruised and bloody knuckles. She didn't remember injuring them. It must have happened in the fall. The abraded skin burned where the fire touched it. Her own body—her own magic—was betraying her. And she couldn't stop it.

A slow, steady tread crunched over the rubble, advancing on Echo like a predator lazily circling its prey.

"Such a shame, really." Tanith's voice was close, coming from somewhere behind Echo and to the left. She could have dug her sword into Echo's back and Echo couldn't have lifted a finger to stop her. So great was her pain. So exquisite was her agony. "It was a marvelous library."

A heavy hand came to rest on Echo's shoulder. Golden gauntlets dug into her muscles, the armored fingers tipped like claws. Tanith leaned down to whisper her next words into Echo's ear.

"Tell me, Firebird. Does it hurt?"

Echo had never quite understood what people meant when they said they were seeing red. It had always seemed to her a cartoonish idiom. But a hot wave of rage rushed over her at the feel of Tanith's warm breath on the shell of her ear. At the sight of the library, half in ruins. At the sound of people who trusted her enough to follow her into battle falling under the onslaught of the kuçedra's vile creatures.

Her anger seethed. It bubbled and spilled over, sparking into her hands in white-hot pulses of flames. Still on her knees, Echo pivoted with a snarl that sounded, even to her ears, more animal than human. The power rolled from Echo in waves, knocking Tanith off her feet. The sound of armor scraping over pavement was loud, even in the din of battle.

Tanith pushed herself up, wiping at a split lip with a gauntleted hand. Black ooze seeped through the broken skin, leaving a smear like shadow dust across her pale cheek. She looked at the blood that was not blood, so dark against her gilded armor. "It feels good, doesn't it? The rage. The bloodlust." She smiled, licking at the black not-blood on her lip. "I used to try so hard to contain it, to hold it back, when all I wanted was to bathe the world in blood until there was no one left standing. But no more. I don't have to hold back." Her smile widened. "And neither do you."

"Oh, fuck you," Echo spat. Angry tears burned at the corners of her eyes. She hated that Tanith was right, but it *had* felt good. Letting the magic pour out of her hands, fueled by pure emotion, felt like nothing she had ever experienced before. It felt raw. Immediate. She felt like she was overfull of power, and it wanted nothing more than to be let out.

And so she would let it out. Right into Tanith's smug face.

Echo rose to her feet. Her fall had been cushioned; she'd felt someone's magic buoying her, but she hadn't seen who had done it. No matter. It had saved her, and now she would put a stop to Tanith's insanity once and for all. Whatever it took.

"It didn't have to be like this," Echo said. "Your people— and mine—are in more danger now than they ever have been, and it's all on you."

"What an awfully myopic worldview." Tanith shook her head. "This is the only way it was ever going to be. I just gave the world the push it needed. It will be cleansed, and we will have a blank canvas on which to paint our new world. That you cannot see that tells me you were never worthy of the power given to you. If only you had known how to wield it properly. The prophecy was true. The firebird was the catalyst for our salvation, the harbinger of our future. The future simply does not include you."

"You really love the sound of your own voice, don't you?" Flames manifested in Echo's hands. She would need to call more of the power within her than she ever had. Her blows had been as effective as a mosquito stinging an elephant;

Tanith had brushed them off with minimal effort. The fire burned, brighter and brighter, until even her own skin was sweltering under the heat of it.

Black tendrils swirled around Tanith's form, creating a cloud of impenetrable darkness. She approached, stepping over snapped power lines and fallen cables, and the darkness moved with her, dancing around her in a frenzied mass of movement. "I can feel all that light inside you. Burning. Wanting to destroy." The darkness fragmented into different shapes. Dark veins raced down the unmarked skin of her neck. It was as if each deployment of the kuçedra's power meant that the monster within her was claiming more and more of her, marking its territory. With enough time, there would be nothing of Tanith left.

"What are you waiting for?" asked Tanith. Her feet, encased in plated sabatons attached to the gold grieves on her legs, came to a halt right next to a severed power line; one of them was squarely in the middle of a puddle, inches away from where sparks of electricity sputtered from the exposed end of the cable. It was a hell of a fire hazard if Echo had ever seen one.

"This," said Echo. She bent down and reached for the end of the cable near her. The rubber melted under her touch as her flames ran the length of it, all the way to the sparking tip. It took only a second or two for Tanith to realize what was happening, but it was enough. The exposed coils caught fire and exploded.

Echo was glad Tanith had headed into battle wearing armor. Metal was a fantastic conductor of electricity. As was water.

The shock sent Tanith crashing to the ground, her body

writing as electricity coursed through her. The black cloud-like beings around her evanesced like a fleeing mist. Her black irises rolled back, exposing the pale whites of her eyes, laced with capillaries gone dark. The acrid smell of burning hair wafted over Echo.

She approached Tanith, careful to avoid the flailing power lines, grateful that the rubber soles of her boots protected her far better than the metal of Tanith's sabatons.

"I was waiting for you," Echo said. "This is my city. This is my world. I know it better than you ever will." She unleashed another volley of fire at Tanith's vulnerable, prostrate form. A scream tore its way from Tanith's throat as flames and electricity seared once more.

Echo tried to ignore the thrill of satisfaction she felt at the sound of those screams. It was a horrible sight to behold. No one should take pleasure in what she was doing. And yet . . .

She reached behind her, rucking up her leather jacket. The dagger was still tucked safely into the waistband of her pants. It had dug painfully into her spine when she fell, but she was obscenely glad she hadn't lost it when the roof had collapsed. She slid it out of its scabbard. As Helios's vain attempt at an assassination had proven, a simple stabbing wouldn't stop Tanith. But Echo would saw through her neck, through bone and tendon, if she had to. *Let's see how well you bounce back without your head.*

Tanith's screams quieted as she fought to roll away from the sparking cable. Her hair was a frazzled mess, and she reeked of an odor straight from Echo's—and Rose's—nightmares: burnt flesh. Echo had done that. Another surge of gratification shot through her. A detached part of her felt sickened by the thought that she was the one turning the tables and inflicting the same damage Tanith had on Rose so many years ago, but it was a small part. Easily ignored.

Tanith rolled onto her knees, shivering with the aftershocks of electrocution. Burn marks were scored into her armor. With unsteady but quick hands, Tanith unbuckled the chest plate and let it clatter to the ground. Without the heavy armor wearing her down, she knelt back onto her heels and inhaled deeply. "There. That's much better."

You have no idea, Echo thought. Before Tanith could recover any further, Echo ran at her, the dagger naked in her hand, the magpie wings on the hilt digging into her palm. Tanith's corrupted eyes widened as she struggled to get into a defensive stance, but Echo was too fast. The blade found its target—an opening on the side of Tanith's armor—and sank through her leather tunic with ease. Echo felt the air punched out of Tanith's lungs with the force of the blow. Steel scraped against bone as Echo drove the dagger between Tanith's ribs, aiming for the heart. If Tanith even had one.

Resistance slowed the dagger down as the widest part of it reached the space between Tanith's ribs. Echo tried to drive it deeper, but Tanith's hands came up to trap hers, stopping her.

Tanith grunted in pain, but her lips curled into a wobbling smile. "Is that all you've got?" She leaned forward and yanked Echo's hands—still closed over the hilt of the dagger—closer, burying the blade even deeper into her own chest. Black bile bubbled from her mouth. "I told you it felt good."

That same black ooze poured over their joined hands, pulsing with each beat of Tanith's heart. It scorched Echo's skin, burning a thousand times worse than any fire she had ever felt before. Echo tried to pull her hands back, but Tanith held firm.

"You want to kill me? Make me suffer?" Tanith's voice cracked with the effort of speaking, but there was a clarity in her eyes that sent Echo's stomach plummeting. "Then do it."

That small part of Echo that screamed at her to stop, that this wasn't what she wanted, faded to silence.

She *did* want to kill Tanith. She *did* want to make her suffer. And so she would.

Echo cast her gaze around at the shattered facade of the library, at the still bodies that littered the street, at the white-feathered head darting between the fallen, trying to see who could be saved and for whom there was no hope. She thought of Caius, tumbling from the rooftop. Of Dorian, his handsome face a carved-up ruin. Of Jasper, begging him to stay awake. Of the homes lost and the hearts broken and the lives destroyed because of one person's thirst for power.

The tips of Echo's fingers tingled with magic. She didn't try to hold it back or rein it in. She simply let it go. Fire erupted from her hands in swaths of black and white, like the feathers of a magpie. It ran down the length of the blade as if the steel were a conduit channeling her magic into the wound on Tanith's chest. Tanith angled her head up and looked at Echo through the flames. For a moment, the black seemed to flee from her irises, leaving them the red they used to be. Her brow wrinkled in a frown, oddly delicate on her features. But in the next moment, her eyes were black once more. An illusion, Echo thought. Her mind playing tricks on her.

"This ends now," Echo said. She pushed the fire toward

Tanith, who was still kneeling on the ground, weak from electrocution. Who was the most vulnerable Echo had ever seen her. Who was . . . smiling?

The fire did not burn her.

The metal of Tanith's remaining armor began to glow, hot as an ember, but her skin was radiating with Echo's light. It didn't char her flesh. It sank into it. Tanith was absorbing it.

All of it.

Echo tried to pull back, but it was too late. Tanith lurched forward and grabbed Echo's arms, pulling her into a gross parody of an embrace.

"You're not wrong." Viscous black liquid escaped from the corners of Tanith's mouth. "This ends. This war. This thing between us. And so does everything else."

Tanith's fingers dug into Echo's wrists. Sharp pinpoints of pain lanced through Echo's arms, straight to her core. Something tugged at her—not physically, but at the deepest recesses of her being. It felt like a hook had been sunk into her gut and was pulling her organs out. But she had no wounds. She didn't bleed.

The tugging sensation grew stronger as Tanith's smile grew darker, more feral. Again Echo tried to pull her hands away, and again Tanith tightened her hold, refusing to let Echo go.

Tanith leaned in and spoke into Echo's ear, her voice a harsh whisper. "Look around you, little firebird. Your friends are dead and dying. Your allies fall, one after another. The humans you tricked into trusting you are crumpling like toy soldiers."

Echo looked. A man in fatigues—no, a boy, for he could

not be a day over nineteen—was lying on the ground, his face toward the heavens, his eyes open and unblinking. The front of his uniform had three long gashes, from one shoulder all the way to his waist. Blood smeared the greenish camouflage, but his heart had ceased its beating and the blood trickled to the asphalt in an unhurried descent. Not three feet from him was an Avicen soldier, facedown in the street, white cloak stained crimson, sword still clutched in lifeless fingers.

The fighting had not come near them, and only then did Echo realize why. A ring of shadows had sprouted all around, an impenetrable barrier of velvety blackness cutting them off from the world beyond its border. The only people in the circle were Echo, Tanith, and the dead.

She couldn't see through the shadows as they rose higher, as if sensing her attempt to spot a familiar face through the darkness. Caius may have survived the fall, but they were hopelessly outnumbered. Ivy was no fighter. Rowan was still green, despite his conviction. Dorian was probably already dead. And Jasper. Jasper would do something stupid seeking revenge and get himself killed. They didn't stand a chance. Not one of them.

Not unless Echo put an end to it. All of it.

That blinding rage returned, churning in her blood with the ferocity of some ancient war cry, pulsing through her veins like the beating of a battle drum. A snarl rose from deep inside her chest, and she shoved every ounce of magic she had at her disposal into Tanith, wildly. Desperately. The tugging ceased as she opened the floodgates of power, hoping to overload Tanith just as she'd done with the fire and electricity.

But Tanith's smile only widened, her lips cracked and oozing tar-black blood. The ground shook beneath them, like the warning shocks of an oncoming earthquake.

And Echo realized that she had been mistaken. Tremendously, catastrophically mistaken.

The scar on her chest burned, as if trying to tear a hole in her heart to match the one in the sky.

It was not a scar at all.

It was a seed. A small kernel of shadows, left to germinate in her soil, where it would be tended, where it could grow. Echo felt herself cracking like concrete losing a battle to stubborn roots.

It was a scar. It was not a scar. It was a seed. It was not a seed.

It was a keyhole.

The shadows reached inside her and *turned*. Tanith smiled.

"Yes, that's it. Just like that. Embrace your darkness." Her fingers dug deeply enough into the flesh of Echo's wrists to draw blood, a screaming red against her skin, so unlike the unnatural black of Tanith's. "Let. Me. In."

CHAPTER FORTY-NINE

The world froze.

Cold seized Echo's bones and made them brittle. It stole the air from her lungs, and her blood trickled to a slow, icy sludge.

A word drifted through the tundra of her mind, distant, as if it belonged to someone else. To some*place* else.

Curglaff. Scottish. The shock one feels after plunging into cold water.

She froze. And then she cracked, like an icicle smashing against concrete. She was no longer a girl, a single entity in the greater tapestry of the universe, but a collection of shards floating in space.

All around her was darkness, a vast unfathomable nothing heavy with malice. The fractured pieces of her being drifted into the abyss, and she willed herself to stay together despite the overwhelming pull, as strong and as undeniable as gravity, trying to tear her apart, piece by fragile piece.

Awareness of her body as a physical thing came back to her in inches. Sensation prickled up her limbs. There were her toes and her fingers, unbearably cold in the harsh frigidity of the void. An experimental roll of her wrists proved that they were still there. Her knees ached, a hundred points of discomfort from where they'd slammed into gravel and cement. Shoulders stiff with tension and fatigue fought her disjointed movements, but the unpleasantness of forcing her body to move meant she was alive.

As her mind sealed together her disparate parts, the unreality of what was happening hit her. Hard. She closed her eyes, hoping that the darkness would dissipate, then opened them, but it remained stubbornly unchanged. If colors had a noise, the nothingness that surrounded her would be a screaming black so loud that nothing else could survive in it.

It was too much. It wasn't like the in-between. The space between all the heres and all the theres was neutral in the truest sense. There was a presence to this darkness. A sentience. It cradled her tenderly, but the tenderness was an illusion. It seethed, rife with the taste of what Echo had come to know in Tanith's eyes as they'd stared each other down. It was a hungry void, one that would never be filled but would only take and take and take, until there was nothing left to be devoured.

Echo opened her mouth to draw breath, to scream, to cry out into the great unfeeling nothingness, but there was no air for her to inhale. No atmospheric substance through which to transmit sound. The nothingness rushed into her open mouth like ocean water, clogging her throat and filling her lungs to bursting.

She was drowning, choking to death on the vile blackness that had poured out of Tanith's beating heart.

Let me in, Tanith had said. And like a fool, that was exactly what Echo had done.

She could feel another presence in the darkness with her, a malevolent force eager to leach the magic from Echo's body, from her soul. It pressed against her, oily and insistent.

She felt like a single candle flickering in a strong wind.

You have to fight it, Echo.

The voice was muffled by the darkness, practically inaudible. But Echo recognized the whispered tone.

Her mind was too much of a scramble for rational thought. She tried to call out Rose's name, but she couldn't speak. Her lungs burned in the absence of air. Her voice was stolen by the endless night.

It is a cage, cha'laen.

A different voice this time, not as familiar, but still one she recognized. The woman in the cave, with the warrior's braids and the bow and arrow and the scales that caught the firelight just right. The Drakharin.

She put you here, so you do not struggle while she drains you dry. Rose again. *Open your eyes, Echo.*

Echo's eyes were open.

No, cha'laen. The Drakharin woman's voice was quieter now, more distant. *You only believe they are.*

The blackness pressing against Echo squeezed her tighter. Her bones felt like they were being ground together. Her muscles twitched against the unrelenting pressure.

The only way out is to remember.

Remember? Echo couldn't form the words, not aloud or

in thought. But the sentiment seemed to reach them, the other vessels. The ones who were still here with her, at the end of all things. Remember what?

Everything it wants you to forget.

A single point of light pierced the darkened veil, so far away that Echo thought she would never be able to reach it, even if she strained against the oppressive shadows with all her might.

But the flickering image grew brighter and larger, not waiting for Echo to reach toward it, but rather reaching toward her. The closer it got, the looser the void's hold was on her. She could think a little more clearly, in words instead of frantic, half-formed images.

What is that?

Rose's voice felt closer, her words clearer in Echo's mind. *That's the part of you it hasn't touched. The part it wants to snuff out so that nothing is left to stand in its way.*

The thing glowed like an ember in the darkness. It inched closer and closer to Echo, or she inched closer and closer to it. Distance held no meaning in this place. No logic seemed to govern the nature of the space, no rules of physics or limitations of magic. The more Echo thought about it, the less real it became, as if her consciousness was chipping away at it bit by bit. But the light never crystallized into something substantial. It sat there, waiting for Echo to act upon it, to give it form.

Remember, Echo.

I don't know what to remember, she wanted to say. She couldn't remember where she had come from or how she had gotten here. It was all a pale blur, indistinct and shapeless.

Then let us help.

With a sudden burst of speed, the light slammed into Echo with surprising force. She'd expected the impact to hurt, but in a rush, the pressure that had been crushing her evaporated. The relief she felt in its absence was nearly as overpowering as the unbearable weight that had been wrapped around her body, squeezing her skeleton nearly to the point of fracture.

She blinked against the onslaught of light. When her eyes adjusted, she could see forms taking shape, figures she knew even by their roughest outlines.

The Ala bending down to wipe a smear of dirt off Echo's cheek. Echo's scraped knees dotted with blood, her nose runny. Her hair half out of its braid, so neatly plaited by the Ala that morning, now in utter, shameful disarray.

"The cruelty of children is a truly remarkable thing." The Ala's voice was faraway and fuzzy, a remnant from a half-remembered dream.

Only the sparsest details of the circumstances surrounding her scraped knees and mussed hair remained in Echo's memory. Some Aviceling had tried to prove himself to his friends by picking on the human girl, most likely. But what had stood out so strongly to Echo was the Ala's endless compassion. That she hadn't chastised Echo for fighting back. And especially that she had not shamed her for losing. The Ala had merely bandaged her bloodied knees and sent her back into the world with a handful of chocolate chip cookies and a promise that she would always love her, no matter what the other Avicen said.

The light flared bright and coalesced into another shape,

another scene. A tableau of laughing faces, Ivy's chief among them. The feel of Rowan's hand in Echo's own, his thumb pressing into the fleshy part of her palm at the base of her thumb. They'd snuck into the movie theater at Union Square—Echo had forgotten the movie, but she remembered everything else that mattered. The way Rowan had waited for the lights to dim before reaching out to take Echo's hand. The way Ivy had staunchly pretended not to notice.

Another shift of light. Jasper, his feathers so bright against the blinding whiteness, surrounding his head like a Technicolor halo. His lips moving, making fun of her, probably. It was his favorite pastime. Echo hadn't minded. She gave as good as she got, and there was a certain comfort in the way he treated her. Not like a human. Not like an Avicen. But just as herself. He didn't care about alliances or tribal delineations. All that mattered to Jasper was one's abilities. Prove yourself to him and you had a friend for life—or for as long as he felt like it. But Echo had known, even before his loyalty had been tested and Dorian had given him a reason to stay, that she'd found a friend in him. A true one.

And then there was Caius.

Oh. Rose's voice breezed through Echo's mind like a gentle wind.

Caius, sitting on the beach, watching the waves lap at the shore. His shirt was off, lying on the sand next to him beside his discarded boots. Sunlight glinted off the scales running down the column of his spine, disappearing at the waistband of his breeches. His hair looked like chocolate in the sun, shot through with strands of gold. He was smiling, a soft, reverent smile that had died along with Rose.

Remember, cha'laen. Let them be your anchor.

I remember, Echo thought. And nothing was going to make her forget.

She let the light envelop her in its warmth. Her eyes drifted closed. It seeped into her pores, sinking deeper and deeper, all the way through to her bones. It drove out the darkness that had tried to drown her, and in its screaming brightness, she let herself burn.

CHAPTER FIFTY

When Echo opened her eyes, it was to stare into Tanith's wide ones. Red eyes, not black. A frown creased Tanith's aristocratic brow, marring the features that still managed to be beautiful, even with the network of black veins cutting across her pale skin.

"How?" The word escaped Tanith's lips more as breath than sound. Her hands fell away from the hilt of the dagger still embedded in her sternum. Echo hadn't the foggiest idea how much time had passed in the real world; the prison in which she'd found herself hadn't a notion of time as she understood it. It could have been minutes. It could have been seconds.

Echo didn't offer a response. She barely understood what had transpired. Her entire body trembled with exertion, as if she had just completed a marathon in record time. The hilt of the dagger was slick with the oily black substance that had poured from Tanith's wounds. Echo tightened her grip on it and pulled it free. It came loose with a sickening squelch.

She pushed herself back, away from Tanith, who was still staring at her, her expression a mix of disbelief and calculation. Echo could very nearly hear the gears in Tanith's head turning, trying to puzzle out how she'd broken free of the kuçedra's shackles. If Tanith attacked her now, it wouldn't be much of a fight. Echo felt drained, like a well run dry.

The barrier of shadows had fallen, but two things had changed in Echo's surroundings, fundamentally altering the landscape of Fifth Avenue and Forty-Second Street.

Just feet away, a rift had opened up in the middle of the avenue, neatly bisecting the road. It separated Echo from the library like a canyon. She peered into it; the chasm had no bottom, only endless black sliced deep into the fabric of the earth itself. It wasn't as wide as the tear across the sky, but as Echo watched, the rift expanded. In centimeters and slowly, but it expanded nonetheless. It was growing, eating away at the asphalt like a black hole.

"Is this it?" Tanith's voice had gone soft with wonder. Echo glanced back at her; she looked like a completely different person than she had mere minutes before. Her eyes were scarlet, with only the slightest tinges of black at the edges of her irises.

The "it" to which she referred was actually more of a them. Motes of light danced in the air, casting a white shimmer over the devastated street.

Echo reached out and let one of the luminescent motes land on her fingertip like a snowflake. It clung to her skin, then seeped into it, flooding her with a sense of recognition. Instantly she knew that it was the thing that had been inside her. The being of energy and light that had rushed into her when she'd plunged that dagger into her own heart in the Oracle's cave in the heart of the Black Forest.

This was the firebird, in its purest, wildest form. Untethered from a vessel and left to float free, aimless as a child. It had been inside Echo, but Tanith had tried to unmoor it, to steal it for herself. She had managed the former but not the latter. Now it was simply there.

The firebird was neither good nor bad, the Ala had told Echo all those months earlier. Its nature was determined by the one who harnessed it. There was a quality to the floating luminescence that Echo had tasted before; it was hungry, just as the kuçedra was hungry. It wanted to have a home, a purpose. It needed it.

A surprisingly girlish giggle burst from Tanith's lips. She too had touched the light, and it had been absorbed into her skin. The tips of her fingers glowed with it, sending the blackened veins in her hands into grotesque relief.

"It feels like champagne," Tanith muttered, mostly to herself. "Like flying."

The dusting of light—like glitter, Echo thought, half giddy with wonder—drifted down toward the rift in the street. Where it touched, the blackness writhed, growing and shrinking in undulations of movement. They were drawn to each other, the Light and the Dark, but they were not enemies. They complemented each other. They completed each other. Two sides of the same coin.

A sudden movement caught Echo's attention. Tanith rose to her feet, her hands swirling in the radiant mist. She twirled, her cloak winding around her legs, her face upturned in something akin to ecstasy.

"Yes," she was saying over and over. "This is what I needed. This is all I needed. So close. We are so close now."

Echo tried to push herself to standing, but there was a weariness in her bones greater than any exhaustion she had ever felt before. It was as if a part of her was missing, as if something vital to her existence had been amputated. There was an ache in her like the phantom pain of a missing limb. She had rearranged herself in the months after the Black Forest, had made room for the thing living inside her body, and now that it was gone, all she felt was a great yawning emptiness where it had once been.

Tanith could not be allowed to claim the power of the firebird, in all its wild effulgence, for herself. She was powerful now, but with the dual powers of light and dark on her side, she would be unstoppable.

We have to seal the rifts, Echo realized. *We have to close them off the way they did way back when.*

Some power was too great to exist in the world, free for the taking. People—human, Avicen, Drakharin—were fallible things. Easily corrupted.

The power seemed to respond to Echo's touch, but she had no idea how to control it. It wasn't as though the firebird had come with an instruction manual. That would have made her life much easier.

Echo finally got to her feet, thoroughly winded. How the hell she was going to battle a centuries-old warrior halfway to becoming some kind of unstoppable demigod was a perfectly valid question, considering that it was taking every ounce of her strength to simply remain standing.

The sound of gunfire cut through the bubble of light and magic and shadow that had formed around them. Then shouts and the far-off roar of a dragon. Time may have felt as if it had stopped for the two of them, but the world had kept on spinning and the fight had continued to rage without them.

"Echo!"

She turned, immediately regretting how quickly she'd whipped her head around to find the source of the cry. Clambering atop an overturned car was Caius, his left half awash with blood. It caked the ridges of his leather armor. The blades of both his knives were equally drenched, in blood and darker things.

He ran toward her, skirting his sister, who seemed not to notice his presence—or if she did, she couldn't be bothered to care. Tanith was drunk on magic, a state of being that benefited them now but would turn detrimental when she figured out what to do with all that power.

When he reached Echo's side, he stared down at the still-widening rift with horror. "How did that happen?"

"I'm not entirely sure," Echo began, her voice wavering with fatigue, "but it happened when Tanith tried to steal my power. Contact with it made her stronger, and then"—she waved a hand at the chasm helplessly—"this."

"How do we close it?" He looked at his wrists as if contemplating how to use his blood to lock it shut, just as the mages had done with the broken seals. But this was far bigger than a broken seal, and even all the blood in his body might not be enough.

"You don't." The childlike awe had fled from Tanith's voice, replaced by the bitter malevolence Echo expected from her. Tanith stalked toward them, waves of light and shadow dancing around her form. "It will grow and grow and leave nothing in its wake. Then we can start fresh." She paused a few feet away.

Caius stepped in front of Echo and slipped into a defensive stance. He gripped the knives tightly, but Echo was close enough to see the slight tremor in his arms. "There is no 'we.' Not in starting over. The only thing you'll achieve is complete destruction. There's no room for creation after that."

"You can't talk sense into her, Caius," Echo said. The dagger in her hand seemed pathetic next to the long, elegant wickedness of Caius's blades, but it was all she had. If only she could marshal the free-floating energy surrounding her. "She's delusional."

Tanith cocked her head to the side like a curious bird. "There could be a place for you beside me, Caius."

He shook his head, an expression of unbearable sadness settling on his face. "No," he said. "There isn't."

"Then you've made your choice," said Tanith. She drew her sword from its sheath. She hadn't bothered using it yet, as far as Echo knew. Perhaps there was a part of her that wanted to meet her brother in a fight that was as fair as she could make it. Fire crackled to life around her, dancing up her gilded armor, snaking around her gauntlets, licking up the length of her blade. "We could have ruled together, you and I. Your passing will be dutifully mourned."

With that, she sprang forward, a dizzying whirlwind of shadow and flame trailed by a cloud of wispy light.

Caius met her halfway. Their blades clashed. The sound of steel ringing against steel was loud, even in the midst of all the chaos along the avenue. Echo darted out of the way.

She was hopelessly out of her depth. Tanith and Caius were tangled in each other, blades locked, moving so quickly that Echo could hardly follow what was happening. She couldn't tell who was winning, so evenly matched were they in skill. Caius moved with the grace of a dancer, while Tanith preferred to throw her strength into her attacks with all the finesse of a blunt instrument. It was inelegant but undoubtedly effective.

Echo tried to spy an opening she could slip through to aid Caius, but it was futile. Without her magic, she was just a girl waving around a dagger she only barely knew how to use.

And then Echo saw the blackness growing faster, spreading. Reaching.

The fissure opened wider and wider, a mouth demanding to be fed. It inched closer to the spot where Caius and Tanith tussled, locked together in combat.

It was so close to them. Too close.

Echo drew in a breath, and the magic around her rushed into her lungs. She was a vessel; the power was drawn to her. Light and dark. The magic smashed into her with enough force to send her to her knees. Even then, she didn't stop breathing it in. She drew it into herself, every mote she could reach, and she pushed it *out*.

The crack in the street stopped growing. Every fiber of muscle in Echo's body strained to hold the rift together. She couldn't close it, but she could keep it from getting larger. From reaching Caius.

Echo could not move without snapping the tenuous tether she had on the rift. She could only watch.

A pained grunt escaped Caius as he parried away from one of Tanith's artless lunges. Blood trickled from a gash on his cheek, a neat diagonal line that ran from cheekbone to chin.

Tanith stepped away from him, one hand coming up to her mouth. Her eyes faded back to red, and an expression of horror stole across her face. "Caius?"

Her voice sounded weak and confused, like that of a lost child. A ruse, Echo thought. It had to be. But Tanith was backing away, shaking her head. When she looked at the tear in the in-between in the ground, it was as though she were seeing it for the very first time.

"Did I do this?" Tanith asked.

Echo didn't buy it. Not for one second. "Yeah, you did," she spat, wishing she could get up and wipe that lost look off Tanith's face with a well-aimed punch. "And you know you did."

Caius frowned, puzzled. "Tanith?"

Tanith peered at him as if she were seeing him, too, for the first time. "Caius?" She looked down at her hands, her gaze roving over the tracery of black veins and the dusting of bright white light clinging to her skin. "What's happening to me?"

"You don't remember?" Caius asked. He didn't relax his stance or lower his knives an inch, but he didn't charge her either. Even though she was as vulnerable in that moment as they were likely to ever see her.

"I— Bits and pieces—broken fragments . . ." Her eyes snapped up. "I left you there. In the temple. I knew she would come find you." She took a step forward, a tentative one, as if she didn't trust herself to pilot her body of her own accord. "She found you."

Caius dipped his chin in a slow nod. "Yes. Tanith, that was days ago."

"Was it?"

Echo wanted desperately to step toward them, but the magic held her in place. She was all that was holding the street together. "Caius," she hissed quietly. "This is a trick."

"She doesn't have anything to gain by doing this," Caius hissed back. With painstaking slowness, he sheathed one of his daggers and lowered the other. He walked toward his sister, who was staring at the rift in the ground, her brows pinched in horror and confusion.

"You have to stop me, Caius." She angled her head toward his approaching footsteps, but she kept her gaze on the black gash cutting across Fifth Avenue. "Promise me you'll stop me. This isn't what I wanted."

"Caius," Echo called out. Then, again, less quietly: "Caius. Don't listen to her. She's lying."

He shook his head as he advanced toward his sister. "I don't think she is."

Tanith dragged her gaze away from the breach. She reached for him, her black-veined hand extending in supplication. "Brother . . ."

Alarm bells sounded in Echo's head just as the voices of the vessels rose to a fever pitch.

"Caius, no!"

But he reached for his sister anyway, and there was nothing Echo could do to stop him. The second his hand touched Tanith's the black bled back into her eyes and she twisted his arm with a vicious wrench of his wrist. He cried out in pain, but Echo still heard the telltale sound of something cracking. The bone must have broken.

"Tanith," he choked out. "Tanith, you can end this. You opened the rifts. You can close them."

"Oh, Caius." It was as though a completely different person was speaking now. The pitch and cadence of her voice were entirely distinct from the woman who had so plaintively called out to her brother to help her. "Why on earth would I want to do that?"

CHAPTER FIFTY-ONE

Caius had always appreciated the symmetry of a good story. There was something beautiful in the circularity, the wholeness. A good story made him feel like the world and all its fundamental truths were encapsulated within its neat enclosure.

He supposed he'd always known how his story would end, even if he had not realized it until the moment it did.

His sister's eyes gleamed black. Darker than the night sky above, darker than the velvety shadows of the in-between, darker even than the rift she had torn open in the world. They were unfathomable. Alien.

Pain lanced up his arm. His wrist was broken. But pain was a physical concern, the body crying out against some unpleasantness. Decades of Caius's life had been spent training to push pain away, to lock it behind a seal to be dealt with at a later time. The pain was nothing. The pain would not win, would not make him pliable, would not soften him for the shadows to claim. Not this time.

Tanith's power—not hers, not truly, but the power that rode her body like a knight rides a horse—pushed at the boundaries of his body, aching to tear them down, to spill across his skin, into his veins.

He held it off with all his might and choked out his sister's name, even as the syllables were crushed in his throat by the power clawing to get in.

Golden eyebrows furrowed, oddly pristine against the charcoal-veined ruin of her face. A flash of red fought through that black gaze. A glimmer of truth stealing an illicit peek through a curtain of darkness.

"Caius?" Her tone was soft, tentative. Confused. Her grip on his shattered wrist loosened.

He could hear Echo calling out to him, shouting that it was a ruse. Not to trust it. Not to trust his sister, his blood.

Her reddish eyes rolled to the side, then upward, taking in the horror she had wrought. The wound in the heavens. The fissure in the street. The ravenous creatures of darkness and despair she had birthed in her frenzy of violence.

Moisture gathered on her lashes, tears threatening to spill.

More than a century had passed since the last time he'd seen his sister cry. And this *was* his sister. Not a monster wearing her skin like a mask. He knew it as surely as he knew the sun would set and the moon would rise.

"I don't want this," she said. She was herself once more. The darkness had receded, pushed back by the strength of her emotion. But how long her reprieve would last, Caius did not know. Tanith's grip on herself seemed a tenuous thing.

There one moment, gone the next. But Caius would not let it claim her. Not again. If she died here today, she would die as herself and no other.

Darkness be damned.

Caius sagged against his sister. She supported his weight, as they had so often done for each other over the years. As they had forgotten to do, torn apart as they were by time and tragedy.

"You can stop it," he said, his forehead falling to rest against hers.

Her eyelashes brushed against his skin. She shook her head, blond hair falling around their faces like a curtain, shielding them, this moment, from the broken world beyond.

"I can't," she said.

"You can," he countered. "You—"

"Not by myself."

Her words halted his reassurances. The truth in them rang as clear as a bell, too loud, too resounding to be denied.

She pulled away, enough to force her slightly less reddish eyes to meet his. There was a battle raging within her, and she was losing ground to the enemy. *Their* enemy.

"I'm sorry, Caius. I'm so sorry."

The apology was too big for words, but still, she tried. He heard all the things she didn't—couldn't—say.

I'm sorry for Rose.

I'm sorry I failed you.

I'm sorry I failed myself.

I'm sorry for this.

She was not wrong. He hated how right she was, but not even he, the Dragon Prince newly crowned, could defy the truth when it was so abundantly clear.

She could not close the rifts. Not alone. It had taken both their magic to crack the seals, to open the gaping chasm in the world that was consuming it with the inexorable hunger of a black hole. It did not matter than his magic had not been willingly given, that she had stolen it for herself and her own selfish desires.

It had taken both of them to open the rift in the world, and because the universe also loved the symmetry of stories, it would take both of them to close it.

His blood had begun to mend the wounds the broken seals had inflicted, but it wasn't enough. It was nowhere near enough. The universe demanded a more potent power to cage what had been unleashed, to close what had been ripped open.

Caius spoke the words he had heard Echo say, the words of a spell as ancient and as fundamental as the changing of the tides, as the elements that gave life to the natural magic of the world.

"By my blood."

He felt the ripples of magic those words created. Sensed the electric potential they carried.

The magic swelled in the air around them, a glittering crescendo to the grand finale.

Caius wrapped his arms around his sister. Over her shoulder, he saw Echo kneeling, holding the fabric of reality together with little more than the force of her will. Her hair—as brown as rich soil—tumbled around her face, freed from the ferocity of her fight. Her eyes were rimmed with red, and tears had tracked through the soot and ash on her face, leaving trails of pristine skin in their wake. He could see the plea forming on her lips, and he hoped that she would not cry out for him to stop, to not do what he knew he must. He was only so strong. Oh, how beautiful she was. How brave. It was a privilege to love her.

Caius had indeed always loved the symmetry of stories. He had lost a love and found another. He had lost a sister and found her again. He had lost his crown, his title, *himself,* and found the role he was meant to play, the piece of the tapestry into which all their lives had been woven. He was but a collection of threads, unable to see the totality of the image until he stepped away from it, but now he saw.

He should have seen it coming. He should have known the familiar lines of his tale, one as old as time itself: a king sacrificed so the rain would come and the crops would grow and the sun would shine and the world would keep on spinning another turn.

The wholeness of his story was laid bare before him, and he knew his story would end just as it had begun.

He stepped back, guiding his sister with him. One step, and his foot felt the ground give way beneath him, drawing them both into the abyss. Another step, and there was only air and darkness.

Caius and Tanith—his sister, his twin, his blood—had entered this world together. And that was how they left it.

CHAPTER FIFTY-TWO

The pivotal moments in one's life happened in slow motion. It was the universe's way of forcing every moment to be experienced in its fullest, most excruciating detail. The speed of objects slowed to a molasses crawl. The air stilled. The earth held its breath.

Watch, the universe said.

Watch him fall.

Watch him take the demon with him.

Watch the darkness follow.

Watch the blackness swallow them up and disappear behind them.

Watch nothing stand in the place where someone had once stood.

Echo watched and felt threads of magic slip between her fingers as the ripped seam in the fabric of the world sewed itself back together because of Caius. Because he had been there and now he was not.

He mended the holes in the world only to tear one open in her chest.

The sound of gunfire rattled against the night, petering out as the shadows broke apart. The sky shuddered, heaving a great sigh as its broken shards re-formed into something whole. The ozone tang of the in-between faded like a bad dream.

Echo couldn't tear her eyes away from the spot where Caius had stood, where he had offered her one last piercing look before plunging himself and his sister into the abyss, taking the kuçedra with him.

Her heart sputtered against her ribs, an engine that wouldn't properly start.

Caius was gone.

Caius was gone.

Echo pushed herself off her knees and stood. Her body was still swollen with magic, far too much for any one person to bear. Her bones were as heavy as stone. With unsteady steps, her feet carried her along the fissure still wide-open in the asphalt. But it was a mundane disruption in the topography of the street. A wide crack running the length of Fifth Avenue as far as Echo could see. No shadows leaking onto the cement. No unfathomable black depths threatening to spill over into the world. The avenue was ruined, but it was a normal ruin. It could be repaired with gravel and tar and paint, a scar scabbed over.

She dropped to her knees. Her fingers traced the ragged edge of the pavement as if she could tear the world back open and pull him out. The knowledge that she couldn't stole the air from her lungs, suffocating her in its terrible immensity.

To be lost in the in-between was to be claimed by the

great tracts of nothingness in the void. To be lost in the in-between was to be lost forever.

"Echo!"

She didn't turn at the sound of her name. She couldn't shift her gaze from the spot where Caius had been seconds, minutes earlier. Time had become elastic for her.

How long had it been since his hands had been on her hands, lacing their fingers together as they fell asleep in the library of Wyvern's Keep? How long since his lips had traced a path down her throat from the patch of skin just below her ear to the juncture of her neck? How long since he had played the magpie's lullaby for her on the piano? Hours. Not even a whole day.

"Echo."

The voice was closer now, cutting through the shrill ringing in her ears. Hands landed under her arms, trying to pull her up. Echo reached behind her to brush them away, but the owner of the hands was persistent.

"Echo."

Someone dropped down to a crouch next to her.

"Look at me," came the voice. A hand gently pressed against her chin, forcing her eyes away from the spot to which they had been riveted.

The Ala gazed at Echo, her raven-black feathers matted with soot and sweat and blood. Her obsidian eyes were unspeakably sad.

"He—"

Echo couldn't get the words out. Words had a power all their own, and if she spoke the ones she could not say, then they would be imbued with a power she did not want them to have. They would accelerate the moment, solidify its reality. They were a finality to which she was not ready to commit.

He's gone, she did not say.

But the Ala didn't need her to say it. She knew. She must have seen. No one understood magic or the in-between like the Ala.

Echo was distantly aware that a trembling had taken her chin. Her vision blurred. Her head swam. She was going to be sick.

The Ala's brow creased. Wordlessly, she pulled Echo into her arms, whispering soft Avicet words into Echo's hair as Echo shattered against her, a wave breaking against rocks.

"I'm so sorry, *dah re'ain.*" "My child" in Avicet. Not a phrase the Ala used often. The power in those words prodded at Echo's wounds. "But there is work yet to be done."

Gently but firmly, the Ala pushed Echo inches away, just enough for her to look upon the devastation that remained.

The broken sky had been healed, but all around them was ruin.

"They need you, *dah re'ain.*"

Echo lurched away from the Ala, falling back against the street, the scrapes on her abraded palms reminding her of their existence. Who needed her? What else did she have to give? She had nothing. Nothing, nothing, nothing.

As if she could read Echo's thoughts, the Ala took Echo's hand in her own and said, "Look."

Echo looked.

Her veins were not black.

They burned brilliantly, subdued by the shield of her skin, but bright enough to make it look like she had light flowing through her veins. Her skin had taken on a strange luminescence.

"What is this?" Echo asked, staring at her oddly translucent flesh. Those words came easier. They were less awful. Now that she had seen the light in her veins, she *felt* it. Her body burned as if she had the world's worst fever. Her skin was too tight against her skeleton.

"Magic," said the Ala. "You took it into yourself. And now you have to release it."

Echo shifted her gaze back to the Ala, swallowing past the sickness threatening to rise. It was too much for her. It was all too much. "How?"

The Ala answered as if it were the simplest thing in the world. "Share it."

She helped Echo to her feet, bracing Echo's elbows with her cupped palms, holding her steady as if she knew that Echo would crumble without her. The Ala guided Echo away from the gravitational pull of the place where Caius had disappeared into the blackness of the in-between, her arm a solid weight against Echo's shoulder blades, pressing Echo onward to witness the chaos Tanith had left in her wake.

The sickness swirling within Echo swelled with every step she took. There were bodies all along the street, draped in white cloaks and clothed in camouflage. Armed with swords and guns. Not bodies, she reminded herself. It didn't help to think of them as bodies. People had bodies. These were corpses. If they'd had souls, they'd long since fled.

Echo reached out to touch the sloped shoulder of a fallen Avicen she recognized but whose name she could not remember. The pulsating glow of the magic in her veins dimmed the closer her hand got. The Ala placed a hand on her wrist, pulling her away.

"It's too late for them. But there are others you can help."

The Ala led her to a small huddle of humans. Two men leaned over the body of a boy. Blood soaked the front of his uniform, so much that the fabric was almost black. Most of the skin she could see was covered in wicked gashes made by something with claws. It took a moment for her brain to assemble the pieces of his face into one she knew.

The boy who had covered her with gunfire. The boy who'd saved her.

He was near death. Echo slid to her knees beside him. The light inside her brimmed, eager to be let out of its mortal cage.

"How do I help him?" Echo asked the Ala.

"Put your hands on him," the Ala replied.

Echo did as she was told, placing one on his hand, the back of which was curiously pale, the other on his cheek. Her fingers slicked with blood. The soldiers didn't stop her. They seemed numb as they watched her.

"And push."

Echo pushed.

The magic didn't need much coaxing. It flowed outward from the core of her body, through veins and arteries, over bone and muscle. It spilled from her skin and across the boy's, motes of light dancing with joy, put to a purpose.

A moment passed in tense silence as the Ala and the soldiers and Echo watched. Then another moment.

"It's not wor—"

A ragged gasp burst from the boy's lips as his chest heaved with breath.

One of the soldiers, the one who'd been cradling his younger comrade's head in his lap, shot Echo a bewildered look. "How did you . . ."

But his question died on his lips. Perhaps he knew she wouldn't be able to provide an answer.

The Ala helped Echo up and led her to the next victim, and the next, and the next. Every time, Echo put her hands on someone near death and breathed her magic into them. But it wasn't really her magic. Magic, despite what Tanith and so many like her believed, could not be collected. It could not be hoarded. It defied ownership. The magic belonged to Echo as much as it belonged to the Ala and the human soldiers and the Avicen civilians who had taken up arms to defend the only home they had ever known.

The magic left Echo and went into them, healing their wounds, filling them with life like sunlight on soil. With every wounded person she tended to, she felt a tether in her snap, like an anchor had been severed, leaving a boat to float free, far away from her. She recognized the sensation as she felt the presence of the firebird vessels lessen. They had lived in her like white noise—her own private Greek chorus, bearing witness to her triumphs and her tragedies—and now they were falling silent, dissipating with the magic she was releasing into the people who needed it more than she did. The Ala helped Echo stand and walk and heal.

Somewhere in the distance, a broken sob cut through the sound of survivors scuffling about, dazed. Echo stumbled.

She knew that voice. It was broken and jagged, but she knew it.

Jasper.

Echo pushed away from the Ala and the huddle of soldiers and broke into a run, careening toward the source of that horrible broken sound.

When she found them, she almost couldn't bear it.

Jasper knelt on the ground, his jeans torn, his shoulders shaking, his arms streaked with blood. Most of it was not his. His feathered head was bent over Dorian's face, partially hiding it from Echo's view. Ivy knelt beside Jasper, one hand on his shoulder, the other holding a cloth to Dorian's face. She raised her eyes to Echo, and there was a hopelessness in them Echo had never seen before.

Echo let her legs fold under her as she joined them. Dorian was so still.

"Let me see," she said.

Jasper wrapped his arms tighter around Dorian, his shoulders shaking.

"Jasper," Ivy said gently. She pulled the cloth away and pried his arms looser as he finally looked up, seeing Echo for the first time. Confusion flitted across his face at the sight of her still-bright veins, but it was swiftly replaced by absolute, utter despair.

Echo had never seen him look so wretched. She looked away from his stricken expression and down at Dorian's face, and that was worse.

There was a mass of blood and flesh and bone where his one good eye had been.

Jasper's voice was hoarse from crying. "Help him."

She could. She would.

Echo reached for Dorian's face. Her hand hovered over the worst of the wounds. She didn't want to touch him. He wasn't moving. His chest rose and fell in the shallowest of breaths. He was, perhaps, past the point of pain, but she didn't want to cause him any more.

"Please," Jasper breathed, his nose pressed to the crown of Dorian's head, his voice muffled by silver hair.

Echo laid her hand against Dorian's bloodied face. It didn't look like there was much left to salvage. Skin against skin, she could feel the thread of life left in him, flimsy and weak and almost worn down to nothing. He was nearly gone.

The magic in her reached out. It was thinner now, but she gathered it around herself and fortified it with her own reserves of strength. And she pushed.

She had saved so many. And none of it would matter if she couldn't save him. If she couldn't wipe that despair from Jasper's expression, the hopelessness from Ivy's.

All those lives saved. And still, she was powerless to help the one person she so desperately wanted to save.

Caius was gone.

The in-between had claimed him, and there was nothing she could do. The magic flowed through all of them, as bright as starlight.

The vessels left Echo. They let her go, finally finding their own peace after all those years, centuries, millennia tied to the firebird and its magic.

She poured the last vestiges of magic left in her body into Dorian, guiding it with her will. Wishes, the Ala had told her a lifetime ago, had power. And she wished for Dorian to be whole, wished it with every last spark of strength she had.

The world went dark at the corners of her vision as the magic grew stronger and her body grew weaker.

Lashes fluttered against her palm.

The last thing she heard before darkness—a gentle darkness, so different from the malevolent one that had done all this—was a familiar voice. One that had sung the magpie's lullaby Echo so loved a century before she had even been born. A voice she knew as well as her own, that inhabited the place between life and death, neither one nor the other. In-between. A voice Caius had loved as he had come to love Echo.

Rose's presence hovered at the edges of Echo's mind, lingering long after all the others had faded, and made a promise.

I'll find him.

EPILOGUE

The battle came to an end and the rebuilding began. Together, Avicen, Drakharin, and human tended to their wounded and mourned their dead. Nothing would be what it once was, but that was perhaps not the worst possible outcome. Days passed in a fragile camaraderie, burdened by the weight of all that had been lost.

Echo made her way to the roof of the ruined library—or what was left of it—scaling piles of rubble and partially collapsed stairways until the sky opened up before her. Clouds the color of smoke and ambient light crowded the heavens, obscuring her view of all but the most stubborn stars.

It was easier to think up here. She felt closer to the sky.

Slowly, she let herself relax. Her body felt the strain of the past few hours, days, months. She ached in places she didn't know a person could ache. But despite her bruised and battered body's litany of complaints, she felt the weight of all that had transpired slip away like grains of sand between her fingers. She knew that the worst was yet to come. The burden of those who survived the war was dealing with the ruin it left in its wake. Loss was not a wound that could be carefully sutured. It would rise up like a flaring infection once the thrill of adrenaline worked its way through her. But for now, she had the relative silence of the city and the quiet companionship of the stars.

Things were quieter this far above the ground. She wanted quiet. Needed it. But she also needed a place that had made her feel like herself. And the library was that place. It always had been. It was broken, but then, so was she. The library would bear the scars of its suffering for the rest of its existence, but then, so would she.

Echo closed her eyes, shutting out the night sky and the stars and the crescent sliver of the moon that peeked out from behind a veil of clouds.

"Are you there?"

She asked this aloud, though she knew she was unlikely to get an answer, much less one spoken out loud, with all the body and volume of a person's voice.

She waited.

Silence greeted her words, and her heart sank a few centimeters.

It was possible that her mind had been playing tricks on her ever since the battle. Trauma had a way of addling the brain. Loss wreaked havoc on the human mind, and Echo, it would seem, was not immune to its influence.

She let out a sigh, preparing herself for the climb back down. There was so much to be done. Explanations to be made to the human residents of New York, who were still reeling from the revelation that an entire society had existed beneath their feet while they had been none the wiser. There were injured people who needed looking after. Dragons to find. The one that had joined the fray had taken off after the last shadow beast had dissolved into nothingness, its great and terrible wings carrying it far away. Echo suspected the human military had tried to capture it, but like any magical creature worth its salt, it had evaded them. Just as the Avicen had done for millennia. Until now.

Echo stuffed her hands into her pockets and turned away from the edge of the roof.

There was nothing for her to see. Nothing for her to hear. Nothing for her to feel.

She hadn't gone more than three steps when she felt it.

She stopped. Closed her eyes. Strained her senses, both mundane and magical, as far as she could.

There.

A tiny tug.

The vessels had left her days ago. The firebird had done its job. It had brought about the war's end. It had made room for a new future to grow. But when she was tired—which was always—she felt a shadow of their presence, like a perfume hanging in the air after its wearer had left the room.

Sillage, she thought. *French. The trace of a person left behind after he is gone.*

Her ears strained and she heard it. A faraway voice, as soft as the chiming of a distant bell, humming a tune almost too soft to hear.

Echo hummed along, reciting the words in her head.

One for sorrow.

Two for mirth.

The tug grew stronger, as if it were trying to pull her in a particular direction, but not one that was restricted by the limits of the physical plane as she understood it. There was a sense of summoning to the tug. A persistence that verged on obstinate.

The vessels had left. All but one.

Echo breathed the name into the evening air, her hope almost too much to bear. "Rose?"

She didn't get a response, but she didn't need one. She knew.

Rose had made her a promise, and Echo knew there was nothing in the world that would stop her from keeping it. Not the laws of physics. Not the known limitations of magic. And certainly not something as pedestrian as death.

"Where are you?" Echo asked.

Again, there was no answer. Not yet. But Echo thought that one was on its way, striving toward her. She could feel the shape of it in her dreams, and for once, she didn't run from them.

The first night after the battle had been the worst. She thought she would be fine never sleeping again. She hadn't wanted to face the morning when she knew she'd be forced to remember all that had passed. All she'd lost.

But that wasn't what happened.

So fiercely had she dreaded the first morning in a world without Caius that she'd almost missed it, nestled as she was in that liminal space between sleeping and waking, when nothing was certain and all things were possible.

A ghost of a touch. A phantom breath on her cheek. The quiet humming of a lullaby in a voice that was decidedly masculine. All of them too real to be the product of an imagination desperate to cling to even the slimmest hope.

Echo knew better than anyone that death wasn't always the end. Sometimes, death was a beginning.

The tug faded, but it would come back, stronger and stronger, just as it had every day since the battle.

Patience was not one of her middle names, but maybe it could be, if the cause was just.

And so Echo would wait. She'd wait as long as it took for Rose to fulfill her promise. The tether that connected the two of them had thinned, but it had not snapped. Rose could reach her. And if Rose reached Caius, then Echo could reach him too.

Nothing was ever so lost that it couldn't be found again.

After all, she had found herself, and that had been hardest of all. She had been many things in her life:

A lost child.

A lonely girl.

A survivor.

A savior.

A thief.

This last descriptor felt the truest in that moment and every moment before it. She stole things. And she was good at it. And when something was stolen from her, she always found a way to steal it back.

A childhood.

A life.

A love.

She'd never been much good at taking no for an answer, even when the laws of physics and magic were determined to say it.

She'd changed the world once, and she would bend its rules once more if she had to.

Echo opened her eyes and breathed deeply. The air was still thick with smoke and dust, but there was something else there. Possibility. Potential.

There were so many stories left to tell. This one was not over.

No, this one was just beginning. And what a beginning it was. Echo let herself mull over the threads of the story they had started, all of them together, her heart sputtering because Caius wasn't there to see it.

Yet.

A crown needed a head to rest upon, and in the vacuum left by Caius's sacrifice, his closest friend had risen to take his place, at least until a proper election could be held. As far as Echo knew, not a single Drakharin soul objected to Dorian's ascension to interim Dragon Prince. He had remained loyal to his prince when so many of them had proven faithless. Jasper had accompanied Dorian to Wyvern's Keep, and no one had objected to that either, but Echo suspected that had less to do with the respect they felt for Dorian and more to do with the glares Dorian was capable of leveling at anyone who so much as looked at Jasper with anything but the utmost reverence. The ferocity of these glares was lessened not one bit by the fact that he had only one eye. Echo's magic had healed the wounds from the battle, but nothing older. Dorian had thanked her and said that was enough.

A Dragon Prince with an Avicen consort. They truly had changed the world, in the most unexpected of ways.

The war was over. There would be other wars in the future. There were always other wars. But for now, there was peace.

And so it goes, Echo thought. It was a line from one of her favorite Vonnegut books. A pithy phrase summing up the tragedies of life and death and the incalculable cruelties people were capable of inflicting on each other. Tomorrow the moon would set and the sun would rise and the world would keep on spinning, held together in all its delicate fragility, so easily shattered.

She looked up, raking her eyes over the familiar constellations she recognized. There was comfort to be had in familiarity. In her mind, she drew lines connecting the stars. A frown creased her brow when she noticed a star that had not been there before.

It was possible that it had been there and she simply had never noticed. It could have been obscured by clouds or pollution, or maybe its flickering light had only just made its way to Earth. But there was something that felt new about it. It burned brighter than the stars around it, as if beckoning for her attention.

The Dragon Princes, Caius had told her, were said to ascend to the heavens at the end of their reigns. It was one of the many stories he had shared with her as they had lain awake on a rooftop of a warehouse in London, hiding from those who wished them harm, surrounded by safety that had proven to be an illusion. The war had found them. And it had claimed him. Perhaps, in death, Caius had taken up his rightful place among the stars.

Her throat constricted. She drew in a breath, and longing

filled her lungs. She was no stranger to the optimistic ache of wishful thinking, but this felt different. Her eyes were locked on that star, the sight of it knocking loose something that had been trapped inside her. She felt something give in her chest. She exhaled, and that sick cloud of sorrow began to thin. Hope—pale and weak but there—unfurled deep inside her, blossoming like a trampled flower.

I'll find him, Rose had promised. And Echo was beginning to believe that maybe she had.

"Thank you." Echo breathed words into the smoke-laden air and hoped that wherever Rose was, she heard. A cool breeze carried the words up into the night sky as if lifting them toward the stars.

Echo heard the scrape of boots on gravel. The footsteps were slow, as if the person was taking deliberate care not to spook her. Or perhaps they were unsure of their welcome.

Echo let them approach, but she did not turn around. There was no sense of danger now. Everyone who wished her harm was dead, dying, or detained. And she did not have the power of the firebird anymore. She had turned it over to people who needed it more than she did, and now she was free. Free of its prison. Free of its potential. She was just a girl standing among the ruins of a demolished library, staring up at the stars.

The person stopped a few feet behind her. "I can come back," said a familiar voice, "if you would rather be alone."

Rowan.

She had come up to the roof seeking solitude, but he was a warm presence at her back and she had no wish to send him away.

"It's all right." Echo turned to look at him, forcing her

lips into a small smile. It wasn't as difficult as she thought it would be. "I don't mind the company."

Rowan nodded, his hands thrust into his pockets. He looked different. It wasn't merely the cut on his brow—hastily stitched by the battlefield healers working frantically below—or the plaster dust that clung to his skin and clothes. It was as if something fundamental within him had shifted. He was not the person he had been. And neither was she.

"Are you okay?" Rowan asked.

"No. Not really." Echo kept her answer honest. "But I will be. Eventually."

Another nod. His hazel eyes drifted to his feet. He scuffed at the cracked masonry with the toe of his boot. Silence stretched between them, punctuated by the shrill wail of sirens in the distance. The city was stunned, but it would recover. It always did.

"I have an idea," said Rowan. "Let's start over. . . . I'm just me and you're just you and we're meeting for the very first time."

He stuck out his hand. There was dirt caked under his nails and the black dust of charcoal smudged on his skin. "I'm Rowan. What's your name?"

There was power in names. To give your name to a stranger was to give them a little piece of yourself. Years ago, Echo would have hoarded her truth, clutched it tightly, afraid to share it, afraid that breathing a part of her soul into the air would cheapen it. But Rowan was safe. Like Ivy and the Ala and Dorian and Jasper, Rowan was home. He would take that little piece of her and cradle it with gentle hands.

She took Rowan's hand in hers, committing each old callus and fresh scar to memory. His wounds told the story of who he was and who he was becoming, just as hers did. Her mind was already churning with plans to do the impossible, and she knew she wouldn't have to do it alone.

There was power in names, and power, she had learned, was to be shared, not hoarded.

"My name," she said, "is Echo."

ACKNOWLEDGMENTS

When I was twelve years old, I scribbled some awful poetry in a Winnie-the-Pooh notebook and decided I wanted to be a writer. There were many people who told me it was a silly dream, a waste of time. Some of those comments stung, but they just made me want it more. I owe those people as much as I owe the people who supported me, in a weird, twisty sort of way.

But only one of those groups merits being mentioned by name.

First, I want to thank my agent, Catherine Drayton, without whom Echo and her friends would never have found a home. She took my dream and cradled it in her hands and made it come true.

My editor, Krista Marino, helped mold these books into what they are. Without her, I don't think I would have survived this trilogy with my sanity (mostly) intact. She is the best editor a scared debut author could have asked for.

The team at Random House, especially Aisha Cloud: thank you for guiding me on the crazy journey that is publishing; Alison Impey and Jen Wang, thank you for making these books beautiful. Lyndsey Blessing of InkWell Management: you are a foreign-rights rock star.

Virginia Boecker, thank you for helping me survive the

this-is-the-worst-writing-sin-anyone-has-ever-committed phase of drafting and the burn-it-with-fire stage of revisions. Amanda, Idil, and Laura, thank you for believing in Echo's story from the start.

Compiling Echo's lexicon of esoteric and untranslatable words wasn't easy, and I'm deeply indebted to the curators of Other-Wordly (other-wordly.tumblr.com), Wordstuck (wordstuck.co.vu), and Haggard Hawks Words (twitter.com/HaggardHawks).

Last, but never least, I would like to thank you, the reader, for being curious enough to pick up *The Girl at Midnight* and caring enough to see this story through to *The Savage Dawn*. Echo and Ivy and Caius and Dorian and Jasper are as much yours as they are mine. Books may end, but characters carve out spaces for themselves in your heart, and I am so incredibly grateful that you allowed mine into yours. Thank you.

ABOUT THE AUTHOR

Melissa Grey was born and raised in New York City. She wrote her first short story at the age of twelve and hasn't stopped writing since. After earning a degree in fine arts at Yale University, she embarked on an adventure of global proportions and discovered a secret talent for navigating subway systems in just about any language. She works as a freelance writer in New York City. She is the author of the Girl at Midnight series: *The Girl at Midnight, The Shadow Hour,* and *The Savage Dawn.* To learn more about Melissa, visit melissa-grey.com, follow @meligrey on Twitter, and look for melissagrey_ on Instagram.